BABEL

The Story of the Tower and the Rebellion
of Man

BRENNAN S. MCPHERSON

BABEL

The Story of the Tower and the Rebellion of Man

Copyright © 2019 by Brennan S. McPherson

ISBN: 978-1-7324436-3-1 (softcover)

ISBN: 978-1-7324436-4-8 (audiobook)

Published by McPherson Publishing

Sparta, WI, USA

Cover design by Josh Meyer Photography and Design

Edited by Natalie Hanemann, nataliehanemann.com

Author's Note

This is a stand-alone novel that covers the events of the tower of Babel, mainly from the perspective of Noah, who the Scriptures say was alive during this time. I have never heard a single sermon preached on Noah's failure to stop his progeny from rebelling against the Almighty. Nor do many discuss the oddity that the Bible doesn't include what Noah, Shem, or Japheth were doing while the world was unifying in rebellion against the God they served. The last we hear about Noah in Scripture, he is getting drunk and letting his family fall to pieces.

This book is, as it must be, a work of fiction written to explore some of the possible reasons for Noah's seeming absence and lack of accountability for his offspring's revolt. The last thing I want is for my own imaginative additions to become canonized in readers' minds. So please keep in mind that what you're about to read is not a recounting of history. It is only me applying my imagination to the text to help us grapple with the central truths of the story. My paramount goal is always to inspire readers to engage more with the Scriptures.

At the end of the book, I offer a more comprehensive examination of the Scriptural text, along with an explanation for the creative decisions I made, the source of those ideas originating within the text of the Bible.

Also, I write a weekly devotional at my website, brennanmcpherson.com. If you sign up (https://brennanmcpherson.com/newsletter/) to get the devotional sent to your inbox every Saturday morning at 6:00 a.m., you'll also receive a free e-book, Book 1 in the Psalm Series.

The whole world had the same language and the same words. When they were migrating from the east, they came to a valley in the land of Shinar and settled there. They said to one another, "Come, let us mold bricks and harden them with fire." They used bricks for stone, and bitumen for mortar. Then they said, "Come, let us build ourselves a city and a tower with its top in the sky, and so make a name for ourselves; otherwise we shall be scattered all over the earth."

The LORD came down to see the city and the tower that the people had built. Then the LORD said: If now, while they are one people and all have the same language, they have started to do this, nothing they presume to do will be out of their reach. Come, let us go down and there confuse their language, so that no one will understand the speech of another. So the LORD scattered them from there over all the earth, and they stopped building the city. That is why it was called Babel, because there the LORD confused the speech of all the world. From there the LORD scattered them over all the earth.

—Genesis 11, NABRE

PART I

Fractured Dust

120 YEARS AFTER THE WORLDWIDE FLOOD

1

Noah

Noah woke moments before sunrise. The light of the moon and stars glowed dimly through the curtain that hung across the open doorway to his mud-brick home, though the sky itself was blocked from view by his roof. His old bones ached from lying on a reed mat in the same position all night. He blinked and yawned. It was bright enough that he could just see the outline of jars lining the shelves to his left and the shape of the small table resting against the wall on his right. His chest expanded, and he sensed a weight across his belly. He reached up and realized it was the arm of his wife, Jade.

Of course. They had spent the previous night worshipping the Almighty around a small fire before pouring their best wine into the flames as an offering for his faithfulness. Then they'd fallen asleep inside the home they'd lived in for over a century, her white hair splayed across his chest like a frosted fern over winter soil.

He clasped her weathered fingers, longing to hear her voice speak his name, but as he touched her skin, his breath seized.

Her fingers were cold and stiff against his.

He let go and craned his eyes toward her face.

Yes, she was there next to him. Even in the dim lighting, he recognized the contours of her wrinkled cheeks. Whatever remained shadowed, his memory completed. Her chest pressed

3

against his right side as his right arm cradled her back. He held his breath and closed his eyes, trying to sense any movement.

He felt nothing.

A spear of panic lanced through his abdomen, and he thrust himself away, scrambling backward till his shoulder met the wall. Was he dreaming? Was this some dark, terrible nightmare?

He stared at her form, lips shaking as he whispered, "Jade," over and over.

But there was no response.

He blinked hard, rubbed his beard, and shifted his feet across the dusty floor. The sound of the wind and the creak of distant wooden buildings were too nuanced and calm for a nightmare. And his mind held none of that blurred confusion that lucid dreams often gave you. Everything around and inside him screamed that this was no dream.

So he waited, hoping instead that he was simply mistaken about her stillness.

"Jade?" He crawled forward on hands and knees, daring to test reality once more. "Jade!"

But there was no response. No movement.

He stood, rubbed his face, feeling heat rush to his cheeks and a quivering wetness to his eyes.

"You can't take her from me," he said, swallowing his tears to make way for anger.

But he knew that wasn't true.

He walked to the door and parted the curtain to look across his vineyard, desperate for some way to replace the pain flooding his senses with the sight and sound and smell and taste and feel of the natural world. The sunrise glowed violet across linen clouds and cast a hopeful silhouette across his land. Everything felt so normal. *So like it always had been.*

He walked out of his home, limbs wobbly, head spinning. Birds chirped outside their—no, *his*—home. A slight breeze rasped between branches and leaves. Everything looked the same, though he knew a sword had been thrust through reality.

For Noah was now, after the great deluge, the father of all living people. And she the mother of all. The entire world would feel the sting of loss today. Though none but he yet knew it.

The sense of responsibility bowed his shoulders. He should send messengers to his children immediately, to honor Jade before too much time passed. But the only thing he wanted to do was bury himself in his work.

He stared at the curving vines that bore the grapes that had kept them alive, then at the workhouses that lay motionless in the morning. Today was supposed to be a day of rest. It would be some time before anyone crossed his path if he went to work now. What would they think, once he told them? How could he explain any delay?

He cleared his throat hard and turned slowly away from the vines, as if fighting ropes tied to his shoulders. He focused every thought on the next step. The sun warmed his back until the heat became an unbearable weight.

"The Almighty gave her, and now he has taken her. Blessed be the name of the Almighty." Noah spoke the words to quell pain's gravity, but even as the final words left his lips, the ache fell again around his throat like a millstone.

He arrived at the communal living area for his workers and woke Abbiar, his primary overseer, with a hand on his shoulder. The tall man with dark eyelids turned his way and rubbed his beard, shifting up on one elbow. "Noah? What is wrong?"

Noah opened his mouth to speak, but nothing came but a guttural croak. He fell forward, and Abbiar, Noah's great-grandson, caught him. Noah's shoulders shuddered with quiet sobs, and Abbiar patted his back.

"Jade," Noah managed. "She's gone."

Soon, Abbiar wept with him, until both of their shoulders were completely soaked by grief.

They let go of each other, and Abbiar lit a lantern and stared at Noah, shaking his head. "How?"

"I don't know. We must gather Shem, Japheth, Ham, and their families. Please, send your fastest couriers."

Abbiar nodded and pulled on his brown work tunic from the day before, still dotted with mud at the hem. "The world will arrive in your courtyard before days' end."

Noah focused all his attention on the sound of Abbiar's feet scraping the dusty ground as he went and woke his two brothers, then passed the news to the rest of the two dozen workers who lived there. Abbiar and his brothers bound sandals to their feet and left in a hurry, one going West, another North East, the last South.

They had survived the world's purging at the hands of the Almighty and outlived the murderous Others who'd slaughtered all those faithful to the Old Way of the Almighty but for them and their children.

How could something so innocuous as sleep claim her now?

Surely, they were old enough to feel death's approach. But young enough to believe they could still outrun it. At least for a while. Or so he'd thought.

How cruel the world could be.

Noah rose and exited, eyes scanning his land and stopping once again at the home that had become Jade's temporary tomb. They had built it near the foot of the mountain that the ark had landed on nearly a hundred years earlier. The wood from the ark had been cannibalized for firewood, buildings, and tools. Now nothing was left but a skeleton rotted by harsh weather on the rocks above.

Noah had planted the vineyard and gardened as his father, Lamech, had so many years earlier. Though he didn't have the same talent for gardening as for construction, he knew enough to do what was required. As his grandchildren and their children grew more skilled than he at farming, he focused on what was most needful: producing enough wine to purify their water.

In the wake of the destruction from the flood, clean water had grown difficult to find. Watered wine had been, by far, their most frequent drink of choice, as it rendered potentially dangerous water clean. Now that the world had settled, he continued his trade out of love for the labor.

He often walked the rows as he did now, feeling the texture of the leaves, tracing contours on the vines, and plucking ripe grapes from their place. With his bare feet on the soft, damp earth, he felt he belonged.

But now, as he walked those roofless halls of grapevines on fencing, he desired nothing but to tear their roots up and throw them in the fire. He plucked grapes instead, hoping it would assuage his aimless anger. The sun grew hot overhead, and he began to sweat profusely, his tunic sticking to his skin.

After passing half the length of his land, he realized he'd also been checking the new growth and pulling weeds. He reached for a particularly thick weed with both hands and saw the vine beside it was sickly. He began pruning the rot before it spread. His workers were supposed to keep better track. He had taught them that if they found one ill plant, they missed five besides it.

And so his work expanded, and the sun rose high. When the back of his neck began to burn in that pleasant sort of way every gardener knows, the thought struck him strange that he hadn't seen Jade. Then he remembered that she had died, and his eyesight dimmed and he stumbled to his knees, breath coming in shallow, furious pulses. He passed a hand over his face and rose again, for if he gave himself to the pain it would wash him away.

The old bones in his feet were sore from labor. But he'd grown to distrust the flat, wooden planks his young workers tied under their feet. They were different from the leather sandals he'd grown up wearing. And being barefoot helped him work longer before the pain set in.

At the end of several more hours of work, he slammed his final basket down and kicked it. His tears had long since dried, and all that was left was a fiery rage. Sweat stung his eyes, and he was desperately thirsty. Though nothing remained in his storehouse but barrels of undiluted wine.

He took several deep breaths to calm the ire, grabbed a clay cup, and filled it with pale, pungent liquid.

He drank until he gasped for breath. The liquid burned his throat, leaving him thirstier than before. So he refilled his cup and drank again.

Then he sat and thought of her. After a while, the anger lessened, along with the pain.

He knew why, so he stood and filled his cup again.

And again.

And again.

Until he could barely see, and he stumbled to his work tent where he often sat to answer his workers' questions.

But no one was working today.

He remembered her, then, in only beauty and glory. She looked, to his blended thoughts, as stunning as the sun. He lay on the ground and focused his mind on how her lips had moved when she spoke, and how her hands had flowed in rhythm to her conversation.

"I love you," he whispered. "And I will never forget you."

He tore his tunic in honor of her, and lay naked on the hard ground until he slept in a drunken stupor.

2

Ham

Ham gripped the reins of the loping camel beneath him and leaned into the wind. They were crossing the plains toward a cliff that descended to Noah's vineyard at the foot of the mountains the ark had landed on a century earlier. Dark clouds dashed across the distant horizon, dragging a gray skirt of rain across the hills half a day's journey east. The storm would miss them, but the power of those billowing giants spawned little dust eddies that twirled across the packed dirt road in front of him and tossed silt into his eyes.

His camel brayed, its sides contracting beneath Ham's legs as he pulled his thin, sheer scarf over his face. His sons, Cush, Egypt, Put, and Canaan followed on their own camels, as did all of his grandchildren and those great-grandchildren old enough to ride. Cush's wife had stayed back with their newly born infant, Nimrod, while all who were able made ultimate haste to pay homage to the death of their matriarch.

Being the youngest of three sons and many girls, Ham had loved his mother and had relied on her heavily because in the formative years of Ham's life, Noah had been most preoccupied with discipling followers of the Old Way. Ham's earliest memories were of wondering if Father was still alive because many days had passed since any had seen him.

Now that Mother was gone, though Ham had long since

become his own man, he felt the world had been tipped on its side. He did not cry, for he had long abandoned tears. But he felt a cold burning in his chest.

"I am ready," he whispered, the words muffled against his scarf as the group began to descend the steep, winding road. His camel kicked a large stone to the side, over the ledge. But the beast was surefooted and kept Ham safe as they navigated the path.

He received no answer from the presence he had felt the previous night as he sacrificed. Of course, that meant nothing. What mattered was his obedience. The silence was a test. And he would pass this one as he'd passed every other test since the start when they'd ridden in the dark, musty ark atop violent waters.

They reached the bottom of the cliff and the way widened and led them up a small hill. At the crest, he pulled the reins and the entourage skidded to a stop. There, cradled in the lap of the mountains, stood Noah's vineyard.

Cush pulled his camel beside Ham and raised one brow. "Should we not make haste?"

Ham nodded and pulled the scarf back. "Today."

Canaan joined them and exchanged a meaningful glance with Cush.

"Do you mean . . . ?" Cush said.

Ham nodded. The day was late, and the sun hovered just above the peak of the mountain atop which he could see the bitter remains of the ark like so much rotted refuse. "Today, we make known the truth." He was feeling again the presence of that living clot of darkness he had first seen in the corner of the room inside the ark, as they were thrown to and fro. That was when his Master first revealed himself and offered a revelation that reinterpreted all the events since the foundation of the world.

Canaan nodded, mouth curling into a smile, nostrils flaring with sudden, heavy breaths. He could feel it too.

The Light Bringer cast a heavy shadow.

"He visited me last night," Ham said. "And confirmed that never again will we have such a gathering." He nodded toward the vineyard; noticed a single star stabbing through the blue expanse above. Ham pointed and Cush, Canaan, and several others looked up and gasped. The star hovered directly above Noah's vineyard. "Already we are given a sign that the age of the Light Bringer—the Morning Star—is dawning. Come, let us make haste to our matriarch."

Ham yelled and commanded his camel forward. His children and grandchildren flowed down the hill, across the valley, through the gates behind him.

The rows of grapevines rushed passed, and Ham pulled on the reins, angling toward the group amassed just outside the workers' quarters. Shem was there with hands raised as if conducting a worship service, the man's broad shoulders and perpetual frown instantly recognizable. Japheth's long neck thrust his dark face well above the rest, and as Ham stopped and dismounted, Japheth extended his hand. Ham didn't shake it.

"Where is father?" Ham said.

Japheth retracted his hand and ran his fingers through his long beard. "He has yet to show himself."

Shem approached. "You traveled fast."

"Camels' feet *are* faster than men's. Where is mother's body?"

Shem paled, and his frown deepened until the lines seemed scars dug into the underside of his chin. "Have you no decorum?"

Ham's eyes narrowed. "Was my question too simple?"

Japheth stepped between them but kept his voice low so only Ham would hear every word. "She is still lying on her reed mat. I found her when I first looked for father."

Ham met the eyes of the onlookers and lifted his chin at Japheth, voice strong and clear. "And you just left her there."

Japheth winced and shifted on his feet.

"You've not even thought to prepare her body for burial." Ham spit on the ground and pointed at Shem. "Yet insult *me* for lack of decorum." He handed the reins of his camel to Cush and spun on his heel, heading down the line of work buildings. His Master had been right. This would be easier than he imagined.

Japheth followed first and laid a long hand on his shoulder. "Where are you going?"

"To find Father."

Shem tried to settle a rising murmur from the crowd of gathered family. "All is well. Ham often speaks thus, but he means well." He lifted his tunic and jogged to catch up. A few children coughed in the dust their arrival turned up, and a baby cried as its mother tended it.

Ham reached the first storehouse and tossed aside the covering over the doorway. Light stabbed through columns of dust to illuminate earthenware vessels stopped with wax seals. Tools hung from walls, and clay tablets rested against the vessels with carved markings to differentiate their contents.

"Father has endured a great loss today," Shem said. "We chose to offer Father several hours out of kindness."

Ham met Shem's gaze. "It is no kindness to let our mother's bones rot." He neared Shem and bent over his older, shorter brother.

Shem leaned back at first, then straightened, fire dancing in his eyes, though he kept his tone calm. "Father had hoped to put her in the side of the mountain, but there will not be enough time to carve a tomb."

"Stay out of my way," Ham said, the corner of his mouth curling like a leaf blade. "I didn't come today to be lectured like a babe still suckling at his mother's breast. I came to talk to Father."

Shem took a deep breath and raised his chin. "Not alone, you won't."

Ham laughed. "Don't worry. I want everyone to hear." He spun on his heel and moved to the next storage building as Shem and Japheth exchanged quiet words, Japheth rubbing the back of his head.

He tossed aside the curtains on each storage building.

Finally, in the fifth and final one, Ham found wine stains on the packed earth floor. He followed the trail toward a work tent about fifty paces north while Shem and Japheth followed slowly after.

Ham pulled open the flap of the work tent and passed within. A dark figure lay against the far canvas wall. Ham squinted, waiting for his eyes to adjust.

Slowly his sight sharpened, and he saw the hairy legs of his father, and the remnants of a torn tunic still partially under him. Ham dipped and lifted a small, empty wine flask, noticing his father had spilled wine on himself and it had dried on his bare chest.

Ham took a deep breath and kicked his father in the side.

Nothing. Not even a moan.

Ham looked into his father's face, seeing the evidence of wine-induced stupor, hearing the slow intake of breath. His hands clenched to fists, and his nails dug into his palms.

Ham knelt and put his face within inches of his father's, until the heat from his skin radiated on his own. "Pathetic old drunk." And he spit in his father's face and slapped him hard across the cheek.

Father moaned and shifted subtly before falling silent once more.

Ham stood and spat on his father's naked body thrice more before exiting to see Japheth and Shem staring at him. Ham motioned with his chin. "He's in there."

"Is he not well?" Japheth said.

"Drank himself into a stupor. The fool is naked. So drunk he didn't flinch when I spit on him."

Shem gasped, and his hands clenched and unclenched. Footsteps sounded, and Shem's face reddened as a few of Japheth's children, along with Ham's youngest, Canaan, appeared.

"Why would you . . . ?" Japheth stopped himself because he knew Ham's temper well enough. Japheth motioned for one of his children and said, "Meshech, I'm glad you've come. A covering for your grandfather, please." Meshech's brow furrowed before he bowed low and ran off.

"Believe me," Ham said, "he deserves more."

"He is grieving. On what authority do you judge him?" Shem said.

"On the authority of a son grieving the loss of his mother. Have I suffered any less? And yet I am sober. Think of the monumental responsibility he holds as father of all and prophet of the Almighty. But I forget . . . when has he ever been there for his family?"

"The way you speak is shameful," Shem said.

"You only say that because you're too afraid of the Almighty to question his chosen worker prophet."

"And you aren't?" Japheth said, his voice low, cautious.

Ham waved Canaan close. His son neared, chest rising as Ham clasped his shoulder. "Why should we fear what does not exist?"

Both Shem and Japheth stood speechless. Mouths agape.

"Tell me," Ham said. "Have you seen the Almighty work any miracles?"

"I have not," Canaan said, eyes alight with confident passion.

"What are you saying?" Japheth said.

"As prophet of the Almighty," Ham continued, "should his god not have brought his beloved back to life?"

A strange noise burst from Shem's throat, halfway between a cough and a groan. This time, even Japheth had to take a deep breath to calm himself.

"You were there at the cataclysm," Shem said. "Do you not remember?"

Ham chuckled. "The flash of the star that fell and broke the world, tossing plumes of water into the heavens? Or perhaps the ark we rode, as it was tossed on violent currents for over forty days?" He narrowed his eyes and lowered his voice. "I remember better than you, for while captive in that ark, I was visited by the true god of this world and shown the real purpose for the flood."

Shem scoffed, his brows raised in disbelief. "The Almighty sent the Flood to protect those faithful to the Old Way from slaughter."

"The Almighty had nothing to do with the Flood," Ham said.

Shem tossed his hands in the air, voice reaching higher like a fist about to fall. "Then who threw the star to the earth?"

"The Morning Star himself: the Light Bringer."

Shem took a deep breath and his face paled. For a moment, his lips moved, but no sound escaped them. Then he shook his head and the heat returned to his eyes. "I've heard that name before, but never from my own family."

"The Light Bringer was the god of the Others," Japheth said. "The Others—those beasts with horns on their heads—were the ones who slaughtered our friends. How could you give your allegiance to such a false god?"

"Have you never wondered why the Others—a race so superior they nearly obliterated us—followed the Light Bringer?" Ham said. "They would not have worshipped anyone who failed to offer power and knowledge of the inner workings of the universe. Indeed, the Light Bringer was the source of their genius. And he has offered power to me, in exchange for my service as his mouthpiece."

Shem nodded slowly. "So, you think yourself a prophet."

"I know myself a prophet. And before the end, you will see it proven in action as well as in word."

"Why would the Light Bringer destroy his own servants with a flood?" Japheth said. Voice measured, calming. Still trying to convince.

Ham smiled and spoke low and slow, as Shem had spoken to him earlier. "My dear Japheth. If given the ability, you would always choose the space *between* sides, wouldn't you?"

Japheth merely blinked at him. Obviously disliking where this was going.

"But today," Ham continued, "there will be no twilight left to hide in. Only the black of ignorance or the burning revelation of the bright Morning Star. Your desire for peace is nothing more than a childish fantasy."

"You never answered me," Japheth said, voice finally devoid of that pandering tone.

"The Others grew too greedy," Ham said, smiling that he'd broken his brother. "After the Light Bringer gave them strange gifts, they sought to abandon him. So well did they achieve their goals that the Light Bringer needed to intervene, lest the whole world forget him for the God-King, who sought to usurp his place."

"That's a lie," Shem said. "I am older than you and saw more than you remember. The God-King was the Light Bringer's servant."

"You remember what father taught you. The God-King was a usurper. Nothing more."

Shem and Japheth were both struggling for some way to

counter his arguments. But after a moment, Shem flung his hands in the air and said, "Enough! Today is the day of our mother's funeral. You would defile it with a public declaration of your apostasy from the Almighty?"

"I never served the Almighty. You cannot betray one whom you never claimed to serve."

Japheth tugged at his beard. "Where is this coming from, brother? I don't understand—"

"Our family can choose well enough for themselves," Ham said. "They may listen to the prophet of the Almighty, who is currently stark naked and unconscious in a drunken stupor, or maybe they'll listen to the prophet of the Light Bringer, and the truth that has been suppressed by our patriarch."

Footsteps pounded close, and Meshech rounded a corner with a covering rolled in both hands. The young man knelt before Japheth and offered the roll. Japheth and Shem glanced at each other, then nodded and unrolled the fabric, holding it high to avoid dragging it in the dirt. They passed into the tent backward, faces toward the exit so they would not see their father's nakedness.

Ham smiled and patted Canaan's shoulder. "Come, let us go to the others." And he and Canaan turned and made their way back to the rest of the gathered family.

3

Noah

"Father."

Jade was holding Noah's hand and laughing. Wild blue and yellow flowers he'd picked were in her braided hair. Her eyes, so alive, gleamed with joy that sparked his soul back to life.

"Father?"

Her fingers slipped away, and she spun, arms stretched in the warm breeze that blew across the hills outside their vineyard. All was kissed gold by the cloud-dappled heavens, even as he felt the universe being fit inside his chest at the sight of her.

"Father . . ."

He certainly would burst. How could his body contain such violent emotion? Such relentless love? The heart that thumped in his chest did so to the rhythm of her movements. As she skipped back to him and laid her head on his shoulder, he felt time stretch endless in a moment he could have lived and died in.

Then his side began to ache.

"Father!"

Where was the pain coming from? He didn't remember feeling any pain as she danced with him. But his side hurt worse. And there was a pressure on his chest. Not from inside, but from out. As if someone were resting their elbow on him.

He moaned and ran his hand across his aching eyes, wiping the vision away.

His sight was blurred, and he heard the intake of breath above him.

"Father, are you alright?" A low voice. A man's voice.

Noah was staring at tent canvas. He closed his eyes to try to hold onto the memory of her. But she was gone. Only, why should she have to be gone forever? Surely he could just go back to sleep and find her again.

But hands shook him hard, and he opened his eyes and looked up to see his son, Shem, bending over him. Forehead creased with worry.

Noah turned away and curled his knees to his chest. Now that he moved, his head throbbed horribly, and his stomach quivered. He moaned again, and pressed his palms against his temples. "Pain," he whispered.

Shem sighed and backed away. "You drank too much."

Noah tried to ignore him. But he was right. Noah had failed. Miserably.

The pain of loss had been too much to bear. How could he cope with it unaided?

He knew the answer. The Almighty was faithful. If he had abided in the Almighty, he would have found the strength to cope. Not on his own, of course. Never on his own.

"Yes," he said. "I'm sorry, son."

"The whole family is gathered. We waited. But Ham was not so patient."

Now Noah felt true shame. "What day is it?"

"The same day you called us. But the sun will soon set. It is late, and some of us have been waiting long."

Noah bit his cheek and shook his head. With great effort, he pushed himself up on his elbow and realized a covering had been thrown over him. It slid down, exposing his naked midsection, and he pulled it back up and looked at Shem questioningly.

"Ham was the one who found you. He . . ." Shem looked away and shook his head. "He tried to wake you. When you didn't respond, he spat on you. After he left your tent, he ridiculed you and the Almighty, both."

Noah's sight dimmed. His mind struggled to grapple with

what Shem was saying. Why would Ham do such a thing? And on the day of Jade's death?

Shem seemed to read the confusion in his face and said, "I assure you, I would not make such a false claim. You know me better than that."

Indeed. Shem never said more than what truth could support. Even as Japheth always talked better of everything than he should.

Noah felt a burning sensation coil in the base of his throat, like a serpent ready to strike. How dare Ham defile such an occasion. He had never been affectionate with Noah. But this was something else. Something evil.

"There is more," Shem said.

"I cannot handle what you've shared with me already," Noah said.

"And yet, what choice do we have? We must face the day, or crumble."

Noah took a deep breath and nodded.

"Ham claims to be a prophet."

"What? A prophet of the Almighty?"

"Of the Light Bringer."

A chill crawled up his spine and nipped at the nape of his neck. Sweat moistened his palms, and his fingers twitched against the fabric of the covering laid over him. He opened his mouth, but at that moment, the tent flap opened and Noah squinted in the light.

"Here," said another familiar voice—Japheth's. "I brought a new tunic . . . from Father's home."

"Did you see her?" Noah said, and they fell silent.

Japheth took a deep breath, neared, and held out the spare tunic for him. Noah took it, slid it over his head, and pushed it beneath the covering.

Japheth held out his hand, and Noah grabbed his forearm and struggled to a stand with his help.

"Thank you," Noah said. And he tried to take a step, but stumbled, so Shem caught him.

"Come," Shem said. "I can perform the funeral in the Almighty's name, so that you need not worry."

"Not before I speak with Ham," Noah said.

"Ham is grieving," Japheth said. "You can wait until after."

"I cannot," Noah said. "Jade would be furious if I ignored this. He must face his evil and turn from whatever madness has possessed him."

Noah looked at his tallest son, Japheth, whom no one could deny lived out the love of God more than any other. Then at Shem, whose frowning expression hid a heart bursting with passion for the Almighty's righteousness. "Thank you. Both of you."

They nodded in respect and helped lead him from the tent into the dwindling daylight.

Each step from the work tent to the servant quarters was deadly difficult. If not for Shem and Japheth on either side, his legs would have failed. His sight still spun from the liquor, and his head throbbed and his insides churned. But the worst part was the sense of doom that hung over Shem's words about Ham.

How could Ham claim to serve the Light Bringer? The Light Bringer was the defiler. Deserving of nothing but damnation. The very reason the Almighty had drowned the world. If such an evil had been given a foothold in Noah's own family . . .

They rounded the final corner, and Noah spotted his many children, grandchildren, great-grandchildren, and more. His family had grown and spread over many lands in such a short time. Building cities. Organizing their lives. Noah had become so distanced from them that he failed to recognize a few of those gathered.

He shook his head. How quickly the world had changed since they stepped from the ark to a world baptized. It seemed like only last year. And yet . . . how long had it been? Certainly over a century. Oh, how time bent with age.

How had he failed to recognize any warnings in Ham's life? How could any of his family abandon the Almighty?

It was heinous. Unforgivable.

"Ham," Noah called as he, Shem, and Japheth stopped approximately thirty paces from the family.

Ham stepped forward, his dark eyes and brows like obsidian in a desert cliff. "Father! Where have you been?"

Noah dipped his head, momentarily fighting a growing burning in his eyes. Now that he faced his son, some of his fury waned in the presence of shame, which was exactly what Ham had intended.

Still, the Almighty knew his heart. That never would he abandon the Almighty, as Ham so boldly had.

His Lord, who was his love, and now the greatest thing he had left. He raised his voice for all to hear. "What have you done?"

"Demanded you do what you failed to do: be present with your family."

Noah held Ham's frowning gaze. So, this was how it was going to be. Pointed fingers, taking the attention from his own evils.

Noah would not allow it. "Shem tells me you believe yourself a prophet of the Light Bringer."

Ham raised his chin and, surprisingly, smiled. "I am."

"You have chosen today to defile your family's name. And the name of the Almighty. This, the day of your mother's death!"

"I have only ever honored Jade."

Noah blinked as the rest of his anger bled away to make way for the fear that his son had truly gone mad. "What evil has gripped your fragile mind?"

Ham snorted. "Fragile mind?" He spun to the family, not bothering to address Noah anymore. "I have come to bear witness about the truth."

A murmur rose through the crowd. But Ham's son Canaan crossed to his father's side and said, "Listen to the voice of the Light Bringer!"

Many threw Ham confused looks, clearly unfamiliar with the name. For Noah, Shem, and Japheth had refused to speak that demon's name since the world was changed, and only they and their wives remembered through experience its true significance.

"You have been taught that the Almighty created the world," Ham continued. "That he demands our allegiance. That it was on behalf of mankind's apostasy that he sent the Flood to purify the world."

Heads bobbed in tentative agreement. Noah was so confused

by Ham's words that he didn't know how to respond. He felt paralyzed, convinced he was watching a horrible dream where trees grow crooked and men forget their fathers' names.

"And it is a lie."

Now there was a rumble of disapproval, and a young woman cried out, "Heretic!"

Ham raised his arms. "Silence!"

Noah breathed deeply and shouted, "Let him speak. If he wants to defile himself, let him dirty his soul for all to see."

Ham looked back. "Wise words from our inebriated patriarch." But the words were quiet, and though it drained the warmth from Noah's cheeks, the greater group failed to hear.

Again Canaan raised his voice. "Listen to truth!"

Ham laid a quieting hand on Canaan's shoulder and stepped forward, pacing, head swiveling to address each person individually. "As I rode the violent waters in the ark, the Light Bringer appeared and offered me a revelation. What he showed me, in visions, convinced me that what we've been told is no more than a delusion perpetuated by the prophet of the Almighty, whom I found today naked in a drunken stupor on the floor of his work tent."

A few shook their heads and looked to Noah as if to question if that could be true.

Noah resisted the urge to dip his head. He felt shame for his weakness, even as he knew his own evil was nothing in comparison to what paraded itself before them all now. *Lord*, he prayed, *do not let my mistakes disqualify your Word.*

"The Almighty did not send the Flood," Ham continued. "The Light Bringer is the one who tossed a star to the earth to drown it in water, because the God-King, who ruled the earth in my father's day, was a great deceiver who sought to usurp the Light Bringer's place. The God-King sought to be worshipped as the true god of the world. And he used all the gifts the Light Bringer gave him to steal the glory rightly attributed to the Light Bringer."

Now Ham turned back to Noah. "The Light Bringer is a jealous god." He pointed at Noah. "As jealous as Noah's Almighty. Therefore, all of us must choose. Abandon ignorance and choose the Light, or continue in the Old Way and war against progress. But you may be certain of one thing—those who follow the Old Way will end up just like its prophet, drunk and confused."

Silence. They all just looked at Noah, then back at Ham.

"Well," Shem said. "I made my choice long ago."

Much of Shem's progeny murmured their approval.

"As did I," Japheth said. And roughly half of his progeny agreed without pause.

Canaan stepped forward and raised his hands. "And I have made mine! Nothing now will change it, for I have gazed into the Light."

The family shifted uncomfortably and some seemed to murmur approval to Canaan's words. The family looked at each other and the resolve in their eyes faltered. Little conversations burst out amongst them. Noah caught snippets.

"What did you just say? You can't be—"

"No! I didn't say anything. It was—"

"How dare you nod your head at such blasphemy—"

"But could it be true? What if—"

Noah stepped forward out of the grasp of his sons, who were now preoccupied. He had sobered enough to stand on his own and knew he no longer had the luxury of embarrassment at the thought of baring his darkest sins to them all. He spread his arms, as if inviting them to look beneath his chest and see his flaws—for there they would also see his passion for the Almighty's righteousness. "Who among us is without sin?" he cried out, and several of the younger ones jumped. "Yet cursed be Canaan! A servant of servants shall he be to his brothers." With each step, Noah's voice gained strength. "Blessed be the Lord, the God of Shem; and let Canaan be his servant. May God enlarge Japheth, and let him dwell in the tents of Shem, and let Canaan be his slave. Truly, I tell you that any who follow the Light Bringer in their hearts will crawl on all fours like beasts until they are beaten back to the dust from which they were formed."

Ham faced him and stepped close. "You fear me."

"I think you are dangerous."

Ham shook his head. "Is it dangerous to find love, acceptance, meaning?"

"You have abandoned the Almighty."

"You mean your lover? Yes, you loved him more than you loved me, more than you loved any of us. And you left us for the duties he imposed on you."

"I did what was needful."

Ham raised his voice, face red, veins bulging across his forehead and neck. "You abandoned me!"

The echo reverberated off the mountains behind and the cliffs before, leaving nothing but shocked silence in its wake.

"Son," Noah said. "Is that really how you felt?"

Ham calmed, but his voice remained strong. "You no longer hold authority over me. After I realized the truth about you while riding in the ark, I abandoned the idea that I am your son at all. Instead, I am a child of the Light Bringer."

Noah's eyes blurred. His fury rushed back with teeth bared. How could Ham accuse him of abandoning any of them? He had been there for them. Had provided for them. Had protected them and served the Almighty faithfully. And this was how his son repaid him? He opened his mouth and before he even realized what was happening, heard himself scream, "Then it is clear that you were never my son at all."

No one said anything.

Ham nodded. Eyes glossy.

Noah gazed into the blacks of Ham's eyes and saw in them the distant reflection of his own face swallowed by darkness.

Then his son turned. "Come," Ham called to his children and grandchildren, and reluctantly they obeyed. "Never again will we commune with the followers of the Almighty. Never again will we speak to them, for the evil their prophet spoke over us today." He stopped and turned back to Noah. His limbs shook as he ground his teeth together. But it was Ham's eyes that caught Noah's attention.

They were filled with tears.

"Good-bye." The word was barely a whisper. In that moment, Noah saw the little boy who'd held Jade's hand and slept on their chests.

Noah did not respond. He was too disturbed. Caught between rage and the deepest of griefs. Between horrible anxiety and a sense of holy duty.

What had happened to his family? Noah's family's story was not supposed to be that of Adam's. For that first family had been built of dust, while Noah's family had been washed in the flood-waters. The world was supposed to begin anew with them.

But now, Noah's family had become just like Adam's. Nothing more than a pile of fractured dust.

He bowed his head and grieved the perversion in his son's heart. He was not only experiencing the death of his wife, but also the death of his relationship to his youngest son.

He knew only one thing for certain. This . . . this was not his fault.

4

Noah

Ham and his children departed, along with many of their descendants, though a portion remained. Shem and Japheth reverently carried their mother's body out of the home on a reed mat and set her beside the hole that Noah's workers dug with heavy bronze tools.

Noah stood in the failing sunlight like an old tree battered by hailstones. The hole was now deep enough for a man to stand in, shoulder-high. Japheth lowered himself into it and looked up at Noah as if feeling for the first time the weight of it all. Japheth's son, Meshech, did the same. Together, they carefully lowered Jade into the pit and then stood staring with eyes shining with unshed tears.

Shem stood with hands raised and eyes closed. "Great Almighty, we thank you for the life you gave to our beloved. Though you have taken her, our hearts are slow to follow. So, in this moment, we release our hold. We surrender to your will, and ask that you comfort our afflicted souls."

Noah dipped and raised a handful of dirt. He held it in his fist, hard as he could, imagining how the Almighty had formed them, in the beginning, from dust and breath. Then he pictured Jade's smiling face nodding at him, exhaling one final time. Waving good-bye. He nodded and let the dust sprinkle her shoulders.

Shem looked at him with some interest, likely thinking through what the gesture meant. Then he grabbed a handful of soil while Japheth and Meshech crawled out of the grave.

Japheth stood and brushed himself off, then dipped and did the same. One by one, every person in the family dropped a handful of soil onto their matriarch's body, until the workers took up their shovels and finished pushing the last of the earth over her.

Noah turned away and walked slowly back to his home as twilight transmuted to the gray pall of moonlight. He had imagined the ceremony would make Jade's death that much more real, but it hadn't. The better part of him still felt certain that he would find her inside, healthy as she'd looked on her last day.

He knew it was impossible, and wondered if his mind and heart would ever agree over such an unnatural evil.

But he had work left to do. He had a family. A vineyard.

Thank the Almighty for his vineyard. He turned from his home toward those roofless halls again. The vineyard had saved his family after the deluge. Maybe it would save him now.

He had fallen to the lure of wine and tasted the bitterness of drunkenness as fully as he imagined any man could. The shame of Ham's ridicule, and his entire family seeing his brokenness, still singed his ears. It was enough to make the idea of drunkenness appalling.

But perhaps the vineyard could be the escape he wished it to be without imbibing another drop. He placed his hand on a trellis and felt the dry wood fibers. With his other hand, he rolled the fibrous vines between his fingers and, for the first time since Jade died, he smiled.

5

Ham

The wind whipped Ham's face as he led the procession of camels back across the plains by starlight. Ham hated himself for having felt such emotion as he spoke to Father. The flat edge of the reins dug into his palms.

Had he not hardened his heart? Had he not chosen the way of violence and fantasized about his encounter with Noah for years?

Indeed, he'd known every word Father would speak before he'd spoken. Ham had chosen this path for the treasure laid before him. Still, at the end he had battled tears.

"Master," he whispered, "reveal to me your will."

He heard, as if from far away, the hissing intake of breath growing closer, closer. A chill wind crawled across his hands and frosted his knuckles. He smiled and rolled his eyes back into his head in anticipation of what would come next.

That familiar dark presence entering his nostrils like ice water. The pressure of his soul being forced out and away, into the void where all was black like the dark between stars made liquid and bottled in an endless pit.

The rush of terror came, but it lasted only a moment, until he floated in that embryonic darkness once again.

"You came," he whispered. For his Master had finally responded to his summons and possessed his body as requested, thereby placing Ham's soul into what he had come to call the void. "An honor," Ham said.

It was the greatest honor that could be bestowed. The void was everything, because it was nothing. No fear, no pain, no joy, no laughter. Just endless, infinite emptiness.

Noah had never found such freedom. Noah had never been chosen by Ham's Master. Noah had never been placed into the void. No one had. He was certain of this, for his Master had told him.

Because the Master had chosen *him* only.

Noah's Almighty chose everyone. Was that supposed to make them feel special?

"Quiet your mind," his Master said. *"And I will give you a vision."*

"A vision of your will?" Ham's pulse pounded in his throat with excitement.

"Of my will," his Master said.

It was all he could do to hold back laughter. But he was in the void. The most holy of places. Where emotion was to be drained, not indulged.

He closed his eyes and focused on breathing deep and slow, though he risked letting the smile stay. The vision came immediately, and with such violent force he thought he would burst.

He saw a baby wriggling in his mother's hands. She swaddled him. Already his arms were fat with rolls. The mother dipped close and rubbed her nose on the baby's.

"I want the baby," the Master said. *"He will be mine."*

Ham felt his smile crack and bleed. He cleared his throat. "You have me. What do you need this child for?"

"To be my vessel."

Ham was silent, staring at the baby's tiny fingernails. Wondering if he should find the child and destroy it. Toss it from a rooftop so it could never replace him.

"Ah-ah-ah," the Master said. *"You think I haven't thought of that? Crush him and I will crush you."*

Pain descended on his limbs like boulders. Ham cried out in agony and tried to see if his bones were being turned to dust, but he could see nothing but what little he glimpsed through the window to the vision of that baby boy.

The mother dipped again into the frame and whispered softly, "Nimrod, my dear Nimrod."

As quickly as it came, the pain and vision were gone.

"Don't worry. It will be many years before he's ready. He must be prepared by his father. Afterward, he must prove himself a willing and able vessel."

"What can he do that I cannot?"

"A generation dies and another takes its place. You are still mine. You will be until you die . . . so long as you obey me."

Ham nodded, eager to please, even as desires warred inside him, kept back only by the fear he felt for his Master.

"Good. Now, when you wake, you will speak the words I give you, but only to Cush. Cush's son, Nimrod, and his daughter, Hava, must be prepared. They will marry, for together, they will unify the world. But I have not chosen Hava. She is ruthless, yes, and she will use that ruthlessness to pressure Nimrod. But she has never felt care or regard for others, for she was born broken, an imperfect vessel who could never be my chosen servant. She is blemished, but Nimrod is whole. And so the blemished one shall break the whole, and I will enter through the fractures and my rule shall be complete. Will you do this, my chosen *servant?"*

Ham took a deep breath and let it out slow. "Of course, Master. Anything for you."

PART II

The Tower Grows

290 YEARS AFTER THE WORLDWIDE FLOOD

6

Noah

Noah woke before sunrise on the same style of reed mat in the same part of the same room of the same house he'd lived in for centuries. However, instead of early morning silence, he heard distant yelling and sounds of discord.

He rose from the mat, body creaking like a weathered tree in autumn wind, eyes struggling to pierce the darkness around him. He paused with his breath held to hear faint words.

"Resist and die!"

Noah shook his head. He couldn't be hearing right. But any sound so late at night in his vineyard was unusual.

He shuffled to the edge of the room with arms outstretched through the void-like dark. His fingertips found cool uneven brick, and slid down to the packed dirt floor, patting until he found his sandals.

He sat again, cross-legged, tied the sandals to the bottom of his feet, then rose and tossed aside the double door covering designed to protect the house from the brisk weather this time of year. Chill wind blasted his face, wrenching the breath from his chest. Stars shone like a million torches lodged in the black sky above, and the voices came louder and closer than he expected. Shadows danced in orange torch light from behind several of the larger work tents.

"Tell me who sent you," said a familiar voice. Noah was quite certain it was Aran, a young man he had hired years earlier to guard his vineyard from thieves.

Noah lifted the long hem of his sleep tunic and jogged over the frosted soil as fast as his limbs would allow so early. The shadows ahead shot back and forth violently as Noah heard men grunting. Noah's breaths came shallow and quick.

He rounded the work tents and saw a cluster of men locked together as if holding each other's arms. A young man—was it Aran?—thrust his fist into a bound man's midsection. The bound man, whom Noah didn't recognize, coughed and spit as the rest of the men held him upright, forcing him to stay in place.

Noah stepped into the outer halo of the lantern light and said, "What is going on?"

Several of the men jumped, and the man who was punishing the vagrant turned and lifted a burning lantern from the ground to see who had addressed them. As Noah had guessed, it was Aran. They recognized one another, and Aran nodded.

"Noah," Aran said. "You frightened me."

"Likewise," Noah said.

"We caught this man here with another, attempting to drag a woman away," Aran said.

"Who were they trying to take?"

"Elena. She's safe, though it may take her a while to recover from the terror of being stolen from her own bed."

Noah shook his head and looked again at the man they held. "Why?"

"Supposedly, they'd spoken of their desire to sacrifice her."

"We were bringing her to the tower," the man said.

Noah's eyes narrowed. The tower? The man looked like any normal youth. He could hardly even be older than nineteen. Noah stepped toward him. Aran placed a cautioning palm on Noah's chest.

Noah gently pushed Aran's hand away. "I've faced worse than this in my many years." Though he was careful to keep his distance. "Young man. Do you know who I am?"

The youth's face twisted into a sneer, and he chuckled. Bruises were already rising across his cheeks and face. His one eye was swollen nearly shut, and blood dribbled out of his nose and stained his teeth. "The shame of the world." The youth's body suddenly went rigid, and his eyes rolled back into his head as a horrid clicking sounded in the back of his throat.

Several of those holding him let go and stepped back, disturbed.

But that was exactly what the young man had wanted. His eyes returned to normal, and he lurched, bound hands deftly wrapping around the handle of a dagger sheathed in one of the workers' belts. He whipped the dagger out and, as the others realized what was happening, he yelled, "Praise the Light Bringer!" and thrust the blade straight into his heart.

Aran threw out his hands and yelled, "Get away from him!"

The group let go and ran away as the youth dropped onto his back.

Noah grimaced at the youth's writhing form as dark, flowing wetness soaked the earth around him. His breaths were ragged, and from time to time he moaned.

Noah stepped closer and they met each other's stare. The youth's eyes were glazed. "What is the 'tower'?"

The youth's eyes lost their focus.

Noah nudged him with his foot. "Tell me, quick."

But the youth only shook his head, and after a few moments he stilled, his eyes wide to the starlight he apparently worshiped.

Noah looked at Aran, who still stared at the body, eyes narrowed in disgust and suspicion. "Where is the other man you mentioned?" Noah said.

"He escaped."

The group looked at Noah, their eyes gleaming expectantly in the dim light.

It had been many years since last he heard the name of the Light Bringer. He had maintained little contact with anyone outside of his vineyard, and long ago Shem and Japheth had stopped mentioning anything about it. So he had assumed that the Light Bringer's evil name had not grown in popularity. Until moments ago, he would have guessed that he no longer posed any threat to their lives.

But to hear those words again, bathed in blood in the middle of his vineyard . . . it made fear pour like oil down the back of his neck.

Noah straightened and raised his voice so all could hear him. "You must tell me exactly what happened. From the smallest possible detail."

7

Nimrod

Nimrod walked his garden courtyard at a brisk pace. The crack of his sandals against the polished marble tiles reverberated against the inner wall that separated the garden from the rest of his home. He had been consulting the Light Bringer in his secret underground temple, for the tower's capstone was half a year away from being placed, and already well past their original desired finish date. Its massive shoulders tossed their shadow across half the city from sunrise to sunset. And he needed to maintain his devotion amidst the flurry of activity toward the end.

That was when his servant arrived and told him that a recently famous follower of the Old Way had come to Nimrod's home seeking asylum because of the persecution he received from the followers of the Light Bringer.

Nimrod smiled at how the Light Bringer orchestrated the behavior of little men. How thankful he was that he'd exerted the effort necessary to convince the public he had no connection to the Light Bringer—even as he was one of two commissioned by Ham himself to fulfill the Light Bringer's prophecy to unite the world and slaughter the followers of the Old Way.

Because now, Nimrod had his own enemies coming to him, expecting deliverance. What they would receive would be altogether different.

Nimrod rounded a corner and pushed open the gate that led to the main entrance of his home. A camel was tied to the post out front, which meant his guest would already be seated at the dinner table amidst poisoned food, awaiting Nimrod's audience.

The acolytes of the Old Way had caused him too much trouble recently. That was why he had given the order for all priests of the Light Bringer to do away with them secretly, by any means necessary, until the day they revealed themselves when the tower was finished. Today, however, Nimrod would finally be able to dole out punishment in person. Part of him even hoped the man would refuse the poisoned food so he would be able to kill the man with his own hands.

From the entryway led two halls, one east, one west, both of which eventually turned south to hem in the garden courtyard. Nimrod entered the west hall and made for the dining room. The guards beside the door saw him but made no movement as he neared. They opened the door and stepped aside as Nimrod entered and crossed to the head of the long, rectangular table.

His guest was there, standing at the far end, wearing a simple travel tunic. The man held his hands behind his back, bowed low, and said, "My lord."

Nimrod smiled and searched his memory for the man's name, but failed to find it. "My dear friend," he said. "I apologize for making you wait. Have you been here long?"

The man straightened and shook his head. "Not at all."

"Sit, please." Nimrod motioned for him to make the first move.

The man frowned, hesitating.

Nimrod bowed his head low and extended his open hands in a second invitation. "I don't sit before my guests." He waited several long moments until the scrape of a chair and the rustle of cloth indicated the man had acquiesced.

Nimrod straightened and pulled the chair out for himself before sitting, mirroring the man.

They stared at each other. Before them sat myriad dishes overflowing with food. Cured meats and diverse cheeses. Pickled vegetables and wine flasks. Flatbreads, honeycakes, dried dates, freshly cooked fish. The choices appeared endless. All equally deadly.

Neither reached for anything.

"Are you displeased with what my servants have provided?" Nimrod said.

The man licked his lips and leaned forward, for they sat nearly ten paces from each other. "Please, I mean no offense. I have not come to indulge, but rather to seek your aid."

Nimrod nodded. "Ah, yes. You are desperate."

The man frowned even deeper. "I wouldn't say that."

"Oh?" Nimrod leaned forward. "Am I confused?"

"As I'm sure you know, the work I do is important to the stability of the city. But recently, I've been persecuted by certain factions for my religious affiliation."

"Religious affiliation?"

"I converted to the Old Way some years back. I came to you not because I believe myself deserving of your protection, but because I heard you reject religion and seek the unification of all men. However, since the construction of the tower began, the followers of the Light Bringer have become more and more emboldened. Please, you hold the authority and power to speak against such persecution. I beg you to stand against it."

Nimrod frowned at the food. "You aren't hungry. Let's do something else, instead."

The man blinked. "I'll eat."

Nimrod stood and clapped his hands. Eight servants entered as Nimrod said, "No, it is as you say. You are important to the stability of my city. I can't risk offending you." The servants positioned themselves on either side of the table, then lifted and began carrying the table out.

The man sat in his chair, mouth gaping. Too dumbfounded to move.

"They'll need your chair as well," Nimrod said, as two of the servants returned and one grabbed Nimrod's chair while the other went to retrieve the man's.

The man stood. "My apologies."

Nimrod smiled. "You like physical activity?"

"I . . . don't understand."

The final servant left with the last chair, leaving nothing in the room but the two men standing. The door slammed shut and a bolt sounded as it sunk home. "You're a slave trader, no? I began my work as a hunter—the two trades aren't so different, when you consider their core activities."

The man nodded, face suddenly pale. "My work is mainly administrative."

"That's a shame." Nimrod stretched his forearms. "Being in nature does wonders for the soul. I still personally take care of dangerous beasts when they become troublesome."

The man edged subtly toward the door while carefully keeping himself equidistant from Nimrod. "Oh?"

"The largest animal I ever killed with my bare hands was a male lion. Although I did use a stone, I suppose." He stretched his calves and back, grunting as he bent double to touch his hands to the ground.

"I've never killed anything." The man walked with surprising comfort to the door and tried it.

So the fool wasn't totally devoid of courage. At least Nimrod could appreciate that.

"Don't worry," Nimrod said, "my servants will open it again shortly."

The man nodded and cleared his throat, but when he opened his mouth, no words came out.

"Why haven't you?" Nimrod said.

"Sorry?"

"Killed anything? You've struck a man, haven't you?"

Even from so far away, Nimrod could see sweat break out across the man's forehead. "Who hasn't struck someone before?"

"I find it fascinating how easy death comes. The more you experience it, the less you fear it. You even start to enjoy it, in a strange way." Nimrod shook his arms to loosen his muscles. "Here, let me show you a way that you can approach any common animal."

Nimrod walked to the man, who just stood there, arms hanging by his sides. Nimrod lifted both hands and showed them to the man. "Lift your hands like this."

The man lifted his hands, mirroring Nimrod.

"It's all in your approach. For most animals—excluding predators—you should try to make them feel safe until they can no longer escape you." Nimrod stood less than an arm's length from the man, who visibly shook. "Now, wrap your hands around my throat," Nimrod said.

The man coughed, choking on his own saliva. He backed away two steps, shaking his head. "What?"

Nimrod closed in on the man again and said, "Like this." He wrapped his hands around the man's neck. Not hard, but with enough pressure to change the color in his face.

The man's hands reached up, frantic, grabbing at the hem of his garment.

"No," Nimrod said. "My throat."

The man reached up and grabbed Nimrod's throat as hard as he could.

Nimrod coughed and smiled. "Good," he managed. The man's fingers were cold. Nimrod let up a bit, and the man did the same, seemingly hopeful this wasn't going where he feared. "But you'll have to get over your anxiety," Nimrod said. "It steals blood flow from your extremities, and without blood flow, you lose strength. You must act with ultimate resolve. Like this." Nimrod smashed his thumbs into the man's throat, and rushed forward, slamming his back into the wall. Nimrod kept both hands in place, now using his entire body to push himself into the man's throat. The man fought back, trying to do the same to Nimrod, who did nothing to stop him.

The man's face was beginning to darken from red to purple, now to blue. His eyelids closed, and his cold fingers lost their remaining strength and fell from Nimrod's throat. Nimrod coughed. "Come now," he said. "Don't give up."

The man's legs kicked and shifted around. Nimrod pressed until the thumping in his neck stilled. Then he released, and the man's body crumpled to the ground.

Nimrod heard the lock unlatch, and the door swung open. Hava, Nimrod's wife, entered.

"Nimrod," Hava said.

"Yes?"

"I've been trying to find you." Four servants entered behind her.

"I've been busy," Nimrod said. He indicated the body on the ground. "Our guest had an accident."

"So I see," Hava said, rolling her eyes. "Hurry, so we can talk."

The servants bowed, awaiting orders. Nimrod addressed them. "You three, remove the body. You,"—he pointed at the last—"what was our guest's name?"

"Rin."

"Rin." Nimrod nodded. "Tell Rin's wife that he was ill when he arrived, and we were not able to save him. Deliver the body with our sympathies."

The three hauled the body out, and the final servant bowed one last time before exiting. The door shut behind them. Hava stepped in front of it and kept her voice low. "I know what city our daughter is in."

Nimrod shook his head and rubbed his hand through his short hair. "It's been five years since she ran away, yet you still can't seem to move on. You still believe she must be sacrificed to earn us a son from the Light Bringer?"

Hava twirled her hair around her index finger. "I will bear a son, no matter the cost."

"Fulfill the prophecy and you may."

"After we finish the tower and unify the world, the Light Bringer may abandon us for someone else. For what use are we to him after we do all that he demands?"

Nimrod shot her through with a stare as deadly as her own daggers. "Don't do anything reckless." Of course, he knew Hava never did anything without careful planning, but he distrusted her schemes. Hava was not like others. Father said that when she was born, she didn't cry. She just stared up at him like a crow stares at a gleaming jewel. She hadn't changed a bit. In fact, Nimrod had only grown more certain through the years that she'd never felt empathy in her life. Even explaining the concept felt like an impossible task.

Still, she knew more than any other living creature about desire and control. And she used that knowledge masterfully.

A smirk played at the corner of Hava's mouth. "You may be surprised to hear just how useful you might find my long-term interest in our daughter."

Nimrod waited. "Out with it. You know I do not abide your games."

Hava stepped near and ran her nails softly through his hair as she lowered her voice and smiled. "You want Noah."

No matter how many times she did it, the way she read his desires made saliva pool in his throat. "And?"

She chuckled, for his response was as good as an admission. "And our daughter just might bring him to us."

Nimrod peeled her arms away and leaned against the wall. He knew he should ignore her. It would only satisfy her ego to ask her to explain.

But what she was saying could change everything.

"Oh come now," Hava said. "Let me have my fun with you."

Nimrod narrowed his eyes. "Proceed."

Hava smiled again. "About a month ago, I sent acolytes to Noah's vineyard with specific instructions. The same day, I sent two servants to follow our daughter. Soon, the acolytes will strike, and Noah will be stirred from slumber."

"You fail to explain how this connects to our daughter."

Hava leaned in and jabbed a claw-like fingernail into Nimrod's chest. "The only way you'll find out is if you secure a guarantee that I will bear a son before it's too late. Do that, and I will take care of Noah."

She whipped around and flung the door wide, dress flapping as she disappeared.

Nimrod stood a moment, considering his options. Hava rarely asked anyone for anything. When she did, she was in a dangerous mood.

Though they had always had a tenuous relationship, and neither of them had ever loved the other, he had reason to believe she would not kill him—yet. For he had been chosen by their Master, not her. She needed him, for only he could guarantee her lust for a son would be fulfilled.

Even more, the prophecy that came to Nimrod's grandfather,

Ham, specifically stated that Nimrod and Hava would gather the world at the foot of the tower *together*.

It was the moment after they finished the tower that worried him.

As much as her perception unnerved him, he sensed that now she was speaking and moving out of fear. Though Nimrod had feared Hava since they were children, she had not been one to fear anything. He could count the times he'd seen her fearful on one hand. Somehow, she always managed to be in a position of power and control. The very few times she'd faced actual weakness, she always responded the same way: by murdering those who kept her hemmed in.

Nimrod shivered and made his way once more to the secret shrine of the Light Bringer they had built beneath their house. He would need the help of his god to survive these final, tenuous days.

8

Sarah

Sarah hadn't seen Rin in days. Before he left, he'd been especially anxious. Standing at the window in the middle of the night, whispering to himself to sort out thoughts too quiet for her to hear. She slept fitfully that night, always waking to him looming in another part of the room like a thief.

"It's just me," he had said at the sharp intake of her breath. She had calmed, though only a little, for his behavior reminded her of when he used to drink and she would wake to a dark stranger in her husband's skin. And that stranger would beat her until her own skin became foreign in the reflection in the water filling her cooking pots.

But he hasn't drunk since our son ran away. He only worries because his recent devotion to the Almighty has won us both terrifying enemies.

And so she fell back asleep. Because after everything that had passed between them, she loved him, and he loved her.

The next morning, just before he left, he sat on her reed mat. "I have to take care of you," he said.

"You have."

Zeck, their male house-servant, entered and brought them both tea. Rin eyed the servant and nodded, satisfied by the man's presence.

"Zeck," Rin said. "When I leave, keep watch. Make sure none enter this home unbidden."

"What of the chores, my lord?"

"I will send a female servant to care for my wife's needs," Rin said. "But I trust you to watch over this home and keep it safe."

Zeck nodded and flexed his muscular shoulders. "None shall pass without my permission."

Rin made to leave, but Sarah caught him by the wrist.

"You will come back soon?"

He stared into her eyes a moment, then smiled. "Don't worry."

After Rin left, Zeck took his position atop their home with bow and arrows in hand, and a staff slung over his shoulder. For three days Sarah watched him fight sleep, until finally taking pity on him and sending the female servant to seek replacements to relieve him in turns.

But even after the additional guard arrived, Sarah had to physically push Zeck down the ladder.

"You're worthless to Rin without rest," she said.

He grunted and, as the guard's footsteps sounded on the roof, laid down, closed his eyes, and began snoring.

Before the new guard's watch was up, Zeck woke and ascended the ladder with bloodshot eyes. The guard on watch yelled, "Zeck! What are you doing? Go rest." Zeck tried to argue, but after failing, he grunted and descended.

Sarah smiled and tipped her head questioningly.

Zeck shrugged his shoulders, grabbed his staff in both hands, and said, "I'll circle the property, then."

After the others saw what he was doing from the roof, they cursed his obstinacy, but eventually fell silent. For they knew better than Sarah the reasons for Rin's caution.

That their danger was real.

Sarah stared at the wall for hours and tried to keep her mind from anxious thoughts. Until Zeck entered again, only this time he brought a young man with him.

The young man immediately threw himself at Sarah's feet, and Sarah felt her throat seize. The man was dressed richly, even if obviously a servant. And that meant he was not a servant from any common household.

"I bring news to you of your husband, Rin, from Lord Nimrod."

"Nimrod," she said, more a question than a statement. "What business has my husband with your master?"

The servant paused and looked up at Zeck a moment, as if to gauge his intentions. "It is not for me to know such things."

"And yet I perceive that you know. Speak," she said. "Nothing you utter here will find its way back to your master."

The servant nodded. "My life is in your hands."

"Indeed," Zeck said.

The servant bowed his face nearly to the ground. "Rin pleaded with my lord for protection from those who have been harming his workers. He had heard that the Lord Nimrod was a man for peace who sought to unify the world."

Again, the servant paused and frowned at Sarah. When he continued, his voice was cold and dry. "Sadly, Rin was . . . ill when he arrived, and my Lord Nimrod was . . . unable to cure him. I am sorry. He is gone."

Tears threatened to spring from her eyes, but she forced them away and stilled her quivering lips. "Where is he?"

"We brought him. He is outside, wrapped in linen and laid in a cart."

Sarah turned away, then, to hide her eyes for just a moment. She cleared her throat and straightened her back. "I hear you, along with what you fear to speak." She gauged the servant, who again bowed his face to the floor. "You have done your duty. Now go, before my wrath overtakes my thankfulness."

"You speak with grace," he said. "Thank you." And his breath against the ground turned up silt.

Zeck yanked the man up by the shoulder and ushered him firmly—though not abusively—out.

Sarah's thoughts rushed like water from a broken dam. Rin had made a fatal mistake. One that may prove deadly to her, as well. His slave-trading business would need someone to run it. It would be vulnerable to attack without him.

She raised her hand to her cheeks and found them wet. Thankful that she had been alone when they finally broke through, she quickly swiped them away and forced herself past the mountain of grief to grapple with the reality that many lives were now in great danger.

Rin had become an anomaly. He had first entered the business to pile up wealth for infinite drink. But after their son ran away fearing his abuse, the Almighty had made Rin's heart tender, and he'd become a follower of the Old Way. He began to see his work as an extension of his religion, and as the largest slave trader between the rivers, he held enormous power. He'd grown selective with the slave placement process. Only providing slaves to those who would treat them well, and who aided the cause of the Old Way. He also began to use his vast wealth to protect the followers of the Old Way from the growing oppression from the followers of the Light Bringer.

That was when he had begun finding his workers gone or dead, always with a clay tablet next to the body bearing the insignia of the Light Bringer. A quiet war waged in the shadows. Genocide. That's what it was. And they wanted the followers of the Old Way to know it.

She assumed this day would come eventually. Yet she had little money left even to buy food. If she attempted to take control of Rin's slave-trading business now, she would be putting herself and the others at even greater risk, for she would be placing a target on their backs once again. Perhaps, if she stayed quiet and let things settle . . .

Zeck returned and nodded. "What would you have me do?"

"I'm thinking," she said.

She stood and paced, tucking her hair behind her ears once and again. She did not know how to navigate such turbulent waters. She knew only that she could not do this on her own.

She pointed. "I need you to go to my son."

"You . . . have a son?"

"He ran away before you served us. I promised I'd never reveal where he fled, but now that his father is dead . . ." She cleared her throat to rid it of emotion. "You must go to Noah's vineyard and tell him what has happened."

Zeck's eyes widened, but he said nothing.

"Ask Noah where my son is. I pray he is still there, and that you will find him quickly. For his mother has never been in greater need."

"How shall I identify your son?" Zeck said. "When I ask Noah, I must know something of your son, so that when he asks who I seek, I will not stand in foolish silence."

She turned and whispered the name she vowed to never speak again, unless they would be reunited. "His name is . . . Aran."

9

Noah

None of Noah's servants knew anything more about the thief's connection to a tower, though a few shared that a tower was being built in the west. After Noah heard all that Aran and his other servants had to share about the intruders in his vineyard, one of which now lay dead outside the outer wall, Noah gave them orders and laid down to sleep, for half the night still loomed before them.

At first, when he closed his eyes, he had difficulty calming his mind. But he was old, and with age comes an openness to sleep that young men cannot know. The next time he opened his eyes, he realized he was no longer in the waking world.

In his dream, he lay on ice-cold gravel that extended as far as his eyes could see in all directions. Above him hovered a swath of ten million white pinpricks set in a black curtain sky. It looked the way he imagined the sky had looked at the beginning of everything, when the Almighty sent his Voice through the heavens and sent stars rippling outward.

Noah struggled to a stand, and the infinitely flat expanse retracted. Though the ground he stood on did not move, it seemed the whole world bent upward around him like a great cupping hand. Mountains reared around him, and from ahead in the immeasurable distance came rushing toward him a massive tower.

The tower stopped perhaps two thousand paces away, and the changes to the topography stilled. Noah squinted and noticed what looked like many thousands of people standing along the tower's steps and about its foot. In the starlight, their skin looked gray, and none of them moved. A great, dusty city sprawled around him, brick upon brick upon brick.

"Look at the stars," a Voice said, deeper than the deepest of oceans.

The hair along Noah's neck and arms stood on end as if offering praise—for he knew that Voice and had last heard it when the world was washed clean nearly three centuries earlier. It was the Voice of the Almighty.

Noah obeyed. A single star outshone the others, growing, growing—now falling toward the earth. But it did not shoot through the sky and burn itself up in a blaze of finite glory. This star slowed as it fell, until it hovered above the tower itself, and offered its brilliant light to all beneath it.

Only, the light was silver, and strange, for everything it touched somehow became harder to see. Noah had a hard time placing exactly what was wrong with it. Only that it made everything it illuminated murkier, even while making him feel he was seeing in greater detail.

Then all the gray figures moved in unison, their heads swiveling until their glittering eyes reflected the light of the silver star above the tower that cast long shadows from each of the figures.

"Behold," said the Voice again. "The star who hides darkness in light."

"Behold," the gray figures echoed. "Behold!"

Noah sank to his knees at the thunder of their voices and pressed his hands over his ears.

All quieted, until he could hear footsteps approaching him from behind. He turned to see the dark figure of a man he did not recognize emerging from the shadows.

Their eyes met, and though Noah had a hard time making out the man's features in the dark, he felt certain—as one often knows more than one should in dreams—that the man was one acquainted with violence.

Noah nodded. The man nodded back.

"You will wake soon," the man said. But his voice was not that of the Almighty. This was a messenger only.

"Who are you?" Noah said.

"Are you awake yet?"

"You tell me," Noah said.

"You've been sleeping since she left," the messenger said.

Noah saw Jade's beautiful smile in his mind, as vividly as if she stood before him in her youth. He covered his face and cleared his throat.

"You never stopped believing the Almighty," the messenger continued. "But since the pain, you have been like a man in slumber. You must wake, for a man has come to your home. Listen well, for through his words you will understand what the Almighty desires you to do."

Noah blinked, and the vision was gone, and he was back on his reed mat in his home.

"Noah?" a voice called from just outside his home. "Noah."

If he wasn't mistaken, it was Aran again.

"Noah!"

Yes. It was Aran.

Noah struggled to his hands and knees.

"Hello?"

"One moment. I'm old." His knees and ankles popped as he got to his feet. He shuffled to the door and swept the thick curtain aside.

Aran stood there with a torch in hand, the orange light flickering across his shining black beard and the scars along his cheek and brow. "Sorry to wake you, but—"

"A messenger has come to see me?"

Aran blinked. "How did you know?"

"Call me a prophet."

Aran narrowed his eyes. "Do you also know what the messenger has to say?"

Noah chuckled. "No."

"Did the Almighty speak to you tonight?"

"He did."

"Have his words ever heralded good news?"

Noah coughed in the cool air. "You should bring the messenger in."

"To your home?"

"Where else?" And Noah let the curtains fall back into place. "It's cold out!"

Aran entered, and Noah heard the footsteps of another. The messenger must have been standing close beside Aran, just out of view when Noah looked out.

The messenger was large. Not a common servant, for he held himself like a warrior, though the plain travel tunic and staff that he held marked him as a courier. "Greetings," Noah said. "I welcome you as I would an angel of the Almighty. What is your name, and where have you come from?"

The man knelt and bowed his hands and forehead to the ground. "My lord, I am called Zeck. I am a servant of one of the great houses of Erech. I come bearing tidings of woe, for my master has been murdered, and his widow is in great need."

Noah looked at Aran, whose brow was furrowed. After the dream, the man's words made Noah's hands begin to shake with fear. "I am sorry for your loss," Noah said. "Why was your master murdered?"

"He was faithful to the Old Way. His love for the Almighty gained him enemies. They persecuted him relentlessly, and so he pleaded his case before the Lord Nimrod, who is the leader in the land between the rivers. Nimrod is known to be a man of peace. He has dedicated his life to the unification of mankind. But we received word that my master died after arriving at Nimrod's home."

The man let the silence hang in the air as Noah's mind worked through the meaning of his words. He had heard little of Nimrod, or Erech, though he knew where the city lay.

Maybe the messenger in his dream was right. Maybe he had been sleeping awake all these years, blind to what was going on around him. If that were true, what could the Almighty be wanting him to do?

"Alright," Noah said. "Your master has been murdered. What do you ask of me?"

"I was sent to find my master's son, whom I'm told is working in this vineyard."

"That is all?" Noah said.

"That is my task."

"What sort of man is he?" Noah said.

"I have not met him and know nothing of what he looks like."

"If you do not know what he looks like, how could I point to any of my workers and say, 'This is he'?"

"His name is Aran," Zeck said.

Noah narrowed his eyes and shot a look toward Aran, who was eyeing Zeck with the same intensity as before. Aran must have realized as soon as the man mentioned Erech that what Zeck spoke of might concern him.

Aran said, "That is my name. But my father was no lover of the Almighty."

Zeck observed Aran's features, the shape of his face, the form of his shoulders and hands. He nodded. "Now that I look, I see your father's features in you."

"To some, that would be a compliment. For me, it is not. Tell me, is your servant of the Almighty the same who beat me when I was a child?"

Zeck seemed troubled by Aran's words. "My master's wife said you ran away years ago to seek work in Noah's vineyard. I assume that could only be you."

Aran folded his arms. "Perhaps you are confused, or maybe you heard wrong."

Noah looked at Aran questioningly, for though Aran had come to him years earlier, he had never asked the young man what his life had been before coming, for he perceived there was great pain in his past. He had come to Noah to escape something, so he never felt it good to force him to face it again. "Thank you, Zeck. You have fulfilled your duty. You may return to your master's widow."

Zeck paused. "My lord, if this is my master's son . . ."

Aran said nothing, but Noah saw a mass of tumultuous thoughts churning behind his stoic expression.

"I understand," Noah said. "But now is not the time to press. I shall command you to return, if need be."

"My lord, I will obey . . . but—"

"I perceive you are no simple servant. You have a noble, faithful heart. But in the wake of your master's death, his widow needs you by her side now more than she needs you pleading with me for something you have no control over. Return to her. Aran will come. Though he has served me all these years, I release him now to fulfill his duty to his mother, and . . ." He considered again the words of the messenger in his dream. "I will personally see to it that he does just that."

"He's wrong—," Aran began, but Noah raised his hand for silence.

"As I said," Noah said. "I will make certain *the one you seek* comes."

Aran huffed, but that seemed enough to satisfy him.

Zeck bowed, "Truly, my lord, you have dealt graciously with me and my master."

"You are satisfied?"

"I am." And he stood and looked at Aran one last time before leaving.

Aran took a deep breath and let his folded arms drop.

"Aran," Noah said.

Aran stared at the ground, shaking his head.

"Aran?"

"I'm not the one he was looking for." Aran walked to the doorway and thrust aside the heavy curtains, leaving Noah alone.

Noah sat and sighed. He knew that to follow Aran would only fuel a burning fire. For he empathized with Aran's emotions all too well. To this day, Noah still didn't know what his mother looked like. And his relationship with his father had remained strained until the end.

"Almighty God," he said, "give me wisdom to handle this."

Chastisement surely wasn't what he needed. Right now Aran needed . . .

What?

Comfort? Who could give it?

A reminder of his duty? How could that help him grieve?

He was a boy. A fatherless boy who needed time to sort out a mass of confusion.

Noah sighed. What was he thinking? Aran was no boy. Young by Noah's standards, but then again, everyone was young to him, because he was the oldest man alive. Aran was a man. A strong man. Aggressive. Loyal. More skilled than any other with the spear, the sword, the bow.

But even if Aran *were* a boy, Noah was not so old as to forget what it felt like to be a child. When adults spoke to you in belittling ways, as if you felt things less intensely than they—which of course was not true.

Noah had never been one to show sadness. Anger had always come easier. So, in his younger years, fury was the door through which everything entered.

Others might call that simple. But a boy's heart is anything but simple. Especially one wounded by fatherlessness.

I will give him time. As much as I can. Then we must speak.

Though Aran was unsure the servant spoke of him, Noah was convinced. Between his dream, and the fact that Aran's name and home city had been mentioned, there could be no doubt.

The Almighty wanted Noah to accompany Aran on the journey back to his mother.

10

Aran

Aran strode from Noah's home and passed the rows of vines and workhouses to the outer wall of fieldstones that marked the end of Noah's property. It would likely be dark for several more hours, and Aran was reminded of when he first came to Noah's vineyard, how he used to wake in the night absolutely sure that he'd heard Father calling his name. That Mother had broken her promise to keep his destination secret, and Father would kill him as he'd promised.

Those nights felt everlasting. He never fell back asleep. In the summer, the sweat would make his tunic cling to his skin, and he would shake as if feverish. In winter, he would pace outside to cool the fire that burned his veins. Trying to empty his mind of all but the bloom of his breath fogging on the frozen wind.

Just as he did now while sitting on Noah's wall.

He coughed, the cool air sharp in his lungs, and turned to make his way to his sleeping quarters where he kept his wine flask. He was thirsty and needed something to calm his ire. Though he feared his father, he hated him more, and as much as he'd tried to convince himself he didn't care, hearing his father had died brought all the fury back.

He rubbed his side with his hand, mind dim, unclear. His breaths were ragged and desperate as he swung open the wooden door to his sleeping quarters and went inside. His lantern still burned, its clay innards filled with oil that soaked up the wick. He grabbed the lantern and brought it down to search his belongings for the wine flask. His cheeks were hot, and he touched them and brought his fingers away glistening.

He shook his head. Now he was crying. And for what?

The death of a worthless abuser? A man who loved strong drink more than his family? A slave trader, the most immoral of men?

"My life's greatest enemy," he said as he searched madly for his wine flask.

He had decided the moment he fled his home that if Father ever found him, he would kill Father before Father could kill him.

That was why, though small in stature, he had devoted himself more than any other to learning how to fight. With bare hands, sword, spear, or bow, he had learned to wield even the simplest tool as a weapon. He had even begun sparring with the other men with exaggerated limits, for sport. His opponent would take a spear and a shield, and he would take only netting used to keep birds from pecking the grapes.

He seldom lost.

Yet now he felt he'd been caught by his father both naked and asleep, for the pain that punctured his chest felt like that of a broadsword.

He tossed aside another bag before he finally found the wine flask wrapped in his bedding, set the lantern on the ground, and tipped the opening to his lips. The liquid sloshed against his teeth, and he held his breath and let it slide down his throat until the flask was empty. He tossed it, gasping, and wiped his mouth with his forearm.

As much as he wanted to deny Zeck's claims, there was too much in his story that fit. Only, it was maddening that anyone would call his father a servant of the Almighty. Father had served nothing but his love for drink.

Aran spit in the dust. Still, though he tried to blame the pain in his chest on the fact that his option for revenge had been wrenched from his hands, he knew the pain for what it really was.

"Grief." His breath tossed the lantern's flame as he bent over it, staring into the flickering red. Grief over the childhood he never had. Over the family his father's drunken rage had destroyed. Over the world of pain he'd endured, along with his failure to escape it even after running away.

More than anything, he grieved the loss of the father he'd wanted—needed—to love and be loved by. What never was, what could have been—even what little there was.

For he'd seen glimpses of *some* love, long ago.

Like that morning when he was seven, and his father woke him early. Aran flinched at his raised hand, but Father's breath didn't smell like strong drink, and his eyes fell as he realized his open hand did not invite Aran, but repelled him.

Aran's heart broke then, even as it sped with excitement at the thought of his father sober and tenderly inviting him to . . . he didn't care what.

So he grabbed the hand Father offered and said, "I'm sorry. You only scared me."

Father's eyes searched his. They were blue and clear. Not bloodshot, like they always seemed to be. "You were . . . dreaming?"

"Yes," Aran lied.

Father smiled weakly. As if he'd neglected the expression for so long that he'd forgotten how to make it. "I thought maybe I would take you to the market today."

Aran stood, still holding father's hand. "Will we be selling slaves?"

The softness in father's eyes sharpened. "No. Of course not. We merely need to purchase some supplies." A pause, "Would you . . . like to come?"

How strange it felt to be asked instead of commanded. He smiled, "Please."

Father smiled back. "Very well. Put your sandals on and hurry after."

Aran followed Father to the market. They lived close, but that didn't keep their walk from seeming the most significant time they'd ever shared. The thought crossed his mind that Father was being so gentle to make up for striking him in the eye the previous night while drunk, but even if that were true, he forgave his father and was glad for it.

A bird flew overhead, wings spread, gliding gracefully, dark in the bright morning sky. Aran pointed. "A hawk?"

Father looked. Shook his head. "Vulture."

Aran nodded. Father had taught him something. He had answered Aran's question with gentle words. A warmth began growing deeper in his chest, and he walked closer to Father's side. He looked up again for that dark bird and forgot to watch his feet. He stepped too close and Father tripped over him and caught himself on Aran's shoulder, digging his nails in and cursing loudly.

"Look what you did!"

Aran followed Father's pointed finger to a broken strap on Father's sandal. Tears came to his eyes, and he fell to his knees and tried tying it back. "Sorry, Father—"

Father slapped his hand away and said, "Get up. You're just going to break it worse." When Aran hesitated, Father lifted him hard by the arm and shoved him forward. But his voice grew softer again, and Aran could tell he was trying. "The sooner we get to the market, the sooner we can buy a replacement. Just be more careful."

Aran nodded, and though he no longer walked close to his father, he was thankful they hadn't turned back. Normally, he would have beaten him and forced him home. And Aran loved the market, possibly more than anything.

For the market was always filled with colorful people who talked loud and moved fast. They handed strange items back and forth. Peddlers and merchants and patrons and artists and farmers and masons and bakers and tanners and on and on it went. The mystery of it all rushed through his chest.

Because father was a slave trader, he owned many strange metal tools, and when he was gone and Mother wasn't looking, Aran would play with them and imagine their uses. Aran had always been most drawn to the gleam of metal at the market. How the tools and weaponry hung from hooks above rich carpets woven of cloths dyed many colors. Aran hoped they would visit those stalls first, but instead they went to the sandal maker to fix Father's broken strap and buy a new pair.

"Greetings, master," the sandal maker said, and Father nodded in return. "What do you need today?"

Father stooped and slid his broken sandal off, then placed it in the tradesman's hands.

The sandal maker nodded as Father took the other sandal off to even his stance. "I can fix this," he said. "But it will take a moment."

"We can't wait long today," Father said. "But I need it repaired."

"Then I will return this to your slave complex. Perhaps you would be interested in a new pair that I just purchased from a merchant from the great city of Babel?"

"Show me—"

Aran caught sight of the glint of metal amidst the endless stalls, and Father's voice faded. He stepped away from the sandal maker's shop to find the source. Hanging tapestries and pottery and great stacks of fish and vegetables blocked his view, but behind them, several stalls away, was a merchant selling knives.

Aran looked back and saw Father in deep conversation with the sandal maker, haggling over the prices for several pair of elegant sandals. Father hated being interrupted, and after what happened earlier, Aran had no desire to frustrate him further. Besides, he only needed a moment to glance at the knives.

So he rushed off, dodging old women and sunburnt slaves. With the rush of bodies, he was pushed to the side, but his momentum pushed him toward a stack of beautiful clay bowls. He jumped, and though he nearly knocked them over, they stayed upright.

He turned back again—and there they were. Row upon row of gleaming blades arranged on reed mats and hanging from linen ribbons beneath a wooden lean-to. The merchant was a dark-skinned man with gleaming, muscular arms, and a shaved head. His dark eyes followed Aran as he ran his fingers lightly over copper blades the size of his forearm, and then bronze knives far longer and of different design.

"You are interested in blades?"

Aran looked up, unsure how to answer.

"Unless you have money, I suggest you look elsewhere."

Four men arrived, then, and pushed Aran out of the way. They immediately began lifting knives and testing their weight. One of the leaders, a tall brown man with curly hair, addressed the merchant. "You make them?"

"With these two hands." He flexed his fingers and clenched them into fists.

"Where did you learn to smith like this?" said a smaller man, who was testing the sharpness of a bronze dagger by cutting the hair along the top of his hand.

"From my great sire, Tubal, the son of Japheth."

The men murmured their approval and instantly launched into haggling for prices.

No one paid Aran any mind. He was just a silly boy infatuated by the gleam of metal coaxed to a bitter edge.

Aran crouched and ran his fingers along the hilt of a particularly beautiful dagger with a handle wrapped in silk bandages. He picked it up, and though its weight felt significant, it was not too heavy for him to wield.

He looked back to where Father was. He caught sight of him still talking with the sandal maker. He looked back at the dagger, then at the merchant, who was also busy. The weapon merchant looked like a hard and intimidating man, like Father. Surely he wouldn't want to be interrupted, either. And Aran only wanted to take the dagger to Father to show him how beautiful it was.

So he held it in both hands, reverently, to be sure he wouldn't drop or damage it, and began walking back to Father.

He rounded the corner, dodging people who noticed he held a blade and glared down at him as if he were trying to harm them, then passed the pottery merchant whose bowls he'd nearly destroyed.

He was almost within reach of Father when a booming voice sounded behind him.

"Thief!"

It was the weapons merchant.

Father looked their way.

"What?" Aran said, "No, I just—"

The man rushed over and grabbed his wrist, wrenching the knife from his hand. "Thought this was a pretty trinket, eh?"

And then Father was upon him as well.

"Is this your son?" the weapon merchant said, narrowing his eyes at Father.

Father glanced around at the other merchants watching, including the sandal maker—though the sandal maker looked away and acted as though he was too absorbed in his work to notice. Then Father looked at Aran, and all the clarity and openness that Aran had seen in Father's eyes was gone, replaced with the cold edge of fury. "You think it good to steal, child?"

"No, I wasn't—"

Father struck him in the face and sent him flying onto his back, head striking the cold ground. "Don't lie to me." Father picked him up and shook him. "Confess to the merchant!"

"I'm sorry," Aran cried. "I'm sorry!"

Father struck him again, and Aran felt his face swelling as blood trickled from fresh wounds. "Never run off from me again!"

No matter what Aran said, nothing could stop the onslaught.

Father struck him again and again, and after the edges of his sight faded to black, Father dragged him home. Aran remembered nothing of the journey home save for the gleam of jewels on the new sandals Father wore, for his face had remained close to the ground as his father dragged him.

That night, Father drank heavier than usual, and beat Aran again after yelling about how Aran had pushed him to it. That it was Aran's fault everything went wrong that day, that the others had seen him beat Aran.

Until Aran went unconscious.

When he awoke, he lay in a small pool of his own blood, and wondered if he would die, for Mother was weeping over him, and he realized he'd been dragged into the weeds.

He didn't see Father again for nearly a week.

Mother cleaned his wounds as best as she could. But even as an adult in Noah's vineyard, Aran bore scars across his face from that day.

Tears flowed from Aran's eyes at the memories and the bitter fury of the injustice. He wanted only to forget. To never think of Father again. But even in death, Father would not let him rest.

In the quiet of his private room in Noah's vineyard, Aran picked up the wine flask again and realized he'd forgotten it was empty.

He stood, and considered where he could get some more.

11

Noah

Morning dawned, and they were running out of time. The Almighty had spoken no more, and Aran's mother lived in Erech, likely two weeks' journey by camelback. Assuming her servant had traveled quickly, many days had passed already. And if Aran left today, his mother would have to wait that much longer for relief. If she had not saved up wisely, she could foreseeably run out of food.

Noah sighed, frustrated that the acolyte of the Light Bringer had trespassed under cover of dark and broken his peace and defiled his vineyard with spilled blood. He couldn't help but feel the acolyte's death was the beginning of all that had transpired, though not in any physical way, at least in a spiritual sense. Because since that moment, all the peace and ease he'd felt for so long had vanished, and he had been given an evil dream that foreboded ill.

Noah stood and exited his home. He made for Aran's sleeping quarters and, when he arrived, knocked on the door. There was no response. It wasn't like Aran to sleep so late, but the days had grown strange, and maybe he had sought rest after such a long night.

"Aran?" Noah called.

He thought he heard a low moan from within and dark shivers rippled down his shoulders. Something was wrong.

He pushed the door open and saw Aran lying on the floor, limbs splayed awkwardly. Noah fully opened the door, and allowed a beam of sunlight to fall across his face.

"Aran," Noah said.

Aran moaned and rubbed his face. "Too bright . . ."

Noah stepped in and nearly tripped over two wine flasks that he hadn't seen. He looked around, squinting in the dim, smoky interior, and noticed one of the storehouses' wine containers had been dragged into his private quarters. "You're drunk," Noah said. "And on stolen wine."

Aran rolled away to better guard his eyes.

Noah had never seen Aran drunk before. And that meant only one thing—he truly did believe his father was dead. "Do you want to pay me back now, or would you rather I keep your wages until next season?"

Aran grunted and raised himself on his elbow. "I didn't even drink half of it."

"You would have died if you'd drunk all of it." Noah found a cushion and sank into it.

Aran itched his disheveled hair and said, "Can you give me some time?"

"No. Because you need to leave before mid-day. What were you thinking, drinking at such a time?"

Aran chuckled unhappily. "I'm not going anywhere."

Noah snorted. "Then what are you going to do? Lay on the floor and drink yourself into another stupor?"

"Not the floor. My bed."

"You're on the floor right now."

Aran looked up, seemingly confused, then at the bed in the corner. He took a deep breath and let it out slow. "Look, I'll recover soon and continue working."

Noah considered whether to say it. But he knew now Aran had no plans to go to his mother. "You don't work for me anymore."

Aran lifted his head, eyes slanted like the tip of a spear. "What?"

"You have no job. Didn't you listen to what I told Zeck? And that bed in the corner is as much mine as the wine in your belly."

Aran scrambled to his feet, legs unsteady. "You can't do that to me."

"Of course I can."

"I've worked faithfully for years."

"And now I've released you to return to your mother."

"I'll send her money." He fiddled with his tunic, and tried to press out the wrinkles with his palms.

"You aren't listening," Noah said. "There's nothing left for you here."

Aran stared at him a long moment, then crossed to a bowl of water and splashed his face. Droplets dripped from his black hair, down the scars on his brown face to the packed dirt floor at his feet. "What do you want from me?"

"For you to fulfill your duty to your mother. It is shameful to leave her alone in her suffering. To not offer your aid and comfort in the time of her need."

Aran nodded and licked his lips. He opened his mouth to speak, then closed it again. He took a deep breath, clenched his hands to fists, and said, "When I was a boy, my father beat me so hard he thought he'd killed me." Aran pointed to the scars on his cheek, chin, and eyebrows, and Noah's innards twisted and chilled. "Mother never rescued me. Never lifted a hand to stop him. So, what do I really owe her?"

Noah stood and combed his fingers through his beard. Voice softening. Finally, Aran's behavior was starting to make sense. "Your father is dead. Let your grievances die with him."

Aran took up the wooden bowl and threw it against the wall beside Noah. "What do you know of my grievances?"

Noah lifted his hands in self-defense, then stepped forward, veins pulsing with sudden fire. "Enough to realize that you're standing on the precipice of repeating them. To be hurt is to be human. But your wounds are no greater than the ones anyone else has endured."

Aran pressed his temples with his palms and winced. "You're talking too loud."

"I'll talk louder still, until you listen." Noah took hold of Aran's tunic, and as Aran tried to back away, Noah held him as tightly as his old hands would allow. Sudden fear gleamed in Aran's dazed eyes. "Have you ever killed a man?" Noah said.

Aran held his gaze a moment, then looked away. "What does that have to do with anything?"

"More than you realize." Noah brought him closer and said through gritted teeth, "Answer me."

"No, I haven't."

Noah pushed him back. "Well, I have. And I lost most of my childhood to rage and the pursuit of revenge. My obsession nearly cost me everything, until the Almighty healed my pain. And unless you can get rid of your anger, it will cost you everything too."

Aran took a deep breath. "I'm not you."

"Of course not. But all men have a heart that beats to the rhythms of pride."

They held each other's stares. Finally, Aran looked away, and his face softened. His shoulders slumped, and he leaned against the wall and slid to his seat, face in his hands.

Noah wondered briefly if he'd pushed too far. But Aran had needed hard words. He was too panicked to respond to a gentle rebuke.

Aran looked up at him again, eyes no longer clouded by rage. "Have you gotten any more sleep since the messenger arrived?"

Noah felt in that moment just how deep his exhaustion ran. "I needed to consult with the Almighty."

"Did he speak to you again?"

Noah wondered if he should tell him. He sighed and looked again at the wine flask, marveling at how similar he and Aran really were. "I think that I'm supposed to go with you."

Aran looked up. "What?"

"Don't look so surprised. I may be old, but I can still travel."

"I don't understand."

"Neither do I. But after that thief spilled his blood on our soil, I laid on my reed mat and fell into a dream from the Almighty. What he revealed in that dream makes me think that I have stayed here too long. After many years, it is time for me to go and see what has become of my offspring."

"You will go to Erech?"

"I will go with you to Erech, and then beyond to see my sons, Shem and Japheth, for they live near your mother's city. I have not seen them in many years, and I believe they will have answers to some of the questions my dream has raised." Noah turned and laid a hand on the door. "Pack light, and pack quickly. We will travel in haste. If you desire to claim that you have served me faithfully, you will accompany me on this journey. Meet me at my home. This is about more than your mother's need."

12

Nimrod

The stairwell echoed with the sound of Nimrod's sandals against stone as he made for the underground temple to complete the ritual that would guarantee his survival. Water fell to puddles in the dark underground tunnel, illuminated by the crackling dance of the flames on the tip of his torch, which reminded him of the forces he was attempting to conjure and control. So destructive, yet, when handled correctly, so essential to life. As he reached the bottom of the steps, the hall extended, marked by prison doors on either side. He passed them, ignoring the quiet moans from the prisoners, for his destination was through the door at the very end.

As he reached it, he hung the torch in a receptacle just outside, and passed within, latching the lock after himself.

The inside of the secret temple was already illuminated by burning braziers, and the small pedestal in the shape of a star had been prepared by his servants with a live goat. Its legs were tied and thrust into the air, and the beast watched him warily, rectangular pupils dilated to pierce the dark of the smoke-filled hexagon.

Nimrod stepped atop the pedestal and lifted the ceremonial knife, curved in the shape of a serpent. When he was younger, much younger, the musty, heady scents and the moaning, crackling noises had shocked and disturbed him. Now, he realized they were to be savored, as his master savored and fed on the blood of his sacrifices. Because without him, his master would ache and ache, and he had long ago agreed that he would trade power for food.

He lifted the blade above his head and closed his eyes.

"Great Light Bringer, I bid you to fulfill your promise. You know how Hava lusts for a son. That she would kill me to get one, for she believes rightly that a gift of surpassing worth must be met with a sacrifice of surpassing worth."

And he plunged the knife into the goat and spilled its life across the ceremonial table.

He stepped back and watched the liquid ooze and shimmer. Dark and bright, reflecting shadow and flame. A paradox he had long embraced—that life can only come through death.

He knelt and bent closer to watch little droplets form at the tip of the altar before dribbling to the floor. The liquid appeared so beautiful. So perfectly viscous and lovely. How had he never noticed before, how rich its color, how desirable its touch? He reached his hand forward—though he felt as if he were watching rather than acting—fingers shaking as he pressed the line of blood and let the fluid flow over his knuckles, down his hand and up his wrist.

He twisted his hand and lifted it to get a better look at the red liquid filling the tiny maze-like patterns on the pads of his fingers. All sound faded but for the hiss of his breath and the drip of blood to stone. All heat died, replaced by a cold, chill wind that blew through skin and bone and soil and stone.

He tried to look away from the blood, and only then realized his body would not obey. He was locked in place, staring at the goat's blood on his fingers. Fear prickled down the back of his neck as his hand hovered closer, closer to his mouth, which opened to receive it though no part of him desired it.

"Taste and see," he heard, like the echo of a whisper from a terrible dream.

What was happening? He shivered with pleasure as he tasted copper, and cold liquid wetted his lips. He closed his eyes and trembled—how cold, how frigid the room had become.

He fell to his back, sight spinning, breath caught in his throat, chest transmuted to terror. Had the Light Bringer possessed his body? He hadn't experienced such primordial fear since he was a small child in Ham's presence at the first sacrifice he ever made, when he first encountered the presence of his master.

But wait. What was that sound? The slow scrape of skin across stone. It sounded like . . . yes, it was footsteps.

But the door had not opened. It was locked from the inside. Had someone been waiting in the temple?

Was it Hava? Had she poisoned him?

Terror clutched him even harder until an unfamiliar face dipped into view.

"Who," he managed, but then he realized.

This was not Hava. This was a messenger of the Light Bringer.

A messenger in the form of a little boy with gray skin, silver eyes, and silver hair. It smiled at him, then lay beside him and pressed its lips to his ear, its breath the same cold rushing wind he'd felt earlier. "Well done, faithful servant. You see me outside yourself, but I am inside you, for I have taken you as my own. The feelings you feel are my own; the desires you feel are mine. My master, the Light Bringer, has heard your request and sent me to show you the way."

"W-w-who are you?" Nimrod managed.

"The Light Bringer's greatest servant." It laughed and kissed him on the cheek as a father would a child. The gesture made Nimrod's stomach twist as the boy continued. "I thirst for richer blood. In exchange, I will fulfill both your request for safety, and Hava's desire for a son. I will reform her womb and give her a progeny like none in existence. Offspring that will progress the human race. But only if you give me the sacrifice I desire."

Nimrod closed his eyes to quell the fear that shot through his limbs and demanded he thrust the silver boy away. "What sacrifice do you desire?"

The silver boy growled and its voice descended until it shook the earth. "The children of Noah."

13

Aran

Aran's head throbbed when Noah slammed the door on his way out and nausea rose in his gut. He grimaced, feeling as if he'd slept in the winepress and was now having his thoughts crushed out like grape juice.

"Curse everything," Aran mumbled.

He retreated to the corner where his bed lay, and took up his satchel to fill it with light provisions. After a bit of fumbling around the dim room, he found his moneybag under the covers and tied it to his waist inside his tunic.

No matter how much he wanted to stay back, he felt indebted to the old man. First, of course, because everyone on earth owed their lives to him as the father of all. But more importantly, Noah had given Aran asylum for years without questioning him and thereby had become the closest thing he'd ever had to a father. He feared failing his duty to Noah even more than he feared facing his mother.

Aran looked around, mind foggy. What else did he need?

His eyes canvassed his little room. Herbs hung from hooks embedded in the mud-brick wall. Rope lay coiled beside a small table that held a partially molded piece of bread. Beneath it sat his box of clothes.

He crossed to the box, removed its wooden lid, and pulled out his treated leather travel tunic made from camel hide and tanned to keep moisture from soaking through. How could he have thought of a long journey without it? He shook his head, then pulled the tunic on and slung the satchel over his shoulder.

The moneybag jangled as he walked outside and let the door swing shut behind him. It was all the money he'd saved in the years he'd worked here, and he could hardly believe he would soon give the majority of it to his mother. It felt perverse that all his labor would return to the home that he'd believed he would never see again.

Still, he was curious about Noah's god. The old man seemed to believe the Almighty had the ability to do . . . anything. Yet in all his time working at the vineyard, he had seen no proof of the Almighty's power. He just wanted to see something. Anything. Because if the Almighty was true, maybe Noah's claims could mean something for Aran.

He pressed his chest where he'd felt the burning the previous night. It had faded in the light of the morning but had not disappeared.

As he walked through the rows of the vineyard back toward Noah's home, he felt nausea from the wine grow. He stopped several times, breathing deeply and slowly through his nose.

Even before he could see the yard in front of Noah's home, he heard the braying of camels, and his shoulders slumped. He loathed camels. Their stench, the way they looked, their attitudes. Everything about them repulsed him.

Noah was there, strapping bags to the backs of one of two camels who both knelt. Their bizarre legs looked broken beneath them.

Noah waved him over. "That one's yours."

Aran approached warily. The beast twisted its elongated head on its lengthy neck to give Aran a surly look. It growled, and Aran stepped back, staring at its bulging eyes.

Noah chuckled. "He's a loud one, but he's not bitten yet."

"Does he look at you like that?"

"Don't look him in his eyes—he doesn't like it. Approach him from the side and tie your satchel to the saddle."

Aran sighed and tried to do as told. But as he reached out to touch it, it swung its head close, and when their eyes met, the thing yelled and spit a wad of green saliva on his leg. Aran cried out and swiped the liquid off, shivering as he dipped down to clean his hand in the dust.

Noah chuckled.

Aran's face and neck warmed.

Noah finished tying his bags and approached Aran's camel slowly with hands raised. He made a few kissing sounds, and Aran's camel responded with a low moan. It dipped its head and went back to chewing cud, paying neither of them any more attention. "His name is Kavel," Noah said.

Aran nodded and stood beside Noah.

Noah motioned for Aran's satchel, and Aran gave it. Noah tied the bag to the camel's first hump, then rubbed the animal's side. It murmured approval, and Noah said, "Good boy, Kavel." He backed away and nodded. "Alright. Get on."

When Aran touched Kavel, the beast did not react. So Aran grabbed hold of the hump and tried to swing his leg over, but the thing was tall and swayed as he tried to hop up. Aran lost momentum and slid back down, landing awkwardly on his left leg and hopping several paces to keep from falling flat on the ground. He grumbled and watched how Noah swung his old body up onto the other camel with ease.

"Getting on is the difficult part," Noah yelled back. "Just try again."

Aran positioned himself and hopped as high as he could while swinging his leg over Kavel's back. He made it and shifted to find a comfortable position, but the beast's spine felt like it was made of river stones.

Noah clicked his tongue, and both camels rose, back legs first. The momentum tossed Aran forward and smashed his face into the back of Kavel's neck. Aran's body slid out of the seat, and though he tried to stop himself by hugging Kavel's neck, the beast tossed his head and threw Aran back onto the ground.

Aran landed hard on his back and struggled for breath.

Noah laughed so hard that he started to wheeze and cough.

Holding a palm to his aching back, Aran scrambled to his feet. "I've never ridden a camel before."

Noah's eyes widened. "What? I thought you were struggling because of the wine. Kavel, down!"

Kavel knelt again, though he didn't sound happy about it.

"Alright," Noah said, "hop on again, and this time, when he stands, lean as far back as you can and hold tight."

Aran did as he was told, and this time successfully stayed on Kavel's back when the camel stood. Noah looked back and smiled, then urged his camel forward. Kavel followed.

"Sorry," Noah said. "You'll be comfortable soon enough."

"As soon as we stop riding them," Aran mumbled, half-hoping Noah wouldn't hear.

Noah looked back and raised an eyebrow at him, and Aran looked away, feeling his face warm again.

They made their way out of the vineyard, and some of Aran's fellow servants gathered and watched as they exited through the opening in the outer fieldstone wall, then turned north and west.

But all Aran could think about was how bad his lower back and behind hurt as he fought to keep his balance amidst Kavel's jerky gait.

Just as they started to make their way up the rocky hills that surrounded Noah's vineyard, Aran noticed that Noah had crossed his legs.

"Is that more comfortable?"

Noah looked back and nodded, then focused once more on navigating his camel up a risky incline. The camel's feet sent little pebbles skittering down a fifteen-foot fall. As Kavel ascended, Aran clung to the beast even harder with his thighs. Kavel brayed as they went, and Noah called from ahead, "Relax. You're making Kavel anxious."

Aran looked down at the sheer drop and breathed in sharply. "*I'm* making *him* anxious?"

"He is surefooted. Surrender to the rhythm of his walk."

Aran tried, but it was difficult. And soon, the side-to-side motion chafed his inner thighs mercilessly, for Kavel's fur was rough.

After half a day of riding, he decided to try Noah's cross-legged position. It instantly brought him relief, both to the raw skin and to his lower back.

After navigating the perilous hills, their way flattened, and Kavel walked closer to his companion, so Aran and Noah sat nearly side by side. They'd talked less during the first part of their journey, but now they had little to do. It made Aran thirsty.

"Why did you get drunk?"

Aran looked up and wondered briefly if the man could hear his thoughts, though it made sense for him to ask after what Aran had shared of his father.

"Father said he drank to forget. I wondered if it would work for me."

"Did it?"

"Everything that man ever said was a lie."

Noah took a deep breath. "You'll be glad you responded to your mother's summons, in the end."

Aran shook his head. "I didn't come for her." But even as he said it, he was struck by how much he believed the old man's words. As the brisk breeze filled his chest, he realized how terribly he missed his mother. He wanted to find her safe and happy. Because part of him wondered if maybe, after being released from Father's violent grip, she could finally be her true self. Maybe now they could discover the relationship Aran had dreamed of.

14

Noah

The sway of the camel and the dance of the wind urged Noah's eyes closed. Each moment became a battle to stave off sleep, and every passing hour the fight grew more difficult.

He repositioned himself and straightened his posture. He had slept only a handful of moments in the past two days. In his younger years, he would have done so without difficulty, but he had long ago lost his youth.

"Tired?" Aran said.

"Are you not?"

Aran stared at him a moment. "We should make camp."

Noah gauged the softening red ball of light half sunken beneath the edge of the horizon. His eyes burned, and he swiped moisture from his eyelids. "Wait until night falls. I want to make as much progress as possible before resting."

Their camels' footsteps pattered out an uneven rhythm. When a third rhythm interjected itself, Noah watched Aran look behind himself, confused.

"Kavel is defecating," Noah said.

Aran nodded, looking both mildly relieved and irritated.

Noah chuckled. "Frighten you?"

"Last time I traveled the wilds, a lion hunted me."

"When you were a boy?" Noah said.

Aran nodded.

"What drove you to such a foolish task?"

Aran sighed. "Before I ran from home, I purchased a bow and some well-made arrows with money from my father's private stash. I knew what I was getting myself into, traveling the wilds alone. At least, as well as any fool boy could."

The light was dimming, and the growing twilight made it harder for Noah to see Aran's face in detail, but the glint of his smiling teeth was enough to show his pride. "What happened?"

Aran's smile fell, and he shrugged. "I shot the lion. It grew angry. A patrol happened to be riding by and saved my life." He turned toward Noah. "I don't like traveling in the open."

"Well,"—Noah patted his camel—"You're much safer on Kavel than on foot."

Aran grunted. "I'd love to have a spear."

"You could have brought one."

"Don't remind me."

They continued on until only a sliver of the sun remained visible, like the tip of God's fingernail grabbing hold of the world to roll it forward another day.

"Why are you so intent on making progress?" Aran said.

"Because I want to."

A pause.

"Why?"

Noah looked at Aran. "Why are you so curious? You should learn when to leave an old man to his silence."

Aran shrugged again.

"You should also use your words instead of shrugging all the time," Noah said.

"I thought you wanted silence."

Noah groaned and rubbed his face.

When Aran laughed softly, he couldn't resist joining.

But then Aran asked an even more uncomfortable question. "Are you afraid?"

"Of lions?" Noah said.

"Of the Almighty."

Noah twisted in his seat to find Aran's eyes, twin gleams in the twilight. They stared at each other a long moment. Finally,

Noah nodded. "Wouldn't you be? If you saw him destroy the world?"

"But you love him."

"Of course I love him."

But he could not deny that Aran's words had left a slippery coldness in his belly.

Darkness fell, and the stars multiplied. The two rode in silence for some time, and Noah was thankful for it gave him time to remember the Almighty's tenderness in his younger years. Still, a nagging thought dulled the impact.

Is all I have memories?

The Almighty had been Noah's greatest treasure for so long. He had walked in daily, searing heart-intimacy with the God of all creation.

Yet when he tried to think back on the last ten, fifty, hundred years, he recalled only a vague form of adoration without substance.

Could it be possible his heart had drifted? It couldn't have been so long . . .

"Back in my room," Aran said, and Noah nearly jumped. "What did you mean when you said you'd lost most of your childhood to rage?"

Noah took a deep breath and steadied himself on his camel. "I meant what I said."

"What was your childhood like? I know nothing of it from the stories I've heard."

"That's no accident." He knew he shouldn't try to shut Aran down, but all he wanted was to dig into Noah's past.

Come now, he told himself. *Why shouldn't he ask questions? The last thing he needs is fake answers to hard questions*—and that's what Noah had just offered.

Perhaps, in answering Aran's curiosity, Noah could take steps toward solving a bit of his own. "I was a fool most of my life. Maybe now too. But when I was twelve years of age, I saw a man beating a group of women he'd purchased at a slave market. The women were weeping, and they were naked. They were chained together by their necks and ankles, and the man was enjoying harming them."

"That's disgusting . . ."

Noah nodded. "All I could think about when I looked at them was my mother. I never knew her, but Father told me she'd been captured by wicked men, and that she died giving birth to me because of the wounds they inflicted on her." Noah pulled on his reins and breathed in through his teeth to indicate to his camel to stop. It obeyed and knelt, allowing him to slide off.

"So," Noah said as he stretched his back. "Instead of turning away like any normal child would, I took up a spear and murdered him right there, in front of the women." He shivered just remembering it. "The feel of the shaft finding its way through the man's ribs. It was . . . terrible. I felt such horror and perverse enjoyment at once. The sense of total control, of chasing my own sort of righteousness that had only just been darkness bathed in flames. A part of my soul turned to stone that day."

Kavel crouched as well, and Aran stepped off and groaned at the stiffness in his legs.

"You'll grow accustomed to riding soon enough," Noah said.

"I never imagined you were capable of . . ."

"Of being so evil?"

"Of violence."

Noah nodded. "I vowed to never kill again. You think you can justify it, but no matter your reasons for murder, your soul pays a deadly price to claim it."

Aran looked at him, and Noah could see his mind working through it all.

Noah softened his tone. "That's enough for the day. I am weary. Let us get some rest."

Noah lay slowly on the hard ground, bones aching on the lumps of hard earth, skin prickled by harsh grass. He closed his eyes and searched for rest as Aran did the same, shifting restlessly for comfort.

But Noah didn't receive the rest he hoped for.

Because the Almighty gave him a dream even more disturbing than the last.

15

Noah

Noah opened his eyes to a dreamworld. A stairwell lay in front of him, leading to an underground hallway. As he looked at the ceiling, he could sense the same swath of ten million stars that he'd seen in his first dream, even though earth and stone should have blocked his natural sight.

He walked down the last of the steps, his feet making the sound of wooden sandals, though he wore nothing on his feet. He passed through the hallway toward a door at the far end, beside which hung a single burning torch.

On either side of the hallway lay openings guarded by metal bars. From inside them came faint moans, as of wounded men and women. Tears grew in his eyes as he went along. What horror was this? That men and women should be kept hidden in tunnels under the earth? It was for evils like this that the Almighty sent the Flood. To drown out the hidden hovels dug by man's sin, and to wash the world clean.

But his thoughts were cut short when the door at the end slammed open, and he spied from within the room a star-shaped pedestal lit by burning braziers. A naked boy with gray skin and bright, silver eyes sat on it. The creature was genderless, and Noah recognized it for what it was—an evil spirit, or some other representation of the evil stalking this world. It stood and waved at him, sending prickles down his arms. Then it opened its mouth, and viscous, black liquid bubbled out.

Noah stepped back, horrified at what first seemed to be blood vomiting from the boy's mouth, until the flow of the liquid intensified and started to fill the room and spill out. The liquid churned and sloshed and rose higher until the silver boy's body was submerged. Then it flowed out of the room and rushed the boy's body toward Noah in a massive wave that reached nearly to the ceiling.

Noah tried to cry out, to call for the Almighty, but his words were stopped as the liquid engulfed him and sapped all warmth from his body.

Noah was drowning, gasping, choking on the stuff, body instantly made numb in the infinite chill. He knew he would soon suffocate and pass into the next life.

Yet before he did, a searing Light pierced the darkness, and as its rays touched his body, warmth and breath returned to him, and he gasped and threw himself into its embrace. He wept for the pain and the horror of the sense of total isolation that thankfully now felt distant and dull.

"Almighty God," Noah said. "What horror have you shown me?"

The Almighty did not, at first, respond. He merely waited, letting his glory pass through Noah, illuminating his body, piercing his bones. He rested in it. And soon, his tears dried and a thankful smile grew on his face. He raised his hands in worship, and praised his God. As he looked into the Light, he perceived that a Man stood at its source.

"Lord," Noah said. "You promised to never again flood the earth. What, then, have you shown me?"

Finally, the Voice responded. "The same evil that stalked you before the flood has been given a foothold in this world. It intends to drown the world in darkness with the evil false prophecies that spew from its mouth, to separate humanity from the warmth and knowledge of my presence and holiness. Soon, you will face it in the flesh. But your destiny is not to challenge it. You are one of three who shall stand against the tide. And I will be in your midst, to reveal to you at the right moment exactly what my will for you is. But first, you must awake and make haste, for your time is burning like a spent wick. If you do not return Aran to his mother within six days, the enemy will feed on your son's lifeblood, and in the end, you will all become like ash."

The Light, the Voice, and the stars were gone in the space of a blink, as Noah woke on the cold ground beside Aran, shaking with fear and uncertainty.

"My son," he whispered. "Which of my sons is in danger?"

16

Nimrod

Nimrod stood in the middle of Ham's garden and, despite the warmth of the sun and the embrace of a warm breeze, shivered.

He had met Ham in this same spot every season since he had agreed to take his position as the Light Bringer's chosen servant. Each time, they exchanged few words. Nimrod stayed long enough only to see that simple, slow nod showing approval of his recent decisions. For they could not risk being seen together.

This time would be different. Because everything had changed since that silver spirit took hold of Nimrod and gave him new directives. Directives that had, for the first time, not come through Ham, the Light Bringer's prophet. Directives that, if followed, would eventually lead to Nimrod sacrificing Ham himself to the god they both served.

Of course, he could not dare let on that he now had a revelation Ham was not privy to. If he did, he would risk Ham retaliating. It did not matter if the Light Bringer desired Ham be succeeded by Nimrod now. Ham's entire reason for existence had become filtered through his status as prophet. He would let go of that as soon as he let go of his right to breathe.

But that wasn't why Nimrod had come to Ham today, nearly four weeks earlier than he was supposed to. He had come now to decide whether to kill Ham first or last.

He rubbed his arms to swipe away the sweat just as Ham

stepped into the open, flanked by two servants. Ham wore his customary wooden sandals, and walked the mosaic cobbles until he stopped five paces away.

They each raised a single hand in silent greeting.

"I have a request," Nimrod said.

"Speak," Ham said.

"I want Japheth."

A pause. Nimrod could see the thoughts churning behind Ham's glassy eyes. Tension rose in the old man's jaws. "And what do you offer in return?"

Now was the moment of proving. It was a wild risk, and he still wasn't certain he could bring it to fruition. But it was the only way to test Ham's compliance. "I will give you Noah."

Another pause. Ham's tensed jaw suddenly relaxed into a wide smile. "And how do you propose you will accomplish this?"

Nimrod turned toward the tower, now nearly grown to its full height in the distance after years of rapid construction. "Long ago, you told me the tower's true meaning. And yet, we know that to each man, the tower represents something different. To some, the hope for a future. To others, the ingenuity and progress of man. To your father, Noah, it will represent his worst failures. Already, he is being drawn to it like a dog to its wound."

Ham's head bobbed up and down in a slow, approving nod.

Even if Nimrod had no idea how Hava planned to draw Noah, he felt confident that she never spoke so strongly without solid footing. And so he turned away, content.

For it had been decided. Simply, cleanly.

Ham would be the last of Noah's sons to die.

17

Aran

Aran hadn't even fallen asleep when Noah gasped and started to rise, bones creaking like an old tree as Noah's whisper sounded like the rustle of wind through leaves.

Aran raised himself on his elbow. "Why are you rising?"

Noah rubbed his face and coughed into his hand. "We need to continue."

Aran groaned and rested his forearm over his eyes. "Lay down—we are far from morning."

"No," Noah said. "You don't understand. The Almighty gave me another dream."

Aran's breath stopped, and he looked once more at Noah. The man was bent, breaths coming fast and deep. "We've hardly been resting for more than a few moments. How could you have dreamed?"

"We need to get moving. We're running out of time."

Aran sat up. "To do what?"

Noah was silent a moment, seeming to gather his thoughts. "We need to get you back to your mother."

"I'm not getting back on that camel unless you tell me what's so dangerous about us getting one good night of rest. Because unless someone's trying to kill us, one more sleepless night and I may try to kill you."

Noah rested his hands on his hips and started to pace. Moonlight glinted off of the moisture on his forehead.

And now the man was sweating? He truly did seem terrified.

Noah nodded absently, as if coming to a decision on some internal argument. He sat cross-legged beside Aran and stared up at the stars. "I've had two prophetic dreams. In both dreams, the stars were strange." Noah closed his eyes as if to see better. "In the first dream, I saw a great tower being built far away. Men stood on it, but they were like gray statues, and a great light came down and hovered over it. I heard the Voice of the Almighty say, 'Behold, the star who hides darkness in light.' Then I was told that a messenger had come to my home. That if I listened to the messenger's words, I would discover the Almighty's will for me. Immediately after, I woke to you outside my home with Zeck at your side, bearing news of your father's death."

Aran felt his mouth run dry, and his tongue rubbed the roof of his mouth. Could the old man's words be true? He had wanted to see proof of the Almighty's power. Now that he was getting a glimpse, he couldn't stop his pulse from quickening. "But that doesn't explain why you came with me," Aran said.

"The young man who trespassed and attempted to kidnap my young worker had mentioned a name just before murdering himself."

"The Light Bringer . . . ," Aran said, thoughts fitting into each other like bricks into the base of a home.

"Violence in my vineyard, the mention of the Light Bringer, then a dream that pictures a great light as the focal point of a massive tower, the like of which this world has never seen. And above it all, the voice of the Almighty declaring its evil—along with a command that links my destiny to your journey back to your mother."

Aran's arms and legs began to fidget, so he stood and dusted himself off. Grasses swayed in the distance like bulky shadows. He searched the surroundings for any creatures but found none, for he felt as if eyes were watching him.

Noah stood, crossed to his camel, and checked the saddle. The camels groaned and looked at him, clearly as irritated as Aran that the old man wasn't sleeping. "My second dream was worse."

Aran felt dark shivers run down his back and legs.

"I had a vision of an evil spirit in an underground temple. From its mouth spewed blood, until it drowned us both. Then the Almighty said that we were running out of time, and that we needed to get you back to your mother in less than six days—lest we burn away like spent wicks."

Aran stood, mouth hanging open. "Wait . . ." He ran his fingers through his hair. "I don't understand."

Noah sighed. "The world is going to be covered in darkness again—just as it was before the world was washed clean."

"How could the world be that far gone? I've never wanted to cover the world in evil. I don't know anyone who does."

"What do you call your obsession with getting revenge on your own father? Or drinking yourself into a stupor with stolen wine while your mother wastes away?"

Aran clenched his jaw to keep his tongue behind his teeth.

"You may think my words unfair, but they are not. The world is evil because *we* are evil. Once you've lived long enough, you'll no longer be surprised that man, when left alone, will always destroy himself in the end."

Noah swung into his seat on his camel, which yelled in protest. He clicked his tongue, and the camel obeyed and stood. "Get on Kavel," Noah said.

"If we are in such danger, why should we continue following the Almighty's advice?"

"Aran. Get on your camel."

"What guarantee do we have that the Almighty won't destroy us once we do his will?"

"He will protect us. But if we disobey him and stay, the entire world will collapse around us."

Aran stared at him. Then, slowly, he crossed to his camel and mounted.

Noah yelled, and the camels started off into a trot. A moment later, Noah turned and called out, "Finally convinced?"

"No. But if the world falls apart," Aran yelled into the wind, "I don't want it to be because I slept a few hours."

Noah laughed and turned forward once more, teeth glinting in the moonlight as they rode on.

18

Noah

Noah and Aran traveled through the night and into the next day. Finally, as they crossed a cool, bubbling stream, they stopped to water the camels and rest their aching limbs.

Noah splashed his face with water and tried to wash the dust from his hair and beard. But the creek was small, and he couldn't achieve a thorough washing.

Aran pulled his tunic back and splashed the cool liquid on his raw inner thighs, clenching his teeth and sucking at the air as each droplet struck his skin.

"Let me see," Noah said and crouched to get a better view. Blisters had formed across the young man's legs and would take some time to go away. Noah straightened. "Have you been riding cross-legged since—"

"Yesterday," Aran said with a nod.

"It will get worse before it gets better."

Aran groaned and sat beside the stream. "Please tell me we can eat."

Noah considered how much of their journey remained. If he'd accurately calculated their progress, they should be able to reach the first major city, Accad, by nightfall. The camels wouldn't make it much farther without rest, and the rush of fear had since fallen away, leaving only a dull throbbing in his head, and a nearly unbearable heaviness in his eyes.

Noah crossed to his camel and untied one of the food bundles. "I have bread that won't last long. We'll eat that with some dried figs."

He brought both and laid them in front of Aran.

Aran went to Noah's bundle and dug out a flatbread and a smoked sausage. His stomach growled, and he moaned. "Why not the meat?"

"Because that is valuable and will last many days. We'll rest outside Accad, then travel again without entering the city. Four more days of hard riding and we might be able to reach Erech by nightfall. If we stop in the city to purchase food, we'll be at least another day behind."

"Then what's wrong with a bit of rest?"

Noah looked around. "I'd rather we move as quick as we can." But he said nothing to Aran of his worries over his children.

Aran glared at the meat, then shoved it back in the bag and took a bite out of the bread, which was now dry and hard. He shook his head and cupped stream water in his hand to wash it down.

Noah's own stomach started to ache with his first bite. He grabbed at the skin of his belly and groaned.

"I know." Aran shoved a dried fig in his mouth. "And all because of you and your dreams."

"The Word of the Almighty doesn't bring suffering. It heralds the suffering purchased by our mistakes."

The scar over Aran's right eye began to twitch. "Or convinces us we need make ourselves suffer." He slipped his hand back into the bag of meat, and Noah chose not to say anything as Aran hid a sausage in his tunic.

They finished their small meal, and Noah rose and reattached the bags to his camel before mounting. Aran followed reluctantly after stretching his legs and back one last time. When at last Kavel stood, they continued until the sun began to dip beneath the horizon.

Insects buzzed across desert bushes that hunched like the shadows of gnarled old hands with too many fingers. Kavel's soft feet softly crunched the dry branches as Noah pulled his cloak close against the growing chill. By the time they saw the flicker of torchlight atop the high brick walls of Accad, Noah's breath puffed out in clouds. Something about seeing signs of human life sparked a desire in him to continue. To see his children as quickly as possible and make certain they were alive and well.

But the heavy breaths from the camel beneath him brought back the sheer exhaustion that lay on them all. After days of hard travel, they were at risk of pushing the camels too hard. If either beast became injured, they'd never make it in time. Noah was too old to travel so far on foot in such a short time, and neither could a single camel carry such a load in that time.

"Alright." Noah pulled on the reins to slow their approach. "We will rest here tonight."

They found a cleft in a hill outside the city that would guard them from some of the wind, and Noah dismounted and tied the camels to a tree atop the hill. He lengthened the rope so they could graze through the night. But even though they were likely as hungry as Noah and Aran, the camels knelt and bellowed, overjoyed to finally be able to rest.

Noah undid the largest bundle attached to his camel and lugged it next to a boulder near the cleft they'd sleep in. Then he pulled a large linen sheet out of the bag and laid down next to Aran so they could share their body heat and weather the night in relative comfort.

Despite the stony ground and cold air, Noah fell asleep only moments after closing his eyes.

19

Japheth

Japheth had never been so exhausted. As Babel expanded with the construction of the tower, Japheth had offered to serve Babel in its endeavors, for he believed from the beginning that unity was important. That the schism wrought between Ham's progeny and his own had always been an ungodly and evil thing.

But as construction on the tower was finishing in a flurry, preparations for the celebration had become manic. For over a decade, workers had floated materials for brick building downriver. Now, even more supplies came. Piles of reeds for basket weaving, flour for bread, dried fruit and herbs for preparing a great feast to celebrate the new world order. Buildings and booths needed to be constructed on a grander scale, and quicker than he'd ever been demanded to build them before. Even simply administrating the madness was pushing him beyond his limits.

He crawled into bed moments before sunrise, longing to fall into the sweet embrace of blank dreams, when a knock at his door tested his patience.

He waited, hoping against hope that the person would go away.

But there it was again.

"Master," came a voice from the other side, which he recognized belonged to one of his grandsons, and a good servant Elik. He had long ago proven himself kind and reliable.

Japheth slowly got to his feet again, wincing at the ache in his back. He opened the door and met Elik's eyes, which glowed in the light of the torch grasped in his left hand. "Yes?" Japheth said, trying to keep any irritation from showing.

Elik bowed his head. "Forgive me. A messenger arrived moments ago."

"With what news?"

"The Lord Nimrod has summoned you to his home."

Japheth sighed and rubbed his burning eyes. "Can it not wait?"

Elik winced. "The messenger was emphatic that you leave immediately."

Japheth tapped his fingers on the door and pursed his lips. There was nothing he could do about it. Too much was needed. If foregoing rest accomplished the goals they held in common to unify the world and promote peace, what were a few additional hours without sleep?

"Very well. I will prepare myself and go."

20

Aran

Aran woke to the sounds of camels groaning and men whistling nearby. Reflexively, he twisted to his belly and shoved himself to his feet with his palms, quickly taking count of the number of figures on the hill in the dim, early-morning light.

Two men sat atop their own camels, holding the reins to Kavel and Ashbar, Noah's camel. His breath waited, unsure. A moment later, it dawned on him what they were trying to do. For once, he was thankful for Kavel's loud mouth and obstinate disposition, because it was his refusal to budge without the command of his master that woke Aran. And it was now making the men angry and distracted.

Noah grumbled and began to wake, but Aran dipped and pressed his hand hard over his mouth. Noah opened his eyes wide and calmed after realizing it was Aran. Aran motioned for silence, then slipped behind the thieves as silently as he could.

The closest man had dark hair and skin, obviously accustomed to working in the sun. He was sweating profusely in the early-morning cold. He was thin and did not appear to be a warrior. His companion was thicker, but no more battle ready.

Aran approached the thin one, because the man was within distance, and jumped as high as he could, taking hold of the man's thigh and the horn of the camel's saddle.

The man cried out and tried to kick him off, but Aran was

quick and twisted out of the way. His hand slipped onto a hard, metal object, and he pulled it up and heard the swipe of metal against metal.

A curved blade glinted in his hands against the sunrise, and the man cried out as Aran slammed the blade through his leg.

The knife must have gone too far and pricked the camel, for the beast reared and bellowed before throwing Aran off and hurrying away at full speed—with Kavel attached. The second man quickly followed on his own beast.

"No!" Aran yelled as he tumbled down the hill, bashing his head against the stony earth until he came to a stop, blood trickling down his cheeks. He hurried to his feet, sight spinning as he watched the thin thieves crouched low in their saddles, already hundreds of paces away. One man hugging his wounded leg while their camels pulled Aran and Noah's beasts with all their belongings tied to them.

Aran kicked dust at them and spat, cursing their families.

Noah was just getting to his feet, but no longer looked drowsy. His brows were low, and his jaw was set. "Nothing we can do about it now," Noah said.

"They stole our camels!"

"I saw."

"You didn't do anything," Aran said.

"I'd have broken a limb if I fell from that height—then we really would have been without hope."

Aran narrowed his eyes at Noah. "Did you know this was going to happen from your dreams?"

"Of course not."

"Then why aren't you more irritated?"

"Because there's no point in enraging myself." Now his face was reddening. He took a deep, calming breath. "At least now we know why the Almighty was telling us to make haste. We must hurry on sooner than we thought."

Aran steadied himself and patted his body to see what he still had on his person. With a flood of relief, he found his moneybag still tied to the inside of his tunic, along with the sausage he'd pilfered. But he'd lost his travel tunic in case of rain, his extra clothing, and the rest of their food.

He didn't even want to imagine what Noah lost.

He looked around, not seeing Noah where he'd expected, but rather by a large rock and kneeling half-obscured by it. "What are you—?"

"We still have this, thankfully," Noah said, and dragged forward a large bag.

Aran looked at him questioningly.

"I decided to pack our linen blanket alongside my wealth before leaving."

Aran looked at the linen blanket on the ground, then back to the massive bag that was filled to the brim with . . . stones?

"After the dreams, I assumed we would not pass through the wilderness unhindered."

Aran took a deep breath and let it out slowly. "Then you should have taken the other bags off."

Noah glared at him. "Be thankful we have our lives. When I was young, before the world was changed, thieves like that would have slit our throats without a second thought."

"You're supposed to be a prophet."

Noah's voice softened and his face paled as he said, "I thought we could risk some rest. I won't make that mistake again."

Aran grunted. "Well, what do we do now?"

Noah turned toward Accad. "We buy new camels, food, and any other supplies we deem necessary as we hurry through the market."

"New camels will cost a small fortune."

"Fortunate for us, I have enough in this bag. Please, I'd rather you carry it. It's quite heavy."

Aran struggled to lift it over his shoulder. Hard, angular objects inside the bag dug into his ribs, and he coughed. "It feels like a mountain."

"It's filled with silver slabs."

"Silver *slabs*?"

"They're valuable and easy to trade because the metal is useful for many purposes. They're not purified yet, so we'll need to sell them to a metal worker."

"Oof!" Aran stumbled, but kept himself upright with one

hand holding the bag over his right shoulder. "I'm not lugging this around all day."

"Accad is not a large city, though it is a wealthy one because of its placement." After they crested the hill, Noah turned toward the far right side of the wall.

Aran groaned. "We're not even on the correct side?"

"We were going to pass it by, remember? I saw the entrance on the east wall, around this corner." He pointed to the hard angle of the wall ahead.

Aran readjusted the bag to the middle of his back and held onto it with both hands. "If the Almighty wanted us to make good time, why did he let our camels get stolen?"

"I don't know. Perhaps"—he paused—"there's a reason he wants us to go into Accad."

"Then he should have said, 'Hurry to Accad.'"

Noah didn't respond and his silence made Aran uneasy.

21

Noah

Why did Aran have to keep asking questions Noah didn't know the answers to? It was frustrating enough to be thrown into this journey with so little knowledge of the Almighty's will. Now he worried their mistake would cost Shem or Japheth their lives.

As he listened to the silver slabs clunk against each other, and Aran's feet shifting across the dusty desert ground, he considered how much farther he could have pushed the camels. Maybe another half day, at most. But what would have happened to the poor beasts? Would they not have met another setback in due time? And possibly an even worse one.

He purposely crushed a skeletal sagebrush with his sandal to hear the crinkle of dry stems breaking. Perhaps they had rushed *too* far and too quickly.

No, that made no sense. Either it was as he told Aran, and the Almighty had plans for them in Accad. Or he had failed and put his children into peril.

Show me, he prayed. *Show me where I've gone wrong, so that I might right it.*

He listened to the quiet rush of his breathing against Aran's and the patter of their sandals against the dirt and stone and brush. But he heard nothing from God. One foot after the other. Each breath following the next. Plodding. Methodical. Patient.

Yes, he would trudge on until the Almighty sent word or

brought additional revelation through dreams or waking visions. The Almighty had always been faithful to him. Even when Noah had been unfaithful.

That thought released the tension in his chest, allowing him to breathe a bit easier.

He closed his eyes. *Help me, Almighty. Help me trust you.*

He opened his eyes and realized the gate was no more than two hundred paces away. Guards stood positioned with spears in hand beside the gate, wearing bronze helms and mail that hung over thick, protective leather tunics.

Noah placed a hand on Aran's chest, and the young man looked up at him with one eyebrow raised. "Don't let anyone know who I am," Noah said.

"What? Why?"

"I don't know." But he did know. He just wasn't sure how to explain that if evil men were attempting to destroy his children's lives out there, they would likely want to stop Noah from getting to them. He couldn't risk anything—especially after what just happened.

Aran's gaze canvassed Noah's figure. "Hard to hide how old you are."

Noah waved him away. "There are many now who are old and have gray hair and wrinkled faces. Since I've never ventured from my vineyard in all the years since the Flood, I don't think any will suspect that I'm the father of every living person." Noah looked again at the guards and wondered how they were related to him. Were they a distant descendant of Japheth? Or maybe Shem? They weren't quite as dark as Japheth, but most of Japheth's children weren't that dark, for his wife had lighter skin. He doubted they would pose any danger to their own patriarchs, but he now felt sure of nothing. "So," Noah continued, "just indulge an old fool, and don't let any know who I am."

Aran shrugged. "Whatever you want. Can't say it won't slip out, though."

Noah put a hand on Aran's chest. "It won't slip out."

Aran stared at him, gaze hopping from his left eye to his right. "Alright. It won't."

They approached the guards, who hailed them and lowered

their spears to caution them against advancing. "State your names, lineage, and business in Accad."

"I am an old merchant traveling with my servant Aran, the son of Rin, of the city of Erech. Our camels, and most of our belongings, were stolen by thieves within sight of your walls. We have need of more camels and seek to purchase some from Accad."

The guard's voice sounded thick and throaty. "The son of Rin? I have never heard this name. I see blood smeared across your clothing. We resist entry to all violent men."

"Aran is my defender, not a man of violence. He tried to resist the thieves for me, his ailing great-grandfather. I am on a journey to visit my children and am weary." He suppressed a wince, but he couldn't stop now. "He agreed to come to protect me from wild animals or brigands on the road. And so he has. Tell me, why would you not want such a man in Accad?"

The soldier cleared his throat and pointed with his spear. "What's in the bag?"

Noah motioned for Aran to drop it, and he did so and opened the mouth of the bag. When the guards looked inside and saw the silver slabs, their eyes widened slightly, and the one nodded.

"This is the only bag the thieves failed to take," Noah said.

"You are very strange," the guard said. "I do not feel comfortable—"

Noah stepped forward quickly, deftly dodging the tip of the spear and placing a firm grip on its shaft. The guard readied himself for violence but did not attack.

Noah poked him in the chest with a finger and wagged his head in disappointment. "What sort of rabble have they hired to guard this city? I'm old, curse it, and tired. Accad failed to protect me within its realm of dominion. The least you could do is let me in so I can trade and bring more wealth into your city. If, for some reason, you find us guilty of evil, take our silver and turn us out."

The guard regarded him. Clearly displeased at being spoken to in such a way, he seemed a reasonable man acquainted with self-control. Finally, he nodded. "Very well.

You may enter, but you must pay a foreigner's entry tax of three gold pieces."

"Three gold——" Aran began, but Noah cut him off with a raised palm.

"A reasonable request," Noah said. "Pay the guard what he demands, so that we may enter and do our business honestly."

Aran sighed and fished out his moneybag with no small amount of irritation. He uncinched the opening and poured out three precious gold pieces——which had taken him nearly half a year to save——and handed it to the guard.

When the guard took the pieces, Aran glared at him until the guard shook the shaft of his spear and said, "Go. Before I change my mind."

Noah entered, and Aran picked up the bag of silver again and carried it through the city gates.

22

Noah

As soon as they passed within the outer city limits, they immediately entered what appeared to be the poorest section of the city. Beggars lay on reed mats beside the road. What small buildings existed were rickety wooden lean-tos smashed so close together you could scarcely tell where one ended and the other began. The ditches ran with slow sludge that a young boy splashed through with bare feet. His belly protruded, and his lips were cracked and bleeding as he ran off between the alleys.

Aran grimaced at Noah. "Wealthy city, you said?"

Noah shrugged and kept his voice low. "I only repeated what others spoke."

Soon they entered an area with more appropriate housing and passed several crossroads where others walked. Some workers, others merchants. A few were dressed richly, like some sort of city official, for they brought around clay tablets that they marked with a reed pen after knocking on doors and talking to inhabitants.

The houses slowly shifted from sunbaked brick homes to stone slab houses and civic storehouses. Just outside the market square, Noah stopped one of the city officials and said, "Where could I sell raw silver to be smelted?"

The official, who had curly hair and thick eyebrows, pointed west and said, "Three streets down and to the left. Follow the black smoke."

Noah nodded and thanked the man, then he and Aran made their way.

"The city may be small, but this road feels never-ending," Aran said.

Noah tried to help him carry the load by lifting the bottom of the bag.

"Stop," Aran said. "It's just making it more awkward."

Noah chuckled and let the bag drop again, lifting a grunt from Aran. "Don't worry, we've not much farther to go."

Aran grumbled something too quiet for Noah to hear, though he was certain he understood the general intent.

Black plumes coughed into the morning sky from a circular clay furnace outside a small home. A man with soot smeared across his face worked the forge.

Noah greeted the man as he hammered slag from a glowing slab of crude iron.

"Stay back," the smith said.

He was smaller and thinner than Noah expected, making the hammer in his arms look strangely oversized, like a child had grabbed hold of a man's tools. But he wielded it with skill.

Aran set down his burden and leaned against the man's home, watching with seemingly mild interest as he beat the iron to purify it before the metal cooled and the ore coagulated.

Noah was well acquainted with the technique, for Japheth had learned much from the smiths in their hometown before the Flood. Of course, since the cataclysm, ore had become more difficult to find, and they rarely had access to as much materials as were necessary to practice the most sophisticated techniques.

When the smith finished, he took his gloves off and wiped the sweat and soot from his brow. "What brings foreigners to this dirty corner of Accad?"

In response, Aran opened the mouth of the bag and hurled the contents across the ground.

The man spluttered and threw himself atop them as if they were his own newly born children. He lifted them and tested them with a close eye. "Silver? Won't take much to purify, either. What do you ask?"

"Enough money to buy new camels, food for a long journey, and additional supplies to weather the wilds."

The man counted up the slabs of silver and stacked them neatly, chuckling as he rubbed his hands together and nodded. "I'd be robbing you. So, yes, I'll take them. One moment . . ." He disappeared into his home and returned with a bag of gold coins that he poured into Noah's open hands.

Noah nodded, satisfied, then poured them back into the bag with the smith's help. Before he took the bag from the man, he said, "May I ask you a pointed question?"

The smith narrowed his eyes but nodded.

"I heard this city was quite wealthy, but when we entered . . ."

The smith nodded. "You speak of the new additions."

"New?" Aran said.

"They came seeking asylum. At first, we gave them a small amount of land toward the back of the wall. But they kept coming, and we ran out of space and had to find new areas for them to live."

"Like the gutters by the city entrance?"

The man's head dipped, and his voice softened. "Yes."

"And you just live here, not helping them?" Aran said.

The man scoffed. "What more could we give them?"

Aran pointed at the bag of money in his hand. "You seem well off."

The smith tossed the bag of coins on the ground and kicked it as if it were a snake. "Teach us how to eat gold and you'll save many lives. We're all hungry, and you'll likely not find any food in the market. This money has been kept aside for a purpose like today. I have to take care of my family. Now, take it and go." And the man turned and disappeared once more into his home.

Noah picked up the money and counted out a third of the pieces. "Here," he said. "Take this."

"What? Why?"

"We will go separate ways to save time. I'll purchase the camels and see if I can find any food—seems unlikely after what the man said. You find supplies and anything you think will be useful for our journey."

"Where will we meet?"

"The city gate."

"What if I'm done before you and have to wait?"

Noah squinted. "Then you will wait."

"And be stared at by the vagabonds while holding supplies that could probably help them."

Noah hadn't thought about that. "Seems a better idea than any other meeting spot."

Aran thought it over. "Fine. Just don't take your time."

"Believe me," Noah said. "I won't."

23

Zillah

Zillah had followed the two newcomers at a reasonable distance from the moment they slipped through the gates of Accad. Foreigners were the best targets for theft. Many times, they left before even realizing what had happened.

But these two were different than the usual fair. The man was old—very old. And the young man had scars across his face. He looked dangerous.

She'd grown tired of the easy swipes. She'd lived for three years now alone in a hidden cove of a forgotten part of Accad. Forced by those who sought her life to live a solitary life, able to open herself to none, experiencing few of the simple joys of life. Living as a thief on the run was not so glamorous, but she had been forced to it.

With so little excitement, the more challenging targets kept her blood moving. She hated the risk, but she'd seen the money the two men carried. It couldn't be all they owned that held great value. Enough to get her out of this city where she wouldn't be known, and wouldn't be treated like refuse.

But the difficult ones demanded more careful planning. So, as she hunched low atop the building and listened to the two men quietly talk about leaving, she wondered if she would miss her opportunity.

Zillah smiled to herself and slipped silently from the roof. Just as she hopped down, her eyes caught the glint of a flash of blonde hair in the distance, though the wall of the building now obscured it.

Despite herself, her pulse began to pound. It couldn't be possible that the man who'd chased her for so long could have found her in Accad—not after all the work she'd done to confound his tracking.

She stopped and turned back, pausing at the edge of the building before slowly edging her gaze around it until she could see where she'd thought the man had stood. She could have sworn she saw him leaning up against the low wall skirting the dirt road, legs and arms crossed, blue eyes glinting. But there was . . .

Nothing. She sighed, pulled herself back against the wall, and clutched at the skin of her chest. The solitude was getting to her. She was starting to see things. She took a deep breath and walked down the road behind the young man with the scars, matching his gait.

It was more than time to move to a different city. She'd been having dark dreams lately. Disturbing, cold dreams wrought with anxiety. The city was doomed. With all the refugees, food was running out. Life was getting harder by the week. If not for her craftiness, she would have died long before.

The man with the scars stopped in front of her and looked around. This was as good a time as ever to stage a distraction.

24

Aran

The camels were pastured outside the north wall, so Aran took his time perusing the market with wide eyes. It shocked him to find the sheer variety and volume of goods in such a small city. His hometown of Erech was easily twice the size, yet never had he seen such beautiful tapestries or such well-crafted stringed instruments.

He stooped and ran his finger along glazed pottery the color of brilliant topaz. The potter was sitting behind her wheel, coaxing wet clay into a gooseneck pouring flask. A small kiln sat off to the side, and Aran spied glowing coals inside it. Dark clay cups sat on the embers, baking until they hardened sufficiently for daily use.

He continued toward brilliant furs displayed on wooden poles. Then leather stretched on a rack. A worker carefully scraped the animal skin with the rounded edge of a bone.

Then came ivory combs, woven baskets, linen tunics, braided sandals. The more he saw, the more he realized how rich, yet how underfed, Accad's people looked.

Women walked by, their shoulder bones jutting through ornate dresses of purple and scarlet. Some hobbled, including a young man whose legs were bowed from malnutrition.

He had passed nearly every stall in the market, yet still hadn't found a single morsel of food. He continued to the outer border, now looking only for food. Near the end of the market, he found a single wine seller holding a couple skins of wine.

"How much?" Aran said.

"Two gold pieces," the seller said.

Aran's eyes widened. "For one skin?"

"It's all the wine left in the city."

"I could buy ten for that price anywhere else."

"Well, you're not *anywhere else.*"

"Is anyone selling food in this city?"

The wine seller shook his head. "A small shipment comes each day, and none of us see it until the officials deliver rationed bread and—if we're lucky—fruit."

Aran turned away, mind reeling. What was happening? The inhabitants were slowly starving to death while stalls stood lined with luxurious goods. He didn't understand it, but he found one of the city officials and decided to follow him to see the man's work more closely.

The official was welcomed into three homes in a row with smiles and sighs of relief. The people didn't seem to suspect him of mistreating them. Instead, they thanked him as he went on his way. The official appeared weighed by anxiety, so preoccupied with his work that he didn't even notice Aran until the fourth home.

The man looked at him and waved. "Do you need something, sir?"

Aran shook his head, even more confused than before. "No, thank you."

The official nodded and entered the next house.

Aran turned back and noticed a figure turning a corner just before something slammed into him, throwing him back and knocking the breath from his chest. Aran reflexively shoved his knee into the figure's abdomen, drawing a high-pitched "oof."

Aran twisted and scrambled to his feet, looking down at the grimacing face of a young woman partially obscured by a hood.

"What did you do that for?" She grunted and held her midsection, but got up quicker than he expected.

He blinked, confused that she could stand already, because he had hit her hard. "Are you alright?"

Yells sounded from down the alley she'd come from, and she threw a glance back and cursed. "You never saw me." She burst into a full sprint before disappearing into the crevice between two houses across the road. The crack was so small, he hadn't thought anyone would be able to fit. Lucky for her, she was small, and the leather tunic she wore blended in with the shadows so well that Aran could no longer detect her.

Three guards jogged around the corner and stopped. Spotting Aran, they crossed to him. "You there!"

"Yes?" Aran said.

"Did you see someone run by?"

Aran furrowed his brow. "What?"

Two of the guards stepped closer. "What are you doing here, alone?"

"Trying to find food."

The shortest guard scoffed. "You know there's no food in the city. Tell us where the thief went. She stole from our storehouse."

"I'm not from here," Aran said.

Two of the guards stared at him until the third placed his hands on their shoulders and said, "We're wasting time. Let's split up and hurry."

After a moment's hesitation, they nodded and ran their respective ways.

Hardly a moment after the last disappeared, the woman exited her hiding place and pulled back her hood. Her long black hair spilled across her shoulders, and her dark eyes regarded him with a piercing shrewdness he'd encountered in few. Her thin face was the color of sandstone, smooth as polished stone. She was not beautiful the way of some in their softness. But rather in the hard set of her jaw, and the intensity of her gaze, which sent a thrill through his chest. Dust and mud marked her skin and matted her hair. But that hardly marred her loveliness.

"Why'd you help me?"

He shrugged. "You seemed in need."

She stepped near enough to make him uncomfortable. "Where are you from?"

"I'm just trying to find food. My grandfather and I have a long way to travel yet."

She stared at him, then sighed. "I suppose you think I owe you some of the food I stole, for saving me."

Aran shrugged again. He certainly needed food. In fact, it was the primary thing he was looking for. He didn't want to starve during several more days of hard travel.

She narrowed her eyes and said, "What's that supposed to mean?"

"Whatever you think it means," he said.

"That's not an answer. Where are you and your grandfather going?"

A yell sounded from behind them. "I knew it!"

They looked back to see one of the guards running toward them.

The woman cursed again and pulled him hard by the arm. "Follow me if you don't want to rot in prison."

He sprinted after her, struggling to keep up. A second set of footsteps joined the first and gained ground behind them as she led him down two alleyways, through a door into what appeared to be an empty storehouse, then out the back into a courtyard. She bounded up a stack of barrels and over a high brick wall.

Aran followed and the guards burst from the door and yelled for him to stop as he leapt from the wall. He rolled when he hit the ground to avoid harming his legs, then ran after the flash of the young woman's figure.

The guards were yelling, struggling over the wall just as Aran and the woman turned into a small alley that led to a fork in the road. Instead of choosing a side down the fork, the woman opened a door into a brick house and yanked him in, shutting the door quietly behind them.

He was gasping for breath, chest burning from exertion. She clasped a slender hand over his mouth. "Shh."

He felt his cheeks warm at her touch, but as he slowed his breathing and grimaced at the pain, she slipped into the shadows, leaving a tingling where her fingers brushed his lips. The guards ran past and Aran turned and tried to find her.

"Careful," she whispered. "You'll knock over that stack of bowls."

He looked down and struggled against the white shadows

that mottled his sight in the dark from his time in the sunlight. Slowly his eyes adjusted and he saw the bowls merely one step from his feet. He breathed out long and slow, thankful she'd warned him. "Is this your home?"

"No," she said, as he watched her rustle through items in a storage bin.

She really was a thief. "Then how did you know the home would be unoccupied?"

"I didn't." She pulled out a length of rope and shoved it into a little satchel sewn into the inside flap of her leather tunic.

A gleam caught Aran's eyes, and he crossed to the corner where he found a spear leaned against the wall. He ran his fingers across the sharp tip of the bronze blade attached to the wooden shaft with an iron collar.

"You fancy it?"

Her voice, no longer a whisper, made him jump.

"If you want it, take it. But be quick, we're not safe yet."

She crossed to the back door, which presumably led to another courtyard, and peered out through the crack.

He looked back at the spear. Indeed, he did fancy it. He'd been wishing for a spear since the moment he left the vineyard. But he had no desire to steal anyone's valuable possessions.

"What's the matter? Never stolen before?"

"I'm no thief."

Then he remembered the sausage he'd taken out of the food bag the night before. He felt the folds of his tunic for it. There it was, tucked into his belt. He pulled it out and looked at it. Then back at the spear. If everyone in the city was as bad off as they appeared, they'd be glad to find food left in their house. Especially something as valuable as smoked meat.

He weighed the worth of the food against the weapon. If the woman gave him food as it seemed she was willing to do, he would regret not taking the spear.

He set down the sausage, pulled out two gold coins, and set them next to it. Then he took up the spear and joined her at the door. She smirked and said, "Now you're just like me."

"I left money." He thought it better not to mention he'd left food.

She laughed. "Are you jesting?"

He shook his head. "I don't think it's funny."

"Help a thief, then refuse to steal. You're an odd one." She took off her leather tunic, leaving only a white linen covering her body. He saw now just how slim she was, but her arms and dark thighs were strong.

"What are you doing?" he said, and averted his eyes.

She turned the tunic inside out, then put it on again. "When I reverse my tunic, it changes color. How do I look?"

The satchels sown into her outfit now faced outward and looked entirely natural. The hood tucked underneath and disappeared. She softened her expression and smiled at him sweetly.

"Resourceful," he said.

"No more running for us. You're now one of the mercenaries my merchant master hired to protect me as we travel from city to city in search of the items to trade in our hometown of . . ." She tapped her lips with her fingers as she searched for an appropriate city to name.

"Erech."

She raised her brow and nodded. "Is that where you're from?"

"Where I'm going."

She placed her palm on the door. "Then Erech it is."

He grabbed her wrist gently. "My name is Aran." He kept his hand where it was, feeling the rhythmic pulsing in her veins.

She looked up at him. Was it just the lighting, or were her cheeks reddening? "Zillah."

He smiled and let go. "A lovely name."

"Thank you."

She pushed open the door and walked into another courtyard. This one was guarded by a knee-high wall with an open gate. Aran followed and matched her pace, using the butt of the spear like a walking stick.

They turned toward the south wall. Several guards passed but paid them no heed. Officials walked from home to home, occasionally harassed by hungry citizens who clutched at the hem of their robes, begging. Twice the guards had to become involved, but none of the altercations led to violence.

"That's the reason for all the guards," Aran said.

"Pity people are so willing to steal."

"Indeed."

She chuckled.

Several streets down, she led him to a wooden hatch in the ground next to the wall. After making sure no one was watching, she unhooked the latch and opened it, beckoning him in.

"What is this?"

"My home. Hurry, and watch your step, it's dark."

He entered, and she followed, carefully dropping the hatch above their heads and using a thin stick jammed between the hatch and the ground to position the latch so it appeared to be locked.

He widened his eyes, hoping his sight could pierce the black, but the shadows were all-consuming. He heard Zillah's breaths reverberate off the stone walls and the musical drip of droplets into puddles like liquid drums. The air here was cool, and as she slipped in front of him, he said, "How can you see anything?"

She laced her fingers between his. "I can't. I know the way. Here, I'll help you down."

He knew he shouldn't be here. Noah would be waiting. But as soon as she'd run into him, he'd known he was in trouble. If it had been foolish to help her, the warmth of her fingers in his hand made him glad he'd done it.

At the bottom of the stairs, the way flattened and turned right. Fifty paces away, Aran saw a glow coming from a recess in the wall. Zillah's hand slipped away now that they could see.

Aran ran his fingers along the cool, porous rock that lined the passage. The entire place reeked of wet sandstone. "Where are we?"

"Under the wall. When the city was first built, a wildfire swept through the region and destroyed homes. After that, they built the wall, along with a few underground cellars."

"Why?"

"The wall to guard against more fires. Lucky for us, everyone in the city seems to have forgotten about the cellars. Probably because they are horrible places to live."

When they arrived at the recess in the wall, Aran realized it was a door. They entered, and the room inside was larger than anticipated. Several mats littered the uneven floor beside a rickety table atop which sat a burning lantern wick soaking up oil. Random tools and supplies had been tossed about, and a bed sat on wooden slats elevated perhaps a hand's height above the floor.

"Did someone ransack your home?"

"That's offensive," she said.

Aran pointed at the bed. "Why—"

"Floods when it rains."

"Ah."

"As I said—not the most comfortable home."

"How long have you lived here?"

She opened her outer tunic and let it slide off her shoulders before sinking onto one of the mats in a cross-legged position, resting her face in her hands. "Long enough."

Aran resisted the urge to look away. Though Zillah was still relatively covered, he wasn't used to seeing a woman so comfortable tossing away clothing.

Zillah looked up. "Something bothering you?"

"Uh—no—well. I can't stay."

She leaned back on her palms. "Want your food now?"

He paused, searching for what to say. "Well, my grandfather is expecting me."

She stared at him for a few long moments.

He resisted the urge to cover the scar across his cheek.

Finally, she stood. "Well, we might as well get going, then."

He blinked.

"Something wrong?"

He scratched his head again. "Uh—what do you mean?"

"I mean that you're going to take me to Erech."

"Excuse me?"

"Look, I need to get out of this city as badly as I need a bath. Why do you think I helped you back there? Because I was thankful you distracted the guards?"

He ground his teeth together, feeling even more foolish than before.

"I need help. That's the reason I stole food today—I don't

just steal for the joy of it. And the rope I took is going to help me get down from the turret directly above us."

"You're mad," he said.

"Everyone in this city is mad for staying when they're all starving to death for accepting refugees."

"Refugees of what?"

She rolled her eyes. "Fanatics of the Almighty who refused to worship the Light Bringer. They fled to escape persecution, and Accad's people were vocal about helping them. Now no one will trade food with Accad because they're afraid of what might happen in return." Zillah's eyes narrowed. "By the way you look, I thought you would have been a frequent traveler."

Aran turned away, more than ever wanting to hide his scars. "I was young when I got these."

She stood and brushed herself off before gathering up assorted tools and hiding them in the pockets of her reversible tunic. She hummed happily while she packed.

"I can't take you," Aran said.

"If you take me with you, I'll give you your share of the food."

"You said I earned the food."

"No, I guessed that you *expected* food."

"Which I didn't really agree to."

She clapped. "Wonderful. That makes everything easy. No food unless you take me with. Of course, if you don't take me with, I suppose I could just walk the wilds alone."

He glared at her. The problem was, the only food he would be able to get his hands on in the entire city was likely now in Zillah's possession. Noah and Aran needed it, and he'd wasted all this time already trying to win her favor to get some. It would be days before they reached another city, and she would likely be harmed in the wilds if she tried to make the journey herself.

He pursed his lips. "How much do you have?"

She tapped the side of her mouth with her index finger as if thinking hard. "Several loafs of bread, a bit of fruit, and a healthy chunk of smoked meat. I'm sure you're hungry."

Aran's stomach growled. "I could just tell the guards where you live."

She stared at him, gaze skipping from his left eye to his right. She was looking at him as she had before, with eyes like spears. Her voice was quiet and calm when she said, "You won't do that."

He held her gaze. Weighing his options.

"So," she said. "Do we have an agreement?"

Aran turned away and crossed his arms.

She skipped in front of him and smiled. "Yes?"

He ran a hand over his face and groaned. Noah was not going to be happy.

25

Noah

Noah handed thirty gold coins to the camel breeder. "Steep price for two skinny youth."

"Camels double as a good source of meat—even skinny ones like these. You should thank me for not slaughtering them to feed my family."

Noah rubbed his eyes. "True." He bowed. "I pray your family will be blessed with all they need to survive." And he led the camels back toward the gates.

The beasts were mild-tempered. Nowhere near as defiant as Kavel. The thought made him wish he still had those ridiculous, foolish old beasts. He hadn't realized how much he loved them. He'd been present at their births and fed them more than half the days they'd been alive, no matter that he had hired servants to care for them. He enjoyed the presence of animals much more since Jade passed away.

The guards at the gate nodded their greeting as he passed within. He hoped that seeing the new camels he'd purchased burned away any shred of paranoia left in them. He wondered, briefly, if the guard would return the money he'd taken.

But no. If everyone was as hungry as they appeared, Noah would have given them all he had. Everyone in the city had come into the world because of him. It was a strange thing that those who could trace their lineage to him would not know him and would distrust him.

Then again, he didn't trust any of them.

Noah stood with the camels between those ditches running with sludge and looked for any sign of Aran. There were more penniless beggars lining the sides and sleeping beneath unstable lean-tos. He even spotted a boney mother nursing an infant.

Noah turned away and fought a wave of grief that threatened to choke him. How could his offspring live in such squalor? He felt a horrible sense of responsibility for the painful sores across their bodies. He closed his eyes and shook his head.

Could I have stopped this? Could I have done something to keep such suffering from these souls?

He could have. As much as he wanted to scream no.

How many days had he spent lounging in luxury, relaxing in the sunlight as he and his workers piled up wealth?

And all while an infant suckled at a starving woman's breast.

He thought again of the dreams the Almighty had given him. He realized now that the Almighty had been too gentle in revealing this to him.

Almighty, forgive me. Give me the chance to reverse my wrongs and change the direction this world is going. Why should they suffer so?

He leaned against one of the camels and brushed its fur with his hand. It rumbled approval and looked at him with bulging eyes, batting double rows of eyelashes at him. He didn't understand why Aran hated camels so much. They were ugly, yes, but in a way that was endearing.

He examined his surroundings again. Aran should have been here long ago. Noah had walked to the market with him, traveled all the way out the gate and to the camel ranch and back. Despite what he'd told Aran, he'd gone slower than intended because his back and legs ached from their travel.

Had something happened? Perhaps Aran had been injured. Or maybe he'd encountered trouble with some of the other guards they'd seen walking the streets.

Hard footsteps sounded, and Aran jogged into view holding a spear.

"Aran," Noah said. "Are you alright?"

Aran stopped and bent forward, resting on the shaft of the spear and breathing hard. He was sweating and seemed jumpy. "Sorry."

Noah stared at him. "Where are the supplies?"

"Long story."

"If you did something foolish—"

"I didn't. Well, at least I don't think . . . just . . . wait until we exit the city."

"Are you hurt?"

Aran held the spear in one hand like a walking stick while he took up the reins of one of the camels in the other and made for the gate. "I'm fine."

Noah followed. "Where'd you get that spear?"

"Shh!" Aran's face reddened as he glanced at the guards facing away from them out of the corner of his eye. "Not until we're away."

Noah followed, disturbed and a little angry that Aran had failed to get the supplies for their journey. Something had happened. Aran was normally dependable.

As they exited, the guards eyed Aran's spear. But when the guard saw Noah watching, he looked away as if the spear was nothing.

They led the camels across the little hills outside Accad and turned the corner, making their way down the southern wall. Noah kept silent as they went, waiting for Aran to explain himself.

Finally, as they were just about to the end of the southern wall, Noah could no longer hold back. "Enough of this. Tell me what happened."

Aran opened his mouth to respond when a rope fell from the wall near them. A dark, strong young woman slid to the ground beside them wearing a plain tunic with pockets sewn into it. She nodded at Noah and dusted herself off.

Aran indicated the woman. "Noah, meet Zillah."

The young woman smiled at him.

She was beautiful. And dirty. And what in the name of the Almighty was Aran doing with a beautiful, dirty woman when he should have been buying supplies and getting back on the road to help his destitute mother?

Noah cleared his throat. "Aran?"

Aran nodded.

"Come here."

The woman smiled. A charming expression. No doubt she knew the effect it had.

"In private." Noah took Aran aside and whispered into his ear. "What demon has possessed you? Who is she? A prostitute?"

"Of course not!" Aran said. "She was in trouble, so I helped her, then the guards almost put me in jail, and she helped me escape . . ."

"Why were the guards after her?"

Aran shrugged. "She'd taken some food."

Noah slapped his palm into his own forehead three times in a row. "Foolish, foolish, foolish. When did you become so foolish?"

"What was I supposed to do? I helped her. She's a woman. I didn't know what was happening. She had food—I couldn't find anyone selling food in the entire city."

"The city is starving," Zillah said from afar.

"Hold your hands over your ears," Noah said, and Zillah huffed before obeying. "I know, Aran. Food was my job. Supplies were yours, remember?"

"She has the only food either of us could have gotten."

"She stole food, Aran. *Stole*. As in, you brought along a thief."

"She needs help getting to a new city."

"How is that my problem?"

Aran narrowed his eyes. "Isn't she your great-granddaughter?"

"What?" Zillah said, and finally stopped faking that she was stopping her ears. She tried to step closer, but Noah held up his hand and she growled and backed off with arms folded.

Noah bit his lip. Shot her a look and tried to fight the heat threatening to flood his cheeks. "Not precisely."

"Well, she offered food if we helped her to Erech."

"Did you get anything besides food?"

He held up his spear.

"And if she robs us? Steals a camel and runs off into the

wilderness? Aran, I can't even tell you how easily she could destroy everything." His vision shook as he thought of his children, crushed. "Have you not thought even once of the money for your mother?"

Aran whispered back, "Perhaps you should let the Almighty decide, if you are the prophet you seem to be."

"And if the Lord says no?"

Aran chewed the inside of his cheek. "I will support your decision."

Noah nodded and walked away from Aran, who returned to talk quietly with Zillah. Noah sat cross-legged and closed his eyes, willing his mind to calm.

Great Almighty, please. I have no idea what the right choice is. But your will is perfect. If you want us to take this young woman with us, please, tell me now.

Noah waited. And waited. And waited.

Wind rustled the scraggly brush around them and blew grit into his face. He opened his eyes and saw dark clouds rolling in the distant sky.

He thought back to the starving, nursing mother. Had that woman once been a young thief as well? What if he'd found her at her worst and refused to help her? Would that have made him righteous? Or merely prideful and co-evil?

He sighed.

Lord, if it's *not* your will that I take this girl, make it obvious immediately.

He closed his eyes and felt . . .

26

Zillah

"What is he doing?" Zillah said.

Aran looked at the old man kneeling on the loose gravel and broken desert brush. "Praying."

"Is he always in such a bad mood?"

"Not usually."

"You said something when you were talking with him," she said. "About me being related to him?"

"I'll let you ask when he's finished."

"Wait, he's not the Noah who . . ."

Aran's face gave it away.

Zillah felt her insides drop away. Then a rush of excitement.

Noah? The forefather of the living world? The oldest man alive? He certainly looked old, but only as old as the other men and women she'd met who were over 100 years of age. Her mind raced as she took in his figure. "How long will he take to pray?"

Aran shrugged. "He's keen on moving."

"Why is he angry?"

Aran shrugged again. "He's impatient."

Zillah snorted. "I want to get moving just as much as he does." She looked over her shoulder at the rope hanging from the wall. Part of her felt certain the blue-eyed man had been in the city. And if he was, he would find that rope eventually. If the three of them happened to be sitting beneath it when it was found, there would be trouble.

She took a deep breath to suppress a rising wave of anxiety. She could still hardly believe that after all these years, the men her parents had hired to hunt her had found her all the way in Accad. If she didn't evade them soon, she would be worse off than if she'd let those guards catch her.

Noah stood and, after taking a deep breath, his expression relaxed, though he still didn't look happy. "You'll ride with Aran after we eat."

Zillah nearly laughed. It was too easy.

"The Almighty spoke?" Aran said.

Noah shot him a look that Zillah couldn't decipher. "In a way."

Zillah approached him and bowed. "Thank you, sincerely."

Noah examined her with some surprise. "Not the behavior I expected from a thief."

"Neither did I expect hospitality from you," Zillah said and instantly regretted opening her mouth, because her words brought a chill back to Noah's eyes. "I only mean that I've heard stories of why you stayed away from your family. That is, if you are the Noah I think you are."

Noah sniffed. "There's nothing menial about the ways my family offended me. But you could be speaking of only one of my children—from whom I have no doubt you originated, judging by your moral fiber."

Zillah couldn't stop her eyes from widening. "So, you really are Noah? *The* Noah? The father of my father's father's father?"

"If you counted right, yes," Noah said.

"Wow. So—is it true?"

"That I will never speak with Ham again? Yes."

"No, that you haven't left your vineyard in over a hundred years."

Noah pursed his lips and creased his brow. "First, where is the food?"

"Oh," Zillah said and opened her tunic and dug the food out of her pockets. "Sorry, I forgot."

She handed Noah and Aran each a loaf of bread and a

chunk of meat, then grabbed the same for herself and started eating.

Noah stared at the food in his hands as if it were a dead child. "Why did you steal this food?"

She stopped with a bite of bread in her mouth as the anxiety returned and her appetite waned. She tried to swallow, but her body resisted, so she held it between her teeth and cheek. How could she explain that she'd run away from her family and lived as a fugitive in a city filled with refugees? They would wonder why she couldn't receive food like the rest of the people there, and if they asked too many questions, they'd come to understand that by helping her, they were endangering their lives, because the ones who hunted her would do anything to get her back— and now might just have a trail to follow. "To survive," she said and managed to force the bite down her throat. It slid slowly, threatening to stick to the inside of her throat as she again stared up at the rope dangling from the wall. Could there be some way to cut it down after using it? Or of making it come loose?

Too late, now. Besides, the guards would never have let her out.

She took one more bite and struggled to swallow before shoving the rest back inside her tunic. Her stomach ached, but she couldn't eat with so many thoughts pressing against her.

Noah still hadn't taken a bite. Aran was tentatively eating, though.

"No one will starve because of what I stole," she said. "But I would have, had I not taken it."

"If the Almighty wants her with us, who are we to refuse the food she offers?" Aran said.

Zillah looked at Aran's scarred face. When he showed her kindness in the city by distracting the guards, she'd looked into his eyes and saw no pretense. Only the shadow of something she recognized in herself. Something familiar.

Now, standing outside the walls of Accad and sharing food with him and the father of all living men, it made her feel they had found each other by more than just happenstance.

Of course, she still had no idea who he was. Not really. But a thief had little but feelings to guide her through life. She had grown to rely on intuition these past years.

"Fine," Noah said after much thought. And he brought the bread to his mouth and started eating.

Sooner than she expected, the two finished their food and began to mount the camels. Noah motioned for her to go to Aran, and she did.

Aran held down his arm and she grabbed hold of it, letting him pull her up into the seat in front of him. He wrapped an arm around her and spoke into her ear, his breath hot on her neck. "Lean back into me."

She did so and felt the warmth of his chest against her shoulders as the camel stood up, back legs first, then front.

Noah's camel stood as well, and in moments, they were off.

Aran kept one arm around her, and she let it stay, because for the first time in years, she felt comfort from the touch of another. It did not matter if the feeling was false. She closed her eyes and wished it would stay. That she could be at peace, freed from the need to run and hide. From the obligation to question motives and distance herself from human need.

Sleeping in the dark chill of that underground chamber, she hadn't realized how lonely she'd become.

27

Aran

They rode in silence for many hours. Eventually, as the light dimmed, Zillah fell asleep and slumped in Aran's arms. He kept having to reposition her head to rest in the crook of his neck so she wouldn't lean too far.

Luckily, he hardly had to direct his camel at all. He'd given it the name Little Kavel, for he was smaller than the old camel who'd borne him faithfully all the way to Accad.

The desert air was dry, and his tongue began to feel like it was wrapped in camel hair. Night settled, and the air began to cool. As the chill seeped into his bones, he was thankful for the warmth of Zillah's body against his. Though she slept fitfully, shivering and waking with chattering teeth before settling into him and falling asleep again.

He envied her ability to sleep while sitting up. He'd never learned the talent and was certain he'd never be able to sleep in *her* arms while traveling the road. Imagining it made him chuckle, and Zillah woke and took a deep breath, rubbing her arms.

"How long until sunrise?" she said, voice croaking in the dry, cool wind.

"Too long," he said.

She tried to sleep again, but kept repositioning herself. With a sigh, she stretched and sat up. "Do you have any water?"

"No."

Zillah groaned and ran her tongue against her teeth.

"I wish I'd paid the wine merchant two gold coins for a skin," Aran said.

"I'd pay with my own leg."

Aran looked up at the sky, and the dark clouds they'd seen far off were now blocking half the stars. The wind was picking up and began to blow grit into their faces, even as high as they sat atop their camels.

Zillah pulled her hood low about her face and huddled forward over the saddle. Aran wished he could do the same. He closed his eyes, instead, to guard against the sand and dirt. Opening them only occasionally to make sure they were still within sight of Noah.

The night trudged on to the rhythm of Little Kavel's feet, until color grew at the edge of the horizon, and the sun rose. But the light only lasted a moment for the dark clouds hung low and soon the sun plunged into them. The light was not strong enough to pierce the billowing squall, and in the distance, Aran spied a sheet of rain falling like a shifting shadow.

Aran braced himself as the first droplets struck his face. Then, in the space of four of the camel's steps, the rain intensified until it soaked his tunic through.

Zillah muttered curses as they clutched each other in the wet chill. The sun hadn't been up long enough to warm the rain, so it felt as though the clouds had diverted a frozen river onto their shoulders.

Soon, the road started to run with little creeks rushing fast enough to dig ditches. Twice the camels nearly rolled their ankles, until Noah pulled his camel to a set of large boulders and slid off.

Aran and Zillah got off as well after Noah yelled above the tempest, "We'll take shelter here until the storm passes!"

They pulled the camels into the alcove as much as they could, and huddled together behind them. Still, though it protected them from some of the bitter wind and stinging rain, they couldn't change that they were soaked.

Aran wished more than ever he had remembered to purchase

new rain tunics at the market before leaving. Even more that he'd never let those thieves get away with all their supplies. He hoped they were drowning in the storm too.

Noah cupped his hands and, each time they filled with water, he sucked the liquid down. Aran and Zillah did the same. "At least we don't have to be thirsty anymore," he said.

Zillah laughed, but Aran didn't find it funny.

They waited and watched for quite some time. Just when Aran thought the storm couldn't get any worse, it did. Now they couldn't see more than a few feet in front of them. And it just kept falling.

Zillah held herself and shivered. Aran wrapped his arms around her as Noah put his back to their sides. Zillah looked up at Aran, their noses hardly a finger's width from each other.

Water ran down her face, matting her black hair to her cheeks and chin. She pushed a lock of hair from her eyes and smiled. Aran smiled back and shook his head. "I wouldn't have guessed a day after you tackled me we'd be sitting here."

"Not what I expected, either," she said.

She looked away, squinting at their surroundings. The camels sat on bent knees, heads lifted high in the rain. Eyes guarded by double lashes and extra lids.

Noah rose slowly, and he groaned as his joints ground together. He hobbled out and stared at the road, lines etched as deeply into his face as the ruts across the road.

"So," she said. "Why are you journeying to Erech?"

Aran looked at his feet, dug partially through the mud. "My father died."

She slid her feet forward, mirroring his. "I'm sorry."

"He deserved to die," he said.

She looked up at him, questions in her eyes but not on her tongue.

"I ran away from home when I was young. To escape him." He pointed at the scars across his face.

Her eyes widened. She ground her teeth together and said nothing.

"I'm going back to help my mother."

"Noah knew them?"

"Noah wants to visit his sons, who live in that region. He's been having dreams."

They looked at the old man, standing like a sycamore in the rain.

"Dreams?"

"I saw the beginning of the end of the world," Noah said, eyes bright as stars in the storm glow. "My goal is to visit Shem, who lives in the oasis city of Erech, then Japheth, who lives downriver, in another city."

Zillah hugged herself tighter.

Aran did the same, until the rain waned.

Then, as quickly as it had come, it stopped.

The cloud cover broke, and the sun fell hot on their shoulders. Noah mounted his camel with haste, and Aran and Zillah followed. The camels rose, and they began journeying again.

Steam rose from Noah's shoulders, and Aran shivered as warmth replaced the seemingly indefinite chill.

As they went, they saw patches of the road that had been dug thigh-deep by violent flash floods. In places, it was so bad that their camels couldn't even traverse the gullies.

"The surrounding cities will need much time to repair this road," Noah said.

After the sun made its way through a quarter of the sky, their tunics fully dried, and Zillah said, "Are we going to rest soon?"

"Tonight," Noah said. "The camels will need to graze. They're too thin for us to push harder."

The rolling hills gave way to wider valleys devoid of growth. The camels' soft feet easily traversed the sandy soil, and Aran was gladder than ever that he wasn't walking. He remembered this area from when he was a boy. He had walked it, many years ago, with nothing but a bow, some arrows, and a flask of water.

Darkness settled, and Noah said, "We'll rest here."

He led their camels to a wall of stone and dismounted.

Zillah slid off. "Finally."

Aran looked around. "Not much to graze."

"I know," Noah said. "But we've been traveling too long. They need rest."

The beasts were groaning loudly, protesting how far they'd come.

Aran looked up the cliff. "I know this area."

"Yes?" Noah said.

This was where he had been hunted by the lion. He feared the lack of visibility the cliffs gave, and was certain he would hardly rest at all through the night. After the deluge, they would find no wood dry enough to start a fire with, either. He voiced none of this. Instead, he grabbed the spear he'd lashed to his camel's saddle and sat with his back against the cliff wall. "Let's take advantage of the time we have."

Zillah threw herself down on the ground, and Noah yawned and lay on his back with a groan.

Aran kept his eyes wide and stared at the few stars stabbing through the holes in the clouds. He tried to tell himself that nothing was going to happen. They had traveled for many days in the wilds without finding any danger from wild animals. What were the chances they'd be attacked now?

It would be strange to be attacked in the same area where I'd been attacked all those years ago.

He was so busy thinking of the past that he didn't even realize his eyes had closed, and his breathing had settled into a deep, slow rhythm.

...

Aran woke to the scuffing sound of the camels standing. His eyes were partially crusted from the dusty wind, and he rubbed them open, heart pounding as he scrambled up, spear in hand. How long had he slept for?

He crossed to the camels, both of which were staring intently into the dark shadows deep in the desert valley. Then a noise in the distance raised the hair on the back of his neck.

A guttural growl.

The camels bellowed and turned back toward the cliff. Aran's back and shoulders stiffened as he stood his ground. He had heard that lions only make that noise moments before charging prey, and if he was the one being charged, running would be the worst way to react.

Ahead, from the shadows, he heard the scrape of paws against dust as the beast shot forward, its padded feet thudding rhythmically across the earth between them. Instantly, the smell of sagebrush and the taste of sand came to him with all the strength of the friction of his fingers against the dry wood shaft. Starlight glinted across the predator's eyes as its massive, sleek frame shot toward Little Kavel.

Aran knew only one thing to do, for they could not risk losing a camel in the desert. He sprinted to meet the lion midway, but his limbs seemed to be moving through mud, and he was still several paces away when the lion shot past and leapt onto Little Kavel, digging its claws into the beast's shoulders and biting the back of his neck.

Aran was running, screaming as he lifted the spear high and shoved it into the lion's shoulder. The beast roared and fell off Little Kavel. Aran backed away just in time to miss a mad swipe of the lion's claws, but a second swipe tore open his tunic and sent a flash of pain through his abdomen. He shoved his spear into the lion's face, striking it in the eye.

The beast roared and backed away, but Aran pursued it, relentless. He slammed the spear into the beast's throat, right above the chest bone, and drove it deep through its heart.

It lashed out again and cracked the shaft of his weapon before falling forward, spear sticking like a broken twig in its throat. Then Aran looked down and saw a puddle of red beneath him. His sight blurred and shifted. Was that his blood, or the lion's? He tried to turn back as he heard someone approaching, but he collapsed instead.

28

Nimrod

Nimrod stood atop the crest of the great tower nearly finished and looked across the city of Babel. He could see miles in every direction, and the sprawl of the city that had grown to support their vision to unify the world. Slaves—his own brethren—carried piles of brick on wooden skids up ramps to the top of the tower with the hope that their assignment would purchase their freedom. Nimrod had needed their help to finish the tower in time, and his earlier refusal to embrace slavery had forced him to claim that work on the tower would mean their emancipation.

He looked at them and wondered how they could be freer than he had ever been in his life.

For freedom was, like many ideals, an illusion. All men were enslaved to something. For most, their master was what they gave themselves to when free to choose. For some, that became drink or women or food. For others, the weaker ones, the opinions of others.

But Nimrod was different. Nimrod was a slave to destiny. And now . . . maybe to something else.

He tipped his head in an unconscious attempt to shake the buzzing from his skull. He itched his face and groaned at the sudden rush of anxiety that stopped his breath. Because ever since that moment in the underground temple, when he'd beckoned the Light Bringer and encountered the silver boy, something had changed. He couldn't quite identify what it was. He merely sensed that he was no longer in control of himself, as if he was caught in an indefinite waking dream.

He'd not seen the silver boy again. But he'd endured a growing buzzing sensation in his head ever since. And, from time to time in the quiet of the night, he thought he heard whispers. As of little spirits dancing around him, trading secrets to harm him.

It had made him agitated. Tense. Jumpy.

Then his appetite disappeared. Though his stomach ached for sustenance, his body refused to let anything he brought to his lips pass behind his teeth. Vegetables repelled him. As did bread. It had been days since last he ate, and he was starting to crave strange things. New, unnatural desires.

Nimrod looked at the sun's positioning and began to descend the stairs, for by now his servants would have received Japheth into his home.

As his bare feet brushed the brick, he saw a bit of blood he hadn't noticed earlier, smeared across the brick from where a slave had been injured. He felt a nearly irresistible compulsion to get on his knees and drag his tongue across the step to lap it up, but he managed to fight it because he had no time to waste, and could not risk any of the hundreds of workers seeing him. The thought flashed through his mind to return under the cover of night to find it, but already it was flaking in the sunlight and soon another would clean it—for his holy temple could have no blemishes.

Of course, few yet knew that the tower was to be a temple to the Light Bringer, instead of a simple monument to humanity. But they would obey his commands on how to build it.

For they feared him as he feared the Light Bringer.

Oh, yes, he feared the Light Bringer more than anything. What was a god without fear? A god must be transcendent. A god must have ultimate power. A god must be terrifying and violent to subdue a world impaled by the sting of death.

And so he returned to his home to deal with Japheth, who had responded to his request for consultation as kindly as ever. The old man had helped him countless times already, offering his expertise as a builder in the most efficient ways to help construct the tower, then organize his own progeny as labor.

Nimrod made his way up the broad path to his home next to the tower, passing within guarded gates, through flowerbeds in raised clay receptacles being tended by a few workers. Pruning dead growth and watering dry soil.

Then came the steps into his marble entryway. He slid his feet into wooden sandals and made his way loudly down the hall to the same room he'd met that fool slave trader weeks earlier. What had his name been, again? Rin?

Yes, that was it.

Servants nodded at him and opened the door and, after he entered, closed it behind him. He smiled at Japheth, who stood and crossed to him on long legs before extending his hand.

Nimrod grasped it and said, "I regret not coming sooner. Construction on the tower is moving at a furious pace."

"I understand," Japheth said, "and could never be offended by your dedication to our people."

Nimrod nodded and motioned toward a set of chairs placed around a table. "Would you mind? I know you like to sit on low cushions."

Japheth shook his head. "Whatever you desire. I am not so particular as my brother, Shem."

Nimrod sank into one of the chairs and crossed his leg over his knee. "But surely you have a preference."

Japheth joined him in the opposite chair, but did not cross his legs. "It is true that I grew up only sitting cross-legged on small cushions or mats. That was the custom before the world was changed. At least, that was the custom of the followers of the Old Way."

Nimrod resisted the temptation to wince at the name. He smiled wider.

"But now I'm wasting your time like an old fool. For what did you request my presence today?"

"Oh," Nimrod said. "You're not wasting my time. I did not ask you to come today to discuss your services—which, I must say I am ever thankful for how faithfully you've helped me. No, today I want only to talk with someone who might understand my plight."

Japheth's brow lifted. "We all, at times, need another to help bear our burdens, and you have held such a terrible burden these many years. So much responsibility, to hold the hopes and dreams of so many on your shoulders. I will listen—I am told I am good at that—and hope I can be of some use to you."

"I have no doubt you will, Otherwise I would not have summoned you."

"So," Japheth said, and rested his dark elbows on his knees. "What has been weighing your mind?"

"You remember that my father, Cush, and I have not spoken in many years?"

"Indeed. What a loss."

"Recently, he has tried to speak with me again. But I do not know how to respond. And I would like your opinion. However, I do not think you can really help unless I tell you of all that has happened to lead us to this point."

"I will listen," Japheth said.

"Thank you."

Nimrod heard the subtle slide of the lock as he spoke the last word. It had happened just as he commanded, and Japheth had been so focused on his words that he hadn't even noticed the noise.

"It started when I was a child," Nimrod said.

Japheth nodded as if he guessed what that meant.

If only he did.

"My grandfather, Ham, had spoken a prophecy that concerned me. And my father, being an acolyte of Ham's, had repeated it to me and tried to force me to bend my life to its will."

Japheth's eyes widened. "No . . ."

Nimrod sighed, "I'm embarrassed to say it, for what he tried to force me to do was unspeakable."

"Was your mother aware?"

"No. He told me it was something between a man and his son."

Japheth lowered his head, disgusted.

"The strange thing is that the prophecy, in a way, will be partially fulfilled as the tower finishes its construction. And so, that is why my father has been trying to speak to me again."

"Interesting," he said. "What was the prophecy?"

"I do not remember it in perfect detail, nor would I want to speak it aloud. But it demanded that I seal a pact in blood."

"He wanted you to make a sacrifice to the Light Bringer?"

Nimrod nodded, frowning. "When I was young, he had often pushed me to kill any living thing I found and brought to him. My earliest memory was of finding more insects to crush to gain his approval. Then came little animals. That was what gave rise to my work as a hunter. Once he forced me to strangle a rabbit and . . ." He closed his eyes. "He wanted to raise me up to be ruthless, devoid of inhibitions to do what was demanded."

Japheth's long fingers settled on Nimrod's shoulder. Nimrod looked up and saw Japheth's eyes searching his. "I understand."

"But I don't think you do," Nimrod said.

Japheth's hand pulled away.

"Because at first, when I wouldn't obey, he beat me. Then he said he wished I hadn't been born. That instead my sister had been born a son. For she had obeyed him without hesitation. But I . . . lacked the courage."

"That is horrific," Japheth said. "No child should need to endure such abuse. Especially from their own father."

"I wish I could say I remained strong. But he was right. I lacked courage. Only not in the way he intended."

Compassion filled Japheth's eyes like oil in a vessel of glass. "Who would expect a child to do different? We are taught to obey, for obedience is a virtue. To know when obedience is a sin demands the wisdom of years."

"Indeed. But when the prophecy over me was handed down, we learned it demanded that both me and my sister marry and consummate the divination in the blood of a man."

Japheth's eyes flashed wide at that. "You and Hava?"

Nimrod nodded. "I refused. Then Hava visited me in the night and placed her hands about my neck, saying that unless I agreed to do as father commanded, she would murder me. Then she proceeded to strangle me." He still felt the old fear crawl up his spine, and he let it do its work for he had no need to hide it.

Japheth's left eye began to twitch, and the vein across his forehead thumped an uneven rhythm. He stood. "Perhaps I should go."

"But you can't," Nimrod said.

Japheth considered this. Nimrod could tell he wanted to help. Wanted to believe Nimrod innocent. But everything was different from what he'd expected. He crossed to the door and tried it, but it was locked.

Japheth stood staring at the door for several long moments, realizing everything Nimrod had said now stood in a different light. Nimrod could almost hear the thoughts tumbling through his head.

"You can't leave before I explain why I asked you to come."

Japheth nodded absently, breaths coming quick. It reminded Nimrod of Rin.

"You see, after I consummated the prophecy, I married my sister. And now, to finish the prophecy, I have been demanded to spill the blood of another."

"Who?" Japheth said.

Nimrod smiled. "You."

29

Aran

Aran woke to slender hands shaking him. Zillah bent over him, dark eyes concerned, black hair falling across him, tickling his neck and cheek.

"He's awake!"

Noah rushed over and dipped into view. "That was reckless, Aran. Very reckless." He grabbed Aran's shoulder hard, eyes bright and wet. "You saved our camels, but all I can think of is how glad I am that you're not dead. Tell me, can you move uninhibited?"

Aran tried his fingers and toes, then his arms and legs, and sat up when he found everything worked fine, though his head pounded with pressure. He winced and rubbed his face. Several paces to his right lay the dead lion. The spear was still stuck in its head, but the shaft was broken and splintered.

He looked down at his hand and realized he had little shards of wood in his skin. He began pulling them out, and fresh blood rose up and out of the tiny puncture wounds.

Then he remembered the wound on his stomach. He reached down tentatively to find that strips of a torn tunic had already been tied around it. It wasn't as deep as he'd feared. It felt like a surface wound, though it had bled enough to stain the bandages before the pressure of the binding stopped it.

"Are you alright?" Zillah said. "You haven't said a word yet."

Aran looked up and blinked. "I feel like I'm dreaming."

"You are not," Noah said.

"It happened so fast . . ."

"How did you spear it without it killing you?"

"I got lucky."

"Now I know why you wanted a spear so badly," Noah said.

"I'm thankful," Aran said.

The three of them stood, and Noah gazed out across the land while Zillah stared at him. "Are you not well?" Aran said.

She shook her head and rubbed her arms with her hands. "I woke to the lion attacking you. For a moment, I thought your wound was deadly. I realize that you are all right. It just still doesn't feel like it yet."

"We have to get going," Noah said. "Little Kavel bolted after the lion attack."

Aran looked back and saw just one camel standing next to the cliff wall he'd rested against.

At least Little Kavel was probably still alive somewhere. What a waste, though. Because now his spear was broken, and they were as good as stranded. A young camel could never hold three riders.

"Soon, the sun will rise," Noah continued, "and it might be too hot for us to make progress."

"We have no water," Aran said.

Noah nodded. "You should ride first."

"I'm fine," he said.

"We'll ride in turns to stave off thirst as long as we can," Noah said. "We don't have much time left." He paused and counted silently, lips forming the words without speaking them. "Three days left," he mumbled.

"Less than that," Aran said. "We could die in half that with no water."

...

Aran refused to ride, as had Zillah, so Noah was the first to ride.

They walked for hours. As the sun rose, they appreciated the warmth, for the night had frosted the grass. But when it hovered directly over them, they grew burdened by the heaviness of its heat, the transition from hot to cold in the desert wilderness extreme from day to night.

The day stretched immeasurably long. Their lips cracked and bled, since they had been thirsty before the lion attacked them. Aran would have gladly given ten gold pieces for a single wine skin to share.

After Zillah made a comment about her feet hurting, all Aran could think about, aside from his thirst, was the ache in his bones. But he kept his wooden sandals on because the plants here were filled with thorns, and little cactuses hid beneath the sagebrush.

The muscles in his legs kept cramping. He struck his thighs with his fist. Noah saw from the camel and said, "You should ride for a while."

"I'd rather walk," Aran said.

"Really?" Zillah said. "Because you look exhausted."

"I don't like camels," Aran said.

"Right," Noah said. "That's why you rode them the entire journey so far."

"Because I had to keep up with you." But now everything had changed.

Eventually, Aran's skin began to flake and itch, and the rhythmic thudding in his chest came faster than usual. His eyes kept threatening to close on him, which didn't seem normal. He wondered if his loss of blood from the attack had drained more fluid from him than he'd realized.

Zillah now road atop the camel, and Noah walked beside Aran. While they stumbled through a dry creek bed, Aran's sight began to dim, as if a shadow veil had been thrown over his face, and he stumbled on a stone and fell to his hands and knees.

"Are you alright?" Zillah said.

"I'm fine." But his sight was spinning, and as he tried to stand, he fell sideways, flinging his arms in a failed attempt to maintain his balance. "Oof!"

He was on his side, looking up at Noah, who stared down at him with brows raised. "Still too proud to ride?"

After two deep breaths, he rubbed his eyes and managed to get back on his feet. The dark veil passed, and the spinning slowed, but his wound was wet again. He nodded. "I can go on."

Noah sighed long and slow, and now walked behind him, keeping an eye out for if he stumbled again.

Aran had been this thirsty before, and he knew the danger was real. Only, his thoughts were fuzzy and far away. As if the distance between his mind and body were lengthening in proportion to the miles they traveled.

The sun set, to their great relief, and they continued easier under the guidance of the stars. At one point, Noah stopped atop a hill and searched the surroundings. Aran heard him mumble, "Have we been going the wrong direction?"

But he hardly had enough energy to muster fear. And he was thankful when Noah sat to consider their path.

Finally, Noah stood and said, "We're close."

Even still, they continued until the sun rose a second time. The entire day was a miserable, blurred, stumbling journey. Until the sun set, and they rested in the chill for they were beyond exhausted.

They rose again long before sunrise and continued into a third day. As the heat set in again, Aran's legs gave way beneath him, and he ground his elbows into the gravel. Zillah pulled the camel to a stop—she was riding again because Noah refused to ride any longer. As they waited, Noah walked up the hill in front of them.

Aran waited a moment to muster his strength as he picked little bits of sand and stone from of his skin and tried not to focus on how his bleeding arms were just another waste of moisture.

"Aran," Noah said.

Aran grunted.

"Come here."

He looked up.

"Hurry."

Zillah urged the camel to the top and, as she saw what Noah saw, breathed in sharply.

Aran forced himself up the last of the hill and saw, to his

surprise, an oasis spread out in a valley before them, dotted with buildings and swarming with people.

"Erech," Noah said. "Your hometown."

Aran's face contorted at the relief that flooded his eyes behind his hands, though no moisture sprung from his eyes.

He took one step down the hill, and his legs buckled. Darkness stole over his vision more complete than before. It was only after that he came to understand Zillah had made their camel kneel and helped push Aran atop the camel's back. The camel stood, and Aran rested, hovering on the edge of awareness as the beast's awkward gait thrust him side to side.

Then water splashed his face, and the mouth of a skin touched his lips and poured water through his teeth. He drank and spluttered, then sprawled across the camel's back for what felt like an immeasurable amount of time.

Slowly, his mind cleared, and he got off the camel—which he only then realized had been kneeling. He sat with his back against a small stone well, drinking as much as he could in little sips and waiting for his body to recover as Zillah tore more pieces from her under-tunic to give him clean dressings for his wound.

Noah and Zillah drank and rested as well, for they were all exhausted and had been pushed to the brink of their ability.

Aran wondered at how his mind could be so muddled to not even recognize the surroundings he'd known so well in childhood. But as he tried to reconcile his memories with what he saw, he realized much had changed in the years he'd been gone. This well was new, as were many of the buildings in this region.

The current surroundings had previously been uninhabited wild growth. The road they stood on had existed, but was used as a trade route between Erech, whose city walls lay to the south of them, and the little farms and settlements that dotted the riverside to the north.

Zillah stood and looked around, watching those who walked by. "What are we going to do now?"

Aran looked up and said, "You plan to stay with us?"

Zillah shrugged. "I could leave, if you want me to." Then she lowered her voice. "But . . ."

Aran closed his eyes and leaned his head against the well, too exhausted to deal with anything.

"*But* there is no need for you to live alone any longer," Noah said.

Zillah gazed at the old man, and Aran had difficulty telling if the emotions behind her eyes were pride or thankfulness.

"Aran was right to invite you," Noah said.

She shook her head. "I forced his hand."

"If you believe that," Noah said, "you've learned nothing of either of us."

After a moment, Zillah sat next to Aran, shoulder to shoulder. "How do you feel?"

"Alive," Aran said.

"I'm glad," Noah said. "But we still have much to do. I must find my way to Shem, who lives in Erech. But first, we must go to your mother, before the sun sets this very day." He stood and paced, skin pale, fingers clutching at his tunic.

Aran took a deep breath. He'd been so distracted by their journey that thoughts about his family had been distant for days. Now that they had reached Erech, and his mind was escaping the fog that hung over him, anxiety pressed his chest, and his pulse pounded at the knowledge that he would soon face everything he'd fled.

How strange that he wanted Noah and Zillah to leave him. It seemed somehow fitting to be alone as he plunged into his past, for no one had been with him as he faced it the first time. He hated the idea that they would see how weak and broken the memories of his family made him feel.

And yet, he would need them. For they had lifted each other up in their weaknesses on this journey more than once already. Somehow, he felt Zillah would understand his emotions about his mother better than Noah.

It made Aran wonder anew about Zillah's past. He had heard nothing about her family, or who she had been before her life of thievery in Accad. All he knew was that he had found her alone, devoid of family, and so he thought the kinship he felt with her was derived from shared pain. Perhaps she had been rejected by her family.

Aran stood and pushed away his fears. "Well," he said, and faced south. "I know the way."

30

Noah

Noah followed Aran, who now finally rode the camel up the road leading toward Erech, which was partially hidden by a grove of date palms in the distance. Little clouds flecked the sky, painted as blue as sapphire, and they could hear the river rushing near though little hills blocked their sight of it.

He was impatient to see Shem. He knew from the beginning that their journey would be difficult, but he hadn't expected so many delays. And now they only barely had enough time to make it to Aran's mother's house before their time ran out.

Noah coughed hard, feeling a burning rattle in his chest. Not only did he feel somehow distantly responsible for Zillah's plight, and the plight of the starving people seeking refuge in Accad's gutters, but as he prayed for the Almighty's will, he continued to receive only silence. As the sense of his guilt increased, so did his anxiety over the Almighty's lack of response.

He'd rushed their journey, but now felt worse, for the pressure to travel had nearly cost Aran his life and Noah his health. Without Zillah, their days may have gone even worse. Noah may not have had the strength to get Aran onto the camel and carry him that final stretch. In a way, her help was an obvious answer to whether he should have taken her. The Almighty had known the decision he would make if he remained silent.

"I've realized something," Noah said. Zillah looked at him.

Aran kept his face forward, driving the camel, but he knew the boy listened. "Almighty has proven himself faithful, even when I have doubted—even when I have disobeyed him."

"What do you mean?" Zillah said.

"He told me we would make the journey in less than six days, and we have. Even more, he has shown me that I have often chosen comfort over his will. Long ago, when my wife was still with me, the Almighty commanded us to live a nomadic life. He commanded us to spread across the earth and to never settle too long in one place. Yet we planted a vineyard to take care of our progeny and thought that reason enough to remain. I realize now that we stayed long after our progeny needed us to. I fear that is why much of what we have witnessed has happened. Why I have felt distant from the Almighty."

Zillah's steps slowed. "You speak as if your God would walk beside you with his arm across your shoulder."

Noah shook his head. "No," he said, voice low. "Closer."

"How close?"

"I remember feeling his heart pulsing beside my own."

Zillah's face flushed at his words.

"I embarrass you?"

"That sounds terrifying. And . . ."

"Wonderful," Noah said.

She nodded and looked ahead toward the city gates, which had drawn near.

The Almighty had given Noah dreams of danger and bid him to hurry, so he'd hurried, and yet they'd only narrowly escaped disaster the entire way.

I believe it easy for the Almighty to answer me. So has he refused to answer because of my unfaithfulness?

As the silence lengthened again, he tried to focus instead on the date palms that shaded them, or the sparse conversation of fellow travelers passing them, leading donkeys carrying loads of wood, stone, ore, or grain. But his mind inevitably turned back to his anxiety like a tongue to a missing tooth.

He knew from experience that in time, the answer would reveal itself. But after his dreams, he no longer knew how much time was left, and he didn't want to miss the Almighty's guidance out of sheer negligence. Still, he was only exhausting himself searching for answers.

Noah cleared his throat and rubbed his eyes with his thumb and forefinger. Now that they were no longer guarded by the high hills and dry desert wind, Noah could smell the river and taste the moisture, though he could not yet see the water. He felt shaky, but could only do away with those symptoms by eating. First, Noah would have to see Aran to his mother's home. After, he would visit Shem. Perhaps there he would finally have a meal.

The gates of Erech were high arches built of white limestone. Sentinels stood watch atop the wall, but no guards manned the gates. Noah, Zillah, and Aran passed within and found Erech to be much more colorful and varied than Accad. Closer to the river stood small homes built of bundled reeds. Now that his view was no longer obscured by the date palms, Noah could see the edge of the river and long, narrow boats slowly skimming the surface as fishermen tossed nets and navigated with long poles. Further from the river stood mud dwellings, and here and there, well-built wooden homes between larger limestone houses that pre-dated the rest, for their stone was well-weathered by rain and the moist river wind. A newly-built school stood near the main road, built of baked brick. Children stood at attendance, receiving instruction from a teacher in how to count using clay tablets and reed pens.

Dark- and light-skinned people exchanged goods and worked jobs. Some were dressed as servants, others were obviously free men. But though some smiled as they passed, all seemed weighed down by an invisible heaviness.

What was most disturbing was the number of little statues Noah saw being traded. Little idols carved from clay and wood were being peddled on every street.

Noah was just about to ask one of the idol peddlers to what god they gave their worship, that they would carve little idols, when Zillah spoke.

"How long has your son lived here?"

"Maybe ten years," Noah said. "He retired from administrating the affairs of cities long ago to focus on teaching young ones the Old Way, but after the man who commanded this city left to aid a building project in another city, the officials demanded Shem take his place, for he is the eldest in the region."

"Have you seen his home? Or know where he lives?"

Noah let several moments pass as they trudged on down the main road. "No."

Zillah looked at him as if she wanted to ask how he could be so unaware of his own son's life for so long, but she held her tongue.

Noah sighed as he shuffled across the dusty road. "Aran?"

"Yes," Aran said without turning.

"The official who ran this city when you lived here. Do you know where his home resided?"

Aran looked back and nodded. "Atop the hill near the center of the city. It is not a very far walk from my mother's home, though she lives outside the city walls."

Noah nodded, then leaned toward Zillah. "Shem lives in the home the previous leader used."

Zillah mouthed a silent "oh."

They kept walking, up winding streets, a few of them paved, though most were made from dirt packed by the march of many feet, hooves, and wheels.

"I am thankful you have done us no ill," Noah said to Zillah. "But as long as you remain with us, you need to refrain from thieving, or prostitution, or any illegal act."

She regarded him.

"And I will do what I can to keep you secure. What we saw on display in Accad is . . . shameful. No one should live in such squalor."

"How could they not?" she said. "When your son's city refuses to trade with them?"

Noah's frown deepened. "That is what most disturbs me. I must talk with my son as soon as possible. I cannot help everyone. But our lives have become intertwined, and because of that, I will do what I can to help you."

She nodded. "And I will do what I can in return. Though I feel I have little to offer."

Noah placed a hand on her shoulder as his chest warmed. "Your response is offering enough. Only do no harm to Aran."

She looked at Aran and, after a moment's thought, nodded.

Aran had always been reserved, but since they arrived in Erech, he'd been even more closed off than usual. He knew from the little Aran had spoken that his relationship with his mother had been strained. Now he was returning to the home he had fled as a child for fear of his life—to face the fragments of a shattered family.

Almighty, protect Aran's damaged soul.

They traveled through much of Erech and eventually passed the hill where Shem's home stood. Noah was tempted to stop, but knew that he needed to fulfill the Almighty's commands first. They kept walking, out of the cramped inner portion of the city, through the southern city gates to more sparsely populated hills.

It was here where Aran turned down a different road, through fields of grass that served as pastureland for grazing cattle and goats raised for milk and meat.

Along the way, they spoke no words, for they felt the gravity of Aran's steps. He was returning to the beginnings of his life. To a childhood that had been defiled.

Noah had no words of comfort. No one but the Almighty could mend the scar of such loss. To offer anything less would be an insult to Aran.

As they wound up the path toward a limestone house at the end of the road, Aran stopped and turned toward the swaying grasses, which were long enough to have tassels at their tops. Aran ran his fingers across them and stared as if through a window into the past.

Noah was about to ask Aran why he'd stopped when suddenly he spoke. "She saw me," Aran said. "Through the window. I saw her look out, and . . ." He brought a hand to his face to cover his eyes as he bent forward, breaths coming in shallow pulses.

Zillah frowned and reached for him, but when her fingers touched his shoulder, he jerked away.

Noah approached as well, but did not touch him. Aran slumped to his knees. Noah mirrored him, joints grinding. Content to wait.

Zillah watched intently. Noah could tell she wanted to ask why he was so emotional, but the moment was too sacred.

After a moment, Aran breathed deep and composed himself. They sat together in the dust beside the grass. No one spoke. Finally, Aran nodded and stood.

Noah looked up but saw no one looking out of the windows or standing in the courtyard. Strange that she would not come out to greet them if she'd seen them. He and Zillah stood. "We should go to your mother."

"Yes," Aran said.

But Noah was the first to move, and Zillah slipped her hand into Aran's and pulled him forward.

Finally, after they entered the courtyard and arrived at the door, Aran's mother opened it and waved them in. "Hurry," she said. "Before anyone sees." Her beautiful, youthful face was lined with a few wrinkles, the only proof of her age—though he wondered if they were due instead to the anxiety that gnawed at her thin figure even now.

Noah narrowed his eyes, wondering what she was worried about, but entered the house. She shut the door behind them and laid her back against the wood. Her eyes took in Noah first. "You are . . . Noah? I didn't expect you to come with. Is something wrong?"

"I have business to attend to in Erech." He almost told her he needed to leave immediately, but her secrecy worried him, and he didn't want to leave both Aran and Zillah before finding out what was agitating her.

Aran stood staring at his mother. He did not speak, nor did he reach for her. Only stood with his hands clasped in front of him, shoulders tense, jaw clenched.

"I see," his mother said. "Thank you for returning my son."

"He chose for himself," Noah said. "He is a free man."

His mother nodded, seemingly pleased by this. "And this young woman, she is Aran's wife?"

Aran coughed.

Zillah's cheeks reddened. "A fellow traveler."

"Well, I can't afford to take care of anyone else. You should go with Noah when he leaves." She looked at Noah. "You will leave soon?"

"As soon as I am able. We had a hard journey. Our camels were stolen, and we were stranded in the desert after our camel was attacked by a lion."

Her eyes widened. "A lion?"

"Aran killed it," Zillah said.

"Do you have any food?" Aran said.

She blinked, appearing to take in all the information and decide what was most important to focus on. "No, I ran out days ago."

She walked deeper into the home, and the others followed. Noah noted that the walls were bare. There were no tables, no cushions, no chairs, no boxes filled with supplies, no jars. Though the home was large and built from solid limestone, it was no more than an empty box. "I suppose I forgot to introduce myself." She turned and bowed. "My name is Sarah."

Zillah and Noah bowed in return.

"What happened?" Aran said, looking still at the home.

"What do you think?" Sarah said. "Your father got himself killed, and I've had to sell everything but a few blankets and jars to survive. Yesterday, I sent the last of my servants out with the final few items of worth, and they disappeared, just like the others."

"The items?" Zillah said.

"The servants," Sarah said.

Noah narrowed his eyes. "Why would your servants desert you?"

"They didn't. They were taken. Why do you think I refrained from meeting you in my courtyard? Ever since Rin died, everything has fallen apart." She was pacing back and forth, growing more agitated—thin chest rising and falling in an uneven rhythm. "I can't sleep. Can't eat. Can't do anything. And now you've arrived, but what can any of us do?"

"Much," Noah said. "Or have you forgotten I am the father of all? You may remember that my son oversees the city of Erech."

Sarah took in Noah's figure with disbelieving eyes. "Erech

won't help me. What could you do against those who would do me violence? Can you protect me from harm?"

"I can sway the minds of those who can," Noah said.

She considered this and though he could tell she wanted to fight him, she changed the subject. "Aran, I do not mean to seem petty, but did you bring any money with you?"

"Yes," he said. "Enough to survive for some time."

She breathed out long and slow, and her shoulders relaxed. "Thank the Almighty."

"Aran and Zillah will stay here to take care of you while I go to do what I came to do," Noah said. "Soon, I will return with aid for you. No doubt, the servant you sent to us will arrive soon, as well."

"You believe he is alive?" Sarah said. "I am not so hopeful."

Noah nodded. "If I am not completely mistaken, your servant is a valiant man. We made better time riding camelback in great haste. If he has not been waylaid, he might return in a week or so. In the meantime, Aran and Zillah need food. Aran could purchase some from the market for the three of you. But now, I must go. I will visit again soon."

Aran and Zillah bid him farewell. Noah walked back toward the city to the home on the hilltop where Shem resided while the city he supposedly led languished in idol worship and secret violence.

31

Aran

How could Aran talk to Mother? After everything that had happened . . . all the years they'd spent separated from each other. Growing in different directions, blind to each other's joys and pains.

Now that they stood in front of each other, he felt both the hatred and the love he'd borne for her through the years. The force of it immobilized him. By the look on her face, he guessed she felt the same.

"Aran," she said. Voice soft and searching, like a foot testing the chill of a river.

He nodded, trying to keep his expression from revealing the fury that boiled his veins after hearing his name on her lips.

Her face paled. "I thought you would have forgiven me by now."

Zillah looked at him, as if begging for an explanation, for context.

"When did you hear father died?"

Mother leaned against the wall, palms against the cold limestone. "The same day I sent for you. It's been long, now." She closed her eyes and rested her head back. "I was just growing used to being alone."

Aran stilled. "I don't want to be here, either," he said.

She frowned. "That's not what I meant, and you know it."

Aran rubbed dust from the corners of his mouth. "How did he . . . ?"

"He was murdered."

"Who told you?" Aran started to walk down the hall, trying to suppress the memories of the place, of it being much larger and filled with riches. Everything looked so dark and pathetic and small now.

"Nimrod's servant delivered the news that he was sick when he arrived at Nimrod's home. He died the same day."

Zillah shifted and cleared her throat. She turned away.

"Yet you believe he was murdered."

"He was healthy, Aran. I'm no fool. Regardless of what Noah may think, justice is dead."

Aran breathed deep through his nostrils to conjure the smells he remembered. But the incense and scented oils were gone. Replaced with what used to be only an undertone of damp stone and dirt. "What do you call his death, then?" He walked into the other room, which used to be their communal lounge, not wanting her to respond to his bitter question. A window sat carved into two adjacent walls, and a slight breeze rustled his tunic.

Mother followed with Zillah's footsteps following slowly after. He wondered what Zillah was thinking. Surely the tension was making her wish she'd gone with Noah. It made him wish the same.

"I understand why you feel the way you do," Mother said. "But what you didn't see is that he had changed. After you left, he stopped drinking—"

"Convenient timing," Aran said, his voice nearly a scream, neck warm, pulse striking like a bamboo rod.

Mother stared at him, blinking.

Zillah held herself and rubbed her arms, face pale. She twisted and exited the room.

When Mother spoke next, her voice was small. "You're so tall now."

Fury stung his eyes. "Don't."

She took three steps, then stopped as he raised his hands to warn her away.

Babel

"If you touch me . . . ," he said, voice quivering.

Tears pooled in her eyes. She raised her hands in surrender. "What am I supposed to do?"

"You were supposed to defend me!" He grabbed her shoulders and shook her hard enough to make her cry out. "When he beat me, you just stood there. You just stood there like—"

His voice cracked, and he shoved her away. She fell back, striking her elbow against the wall and sliding to her seat, glaring up at him in fear and anger.

He turned toward the corner of the room and breathed deeply.

This wasn't what he wanted. This could go a different way.

He looked back at her. "I'm sorry," but he didn't feel sorry.

"You're right," she said.

All he could do was stare at her.

"I should have defended you. I was too much a coward to defend my own son. Do you think I haven't wept myself to sleep half the nights since you left because of it? You think I don't wish that I'd stepped between you and let him kill me instead of beat you half to death? I love you, Aran. It's pained me close to death, what happened."

His face warmed. All these years, he'd convinced himself she didn't care.

To hear her say she loved him, that she regretted anything at all . . . it was easier when she was just a heartless monster, not a frightened mother who cared.

"Where did everything go?" Aran said.

"I told you. I had to sell what was left to survive."

He raised one eyebrow. "The tapestries? The silver idols? The stone statues and carved boxes? What have you been eating? Precious jewels?"

"You wouldn't believe me."

"Tell me."

"It's your father's doing."

Aran snorted. "I don't doubt it."

"After you left, he wanted to kill himself. First, he tried to drink himself to death. Then he vowed to never drink again. For weeks, I heard him cry himself to sleep, sweat matting the sheets to his pale skin as he shivered through the nights. Then he'd wake screaming your name. What he did to you, it haunted him the rest of his life."

"Good," Aran said. But his voice was no more than a hoarse whisper.

"But he started meeting with others who'd extended an invitation to join their gathering. Weeks later, I found him kneeling on our bed, eyes closed in prayer, tears streaming down his face. He told me he'd surrendered his body and soul to the Almighty, that he would serve the Almighty all the rest of his days. Because the Almighty had forgiven and accepted him as his own."

Aran squinted and rubbed his ears. Had he just heard her right?

"It is true," she said.

"He doesn't deserve forgiveness."

She shrugged. "Who am I to say? All I know is after that day, everything changed. He melted our silver idols and sold the precious metal to give to the poor in the assembly of the Almighty. The rich tapestries, the carefully formed furniture. Anything that wasn't necessary, he sold to those in need. And he began to place slaves in homes he knew would treat them with dignity, and he used the proceeds to give more. The reason why I am destitute is because, after hearing of the plight of the faithful who fled to Accad, he sold nearly everything we owned to send food to them. Now that he's dead, and no one is taking care of his business, I fear for those slaves' lives."

Aran blinked hard. "You're lying. This is all an elaborate lie."

"I knew you wouldn't believe me," she said. "If you won't listen to simple truth, what point is there in trying to convince you?"

32

Zillah

Zillah returned to the entrance of the home and set her hand to the door before she remembered what Aran's mother said about people watching the home.

She struggled to take her hand back, caught between fear of those who might harm them, and the animalistic panic that raged inside her chest like a caged lion.

It couldn't be as Aran's mother claimed. There was no way that Nimrod could have killed Aran's father. It was too strange. Too perverse.

Finally, Zillah had found someone who made her feel something. Someone she felt might understand the pains of her past. Someone she had considered opening up to, as she hadn't done in years.

But now their relationship could never go any deeper. Because if it did, eventually he would find out that the man who killed his father was . . . Zillah's own father, Nimrod.

She pressed her palms against her forehead. To blurt out the truth now, blinded by pain and rage, would only deepen the wound and make certain he hated her. But Aran's reaction would grow doubly worse if he ever actually believed what his mother said about his father becoming the man Aran wished he had been all his life. Because it would mean that Nimrod took away the possibility for Aran to know his father as he truly was, without bondage to alcohol distorting his person.

Could the man who'd been following her be aligned with those who had been persecuting Aran's mother? If she stood in the courtyard, and they saw her, someone might be able to recognize her and tell . . .

She shook her head and retreated from the door, chest pulsing as quickly as an overheated dog's. No, she could not let them capture her and bring her back.

She would not be sacrificed to give her mother a son. Which meant there was no way she could run off alone now.

But how could she live with Aran and Noah now that she knew? Even worse, how could she stay in this woman's house? When Zillah knew her own family was responsible for the worst of their pains?

She bent forward, sight spinning. Her stomach boiled, and her throat tensed as nausea rose. She breathed deeply through her nose, then out through clenched teeth. She tried to push away all the thoughts, to empty her mind completely.

But in the void, her father's face floated before her closed eyes, and she thought of Aran and every secret hope she'd harbored unknowingly since meeting him in Accad.

She fell to her hands and knees, and retched the water she'd drunk across the floor.

Her anxiety rose, and her skin began to prickle as if a thousand ants crawled down her back. She stood too quickly, brushing nervously at her skin, and flashes sparkled across her vision. Her legs buckled, and she collapsed as darkness overcame her.

33

Aran

A croaking noise drew both Aran and his mother's attention toward the entrance.

"What was that?" Aran said.

Then came a groan, and the sound of something collapsing.

Aran rushed down the hall and found Zillah crumpled on her side, limbs splayed awkwardly. He skipped over a stream of vomit and fell to his knees beside her. "Zillah?"

Mother breathed in sharply as she realized what had happened. "I'll clean the mess," she said and disappeared toward her bedchamber.

Aran nudged Zillah's shoulder, then rolled her to her back and lifted her head a bit. She winced, and her eyes fluttered open.

"W-wha—" Her words were cut off as she recognized Aran above her, his hands holding her head.

She looked to the side, saw the mess she'd made on the ground, and pushed herself to a seated position. Her cheeks reddened, and she wiped her mouth, though nothing was on it.

"What happened?" Aran said.

"I . . . must have stood too fast," she said.

But no one vomited from standing too fast.

Mother returned and began cleaning up.

None of them said anything. In a way, Aran was thankful

something had broken the tension and given his mother another to focus on. After Mother finished, she took the soaked rag and said, "I will get you some water, for I have no wine."

She brought it back in a little clay cup, and held it to Zillah's lips, though Zillah said, "I can hold it."

"You should rest," Mother said.

"I feel fine. Really, I do."

"Are you sick?" Aran said.

Zillah shook her head and took another sip as Mother offered it. "Thank you, but I don't need water. I am weak from hunger, and I drank too much when we first arrived in Erech."

Aran narrowed his eyes at her. Much of the day had passed since she'd drunk the water. If she'd had too much, would she not have mentioned feeling sick earlier?

"Well," Mother said, "I am sorry that I have no food to offer."

"I will buy food in the market," Aran said.

He stood, but Mother set a hand on his forearm, eyes intense. "How much money did you bring?"

"Enough to survive for quite some time, if you buy only food."

"It would be unwise for you to carry more than what is necessary for immediate purchases," she said.

"Why?"

"Have you been listening? The city is not safe. Especially if anyone knows you have been with me."

"I did not travel all this way to starve with you," Aran said. "I will go purchase food."

"Yes, of course." A bit of irritation crept into her tone. "But first, we should divide the money into separate portions, leaving the greatest portion here."

"You are worried I will be taken away like your servants?" Aran said.

She nodded.

He felt certain that few could take him, unarmed. But if the men who had been persecuting her and Father had taken her servants away, they must have experience and appropriate weapons for the job.

He took out the moneybag and poured the gold coins on the floor. They counted together, sliding pieces into three little piles with their index fingers. When they finished, Mother took up two of the portions and slid the smaller into a pouch, while the other she took into a separate room. Aran put his own portion back into his moneybag, which he tied to the belt inside his tunic.

Aran turned toward the door, and Zillah followed. He turned back and raised a hand. "What are you doing?"

"I'm coming with you," Zillah said.

"You should stay," Aran said. "You're not well."

Zillah was growing agitated. "It won't happen again. The spell has passed."

If there was danger in Mother's home—which there seemed to be—then likely Zillah would be safer with him. Besides, though he had grown to trust Zillah, she was still a thief, and he wondered if she would stoop low enough to steal the money he'd brought to his mother.

"If anyone's unwell," Zillah said, "it's you. We had to pick you up on the hill outside Erech. I should come to make sure *you're* well."

"I can't go in your stead," Mother said. "It would risk bringing too much attention."

"Fine," Aran said and pulled the door open. "But we must be quick."

34

Noah

It had been long since Noah smelled fresh fish. Now that he breathed the riverside air of Erech, he wished he had time to partake, but the rush of blood in his ears threatened to drown out everything. On the cobble street, he dodged white droppings from little flocks of birds that fluttered from rooftop to rooftop, for he had taken off his sandals to rest his feet.

He went slowly because the urgency weighed heavy in his chest and because his old body ached. The travel had taken more of a toll than he had expected. Though he should have expected it, because the last time he'd traveled in such a way had been the year of the Flood, centuries earlier.

He shook his head and struggled up the incline to the top of the hill that Shem's house stood on, wondering how so much could have changed since that catastrophic event. He had found nothing the way he'd expected. What would he find when he reached his son's home? Would Shem be there, and alive? Or worse, would idols line the walls of his own home too? He wasn't certain he'd be able to handle such a betrayal.

Noah steadied himself by running his fingers across the limestone walls, which had been built long after the Flood and were pocked with holes. All the faces he passed were foreign to him, and none of them knew they had originated in the love he had seen in his wife's eyes.

He wondered what stirred in their hearts. Did they bow to idols at home or reject the Almighty and his way of life?

At the outer courtyard of Shem's home, Noah was stopped by two servant guards. They wore chainmail and held long spears. The gate was open, but the heavy doors were studded with bronze nails for reinforcement. Up the hill, a stone house was surrounded by a sparse garden and shaded by date palms.

"State your name and your purpose for approaching the Lord Shem's home."

Noah straightened, feeling the bones in his spine click into place despite the tightness in his muscles threatening to pull them out again. "I am Noah, the father of all. I am here to speak with my son."

The servants examined him with narrowed eyes and mouths tipped in doubt. One retreated up the hill while the other stayed and raised an open palm to warn him back. "Shem will tell us whether you speak truth."

As they waited, Noah stared at the man, who failed to hold his gaze.

Shem appeared at the top of the hill and squinted down at him.

Noah waved.

Shem yelled something incoherent and smacked the servant who'd told him of Noah's arrival. The servant ran back down to the gate and said, "You may enter."

Noah patted the servant's arm. "Thank you."

Shem had disappeared, so Noah walked the remainder of the hill, the rich soil moist and soft beneath his feet. At the top, he crossed between hedges and entered the outer, roofless hall. Several servants bustled around, and Shem appeared in a doorway and waved him in with that perpetual frown running deeper than usual. "I apologize that my servants held you at the gate and that I did not greet you better. I am overwhelmed with duties and did not receive word of your travel."

"Of course," Noah said, looking around, pleased to see no idols stood on pedestals here, so far as he could see. "Instead of sending word, I sent myself. I have come to speak with you of important matters that cannot wait."

"I see," Shem said, and several servants approached him and bowed.

"My lord, what shall we do with the homes we have not gathered accounts from?"

"I need to speak with our guest," Shem said. "Do what seems fitting, and give account when you've finished."

The three bowed and left, while more servants rushed around, carrying items and cleaning floors and walls. Four more asked Shem questions, which he sloughed off.

"Do you do everything through your servants?" Noah said.

Shem's frown deepened. "I could not fulfill my duty to this city without the aid of my servants." Then he struck his palm against his forehead and made a face. "Where are my thoughts? You must be exhausted from your travels."

Noah nodded as his empty stomach ached with renewed vigor.

"And hungry," Shem said.

"Is it written on my face?"

"You look thinner than I remember."

"I haven't seen you in ten years," Noah said.

"Has it been so long?" Shem put a hand softly to the back of Noah's back and urged him down another hall. "I've been so busy I can hardly remember yesterday." They entered a smaller, square room with woven cushions positioned for sitting, just like they used before the Flood. Shem's wife, Aliska, was there.

Aliska stood and blinked at Noah's presence. "Noah?"

"I would have told you earlier," Shem said, "but I only just found out myself. He has come to see us. Please, would you prepare food and drink for him, while the two of us speak?"

She bowed. "Of course. The cook is already stoking the fires. What would my lord like?"

"Anything," Noah said.

Aliska disappeared, and Shem took his seat on a flat cushion. "I have never gotten used to those wooden chairs everyone is so fond of."

"Neither have I." Noah sat cross-legged beside him.

Shem stared a moment before curling his frown upward and shaking his head. "I can't believe you're here." Then his frown returned. "What happened, to draw you so far? You mentioned some important matters."

Noah drummed his fingers on his leg. "First, tell me why idols line your streets as plentifully as refuse."

Shem tipped his head and sighed. "Much has happened here. Ever since I stepped into my role in Erech, I've regretted the decision. Most days I wish I could have lived alone as you have— ignoring the orderings of the world."

Noah scratched the back of his head.

"The other part of me believes that if not for me taking this position, everything would have fallen apart last year."

"Last year?"

"The days have grown evil. Idols line the streets because I've not been able to restrain the peoples' wayward hearts."

Noah nodded. "Now that I've walked the long road between my vineyard and your city, I think I understand a bit of what you mean. Tell me, does, 'The star who hides darkness in light,' mean anything to you?"

Shem's eyes widened. "The words of the Almighty?"

"Yes."

Shem twirled his speckled, gray beard and leaned back. "Has the Almighty not explained it to you already?"

Noah cleared his throat and, after a moment's pause, shook his head.

"Did the Almighty say anything else about a star?"

"He showed it to me in a dream, as a shining light hovering above a great tower, atop which stood men like gray statues."

Shem's mouth hung open, and his eyes widened before looking toward the door.

"You know what the dream references, then?" Noah said.

"Maybe." He lifted his eyes toward the door. "But perhaps you should eat while we talk?"

Noah followed Shem's stare to Aliska, who held a wooden platter piled with flatbreads and fish in the doorway. She dipped and set the platter on the floor beside Noah's cushion, along with a cup of wine. Noah nodded and said, "Thank you."

She smiled but after trading looks with Shem, slipped out again.

"Have you heard of the tower being constructed in Babel?"
Noah shook his head.

"Japheth has been aiding in the construction. I must admit"—Shem watched as Noah filled his mouth with steaming fish and tore a piece of flatbread before dipping it in a dish of honey—"that I also have been having strange dreams. Visions that seem to hold meaning beyond themselves."

Noah tried the honeyed bread and washed it down with new wine. "Perhaps our dreams fit into each other like bricks in a home."

"Perhaps. Each night for the last week, I have had the same dream, though when I wake I can only remember a portion of it. That is what most troubles me."

Noah piled fish on the flatbread and folded it. "What do you remember of it?"

"It is difficult to even put the images into words, as is often the case with dreams. But one distinct element I remember is seeing you standing with two others, holding hands. Only, in the chests of the two sat gaping, black holes. And you are facing something bright." Shem's eyes widened in sudden realization, as did Noah's.

"The light?" they said in unison.

"But what would that mean, if the light in your dream is the same light in mine?" Noah said.

"Within the year, I think, that tower in Babel will be finished. A massive tower, the likes of which has never been built before. A new wonder of the world."

"There were many towers before the Flood." But even as he said it, he thought of what the thief in his vineyard said, and shivered.

"This one is larger yet."

That disturbed Noah. "It would take a great labor to build such a spectacle."

Shem nodded. "And such a great labor has been working tirelessly on the tower in Babel since the leader of Erech left to oversee its construction."

"Ahhhh," Noah said. "So that is why he left. But why is this the first I've heard of such an endeavor? And what does this man stand to gain from its construction? Furthermore, why is Japheth aiding him?"

"Well, you know Japheth. He believes the best. He's too open. The leader of Babel claims his goal is for the unification of mankind. But he is a Hamite, a son of Cush. And for all the beauty of his words, I don't believe he speaks truthfully, no matter what Japheth says."

"Why did you not tell me this before?"

"Oh—" Shem rubbed the back of his neck. "I don't know."

"What kind of answer is that? Come, now. You must tell me why you've withheld such information."

"I should not," Shem said.

Noah set down the last of his bread and leaned forward. "Tell me."

Shem smoothed his long mustache along the downward swoop of his lips and cleared his throat. "Ever since mother died, you've been . . . different."

Noah felt the breath drain from his chest, and his voice came softer when he spoke again. "Different how?"

"I tried to visit you many times after she passed."

"I remember us talking," Noah said.

"Yes, we would talk, but anytime I brought up problems I faced with our family, such as infidelity or violence, or especially when I mentioned Ham's progeny, you would close off. So I grew into the habit of not speaking to you about such issues."

Noah stuffed more food into his mouth to avoid having to respond, though his appetite had disappeared the moment Shem mentioned Jade.

"Afterward, I moved farther away and travel was more difficult. You stayed busy with your vineyard. I came seldom, and when I did, I just wanted to visit with you. To hear about your life."

The bread slid slowly, painfully down his throat. "You make it sound as if I never asked about life outside my walls," Noah said.

"You did. But I didn't want to bother you with what weighed on me. Part of me envied you. The other part wished to keep you in joyful unawareness. I had started to believe it was my responsibility to shoulder it. You have faced so much in your life, and . . ."

Noah lowered his eyes to his hands. Why did that make him feel even guiltier for not remaining involved? His face warmed, and his jaw clenched. "You think I have made a mistake."

"We all make mistakes," Shem said.

"You think I abandoned you."

Shem did not respond.

Noah met his eyes. Dark and speckled with flecks of green like the shadowed trees in the forest he'd married Jade in. "Speak honestly."

"We all felt that."

Noah chewed the inside of his cheek and sighed.

"As I said," Shem said, "the days have grown evil. I have done what I can. I have discipled many in the Old Way, but the rest won't listen. Not anymore. I wield little power now. After Ham's family returned from the east, seeking help to survive the famine, you may remember they struggled to get by. Many sold themselves into servitude. Others were emboldened by the difficulties and held on to their worship of the Light Bringer doubly hard for it. It changed them. It changed everyone. Maybe they might have listened to you years ago, but you were still grieving. You couldn't."

"Couldn't I?"

"You didn't," Shem said.

Noah nodded and fought a burning ache in his throat. "Son, I—"

"What is done is done. I need your help now. Let us focus on the present."

"How can I aid you?"

"I've been growing nervous about Japheth. He hasn't visited in quite some time, and the last servant I sent to gather word from him is nearly a week late returning."

"Why have you not gone to him?"

"I told you. Erech is not well. There have been disappearances lately. We think certain men have been engaging in . . . human sacrifice."

Noah accidentally knocked the dish of honey over. "What?"

"The rites of the Light Bringer are dark, indeed. But that is part of their appeal, I think. To the perverted, darkness becomes desirable, and true light becomes unbearable."

Noah felt the blood drain from his face. "My dreams are no future proclamation, then, but a current fulfillment. I knew that Ham had embraced a false god but didn't think he would stoop so low as to engage in . . ."

Shem nodded. "It is abhorrent, isn't it? But what has changed, that you are so open to hearing this now?"

Noah wiped his forehead. "The night before I left my vineyard to come to you, two young men snuck in and attempted to capture and drag away one of the young women who work for me."

"Adherents of the Light Bringer?"

"One ran, but the other was caught. He spoke of a tower, and yelled the Light Bringer's name before killing himself. I thought at the time he was mad. But you speak as if this behavior is normative."

"It is becoming normative. After hearing of your dream, I believe the tower's construction holds more importance than any of us would like to think. Even as I think back, since construction began, the followers of the Light Bringer have become bolder each passing year. What makes me fearful is that I sense the followers of the Light Bringer may soon become the majority, and the followers of the Old Way the minority. That is why I cannot leave my city. I fear what might happen in my absence. I no longer hold the power to sway the directors of Erech. Though I am their 'leader,' I am merely holding my ground, wielding what power I've maintained to stop undue upheaval. They believe in the vision of total unification, over and above the Almighty's vision for repentance."

"You need Japheth to sway the collective," Noah said.

Shem nodded. "I think it important that you be the one to speak with Japheth, and that you bring him back and stand beside us as we campaign to stop the silent genocide the followers of the Light Bringer have been carrying out. Japheth has been aiding Nimrod and—"

"Wait, Nimrod?"

"Yes, he is the one who has been overseeing the construction of the tower, though I hold the belief that the tower was requested by many in power, including Ham. Japheth and I have disagreed over this for some time. Nimrod has worked hard to show the world he is no acolyte of the Light Bringer. His relationship with his father, Cush, fell apart years ago. They don't talk. Many whisper it is because of Cush's practice of the dark rites. But if the tower is connected with the Light Bringer, that would mean everything we know about Nimrod is a lie."

Of course. How had he not realized the connections earlier?

"Is something wrong?" Shem said.

"I haven't journeyed alone. I came with another young man whose family lives here in Erech."

"What are their names?"

"Sarah and Rin."

"Rin? I know him. He is a Hamite known for selling his own into slavery. He converted to the Old Way some time back. I met with him twice, to speak of the Old Way. He agreed to help the refugees in Accad."

"He is dead," Noah said.

Shem blinked. "How?"

"He went to Nimrod to make an appeal for aid, but died on the journey. Nimrod's servant reported that he was sick. His wife believes he was murdered."

Shem put his face in his hands and did not respond for some time. "You must go, then. You must go to Japheth immediately. If what you speak of is true, I fear Japheth is in a worse plight than I imagined."

Noah placed a hand on his son's shoulder. "Believe me, son. I am as worried as you are. But I need you to do me a favor."

"What do you ask?"

"Send guards to Rin's widow. Have them keep her household safe until I return."

"If anyone else asked me, I would refuse, for I have few men I can truly spare. But for you, I will do this."

"Also, you must tell me where I can find Japheth, then furnish me with supplies and money for the journey. I will need help to travel quickly and efficiently."

"Consider it done."

35

Aran

Aran and Zillah made their way to the bustling market with relative speed. Aran was thankful for the cool breeze that ran through his lengthening hair and short beard because it helped distract him.

After hearing Mother's words, his throat throbbed with such pain he imagined tearing the skin of his neck open would be a relief. He just wanted to turn himself inside out, to break open the depths of his soul and let everything pour out. But he couldn't let it out.

Because I am afraid of what might happen. That the current of my fury will wash away all that is left of me, and I will be left to wander in madness and confusion the rest of my days. Fearing each shadow as I feared Father.

He shrugged away shivers as they walked down the winding road like an island bridge amidst a sea of russet grasses. The breeze made the tassels whisper, and he was glad to leave them behind after arriving at the city.

In the market, they purchased all the rice, fresh fish, and wine they could carry. Aran was still desperately thirsty, and he knew wine would dull pain's blade. But the idea made the wound in his abdomen throb, because it would have been the first thought to cross Father's mind.

Still, he needed moisture, so he tipped one wineskin up and

pressed its lip to his mouth. As the liquid burned his throat, Zillah breathed in through her teeth and jerked him to the side by the collar of his tunic, spilling some of the precious wine across the dirt.

"Wha—"

She smashed her hand over his mouth and put a silencing finger to her lips, motioning with a tip of her head to the left, around the corner. "I recognize a man. The one with light hair and blue eyes."

Aran peeked around the corner and spotted him leaning against the wall of Erech, staring at the gate.

He pulled back. "Did he see you?"

"No," she said. "If he had, he wouldn't still be standing there."

Aran gauged Zillah's posture and tone of voice. "What does he want from you?"

"Nothing good," she said.

"Did he follow you all the way from Accad?"

She pulled her hood back and, for a moment, drilled him with an intense glare.

Aran squinted and said, "Because you stole food?"

Finally, her expression softened, and she took a deep breath and wiped the hair from her eyes. "I don't know. But if he finds me, he won't just put me in jail. He'll kill me."

"What in the world did you do to deserve—"

"If I knew, I wouldn't have done it. Believe me, I committed no sin that deserves the punishment he seeks to dole me."

Aran thought this through. "What are we going to do, then?" Aran peeked around the corner to see the man still hadn't moved.

"I don't know. I'm thinking."

But something wasn't adding up. "How could he know you would come here?"

"I don't know. Shh."

"What are you not telling me?"

"Nothing," she said, her voice too harsh. She winced and sighed. "Just, quiet, Aran. Now is not the time. You don't want him to see us together. Alright?"

He wished he had the nerve to tell her that he would just walk through the gate alone if she wouldn't tell him. But as he looked at her, he knew he couldn't. They had experienced too much together. "Let's double back and use the other gate."

"I was thinking of scaling the wall. It's not that high. You could lift me, then I could pull you up."

"The guards stand on top of the wall beside the gate," he said.

"We'll do it farther away from the gate, then."

"If anyone sees you hopping the wall, they'll know you're a criminal. I'm using the gate." He turned away and started back up the dirt road that led to the little cobble streets farther inside Erech.

She growled and flipped up her hood before jogging to catch up.

Thankfully, the appropriate reaction to seeing a stranger in Erech was to ignore them. They turned down multiple streets and passed several villagers before reaching a dead end.

"Wonderful," Zillah said and spun on her heel to make her way back again.

But Aran stayed put, staring at the wall where the road ended abruptly.

"What?" she said.

"If an enemy were chasing us, everything would be over right now."

"Yes, but he's not, so let's get out of here while we still can."

"We have no weapons," Aran said. "Nothing to defend ourselves with."

"And no time to go shopping for daggers while that snake tests the air of Erech for my scent. Hurry up already!"

But everything in Aran was telling him to get away from Zillah. He wasn't sure why, only that he'd never felt so uneasy around her. Still, despite himself, he followed her back, and they made their way slowly to the other gate. Because she had taken care of him, hadn't she? Had basically saved his life on the road here.

"Wait," she said as the gate came within view. "You go first.

If you don't see anyone, keep walking. If someone is watching, turn around like you forgot something. Alright?"

"What happened last time you saw that man?"

"Not now," she said, and pushed him forward.

Aran felt the rhythm in his chest quicken as he stumbled and slowed, then walked as calmly as he could toward the gate. Each step a struggle to maintain fluidity in his limbs as he carried the bag of food and wine, which suddenly felt filled with stones. He hoped he didn't look as uncomfortable as he felt.

He swept his gaze from left to right slowly, willing his frown to fade. Two teenagers kicked a balled rag in the dust to the left of the gate. Guards stood on top of the wall, as they had at the other gate, but he saw no one else. The alley to the right was empty behind houses built nearly to the wall in this part of Erech.

No one lurked outside the wall as he exited, either. He kept on, then paused and feigned to stretch his legs and shoulders as he waited for Zillah.

He stretched his neck left and right. Then his calves.

He pulled his leg back until he felt the muscles burn, and held it.

Counting slowly.

She should come soon.

He let his leg down, then repeated the same with the other leg.

After finishing, she was still nowhere.

Could that man have followed them as they turned and walked to the second gate? He could have heard them talking. It was conceivable. Zillah had spoken loudly at one point. And Aran had looked around the corner multiple times. If the man's eyesight was better than he expected, maybe . . .

Aran's lips were dry and cracked, and his breath came thin and quick. He was just about to return to the gate when a figure exited.

Zillah's familiar hood flapped in the wind, and all the tension melted from his chest and back.

She passed him and said, "Stop staring at me."

The guards still stood on top of the wall, but were paying no heed. "They're not even looking," he said.

"Doesn't matter. Stop."

He readjusted the food on his shoulder and walked in relative silence through the long grass he remembered from childhood. The same kind he'd passed on that day, when he'd glimpsed the potential in his father for good, and saw the last kernel of love left in his soul before it disappeared into the void because of Aran's simple mistake at the market. It had taken him years to believe it wasn't his fault that his father beat him that day. That it wasn't his fault that Father couldn't continue to treat him with the love he'd seen in his father's eyes that morning.

Because no one had ever explained to him that a monster could never change. That a heart so black and dense with selfishness could never let love pull far enough away to touch those around it.

Aran had seen proof of that blackness in his father's eyes, which darkened and glinted the same way before every violent outburst. He'd come to imagine a void erupted within his father's soul at unexpected times. Always, when he saw it, Aran knew he would taste the violent chill of terror and loneliness.

He tried running and hiding, but Father always found him. And the punishment became twice as severe.

How could he have been foolish enough to imagine his father could change?

And yet . . . what had Mother said? That Father had found God?

And God had forgiven him.

Aran ground his teeth as the grasses tugged at his tunic and scraped his skin. Even if, by some miracle, God had forgiven him.

Aran couldn't.

Suddenly, Zillah stopped walking. "Aran?"

Aran stopped and looked at her.

She pointed. "Who is standing outside your mother's home?"

He looked up, surprised to see they had walked so far. There in her courtyard stood . . . a man.

A memory flashed as vivid as a vision. Yet it was no longer a stranger who stood there, but Father, and he was calling for Aran to return. It was the night Aran ran away, and he'd waited out here, right here in the grass, listening to Father rage. He'd been terrified, lying frozen to the ground, hoping Father wouldn't step out and find him.

"Aran," Zillah said, and struck his shoulder. "What's wrong with you?"

Aran shook his head. "I don't know. Sorry." He wiped his face.

"You're scaring me. I don't know what's going on, but I'm sure your mother wasn't expecting anyone."

"No," he said and looked again at the man, who now was staring at them. "You don't recognize him?"

She shook her head.

"Keep your hood on," he said. "And don't speak."

She was silent the rest of their way up the hill.

The man was standing with his arms crossed, and he nodded as they entered the courtyard.

"Who are you?" Aran said, and dropped the bag of food and wine.

The man smiled. His eyes were set wide, and his eyelids were thicker than usual. His nose was long, and his chin weak. His hair was cropped short and black as coal, but his skin was pale brown. "Hello, Zillah."

Zillah gasped. All the muscles in Aran's body stretched taut.

"You're not welcome," Aran said. "Leave."

"Silence, pig," the man said. "I came for the girl." And he walked casually toward them, smile plastered on his face as he slid a long knife out of his sleeve.

Aran widened his stance, readying himself for what was to come.

The man made his way calmly for Zillah, who backed up.

Several more steps. Aran counted each twitch in the man's body.

At the last moment, the man feigned a step toward Zillah while falling the opposite direction toward Aran, swinging his non-knife hand to distract Aran from the movement of the blade, but Aran anticipated it and sidestepped as the knife slid through the space his torso had occupied.

The man had overcommitted and tipped off-balance. Aran took the opportunity to clamp his hand over the forearm that held the knife and kick one of the man's legs while forcing his knife arm away. He slammed his forehead into the man's nose and shoved him backward, slamming him onto his back and knocking the air from him. Then he twisted the man's arm into a square angle and used the leverage of the man's elbow trapped against his bicep to pressure his bones in the wrong direction.

The man cried out and struck Aran in the back of the head twice, sending white flashes across his vision, but he held on and snapped the man's arm at the elbow, forcing the knife from his hand.

In the pandemonium, Zillah had run past them, calling for his mother.

"Stay inside," Aran yelled, as the man continued to struggle against him, kicking and cursing.

"I'll bleed you both, you filthy—"

The man tried to grab for the knife with his unbroken arm, but Aran smashed his elbow into the man's temple and pulled the man's groping hand down.

He pressed his head into Aran's arm to protect himself. But as Aran shifted his forearm to press the man's throat closed, he jerked and managed to sink his teeth into Aran's arm.

Aran screamed and shoved his knee into the man's side, breaking the man's hold.

Aran had been in this position many times in his frequent fights against the men of the vineyard, but today, no simple disarmament could dissolve the man's violent intentions. He knew this would go badly if he didn't end it quickly, and even as he paused to think through his options, the man's sweaty fingers slipped around the knife and pulled it down, barely missing Aran's face.

He laughed and stabbed three more times, glancing across Aran's arm once, and hitting the ground twice as Aran scrambled away and the man tried to follow.

As the man stabbed down a fourth time, Aran grabbed his wrist with both hands and twisted, but he was strong, and he kicked at Aran again.

Aran reached up with one hand and grabbed the flat of the blade, using the leverage to wrench it way. The man's grip fought him, and the blade cut his hand in the process, but Aran regained control of the weapon, flipped the blade around, and slammed it deep into the man's chest.

The man gasped and jerked, and tried to thrust his knee into Aran's midsection, though the blow was sapped of strength. "You're dead!" he screamed, splattering liquid into Aran's eyes.

Aran bit his lip until blood flowed and closed his eyes as he stabbed the man again and again, until finally everything stilled.

Aran was on his knees, several paces from the man, yet didn't remember how he'd gotten there. His body trembled, cold as snow. He dropped the knife and looked at his bloody hands in horror.

Mother exited the home with Zillah and grimaced. "Oh, Aran."

Aran looked up, feeling bitter tears burn his eyes.

"I'm sorry. But we'll need to clean the mess quickly," Mother said.

Aran's thoughts ran distant, throbbing through a nearly impenetrable fog. He had just killed a man for the first time in his life, to defend both himself and Zillah from peril. But somehow, the pang of regret that ran through his chest felt as unbearable as a mortal wound.

"Before they find it," Mother said.

"Before who finds it?" Zillah said.

"The others," she said.

36

Zillah

Aran's mother seemed to think the man who lay dead in her courtyard had come because of Rin, and Zillah hoped it would stay that way. But Aran knew, now, that she had been fleeing more than just Accad's authorities. If he told his mother the truth, Zillah would certainly be forced to leave. There was no way around it.

But where would she go?

Accad was a dead-end. Now Erech wasn't safe, either. The headhunters her mother, Hava, had hired to bring her home were on her trail, and at any moment, they could finally take her.

Aran's mother said, "I need to grab some tools." After she disappeared, Zillah crossed to Aran and knelt beside him. He looked dazed as he stared at the man's blood on his hands.

"I'm sorry," she whispered.

He blinked and shook his head. "You're . . . sorry?" Then the dim glow in his eyes sharpened, and he nodded. "This is because of you."

He hadn't even thought of it until she said something. How big a fool could she possibly make herself? She wanted to curse herself for drawing the attention back on herself.

He looked again at his bloodied hands, and the lines in his face softened. "I won't say anything," he said. "To Mother."

She closed her eyes and ground her teeth. How could his kindness land so bitter on her ears? "Stop it," she said.

He tipped his head. "What are you . . . ?"

"I need to get out of here," she said.

"We both do."

"No. I can't go with you. Not anymore."

He grabbed her wrist hard enough to hurt. "If I stay, I'll go mad."

She tore her hand out of his grip. "That doesn't mean we have to stay together."

"If I hadn't been here, you would have died."

"You almost died!" she said. "Next time, you might not be so fortunate."

"So be it," he said.

She slapped him.

For a long moment, he did not respond. Then he raised his red palms. "You see this? This was for you. I'm not just going to let you run off and get killed now."

Aran's mother came out again, dragging a massive earthenware jar. "Aran," she said.

He scooted away from Zillah and nodded.

"I don't think we will be able to bury him. I forgot I'd sold the last of our tools. Can you carry him into the brush at the edge of the property? That way I can at least clean our courtyard."

Aran nodded and slid his arms underneath the dead body before lifting and carrying him dripping into the deep grass and brush nearby.

Zillah watched Aran's mother spill the water onto the bloodied earth and begin to wash away the man's life. She moved without hesitation. Mind seemingly clear, unlike Zillah's or Aran's.

Who was this woman?

"Sarah," Zillah said.

Aran's mother nodded. "Yes?"

"Have you seen a dead man before?"

She paused, scrubbing the mud and blood from her hands.

"No," she whispered. "But I choose to believe he was not a man."

Zillah stared at her. At this woman who seemed unbendable. It was difficult to imagine that at one time, she had been cowardly enough to refuse to protect her own son.

Sarah sat on her haunches and brushed the hair from her eyes with her wrist. "When my husband surrendered his life to the Almighty, everything I knew was challenged." She stared at Zillah with those piercing, dark eyes so very much like Aran's. "My husband was a monster. But that monster died, and in its place, the Almighty raised up the man I had always hoped for. Like a butterfly, he emerged from his former life, and outshone me. I stayed the bitter, selfish worm I had always been. I had to die, Zillah. Same as him. I had to kill the 'me' inside my chest, and surrender to the Almighty, the one who wove every fiber of our beings. And now I see." Her eyes shone clear and bright as gemstones.

Zillah did not understand her words, but felt the passion of the woman's heart resonate with her own. She thought for the first time that maybe all the talk of religion she'd heard might have some purpose, might point to some distant reality.

"I see that everything that happens is in submission to the Almighty's will," Sarah continued. "I still fear. I still worry. But I don't hesitate to do what must be done. Not anymore."

And she resumed washing the blood away.

Zillah wiped her eyes and rubbed her chest to push away the ache that had erupted there. She did not understand why the woman's passion so moved her. It made her consider the impossible. That maybe the Almighty could forgive her as well. That maybe she could take hold of that same metamorphosis that Rin and Sarah had experienced.

She closed her eyes.

Let it be, Almighty. If you're real, then change me. Take away this pain. But most of all, don't let me harm innocent people like her and Aran anymore.

37

Noah

After discussing more details, Shem sent four guards with Noah to watch Sarah's home in rotating shifts. A boat would wait for him on the river the next morning. By the time he debarked, he would be half a day's walk from Babel and the surrounding cities, which, as Shem explained, had been partially engulfed by the growth Babel experienced since construction began on the tower.

Japheth lived to the south of the tower, hemmed by a row of cedar trees, which served as a landmark amid the otherwise dusty and lifeless city of Babel. After Noah met with his son, he would bring Japheth back to Shem's home, where the three would speak in detail about the recent events, and together decide what course of action they should take.

As Noah listened to how his footsteps joined the sound of the guards' leather creaking on the road toward Sarah's home, he wondered what Shem's dreams might mean. Shem was a devout follower of the Old Way and had periodically displayed prophetic giftings in the past. Because of this, Noah didn't doubt that the dreams were meaningful. Especially when he considered they'd recurred for seven nights before Noah arrived.

Still, what did it mean? Shem claimed he saw Noah holding hands with two others. Were those two supposed to be Aran and Zillah?

When did the dreams seem to be taking place? If the dreams focused only on Noah's journey to Erech, what was the point of the Almighty giving the dream at all?

No, the dreams must be referring to some future fulfillment. It was all that made sense, especially when he considered that they had been facing a light—perhaps the light from Noah's dream.

But what of the black holes in their chests?

After everything Shem said, Noah felt even more confused. The Almighty had sent no messages. Spoken no words. Given no dreams. And Shem's dreams, which at first had given him hope, now only made his legs heavier. As if each step was a struggle against the Almighty's will. Even though he believed he was walking the road he was meant to walk.

Noah decided he had one choice: do what seemed wise until the Almighty commanded him otherwise. He was done begging for a word.

"If you want to speak to me," Noah prayed under his breath, "you know how to make me pay attention."

But what if the Almighty didn't want to speak to him? Shem said Noah had abandoned them, and the others agreed. He wanted to say they were wrong, but when he thought back to what he had been doing these many years, the details had become hazy. As if after Jade's death, he had become like a man sleeping awake.

Could it be true? Was the Lord angry with him? Was that the reason for his silence?

Noah's breaths quickened and sweat began to grow on his forehead and palms. He swallowed the lump in his throat and focused on his surroundings to distract himself. The sun was already descending when they exited the walls of Erech. He hadn't realized he'd spent so much time at Shem's home, though it felt as though he hadn't tasted sleep in weeks.

They ascended the hill to Sarah's home, and the air settled as the river breeze broke itself on the city's stonework now behind them. Noah was glad for the tranquility after enduring the bustle of the city. In Erech, everyone appeared frantic. It reminded him of why he'd stayed in his vineyard for so long.

Being around so many unfamiliar people was exhausting. It made his mind buzz.

Noah examined the guards in detail for the first time. Three of them looked to be descendants of Shem, while the last he could not place. Two of them were quite short, like Shem, while one was average, and the last was easily as tall as Japheth, though he was fair-skinned beneath his tan.

None of the guards addressed him or even so much as glanced at him. He wondered if Shem had commanded them not to bother him.

As they entered Sarah's courtyard, the two short guards dipped to examine a swath of what looked like mud. Noah cupped his hands to his mouth and yelled, "Sarah?"

38

Zillah

Aran jumped at the sound of Noah's voice calling from outside the home, and Zillah felt a rush of anxiety. She didn't know what Noah was planning, or what his hopes would mean for her. But she was certain he would leave Erech. And when he left, she would do everything in her power to go with him.

Because to stay here would mean falling back into Hava's hands.

Still, the more time she spent in close communion with Noah, Sarah, and Aran, the greater the likelihood they would come to know the truth. The thought made her fingers twitch, for she was certain they would reject her if they knew she'd put them all in danger.

Still, for now, she could do nothing but face them, so she steeled herself and forced her expression to relax as she followed Aran and Sarah out the front door.

There, with Noah, stood four men armed with weapons and leather protection just like the guards in Erech wore. Noah stepped forward and bowed toward Sarah, who knelt and stared.

"I am sorry I doubted you." Sarah reached for Noah's hand to kiss it.

"Please," Noah said and placed a hand on her shoulder. "Shem offered to help because of you and your husband's faithfulness in providing for those seeking asylum in Accad. These soldiers belong to Shem's personal guard."

Sarah shook her head. "Rin and I asked for help many times before, yet none could be spared."

"I am Shem's father. He owes me this."

She stood and bowed. "Thank you."

"Perhaps, with the help of the guards, you can pick up the pieces of your husband's slave-trading business, and wield it toward good instead of evil."

Zillah was struck again by just how utterly sincere Noah was. She had grown so accustomed to hiding beneath layers of lies and half-truths that to encounter someone whom she truly trusted was both shocking and refreshing. Regardless of how he, at times, could be uncomfortably direct, she had grown to appreciate his forthrightness and what warmth he exuded to offset his occasional surliness.

"Perhaps," Noah said, "you should show the guards your home and decide the best positions for guarding its entrances while your son and I talk."

Sarah nodded and motioned to the guards with her hand before turning back into the home. "Come."

They filed in, leather armor creaking, weapons and buckles clanking. But they were respectful, and only spoke when spoken to.

"What is your plan moving forward?" Aran said.

Noah sighed and bent forward like an apple tree bearing too much fruit. "I will rest here tonight, if your mother will have me. I am old, and this journey has been more exciting than I'd hoped."

"And after?" Zillah said, her chest thumping harder, faster.

Noah looked at her, his dark eyes seeming to penetrate every secret harbored beneath her skin. "I will make for Babel. Shem is preparing a boat in the morning to ferry me across. I must wait until then."

Zillah felt the heat drain from her face. Noah raised his brow at her, and she tried to wipe her expression blank.

Aran stepped forward and spoke through clenched teeth. "I'm going with you."

"What?" Noah said.

"I need to leave," Aran said.

"Aran." Noah's tone warned. "Your mother needs you."

"She needs money, and now she has it. With those guards here, I'm of no use to her."

"It is shameful to abandon your family," Noah said.

Zillah's mind raced as they argued. She had hoped Noah would turn back and make for his vineyard. That way, his presence could help shield her until she could find a new home far away, safe from her hunters.

"You're my family every bit as much as she is," Aran said.

Noah pursed his lips and remained silent, as if he hadn't thought of that.

If Noah made for Babel, they would be moving deeper into danger. Still, to run off on her own again while surrounded by her enemies would be the deadliest of mistakes. If she went to Babel, perhaps she would find temporary safety—because why would they ever assume she would return there?

"If I stay, I'll go mad," Aran said.

If Aran left with Noah, Zillah would never be able to wait here with his mother. The guilt of her association with Nimrod would lock onto her like a lion's teeth.

Noah chewed his bottom lip, beard scraping his teeth.

"If Aran goes," Zillah said, "so will I."

Noah placed his hands on his lower back and stretched his spine as he considered their proposals.

Zillah tried to calm her hasty breaths. As terrified as she felt at the idea of going back to Babel, in a way, it felt fitting, as if every circumstance that led her to these two men had been to return her to the place where everything started. To Nimrod and Hava, who had hunted her relentlessly, murdered Aran's father, and subtly turned half the known world to the idol worship Noah abhorred. Maybe she was supposed to go. Maybe, by diving headfirst into her enemies' lair, she'd be given the chance to undo some of the evil that had been done to these people she'd grown to care so much for in such a short time.

"I need to speak with my son, Japheth. After, I will return again to Erech."

"I'll follow you to the end of the world and back," Aran said. "It would be better than staying here."

"I know Babel well," Zillah said and felt her breath seize as both their gazes settled on her. "I . . . uh, lived there once as a child." Her pulse flooded her ears like the wash of a river during wet season, and her eyesight darkened as she tried to push away the panic and focus on Noah's face. She clenched her fists, hoping they would not sense the source of her fears.

Noah nodded. "That would be helpful. But this journey might become dangerous. Talking with Shem has disturbed my spirit."

"I am not afraid," Aran said.

"I am," Zillah admitted. "But I could offer you guidance, and that could be invaluable in a city like Babel."

Sarah came out again with two of the guards, who began to walk the perimeter. Zillah was thankful for the distraction.

"Did you warn the guards?" Zillah said.

Sarah nodded, face grim.

"Warn them of what?" Noah said.

"A man attacked us while you were gone," Sarah said.

"What?" Noah's voice rose. "Who?"

"He had a knife," Zillah said. "If not for Aran, we wouldn't be standing here right now."

Noah observed Aran, perhaps to gauge whether his lack of response was proof of them trying to deceive him. Finally, after glancing again at the mud on the ground, he nodded. "You killed him."

Aran stared at that swath of dark soil. He opened his mouth, then nodded his head. Eyes wet. "You were right," he said. "When you said you pay a price."

Noah crossed to him and grabbed his shoulder hard enough to break him from his thoughts. The two met each other's eyes, but in all Noah's intensity, there was only love. "You protected them."

"I could have subdued him without—"

Noah shook his head. "You didn't kill him out of rage."

"I was furious."

"If not for his attempt on your life, you never would have touched him. Am I right?"

Aran grabbed his garment in his fists. Nodded.

"You protected them."

Aran nodded again.

Noah let go. "But you'll never forget this, will you?"

"No." Aran's voice barely a whisper.

After a long pause, Sarah said, "What are your plans, my lord?"

"That depends on whether you'll abide me for one more night."

She bowed. "Of course. And after?"

"I will cross the river on a boat Shem is having prepared tomorrow morning." He paused. "And . . . Aran and Zillah will come with me."

Sarah straightened, then blinked and jerked her gaze from Aran, to Zillah, to Noah again. "Oh."

"You were just getting used to being alone, remember?" Aran said.

"I was. Yes." She stared at Aran again before turning and heading inside.

39

Aran

Aran stayed outside as Noah and Zillah followed Mother in. He sat on the ground. For the first time since they arrived at Mother's home, the silence and solitude allowed him to think of absolutely nothing.

He had no energy left to grapple with all that threatened to overwhelm him, so he laid back and closed his eyes, hoping to fall asleep. But ants began to crawl across his neck and arms, and the dust made his skin itch. He stood, brushed off the insects, and walked inside.

A few candles burned in the main room, casting a dim glow that revealed Noah and Zillah lying on little beds on the floor.

Mother sat on a cushion in the corner, watching as he entered.

He avoided looking at her, but walked her way and pulled out his moneybag. "This is yours," he said and handed it to her.

She accepted it. "Thank you."

Aran looked around the room, wondering where he should lay.

"I made your bed in your old room," Mother said.

Aran felt a pang of regret. As much as she had infuriated him, she had treated him with nothing but kindness since he'd returned.

How could he say he was sorry? Because he wasn't. Not totally. So he just stood there like a fool.

He turned away to make for his room, but Mother caught his wrist.

"Wait," she said.

He looked back and saw lines of worry at the corners of her eyes.

"I'm sorry."

He ground his teeth together and resisted the temptation to tear his arm from her hand.

"I just hoped you still loved me . . ." She leaned forward, obviously longing for the affection they'd not exchanged since he was a young boy.

He stood motionless and allowed her head to rest against his abdomen.

She wrapped one arm around his torso. Fractured breaths warming his side.

He didn't reciprocate, but as he felt his mother's hand against his back, angry tears sprang to his eyes.

She pulled away. As she took in the rage in his face, her face reddened, and she looked as if he had struck her.

"No, it's him I hate," he said. "Not you."

She brushed the wrinkles from her dress and pulled at her chapped lips. "But you don't love me."

His silence rebuffed her in a way no words ever could.

"Please, promise me something," she said.

"What?"

"That you'll be careful when you go with Noah."

"Of course."

"Do your best to avoid violence."

"Mother . . ."

"I won't sleep if you don't promise."

He stared at her. Her embarrassment was gone. Replaced by the strength she'd exuded when they arrived. The strength she'd failed to show when Father beat him. "I promise."

"Don't go searching for a fight out of hate or bitterness for what happened."

Aran ran his hand through his hair and turned away.

Mother didn't follow, and Aran was thankful, because when he arrived in his room, the cold walls brought back a rush of memories. His pulse washed his ears like an ocean breaking itself on a rocky cliff. He walked to his bed and knelt, then laid with his back to the wall, just like when he was a boy.

He knew Mother sat in solitude in the next room, sleepless and grieving the loss of all she thought she loved. Though he couldn't bring himself to go back out to her, he closed his eyes and remembered long ago, when she came in and laid with him in the dark, telling stories and making him laugh until they fell asleep together. In the solitary dark of his childhood bedroom, he rested in the memory of her love before all went wrong. Because in his memory, any wounds inflicted were final, and any joys were forever safe.

...

In the morning, before sunrise, they bid Mother good-bye. As Aran turned to follow Noah and Zillah, Mother grabbed him by the shoulders and kissed him on the cheek. He pushed her away gently.

"Be safe," she said.

He stood there, dumbly searching for an appropriate response. But his emotions were too muddled, and Zillah called for him from farther down the hill.

Mother waved as he jogged to catch up with Noah and Zillah.

"Your mother is a good woman," Noah said.

"Just like my father," Aran said.

"You will forgive them, eventually," Noah said.

No, he thought. *I won't.*

The violence they'd done to him ran too deep. Before he'd come, he had wondered if his parents' interest in the Almighty would become a comfort. But the more he heard about it, the more bitter he became that Noah's God would welcome such evil with open arms. They didn't deserve forgiveness.

Then he remembered the blood on the soil, and the look of the man's eyes as he screamed in pain. The knowledge that he had murdered a man in cold blood brought back his own guilt. Suffocating. Heavy as a boulder.

It sullied the righteous fervor of his anger toward his parents. Turned it sour and cold.

He didn't know what to hope for anymore. Only that he wanted to be free from the anxiety that crawled under his skin. To find real, lasting peace. If that was what the Almighty offered, maybe someday he could find a way to let go.

Maybe.

But he had more immediate concerns. Like the danger Zillah had brought to them.

Aran tipped his head and caught her smiling.

She noticed him, and the smile faded. "What?"

"Nothing," he said.

Why had those men been following Zillah? Whatever she'd been involved with had certainly been dark, regardless of what she claimed. He wished he could go back to before he knew anything about her. When he could simply enjoy the warmth of her pressed against his chest as they swayed to the gait of the camel.

Just like how he wished he could forget what he'd learned of Mother and Father since returning. To be pushed to admit that either of them loved him opened the door for pain. And he couldn't handle more pain.

Erech was quiet so early in the morning. Crickets chirped, and several women hung their clothes on posts to dry in the rising sun. Workers moved slowly, and few lined the streets.

They found the boat Shem had prepared tied to a post at the riverside. It was a long boat large enough to carry perhaps ten men. Two slaves wearing short pants and nothing else stood with folded arms at the front and back.

They looked between Noah, Aran, and Zillah.

"The Lord Shem said there would be one passenger."

"Originally, that was true," Noah said.

The slaves thought about this. The one at the front shrugged and began untying the rope from the post. "Get on, then," he said. "Before the fishermen wake."

The other laughed at this, and Aran wondered what was funny.

Zillah stepped in, and the rim of the boat dipped for a moment until it was flush with the surface. Noah followed, and the boat bobbed again, allowing some of the water to flow over the top and pool at his feet.

The slave tossed the rope splashing into the boat and motioned for Aran to get in.

"It won't sink?" Aran said.

"Unless you make it," the slave said.

"Come," Noah said. "The boat is safe."

He should know, after riding a boat he constructed himself to survive the greatest cataclysm to ever mar the earth.

Aran lifted his leg, and the slave pushed the boat from the land, so that when Aran set his foot in the boat, he was off-balance, one leg on land, one on the boat sliding away.

"W-wait," Aran said and flung his arms to maintain balance.

Zillah gasped, and Noah said, "He's falling!"

The slave twisted back and grabbed Aran's tunic to pull him into the boat, where he fell to his knees, rocking the vessel and spilling water into it.

The slave shook his head and sucked air through his teeth.

Aran twisted around, nails digging into the wooden sides. "What were you thinking?"

Noah and Zillah were both laughing softly, seemingly relieved and amused at once.

"You pushed off as I was getting in," Aran said.

The slave lifted a large pole that he used to direct them downriver. "Not my fault you move slow."

Noah patted his arm. "I am sorry. I tell you it's safe and then you nearly fall."

Aran sat lower down and kept his grip on the sides of the boat until his hands ached.

Noah noticed and grew concerned. "You are still worried?"

"I can't swim," Aran said.

Noah opened his mouth in a silent, "Oh." Then he said, "Try to trust the boat."

Despite him saying it quietly, the slave heard, and said, "You fear water?"

Aran refused to respond to the man.

"What's your name?" the slave said.

Aran did not respond.

"His name's Aran," Noah said. "He belongs to me."

"I assumed as much. Well, Aran, best way to learn to swim is to be tossed overboard." The slave started to shift the boat, making waves across the surface of the river.

Aran clutched madly at the sides and felt a sliver of wood slide into the flesh of his right palm. "Stop!"

The slave stopped and laughed so hard he nearly fell.

"No more," Noah said, and for once he seemed legitimately angry.

The slave bowed and caused no more issues the rest of the way. Aran could hardly believe the man had conjured the boldness to behave so dishonorably. Aran himself had technically sold himself as a slave to Noah, but Noah respected slaves as voluntary servants, for any dehumanizing enslavement was forbidden in the Old Way. Aran groaned as he pulled the splinter from his palm, beckoning a bead of blood to bubble out.

Shem certainly would consider his slaves in the same light as Noah. Regardless, the commonly accepted and unspoken rule was that slaves never speak so freely with their masters' guests. Specifically to avoid experiences such as this one. It was shameful, and the slave knew it.

But Aran was forgetting himself. The slave had realized Aran was a slave of Noah—it didn't matter if neither he nor Noah saw it that way, culture dictated the setup. And because Aran had spoken back, the slave thought it his place to pressure Aran in return.

He sighed. Wishing to get off the boat as quickly as possible, though he knew Babel was still far downriver.

They rode the current beyond riverside homes and farms. Past grazing cattle and men with yoked bulls pulling carts of goods on the long roads between cities and settlements. Many were merchants obviously belonging to the powerful cooperatives that ruled the region.

Aran remembered from his time here as a boy that the land between the cities was governed by many families, and the roads had been built by the cities as trade routes to support them. The settlements contributed greatly to the wealth of the region, and they traded in groups because it allowed them to gain prestige and wealth behind the protection of many sons, armed and ready to wage violence against any who wronged them.

Though the cities were much more powerful, they respected the families enough to maintain peace. Even one family with forty grown men armed and ready for battle could do great damage to a city's inhabitants.

As Aran observed the countryside at the pace of the river's flow, he considered how unusual his own story was, even in their modern culture. Family was everything to most of those living between the rivers. Fathers protected their sons and sons protected their fathers. Even if there was harshness and little love, there was solidarity. But Aran had experienced none of that.

Noah's hand warmed Aran's shoulder, and he looked at the old man who had long ago become the only sort of father in his life.

Noah spoke quietly, for only the two of them to hear above the rush of the river. "You are grappling with heavy thoughts."

Aran nodded. How could he reconcile his pride in protecting Noah and Zillah with the guilt he felt for killing the man who had threatened their lives outside Mother's home? Or Mother's abandonment with her obvious affection and desire for Aran's love? But more than anything . . . "How could the Almighty forgive my father?"

Noah looked out over the water and let his hand fall until his fingers skimmed the surface, sending ripples behind them. A few fish skipped across the surface of the water toward the reeds at the river's edge. "The Almighty does as he wills. And whatever he does, he does rightfully. You must believe that, before anything else."

"I don't believe it right to forgive a man so evil," Aran said.

Noah met Aran's eyes. "What is forgiveness?"

Aran opened his mouth, but could form no coherent description. He felt he understood forgiveness implicitly, but to explain it was another task.

"Then do you not see how arrogant a statement that is?"

"No."

"What you see of a man's heart is like what we see of the fish on this river. Most men spend most of their lives lurking among the reeds. Your eyes cannot find them, nor see the twists and turns of their movement. But the Almighty . . . his eyes pierce the deepest waters, through the soil and hard rock and whatever lies beyond. If the Almighty forgave your father, he was righteous to do so. For he sees into the heart, and we do not."

Aran rubbed his eyes, which throbbed with dull pain from the tension of constant stress these many days. "My father hated me."

"Maybe. But even the worst of men is not devoid of affection. I am certain that he did care for you. But affection is not enough to keep a man from evil. And so our lives look like a jar of water and sand, twirled together and poured out into a cup. It is difficult to find a pure drink in this world. That is why the Almighty gave us the Old Way."

"In all the time I've been with you," Aran said, "I have seen that you behave differently from the men I knew when I was younger. But I still do not understand your Old Way. I never have."

Noah sighed and slumped in his seat. Finally, he nodded. "It seems in my old age I have failed to be the man the Almighty has called me to be."

"How does it work? The Old Way."

"When you came to me, you bowed at my feet and surrendered your life to me."

"I sold myself as a slave."

"And yet I received you as a servant and paid you consistent wages. I taught you how to work the vineyard until you settled into your primary duties. And you knew you were always invited into my home as a son, though you never came."

"What does that have to do with the Old Way?"

"The Old Way begins with the same such surrender. We offer ourselves as slaves to the Almighty, ordering our lives and actions to please him. But he takes us as faithful servants, instead. And gives us good gifts in return for our love and devotion. We can only serve the Almighty if we love him, in the same way that a servant can only serve his master well if he loves and fears him. It is precisely this love, and the trust it tends in our hearts, that changes our behavior and gives us the strength to live the Old Way. This is what your father embraced."

Aran considered this. He had experienced transformative thankfulness and trust in his work for Noah, and it had been the fuel to push him onward, to give him the energy to fulfill his duties. Through it, he had thought he had healed from many wounds.

Until he returned to Mother.

"Can such love for the Almighty heal hurts so deep as mine?" Aran said, his voice nearly a whisper.

"They can. I am sorry." Noah's voice wavered, and Aran looked at him and saw tears forming in the old man's eyes. "I am sorry that I have not loved you better."

Aran narrowed his eyes. What was he talking about?

"In all the time you spent with me, the Old Way was never clear to you. That is a guilt I must bear the rest of my life. And I fear it is only the proof of a life lived unwell."

"But you have been good to me," Aran said.

Noah shook his head. "From the beginning of this journey, I feared to acknowledge the truth—that in the many years I've lived in comfort, I have forgotten the price I paid in my younger years to be reconciled with the Almighty."

Aran watched Noah and considered his openness. Who was Aran, to be the recipient of such a confession? He was only a hired servant, a slave. And yet, Noah spoke to him as a son.

"You'll remember," Noah said, "I told you once that when I was young, I nearly lost myself to rage."

Aran nodded, chest aching at the pain in Noah's eyes. At the knowledge that he himself was consumed by rage against his own father.

"The Almighty appeared to me and offered to take it all away. All the ache of the loss I'd endured, which was no less than what you have experienced. He told me what it meant to surrender, and at first, I refused him. I thought my pain too intense. Too deep. But the reality was that my pain was too much to *not* offer to him. And when I finally did give myself over, he was faithful to his promise. He took it, Aran. He took it all. And now, in my old age, I have abandoned him and my family, for years of comfort padded by wealth." He hid his face behind his hand, but Aran saw the old man's lips quivering and heard his quiet, uneven breaths. "Forgive me," he whispered.

Tears sprang to Aran's eyes. "Stop."

Noah's free hand slid over Aran's shoulder and squeezed again. "Please," he whispered. "Tell me you forgive me."

"I forgive you, of course."

Noah took a deep, shaky breath, and let it out slow. After a moment, he regained his composure and wiped his eyes. "Thank you. For joining me on this journey. It has been long since I faced such weakness in my own self. Now I see it's always been there. Only I ignored it."

"I gave you my word," Aran said. "I will not abandon you."

"I am thankful. My heart forebodes that what remains ahead of us will be more difficult than anything we've yet faced."

Aran wondered if Noah spoke about the one who had killed his father. Mother had indicated his death was religiously motivated. The followers of the Old Way and the followers of the Light Bringer were oppositional forces, and that violence had now spread far beyond Accad, even to Noah's vineyard.

But why?

40

Zillah

The relief Zillah felt earlier that morning to finally be moving again had given way to a cold, sweaty anxiety. For a moment, as she stepped into the boat, she'd felt certain she saw gleaming blue eyes watching from the shadows. But after the boat stopped rocking, she saw nothing.

She tried to push away the sensation, but as they moved slow and low across the water, the fear that the men had seen her and knew what destination she made for refused to leave.

And now she could do nothing but sit and wait.

As she listened to Noah's words to Aran, her own heart throbbed for the relief Noah spoke of. The ideas he communicated sounded beautiful beyond comparison. To be welcomed in by the Almighty too wonderful to accept as truth. If the Almighty truly could heal her, she would gladly throw herself into an abyss for his name.

But what she had done as a child . . .

She pushed away the memories of crackling flames . . . the screams of the innocent. The dark rites of the Light Bringer. Forced upon her, at first, but after the violence seeped into the cracks in her soul . . .

She shivered. She was Hava's no longer. She would never let herself be twisted to that sick woman's desires again.

I will kill her, she thought. *I will kill the heartless monster so she can never harm anyone again.*

She did not know what Hava and Nimrod had done since she ran from home, but she was certain they aspired toward evil. Hava was an anomaly. A beauty devoid of empathy. Ruthless, cruel, manipulative. She would bleed the world to rule it. And Nimrod, though different, was no less malevolent. He followed what he believed to be his destiny, laid out by Ham's prophecy that together he and Hava would unify the world.

If not for Hava and her ingenuity in denying any connection to the Light Bringer while building the foundations of their dominion, they would never have maintained such positions of power and influence.

But as soon as the tower was finished, and the sacrifices commenced, the world would know. Already their secretive following had grown massive, and their dominance so complete they could afford to let the ruse die.

But Hava would wait. She would never risk herself until she felt confident that she could control the world as completely as a god in human skin. She never risked anything prematurely, but for the knowledge of what she planned to do to Zillah.

Noah cleared his throat, breaking her thoughts. A flock of birds flew overhead, drawing her eyes into the glare of the sun. She winced, then looked down again and saw a city growing on the horizon.

She pointed. "Look."

Aran and Noah followed her finger.

"Babel," she said.

Even from so far away, they could see the tower, rearing like a mountain amid a sea of brick.

"Is that . . . ?" Aran said.

"The tower," Zillah said.

"You lived in Babel while the tower was under construction?" Noah said.

Zillah nodded.

"What did the people of Babel say of it?"

"They are proud. They believe their city the greatest in the world. The center of the new world."

"Ironic that idolatry would find roots in their soil," Noah said.

"Idolatry is everywhere," Aran said.

"But here is its beating heart. I believe the tower's construction was likely commanded by Ham, who still claims to be the prophet of the Light Bringer. It may seem a monument to self-sufficiency to some. To others, however, it's more likely an obelisk to enslavement to a false god."

"Did Shem tell you that?" Zillah said.

"Indeed, he did. And much else." And he looked at Zillah with a knowing expression that frightened the blood from her cheeks.

He doesn't know, she thought. *No one knows who I am. I am a ghost child. Nimrod and Havah kept me hidden from the world, for they feared admitting I hadn't been born a son. There is no way Shem could know . . .*

Unless . . .

"What is the aim of the followers of the Light Bringer?" Aran said.

"I do not know," Noah said. "But I am convinced their goal is evil. And that it has everything to do with the construction of that tower."

Zillah swallowed the aching lump in her throat and straightened herself in her seat. "You are right. In Babel, many serve the Light Bringer. Some in secret, some in public. That is why you must watch yourselves. It is dangerous to wander the city. It is dangerous to speak ill of the Light Bringer."

Noah smiled suddenly. "I am thankful we have you."

Zillah felt he meant it, as he seemed to mean everything he said. For a moment, it made her anxiety wane.

But her relief was short-lived.

41

Aran

As they slid quietly down the river, Aran realized for the first time how everything they faced found its origins in the Light Bringer. First, Noah's son Ham had chosen the Light Bringer over the Almighty long ago, which seemed to have been the central rift between them. More recently, the young man Aran caught abducting a woman in Noah's vineyard had screamed the name of the Light Bringer before killing himself. Then, Father had been killed after seeking asylum from the Light Bringer's followers, whom Nimrod apparently endorsed. Because why else would Nimrod have refused to help Father? And the timing of Father's death—regardless of what he'd said to Mother—was too conspicuous to deny.

It had left Mother destitute, and Aran robbed of the family he'd dreamed of.

But why?

They'd traveled all this way and still struggled to understand why every city remained plagued by what Noah claimed was a false god.

Then there was Zillah, whose past was shrouded in mystery. Still, even she seemed to have had some relations with the followers of the Light Bringer, for she had lived in Babel and understood something of their dark rites.

How could so much trouble spring from one simple name?

There had to be some powerful motivator behind the persecution the followers of the Old Way were enduring. For the Almighty appeared to wield power through his servant, Noah. Surely any god who caused the Almighty's faithful so much trouble must hold real power.

The boat was nearing the harbor to the north of Babel, which sat in the valley inland. Noah and Zillah looked at him as the slaves steered the boat to the left, toward an empty dock.

"We need to figure out the purpose for the tower's construction," Aran said.

"I agree," Noah said. "I doubt it is simply to unify the world. Otherwise, why would there be such disunity in Babel and the surrounding cities?"

"How do you propose we do that?" Zillah said. "Find a group of them performing a nighttime sacrificial ritual and ask them what their darkest secrets are? You'll get yourself killed."

"I think that's a good idea—" Aran began, but Zillah interrupted him.

"You have no awareness of what you're talking about."

"Regardless of who's right, I don't think this is the time," Noah said.

"I don't see that we can just wait around," Aran said.

Zillah leaned forward to see Aran better, tipping the boat as she did so. "First, tell me how you plan to find them."

Aran narrowed his eyes. "Isn't it obvious?"

"No," Zillah said. "And you're a fool to think it is."

"Friends," Noah said.

But neither were listening.

"When do they perform their rituals?" Aran said.

"At night," Zillah said.

"Then we look for them at night. I guarantee you that if they're as plentiful as you claim, I could find a group of them in a single night."

"Even if you could, do you know how many have been killed for less?" Zillah said.

"It can't be so dangerous," Aran said. "I met plenty followers of the Light Bringer as a child, and don't remember them being very frightening," Aran said.

"You never lived in Babel. Babel is different. And things have changed."

"How do you know?" Aran said.

"We will soon arrive at Japheth's home," Noah said. "Best wait until—"

"No, tell me," Aran said. "How do you know, Zillah? You've told us almost nothing of your past. Yet you seem sure enough of this. Explain yourself."

Zillah stared at him as if her eyes were firebrands.

"Watch your hands," the slave said and jumped onto the dock as the boat slid against it. Aran jerked his fingers away just in time, breath quickening as his knuckles were nearly smashed. The slave held the rope and tied it around a post while his companion did the same, pulling the boat to a stop.

The slaves held their hands out for Noah and Zillah first.

Aran helped himself out of the boat, scrambling on all fours up the dock before brushing himself off and spitting in the water behind the boat.

"May the Almighty bless you too," the slave man said, voice drenched in sarcasm.

Aran was about to turn around and continue his interrogation of Zillah when he noticed Noah waving at a man dressed in rich clothing, smiling widely as he approached. The man wrapped Noah's hand in both of his own before kneeling and kissing his knuckles. "My lord," the man said. "It is an honor to meet you. I am Uzza, son of Uz, of the clan of Aram. I received word from Shem and brought a carriage to take you to the outskirts of Babel."

"Thank you," Noah said. "Will you accompany us inside?"

"Sadly, I must attend to business. I live outside Babel and lead a team of merchants for all who belong to Aram." He lowered his voice and eyed the other men loading goods onto boats in the harbor. "I do not enter Babel unless necessary. The air there, something is wrong with it. I believe it accursed, no matter what they say."

Noah nodded. "And yet that is our destination."

Uzza bowed. "I never thought I'd have the privilege of meeting you."

Noah bowed in return. "You are always welcome to visit me in my vineyard."

The man looked up, eyes wide. "Truly?"

Noah chuckled and rubbed the back of his head, bemused. "Well, of course. Why not?"

Uzza clapped his hands once and pressed his lips together. "Then it is settled. I will visit you after you return to your vineyard. Next year, perhaps?"

"Perhaps," Noah said. "If the Almighty wills. My vineyard is open to all visitors—so long as they walk in peace and humility. We could trade wine for some of the goods the Aramites produce."

Uzza laughed and bowed low before motioning farther away, toward a large wagon attached to two horses. "We would give you beautiful horses. The best in the world, and the pride of our family's heritage." Aran, Noah, and Zillah followed as the man chattered.

"My father was the first to tame horses. He has been breeding them for years now. These are two of his favorites. Haffel is the one on the left with the beautiful swatches of color across his coat—isn't he splendid?—and the other is Briggun. They are obedient, for we use them often and my father knows how to tame them. He raised these from their youth, and still owns their sires—he was loathe to give them up, even for great wealth. But he is already wealthy. Here, let me help you." He supported Noah by the elbow as the old man struggled to sit on the back of the wagon. "You two can sit, as well," Uzza said, and Aran could hear the smile in his voice even while his back was turned.

Zillah sat to Noah's left, and Aran to his right, their backs facing the horses.

Uzza commanded the horses to move, and with a grinding creak and the clatter of leather straps, they started toward the outskirts of Babel, which they now could see was not guarded by a wall like many of the other cities.

Aran twisted in his seat to face Uzza. "Why does Babel have no wall?"

"They don't need one. The city is massive—you will see

when you arrive. Few would dare pillage it, either, for the retribution of Babel is swift and complete. I hear word its prisons are filled with corpses."

Aran looked at Zillah for confirmation.

She shrugged. "I always thought it was because the city was growing so quickly because of the construction of the tower."

"So they say, but it is not what I believe," Uzza said. "I believe differently than most about Babel."

"I don't think any of us want to test Babel's prisons," Aran said, and gave Zillah a look.

She glared at him. "What is that supposed to mean?"

Aran shrugged.

"Don't shrug at me," she said.

"You trade with Babel often?" Noah said.

Uzza laughed and twisted in his seat to show them his wide smile. "I may distrust them, but I trust their money. Hah!"

As the wooden wheels skipped over pebbles and grit, Aran tried to imagine how the city of Babel could be so unique.

"Look," Zillah said, voice low. "We need to stay focused. If we don't, there will be trouble when we enter Babel."

"Do you have any tips for what not to do after we enter?" Noah said.

"Yes," Zillah said. "First, don't speak to anyone you pass. And don't meet their gaze for long, either. It is considered hostile."

"How should we respond if someone addresses us?" Noah said.

"Act as though you did not hear," Zillah said.

"Umm," Aran said. "What if they decide to pursue us after we ignore them?"

"No one will pursue us," Zillah said.

Aran narrowed his eyes. "How old were you when you left Babel?"

"Old enough to understand what dangers the city posed," Zillah said.

"Then surely you've seen followers of the Light Bringer who live here?"

"Why does that matter?" Zillah said. "And what has gotten you so obsessed with the Light Bringer?"

"You've seen them yet don't know anything about their ambitions?"

Zillah stared at him a moment. "No," she said. "Now stop asking."

"I don't believe you," Aran said.

"Don't care."

"We spent the last week surviving together."

"So what?"

Aran tried to ignore the ache that was slowly growing in the base of his throat. "You saw the rawest portion of my life. Yet I know nothing of you, and every time I press for details from your past, you act as if I have no right to know."

Zillah's face paled, and Aran wondered if it were possible that she hadn't even thought of how one-sided their relationship had become. "No one has the right to pry into my life."

Heat came to Aran's face, and he resisted the urge to shove himself off the wagon. "I never wanted to show you mine, either."

"Then why did you?"

Noah set a hand on his shoulder and whispered, "Now is not the time."

Aran clenched his teeth as Zillah shifted her glare to the sparse shrubs at the roadside. Refusing to look at him, as if she were an adolescent. Aran concentrated on the river, willing the fury pulsing through his wrists to wane.

How could she be so callous? Did she not realize he had let her see what no one else in his life had?

He had saved her life twice now. First from the potential of being attacked by the lion, and second from the mad man who had tried to gut them with a knife. Had he not earned the right to a bit of honesty and openness? And yet he felt her hiding herself more than ever.

Focusing on it just made him want to explode with fury. He closed his eyes and focused on breathing deeply, slowly. Soon, they would be in the city, and eventually his anger would wane. He would speak to her then. But not before.

She was too stubborn. When pushed, she pushed back harder.

He shook his head. Realizing in that moment that he'd actually grown to care for her. The struggles they'd endured had pressed them toward each other with unique intensity.

It was what made his sense of betrayal so intense.

He knew he shouldn't care, especially after just one week, but when he saw the shadow of wounds deep in the gleam of her eyes, he wanted her to speak of them. He knew they were there, yet during his greatest pain, she had refused to meet him there.

Why?

42

Zillah

Finally, Aran had listened and decided to leave her alone.

What was wrong with him? Even direct commands went ignored by the fool. She wanted to thank Noah for intervening, but worried what would happen once they arrived at Japheth's home. If Noah left them alone, Aran could easily trap her. Force her to lie to him again and again.

The realization that he would even want to push her like that made her belly churn. What right did he have to pressure her so? As if she didn't have enough pressure to endure already.

Of course, he couldn't know that, but after their exchange, he should be clever enough to realize what he was doing wasn't working.

Sometimes, it was hard for her to gauge his mind. At moments, he seemed slow, or overly preoccupied with daydreaming. Other times his eyes punched through her like lances, and his words bit with the speed and the heat of crackling kindling.

Few men had ever drawn such emotion from her. It made her feel vulnerable, exposed. She had to stop talking with him. Stop letting him near. It would only end badly once he found out the truth.

She looked at the scars across his face, which was quivering with anger. A vein pulsed across his forehead as he clenched his hands into fists on his legs.

She nearly slapped herself for visualizing herself slipping her fingers between his to release the tension.

He has been kind to me. I shouldn't treat him so harshly.

A shadow darkened their wagon, and Zillah looked up at a swath of clouds that had floated in front of the sun. She sighed and twisted to see how far they had come.

The buildings loomed close, and the tower now looked like a monstrous monolith, jutting far above the rest of the buildings, utterly uniform in color and shape. Its base was square, and its walls formed gigantic steps big enough for a god. Cut into the steps were four much smaller staircases, one leading up each side of the construction.

Scaffold ramps stood only at the very top, where the last of what Zillah remembered being called "the altar" was being erected. She swallowed hard and felt the rush of anxiety come back full force. If she had to guess, she would say the tower would be finished any day now. The sight of its massive figure sent shivers down her spine.

"I will take you to that house with the wooden shack outside it," Uzza said, "and no farther." But she hardly knew what home he was speaking of, for most of the homes had a wooden shack, and Uzza himself looked only at the tower in the distance.

Zillah addressed Noah. "Did Shem tell you where Japheth lives?"

Noah nodded. "He told me there is a landmark to the south of the tower, a row of ancient trees still standing amid the city. Do you know it?"

Zillah nodded. "It is on the opposite side of the tower from"—she nearly said "where my parents live" but stopped herself—"where the lord Nimrod lives. And we will have to walk around one corner of the tower to get there."

Aran twisted to look back at the tower.

"How long has it been since you've seen Japheth?" Zillah said.

Noah sighed. "Longer ago than when I last saw Shem."

"Are you excited?"

"Anxious."

Zillah nodded. *Me too,* she wanted to say. Instead, she let the grind of the wheels and the clack of hoofs fill the space between them. Noah withdrew into private thoughts, and Aran scratched at a scar beneath his beard. The horses' tails swished, and pebbles skittered in the wind. The clouds widened and darkened until it felt like night was near. Even Uzza was reticent to speak, now that they were within reach of Babel.

Finally, Uzza commanded the horses to stop, and the wagon stilled. Uzza simply turned around and motioned for them to get off.

Aran helped Noah down as Zillah stood to the side of the road and said, "Thank you."

Uzza nodded, neck flushed, and turned his horses, their hoofs striking a slow, ever-quieting rhythm as the three of them faced the city. Though the tower was clearly still far away, its sheer size gave the illusion that it was bending over them.

"Well," Zillah said. "We made it."

43

Noah

Babel was quite different from Erech or Accad. The diversity and color of Erech, and the less sizable but ornate stone homes of Accad, felt quaint in comparison to the alarming size and uniformity of the streets of Babel. Every angle appeared mapped to precision, every baked brick placed with purpose. Yet none of the roads were paved, and the dust from the endless shuffling of feet filled the air and dirtied their teeth.

They saw no trees. But they did see massive piles of dry lumber in great storehouses with servants passing allotments to the citizens who came for wood to heat water and cook food. Even more than in Accad, the city officials controlled every resource and doled out only the bare necessities. Comfort seemed a foreign term, yet many walked the streets dancing and singing, intoxicated, or well on their way to total inebriation.

"Do the inhabitants of Babel always revel during the day?" Noah said.

"No," Zillah looked around. "They must be celebrating some great occasion."

"The tower?" Aran said.

"Maybe," Zillah said.

Young women ran by giggling, clothes tattered as if they had just been slashed open by a lion's claws.

Noah grimaced. "Why do they not cover their shame?"

Young men ran after, wearing nothing but loincloths. Jeering and cajoling one another into catching the women.

Emaciated dogs walked the streets, at times in great numbers. Fleas danced across their boney backs, and with shifting eyes they pranced back and forth to avoid passing feet.

Finally, they climbed a slow incline to a section of larger and wealthier homes. Fewer revelers crowded the alleys. The court-yards had walls, and at the gates stood guards leaning on spears and wearing long tunics and loose, white pants.

They climbed up a second slow incline until they saw the tops of great cedar trees. At their base, a large home built of quarried stone stood out from the rest of the homes like the scars on Aran's face.

"Japheth," Noah said. "My son." And he lifted his tunic and ran, leaving Aran and Zillah to jog to catch up.

His breaths caught in his chest as he neared the courtyard entrance, which was guarded by two tall men who looked as though they may be Japheth's sons, though Noah did not recog-nize them. They had Japheth's lanky features, the same slant to the eyes and structure of the face. But they were lighter in skin tone—as nearly all of Japheth's children were, for his wife had been quite pale.

"Japheth," Noah yelled. "Japheth!"

The guards stepped aside as he ran in, but as he crossed the courtyard and slid through the halls, calling for his son, the empty quiet of the home darkened his sight. Where was Japheth? Or his servants and children? The home around him was simply . . . vacant.

Aran and Zillah caught up with him and said nothing.

Noah turned toward them. "Something is wrong. Where is everyone?"

"Noah," Aran said. "We talked with the guards."

Noah already knew. He heard it in the tone of Aran's voice.

"Dead?" Noah said, his voice a hoarse croak.

"Perhaps not," Zillah said.

Noah grabbed at the fabric over his chest and thanked the Almighty. But the fear that clutched his heart would not flee.

"He left a week ago and has not returned," Zillah said. "The only guards left are great-grandsons of Japheth named Elik and Gom. The rest were dismissed two days ago. Elik and Gom stayed only to wait for Japheth's return and to keep away thieves."

Noah slid to his seat outside Japheth's sleeping chamber. "Please," he said. "Bring Elik and Gom so that I might talk with them."

...

Elik and Gom were twin brothers likely in their early twenties by their look. Neither had married. Why, Noah did not know. But he was glad for it, because if they had families, they surely wouldn't have been waiting at Japheth's home, and none of Noah's questions would have found answers.

Elik bowed and spoke first. "When we saw you running, we recognized you as an elder and did not detain you because we feared to insult you."

"Also," Gom said, "you seemed agitated."

"Yes." Elik nodded. "But we did not recognize you. After we let you pass, we detained your companions. It took only a moment for us to realize they spoke the truth. You are Noah, the father of all."

Elik threw himself to the ground, long limbs crumpled like so many branches. Gom did the same, though he was slower and more reserved.

"Where is he?" Noah said. "Where is my son?"

Elik looked up, and he and Gom met each other's eyes with a nod.

"Japheth left about a week ago," Gom said. "He has not returned."

"So I've been told. Do you know nothing more?"

"We know little. He was going to the Lord Nimrod," Elik said.

"What?" Noah's face reddened, and he struggled to his feet and stepped around the brothers. "Why would he do such a fool thing?"

"He was answering a summons," Elik said. "The Lord

217

Nimrod commands all of Babel. Since Japheth's city was absorbed by the growth brought on by the tower, Japheth's authority shifted. After receiving the summons, we assumed that might change further. Japheth has always been ready to let go of his status. He's never been greedy for power."

"But he hasn't returned," Gom said. "We did not expect that."

"No," Noah said. "It seems no one has expected any of the Lord Nimrod's recent actions. The trust everyone puts in him is in vain, for he has chosen to betray at every opportunity."

Elik and Gom looked to Aran and Zillah, confused.

"What does he speak of?" Elik said.

"Nimrod murdered my father," Aran said.

Elik gasped, and Gom's face sobered. "Surely that can't be true," Elik said.

"I confess," Noah said. "I struggle to hold back anger at your naivety. Has he fooled everyone?"

"Nimrod is silver-tongued," Zillah said. "Or—s-so they say. He has rallied for many years for the unification of all men. The way he orders cities brought wealth, prosperity, health, and community. In all ways, he seems to the public eye to stand for what is good."

"And yet everyone who visits him disappears," Noah said.

"Changes have taken place," Zillah said. "The tower does not seem finished, so something must have happened."

Elik tapped a finger on pursed lips and traded a look with his brother. "We may know."

"The announcement," Gom said.

"Yes?" Aran said.

Zillah crossed her arms and leaned against the dusty wall, casting her gaze about the halls.

When they did not continue, Noah stomped his foot and said, "Do we need to drag everything out of you?"

"Sorry," Elik said. "I am only struggling to understand. Several days after Japheth left, Nimrod announced that the tower's construction had finished. He spoke of representatives from the entire world gathering in a week to celebrate the beginning of a new era."

"The city's been reveling and looting ever since," Gom said, and spat before smearing it through the dirt with his sandal. "Godless drunks."

"The era of the Light Bringer," Noah said.

"What?" Elik said.

Noah stared at the young man. "He is mounting a rebellion against the Almighty."

"The tower is a monument to humanity," Elik said. "Nimrod rejects his grandfather Ham's religion. Always has. We have all seen him prove that he is a servant of the people."

Noah snorted. "Is that why your grandfather and master is missing? Is that why the followers of the Light Bringer run rampant, persecuting the faithful? Or perhaps that is why Aran's father is dead—murdered in Nimrod's very home?"

Gom ran his fingers around the rim of his mouth. "Your words disturb us."

"If what you say is true," Elik said, "why does everyone, including Japheth, believe that he is not a follower of the Light Bringer?"

Zillah rolled her eyes. "Because if the truth was ever known, he never would have maintained his position of power. What I don't understand is that it would have been about a month ago that Rin was murdered. He felt comfortable showing his hand before the tower was finished. Something must have changed. Something big. But what?" She shoved off from the wall and began to pace, kicking little pebbles.

Noah closed his eyes and tried to pray again. He reached for a sense of the Almighty's presence, which he had felt so frequently in his middle years. But there was nothing.

Almighty, where are you? Speak to me. Help me understand what is happening and how I should respond.

He rubbed his face as Zillah and Aran explained their journey thus far to Elik and Gom. Elik periodically gestured, and even exclaimed as they recounted the lion attack. Gom insisted on checking Aran's bandage to make certain it was clean, but Noah convinced him to wait until they were done talking first.

Noah tried to remember the last time he saw Japheth, but his memories had grown murky. Inevitably, he found himself reaching further, further. Until he stumbled toward the day Jade died, and Japheth and Shem visited him with their families to pay respects to her life and legacy.

For years, he had refused to think about the unspeakable—how Ham had defiled the day of Jade's funeral, then publicly declared his allegiance to the Light Bringer, and his family's apostasy from the Almighty.

It still was hard to believe that everything had become so broken. After all the Almighty had brought him through, to let it fall apart like this . . .

It felt like a dream gone wrong and overlong. He wished he could wake and find that all was well. That Japheth could be here, and Shem too. And that he could see Ham smile, instead of spit and ridicule.

But that was only wishful fantasy. For Noah had failed to stand in the gap for his idolatrous progeny. He had neglected interceding for them with prayer and leadership and . . .

His eyes fell, and his heart ached as the guilt washed over him. He had simply failed to be present. To listen to his children, watch them, know them. Jade had taken such good care of them that he had not felt they needed him so much as the men and women he was teaching the Old Way.

But they had all died, and his children had remained. And now what was there to show for it? An entire city filled with nothing but spiritual skeletons.

He remembered his dream, then, and nearly shouted at the others, who had now fallen silent, each mulling through the details in their own private ways. Aran chewing the ends of his fingernails. Zillah pacing relentlessly. Gom sitting cross-legged with his spear in the crook of his arm. And Elik standing, leaning on his weapon.

"That's it," he said. And only Zillah looked at him briefly, before looking away after he said nothing more.

The gray-skinned people were symbols of the spiritual death of the followers of the Light Bringer. And what was the reason for the sheer volume of idolatry?

Ham. It had and always would be Ham.

Wait. What if this entire journey was just God's way of trying to push him to go to Ham? To meet with him. To look into his eyes and see his own mistakes reflected.

That would explain why the Almighty had been so silent. If he had told him anything prematurely, Noah would have caught on and had time to turn back.

But now, what other choice did he have? Shem was powerless without Japheth at his side. And Japheth was either beyond their reach, or dead like Aran's father, Rin. But Ham—Ham was alive. And if not for all the bizarre events that had transpired since that night in his vineyard, Noah would never have considered meeting him face-to-face.

In fact, he had vowed not to.

Yet it felt that his journey to Babel had been for the sole reason of breaking that vow. He visited Shem, and now tried to visit Japheth. What remained but for him to visit Ham? His third and final son?

"I think," Noah said, and their conversation hushed as they turned to him. "That I will go to my son."

"Shem?" Aran said.

"No. Ham."

Elik cleared his throat. "I don't think that would be a good idea."

"I don't care what you think," Noah said.

Elik's cheeks reddened, and he bowed and took Noah's hand. "Please, Ham is the high priest of the Light Bringer. Even we fear him."

Noah was moved by the young man's care. "He is also my son."

"But what if—" Aran began, but Noah cut him off.

"What will be will be," he said.

"What do you stand to gain from going to him?" Aran said.

"I don't know." Noah tried to ignore the warmth that came to his face. "I've not known what would come of any of this. Yet I knew that I needed to walk the road that led here."

"But to place yourself in the hands of the enemy . . . ," Aran said.

"What else can I do?" Noah said, and none of them could answer him. "If going to my son means that I die, then I will die.

I am old—exceedingly old. But I cannot shake the sense that I have played a part in this. Something Shem said has made me consider that maybe . . . maybe Ham's idolatry is more than a rebellion against God." Tears burned his eyes. "Yes, I know in my spirit that this is what I am meant to do."

"You don't even know where he lives," Zillah said.

"But we do," Elik said.

Gom grunted his agreement.

"If you go, so do we," Aran said.

But Noah raised his open palm to ward them off. "No. I must face Ham alone."

They looked at him, confused.

"I will need someone to guide me to his home," Noah said, "but I must speak with Ham of private matters. I must face him alone."

"If that is what you demand, I am willing to guide you," Elik said.

"What if he never comes out?" Gom said.

"I will wait until Ham returns him," Elik said, and his face paled. "Alive or dead."

"Then it is settled," Noah said. "Let us go."

44

Aran

After Noah left with Elik, Gom pointed Aran to the male sleeping quarters before showing Zillah to the women's quarters. In so large a house as Japheth's, many of the male and female servants lived on location in separate dorms.

But Aran did not go up the staircase to rest. Instead, he returned to the courtyard and looked out across the city. From their vantage point, they could see many leagues. The brick homes rolled on toward the tower, which still held some scaffolding, though he could now see workers like little ants tearing the scaffolding apart. A cloud of dust from the reveling rose like a pillar into the sky. Catching the sun like a sheet of brown silk suspended in the air. And voices rose in great cheers as men and women threw their lives into the ebbing tide of pleasure.

He thought then of Father watching from the stars. Long ago, Aran heard Noah say that the faithful dead were caught up into paradise, where they could peer down through a window to look at us.

Are you proud of me? Is this what you wanted?

"I wish I could have known you," Aran spoke aloud as the sun dipped against the horizon. "I wish that drink would never have taken hold of you."

He screamed to the sky. "Will I never be rid of you?"

And he fell to his hands and knees, and then to his face in the dust.

No, he thought. *I will never be rid of you. Because I'm not supposed to be rid of you. You are my father. And beneath all of the hate, I always loved you.*

And now I can do nothing. Nothing but feel the pain, or give that pain back to the monsters who inflicted it on us.

Yes, I vow to repay the beasts responsible for taking you from Mother and me.

I will run Nimrod through. And anyone else named with him.

Then I will gather all the wine in the world and set it aflame.

Aran stood again and stared up into the sky, whispering, "Almighty, if it is all as Noah believes it to be, then forgive me for what I'm going to do. And bring me home to Father if I fail."

45

Noah

The journey to Ham's home felt long and slow. The sun set and darkness hugged Noah and Elik's huddled figures as they skirted the roads. Torches broke the shadows like arrows through the fabric, and the voices of revelers only increased. It appeared that by night Babel was even more drenched in hedonism than by day.

They passed a huddle of men and women writhing in the dark, and Elik turned him quickly down a side street.

"I am sorry," he said. "The city is not usually like this."

But why shouldn't it be? The whole city was controlled by a man who murdered with impunity and built a monument to humanity, or worse, to the Light Bringer—the eldest enemy of the Almighty.

If Noah remembered correctly, Ham had been the one to found the city of Babel shortly after declaring himself the mouthpiece of the Light Bringer. Was it really so hard to believe that Nimrod, who now led the city, had been Ham's pawn from the beginning?

Surprisingly, they did not see very many others, though the sounds of debauchery were ever around them. Most of the revelry was taking place in private courtyards and larger homes.

But then they traveled down a street that lay utterly silent.

"Where are we now?" Noah whispered, for fear of speaking overloud and drawing the attention of eyes in the dark.

"This is one of the poorest districts," Elik said. "Many who live here work on the tower's construction. Or did, before it was finished. The silence here is strange to me. I have never seen this area so dark before."

"Perhaps they seek amusement elsewhere, in the more affluent homes?" Noah said.

After a moment, Elik nodded. "Perhaps." But he seemed to hold back his true thoughts.

They traveled on, until they reached the edge of the city itself. Moon and starlight reflected the hard edges of a massive stone building. It was made of solid granite, though a small circular tower had been built beside it of brick, like the rest of Babel.

A great wall extended around the perimeter so that none could enter, and guards stood stationed at consistent intervals.

Elik stopped Noah while they stood still in the shadows. "Here is Ham's dwelling. None dare approach it for fear of retribution. But perhaps you may find audience where I never would."

"Wait here," Noah said. "And be patient. This may take time. But if I do not return by midday, you must promise to flee and tell Aran and Zillah."

Elik stared at him, considering his words.

"Please. Promise me."

Elik bowed. "Can you not first tell me what you stand to accomplish with this dangerous task?"

Noah looked again at the stone home, massive and imposing and covered in shadow. He thought of all the years that darkness had been tended inside, and Noah had done nothing. Thought of the thousands upon thousands of his own Godless progeny who were indulging themselves in sordid sin even at this very moment.

And where had he been? Had he attempted to guide them? Correct them?

No. He had puttered around his vineyard in slow comfort. Believing himself the most righteous man in the world.

His eyes burned and he rubbed them, and when he opened his mouth to speak, his saliva was thick and his voice wavered. "I am facing the truth I've been running from for a hundred years. I am obeying the will of the Almighty."

Elik nodded slowly. "Then . . . I promise to do as you wish."

And so Noah left Elik for the courtyard entrance of Ham's home.

46

Aran

Aran walked slowly up the creaking wooden steps to the second-floor dormitory for male servants in Japheth's home. The house was quiet, and no candles burned down the hall, which meant that Zillah was either asleep or sitting quietly in the dark. He hoped it was the former, because he could not risk her noticing him sneaking out of the home.

Gom had returned to the courtyard to guard the entrance. When he'd seen Aran speaking to himself in the dust, he'd said nothing. But Aran stood, silenced his breaths, and turned back inside for privacy.

Now, the searing flood of emotions had calmed, and in its place shivered a cold intensity of purpose. He entered his room and crossed to the small window with wooden shutters to keep out rain. He tested their make and found they swiveled open on a hinge.

He judged the width of the opening to be wide enough to fit his shoulders. And the way down was broken by the top of the wall. If he slid out the window, he would not drop far before landing on the wall. It would be a small task to descend the wall after that.

But how would he return through the window after descending?

He did not know, but that was a small detail. The important part was leaving Japheth's home unseen.

He refused to sit by while Noah went to speak with Ham. They were finally in the heart of Babel. Zillah may fear the followers of the Light Bringer, but what did Aran have left to lose? Since that day he left home as a youth, he had spent all his labor building up wealth, only to be forced to hand it over to his mother when her needs became too great for her to bear.

Tonight, he would do something for himself alone. He would find a way to understand the forces that slew his father. And he would exact retribution.

He squeezed through the opening of the window, but his shoulder brushed hard against the hinge of the wooden shutters. As he forced himself out, the hinge sliced open the skin of his shoulder and pulled away from the brick.

He landed hard atop the wall and sucked air through his teeth. He looked down, seeing fresh droplets of blood dripping freely from the wound, and tried to cover it with his tunic. He looked back up and saw the shutters hanging awkwardly by a single hinge at an angle.

Nothing to do about it now.

He shifted his gaze to the window of the female sleeping quarters, holding his breath and hoping Zillah wouldn't look out of it and see him.

A few moments later, he slowly let himself down the back of the wall so that his sandals wouldn't strike the ground too loudly.

As soon as he landed, he strode down the street. Passing from home to home, peering in through the wooden slats that separated the dark outside from the lights within.

He listened to several loud conversations. Most talked only of the simple pleasures of the world. Exchanging drink and food and more. Hedonists lost to the god of self, but not to the Light Bringer.

He moved on, moving slowly across the edge of a marketplace where many had gathered to dance. Several of the men stood atop a table and urged the carousers on. Others tipped an empty stall and set it aflame.

Past the market, Aran found a door leading to a staircase that ran underground. He stood outside the entrance for quite some time, listening, wondering for what purpose a building would be built into the ground in such a place. It was hard to tell if the low murmuring was coming from the homes around him, the marketplace, or from the door leading down.

Then the clouds passed and moonlight shone across a shape carved into the wood of the door. The engraved insignia of a star shining thick rays of light.

He inhaled sharply and ran his fingers across the shape.

What could such a symbol represent but an enclave of the Light Bringer?

He tried to settle the rush of excitement that sent a chill down his arms. He was about to enter when he remembered his arm was injured. He looked down and saw droplets of blood at his feet. He tried to smear it with his sandal, but realized he'd only spread it with each step.

He dipped and undid his sandals, then tore a piece of his tunic and tied it around the wound. He tossed his sandals beside the entrance, where no one would find them until the next day. Then he looked around to make certain no one was watching.

Finally, he opened the door as quietly as he could, the wood creaking as the weight shifted on the hinges. He winced and stopped moving the door, for it was wide enough now for him to slip through.

He angled sideways and shifted into the shadow before shutting the door behind him and plunging into the dark stairwell.

47

Zillah

Who was Zillah fooling? She could not keep the truth from Aran and Noah forever. And the farther she went with them, the more she grew to love and respect them.

She sat on the bed at the edge of the women's sleeping quarters and closed her eyes, but the starlight pierced her eyelids, and the cool breeze beat her bones.

She was exhausted from the effort to maintain the mask. Yet she could not sleep, for her stomach churned and threatened to reject anything she swallowed.

She pulled the woven covers over her chest and shivered. Clouds shifted over stars and moon, dimming the silver glow from the window. She closed her eyes and waited until everything quieted and grew distant. She thought she might sleep, but her body jerked, and she realized the covers were matted to her skin by sweat.

She tossed off the covers and stood at the window, breathing deep to calm her stomach. Her hands shook, and she felt at any moment she would jump from the ledge, screaming.

Why did she feel as though death hovered over her and would soon end her life?

She looked at the flesh of her hands. The strain of the past many days must be finally surfacing. She had endured these emotions before, when Hava hunted her mercilessly. But now there was much more. She faced enemies without, and enemies within. She could share her true self with no one and needed to live falsely toward all.

"What was I thinking?" she whispered. "That was why I lived homeless for so long. So that I wouldn't have to live in such duality, such endless anxiety."

But the longer she delayed telling them the truth, the more miserable she would become, for she would grow to care for them more with each passing day, and in the end, her love would make leaving that much more difficult.

She might as well just go tell Aran now and get it over with while Noah was gone, so that she wouldn't have to tell him, as well.

She took several deep breaths to calm herself. She could hardly bear the thought of harming Aran even deeper. She remembered his reaction after he spoke to his mother and heard of his father's death, and her heart broke for him.

"I am sorry," she said, "that I must harm you again."

She strengthened her resolve and forced each step out of the women's quarters, down the hall to where Aran was sleeping. When she reached the door, she knocked and whispered, "Aran? Are you awake?"

But there was no response. She wondered if she had just spoken too quietly.

But what if he was asleep and she woke him?

Groaning, she rubbed her face and thought, *What does it matter?*

She flung the door open and stepped in, then spoke his name loud and clear. "Aran."

No answer.

She crossed to the beds and touched them to see if he was asleep. "Aran?"

Nothing.

She crossed to the window and stared out at the night sky for several moments before noticing the shutters hung at an odd angle. She reached out to test them, but what she touched felt wet. She pulled her hand back and tried to look at the liquid in the moonlight.

"What?"

She brought her fingers to her nose and smelled.

Tingles ran down her scalp.

"Blood . . . ?"

She leaned out the window and looked down, seeing disturbed dust on the top of the wall, and droplets of dark liquid leading away. Footsteps sounded, and she glimpsed a dark shape fleeing.

She slapped the window ledge and whispered, "Aran, you fool!"

48

Noah

Ham's stone home loomed like a dark mountain before him amidst the many shadows in Babel at night. The building's hunched shoulders were blunt edges jutting into the sky.

Noah approached, feeling as though he would soon be crushed in its shadow. But he knew this was the Almighty's will. As if in confirmation, the guards standing at the gate bowed to the side and motioned him in as soon as he approached. Noah paused at the entrance, considering why they would invite him in if everything Elik said was true.

Then one of the guards said, "Come, Lord Noah."

They could strike him down where he stood. He watched their spear tips gleam in the moonlight. Yet they moved away, not toward him.

He nodded and entered, trying not to imagine the feel of their weapons pricking his skin as he passed. Wind rustled the manicured brush, and he nearly jumped as he turned a corner to see the dark shape of a young female servant with a shaved head. She spoke no word but showed him through a small, lush garden to a bench with a figure resting on it.

The servant bowed her forehead to the road. "He has come, my lord."

The figure on the bench looked up, and even in the dark, Noah recognized the gleam of his son's teeth.

"Ham," Noah said.

"So you haven't forgotten me," Ham said, and sighed.

Hearing his son's voice sent shivers down Noah's spine. Familiar, yet so remote. How strange that his own blood could have retreated so far from him, and now stood in opposition to him. "You knew I was coming," he said.

Ham spread his arms and frowned in mock surprise. "Did I not tell you I was a prophet?"

"Your servants saw me on the river."

The smile returned. "I suppose that's proof you're not a complete fool, yet."

"I know without proof that you are no prophet."

Ham tipped his head. "And yet look around you. See what I have built? See what I have accomplished in the years since you cursed my lineage?"

"I see a garden and a stone home."

Ham's face twitched, and his smile inverted. "The whole city, you fool. I built it. Me. And what have you done? Tended weeds and profiteered off people who are now starving."

"If the city and tower are yours, why doesn't everyone know it?" Noah said.

Ham stood and motioned to the tower in the distance. "For the same reason I have allowed the tower to mean something unique to each person. For some, it is a monument to humanity. To others, proof of our genius and progression as a race. To more, a site of profound worship. Letting others take the credit was a labor of brilliance. It is what draws so many to it." Ham turned back to his father and let his eyes roll up and down Noah's withered figure. "I am pulling the world underneath my wings. I am glad you've lived long enough to see your own mighty achievements eclipsed."

"You cast a long shadow, but only because you've walked so far from the light. You were always so prideful. Ungodly achievements always crumble."

"The tower is not dust yet." Ham snorted. "Tell me, prophet of the Almighty. Do you still hear God's voice?"

Noah blinked. He could not know that Noah had been

worried about the Almighty's silence for days. *A lucky guess. That is all, and no more.*

Ham laughed. "Don't look so surprised. His silence would be the only reason you would come here."

"The Almighty gave me dreams," Noah said.

"Is that all?" Ham shifted to the far side of the bench. "Sit with me. It has been long since last I saw you, dear father. I would enjoy a few moments with you in my garden."

The servant slid away, leaving them alone. He wondered what Ham was planning. The last they had talked, Noah had disowned his son, and Ham had disowned him. Still, he had come this far. If Ham wanted to kill him, he would have done so already.

He sat next to Ham and felt a rush of sorrow. His son was right. If not for the Almighty's silence, he never would have come.

Because even before disowning Ham, Noah had neglected him. And the pain of that truth, even on the day of Jade's burial, had so pierced him that he had forced it out of his mind. Convinced himself it was not true. That all Ham's sins were void of any connection to his own.

That was why the Almighty had brought him here tonight. He considered the possibility of the Almighty wanting him to reconcile with Ham. But now he knew that would not happen. No, the Almighty wanted to humble Noah. To push him to admit his culpability in it all.

Because the world had begun anew with Noah. And, just like Adam, the world was broken because *he* was broken. It was his fault as much as Ham's. As much as he'd wanted to deny it these many years, to refuse to admit it was nothing short of blasphemous.

Ham pointed at the flowers, many of whose petals lay closed in the dark. "I had the flowers arranged by color, so that they seem to be rays of light spreading out from the central mosaic." Ham pointed then to the road, and Noah noticed for the first time that glazed bricks had been laid in the pattern of a multicolored star. "Surely you can appreciate the beauty?"

Noah wiped his eyes and looked into Ham's face. He wanted

to see every nuance of his son's expression as he asked the next question. He needed to get it out of the way before their conversation moved any further. "Where is Japheth?"

Ham's expression went blank, and he rubbed his beard. "Have you not visited him? He's not far from here."

"Tell me the truth," Noah said.

Ham stood and dipped to smell the flowers. "Is that not answer enough?"

Noah stood. "Tell me, son."

They stared at each other. Noah's nails bit his palms.

"I'm not your son. Remember?"

Noah felt the words like lances.

"I don't know where he is," Ham said, and his voice no longer held that haughty air to it.

"How can I believe you?" Noah said.

For the first time, Ham's face expressed the disdain Noah remembered. "I have more to worry about than the location of my fool brother."

"Has he not helped you build this city?"

"Babel existed before he arrived. It will continue without him. In three days, we will publicly celebrate the tower's completion. I thought that was why you journeyed all this way. Now I see you are still lost in little things—blind to the workings of the world and the passing of eras."

"The passing of an age means less to those who have experienced their comings and goings," Noah said.

"You should come to the tower. Then, perhaps, you will witness the substance of my words and be sobered."

Noah nodded. "I will attend the inauguration. But I fear I will see only the descent of the human race."

Ham's eyes flashed like a falling star, and his voice, though calm, held a burning edge. "The human race is progressing."

Memories from long ago punctured Noah's awareness, and he felt disturbing resonance between Ham's words and those spoken by the God-King before the great deluge. "That is what the Others said before God drowned them."

"Perhaps they were right. And the Almighty was wrong."

Noah huffed. "You would test the Almighty?"

"He promised he would never destroy the world again."

So, Noah thought. *He thinks the Almighty a fool.* "You believe in your Light Bringer?" Noah said.

"I have given him my life."

"Then surely he will protect your city from the Almighty's retribution."

Ham laughed. "The world is the Light Bringer's. He has given me authority to rule it."

"And you are certain he will never leave you?"

Ham paused and swayed on his feet. He grunted. "As certain as you are that your God wouldn't abandon you."

"Would you be willing to concede to the victor?" Noah said.

Ham squinted and tipped his head as if he didn't understand the question.

"If you are so confident, you should have no problem yielding if the Almighty shows himself triumphant."

Ham nodded, crossed to Noah, and offered his hand. "If the Almighty proves his strength exceeds that of the Light Bringer, I will bow and wash his feet with my own tears."

"He will triumph." Noah took Ham's hand and felt the strength in his son's fingers. But all he could think of was the infinite value of his son's soul, which seemed now so hopelessly lost. He thought of the dark rites of the Light Bringer and hoped to the Almighty that his son's heart was not too far gone.

"I pray you keep your word," he whispered.

49

Aran

The bottom of the stairwell led to a long hall. At the end of the hall, dim light flickered under a second door. Aran stopped at the bottom and considered his options. Someone was in there, and if they came out, he would find no easy escape.

As his eyes adjusted, he noticed other doors lining the sides, but where could they lead? Surely to more dead-ends.

But he had come this far, and he was certain from the emblem on the door that this was an enclave of the followers of the Light Bringer.

He stepped forward, thankful he had given up his sandals. His breath was louder than his steps as he made his way quickly, like a bat flitting through a cave, and placed his ear to the door.

At first, he heard only the crackling of flames. A torch, maybe? Or perhaps an even larger source of burning.

He could smell smoke from under the door, and he could only imagine how un-breathable the air within had become.

Then a man coughed seemingly less than a hand's-breadth from the door, and Aran jumped. He nearly retreated to the stairs, but if the man was going to come back through, Aran would be in as much danger at the door as he would halfway back to the stairs.

Better to stay and surprise whoever it was.

Then the man spoke. "Raamah succeeded in gathering the builders?" said the first voice.

"Of course, Seba," said the second voice. "The fools had virtually incapacitated themselves celebrating. Father said it was as easy as hobbling sleeping swine."

"Dedan," the first voice, Seba, said. "I think you overly self-confident."

There was silence in response.

"Nephew," Seba said. "You have been given the responsibility of overseeing the guards on the Day of the Tower. You cannot act foolishly. If you do, we will lose control as soon as Nimrod spills Japheth's blood across Hava's womb. The few fools still faithful to the Old Way will put up resistance. And those who have no affiliation may be horrified. We must strike hard and fast to stupefy them."

"Yes, Seba," Dedan said. "We will strike ruthlessly."

"I will be watching you," Seba said. "I will see to it that you do. You know what will happen to you if you do not."

Dedan cleared his throat, and when he spoke next, his voice had raised in pitch. "I will not fail."

Aran's mind was spinning. Spilling Japheth's blood? Across a woman's womb? What horror was this?

A hand scraped the door, and Aran's breath caught in his chest. The door began to swing open, and Aran realized he was much too far from the stairwell to make it there in time.

He flattened himself against the wall and tried to slide behind the door so he would not be seen. But as the door swung wide, it smashed into Aran's foot. The man's eyes shot back to the corner where Aran stood, and he had only half a moment to react.

He smashed the door into the man, who yelled and fell back, head striking the wall. Aran raised his heel and smashed it into the side of the man's neck, dropping him with a dull thump.

Aran took off, but the other man saw him flying away and yelled, "Trespasser! Kill him!"

Additional doors slammed open and booted feet ran after him as he took the stairs four at a time.

He shot out the door at the top and collided with a figure on the other side. They fell to the ground, entangled, and the figure threw him off just as he realized it was Zillah wearing a hooded tunic with the hood pulled low.

"Aran?" Zillah said, holding her midsection and struggling for breath.

"They have Japheth! Hurry," Aran said, and jerked her upright and pulled her into a run as several men burst from the underground cellar, two of them wearing leather armor and armed for violence.

"No," Zillah said, "this way." She pointed to the right, down another alley. Aran turned and held fast, pulling her hard through the dusty dark.

She kept up well, but his muscles were beginning to burn, and the ice that had been injected through his veins when that man opened the door in the underground cellar was slowly freezing his blood and numbing his mind.

He could hardly think. Could hardly breathe. Hardly move. And yet he kept running, as if through wet sand, until Zillah began to nearly drag him.

Footsteps multiplied behind and around them.

She pointed to the right again, but he could hear several men that direction, while the road to the left looked empty.

He jerked her hard to the left, and she cried out, "What are you doing?"

As soon as he turned down the alley, he saw a wall the height of two men blocking their way and knew they were boxed in. He turned around, and Zillah tried to pull him back the way they'd come, but men stepped into view.

Three warriors, and one man dressed in a rich robe. It was hard to tell their expressions in the starlight, but as soon as the man in the robe spoke, he recognized the voice of Dedan, the commander of the guard for the so-called Day of the Tower.

"Kill them," he said.

Aran pulled Zillah behind him and readied himself to fight, but he was utterly exhausted, gasping for breath. And against three men armed with knives and a spear, the likelihood of him surviving was almost nonexistent.

"Wait!" Zillah said and tried to run out in front of him.

241

Aran grabbed her shoulder and whispered, "What are you doing?"

The three were closing in, spreading out to guard the way. There was no possibility that they could escape so many. Maybe Aran could have alone, but not with Zillah.

He wanted to curse her for following him. Rage at her for being such a fool.

But then she pulled back her hood and said, "Call them off, Dedan."

Dedan inhaled sharply, and the three soldiers paused, confused.

"Zillah?" Dedan said.

"You know him?" Aran said.

She ignored him. "You came the wrong direction. The fool ran the other way."

"No," Dedan said, eyes narrowing. "This is the one. He was spying on us, and he struck Seba down. But now I'm even more interested. Last I heard, Hava wanted you."

"What business is it of yours if Hava requested I make certain you do not fail?" Zillah said.

Dedan thought that over. Narrowed his eyes. "Your mother accepted you back?"

Mother? He couldn't mean . . .

What was going on? Aran looked between the two, trying to decipher what was pretense and what was truth.

"I answered Hava's summons," Zillah said. "Why else would I be back in Babel?"

"No," Aran whispered. That couldn't be right.

But Zillah raised her hand as if she'd strike him, and the fury in her eyes silenced him.

"She put a price on your head," Dedan said.

"Until she found a more fitting sacrifice. Hava is nothing if not frugal. Turn around if you want to live through the day."

Dedan scoffed. "I'll go. So long as you give him to me." He unsheathed a dagger hidden in his robes.

"The only way you touch him is by killing me," she said. "Hava assigned him to me herself."

Dedan held Zillah's gaze for several agonizing moments. "You're lying."

She tipped her head, smiled. "Shall I relay your opinion to Hava?"

He thought about that a moment. "I should kill you now."

"Go ahead," she said and took three steps toward him.

He held the blade forward, until the tip nearly touched her chest. Then he closed the remaining space and pressed the edge to the side of her neck.

She held his gaze, not even flinching as he dug a small, red line into her flesh.

The look on her face . . . she appeared in that moment like the queen of the world.

Dedan's gaze jumped from her left eye to her right. His mouth slowly curving into a frown. He growled, sheathed his weapon, and stepped back, flicking his wrists.

The three guards stepped back, and as Dedan turned away, they followed. He looked back one final time and said, "Don't think I can't find you again."

As soon as they were out of view, Aran said, "Zillah." The world spun and he bent forward and rested his hands on his knees. "Who are you?"

But even as the words leapt from his lips, he knew.

50

Nimrod

Blood. Nimrod felt it pulsing in the servant girl's veins. Smelled the fear on her breath as she dipped to pour more wine that failed to satiate his thirst. He grabbed her wrist to tell her to take it away, but her warmth bloomed across his fingers with a thump, thump, thump-thump-thump—as fear flittered across her emerald eyes, littered with little red lines that pulled him like an anchor toward a boat until he nearly opened his mouth to receive the glorious fluid . . .

He closed his eyes and shoved the girl away, breathing deep to purify his chest of the disturbing desires. She shuffled away, whimpering quietly.

He noticed Hava, then, standing in the doorway, watching him. Her voice purred as she said, "What has gotten into you?"

He stood and tipped the wine back until he finished it, then tossed the empty cup and sighed as he looked down at his skin, which he was certain had paled.

She crossed to him and traced the veins on his arms with her fingernail. "For once, I feel drawn to you. The look in your eyes sends shivers down my spine."

He tipped his head in hopes that the buzzing sensation deep in his skull would fall away. "I'm impatient for the coronation."

"Has Shem responded to your summons?"

"The last of my messengers returned this morning with word

that Shem refused," Nimrod said and crossed to the window to look out across the garden. "Shortly after, Dedan sent word that he found Zillah in Babel."

"Oh?"

The lack of surprise in Hava's voice was telling. But he had expected nothing less. He could almost never surprise her—even with his own thoughts. "When were you going to tell me she returned?"

She hung on his arm and rested her chin on his shoulder. "I didn't want to bother you while you had so much on your mind."

"I have delivered Japheth to you," he said. "Tell me what we stand to gain from her."

"She's been traveling with others."

"The young man with scars across his face?"

"Not him," Hava said.

"Who, then?"

Hava wagged her finger as if berating a disobedient toddler. "Guess."

His eyes flashed wide. "She can't be with Noah."

She chuckled. "Still you doubt me."

"No," Nimrod said. "I just don't understand how it happened. You believe they will come here?"

She kissed him on the lips, but he pulled away.

She seemed disappointed. "Why else would they have come to Babel?" Hava said.

Every thought fell into place. Of course, how had he not seen it earlier? Zillah planned to bring them another sacrifice to free herself from constantly being hunted to the ends of the earth.

Finally, he understood the manic intensity with which Hava had pressured and pursued their daughter. She had known that eventually, Zillah would realize the only way to free herself would be by returning to the beginning to settle her debt.

If what Hava said was true, he would be able to fulfill the wishes of the silver boy, of Hava, and his word to Ham in one sweeping move at the pinnacle of the tower.

He crossed to Hava and kissed her furiously.

51

Noah

As soon as Noah exited Ham's courtyard and took several steps down the road toward Japheth's home, Elik slipped out of the shadows and said, "Did something happen? Why are you out already?"

Noah kept walking. "Not until we're farther away."

He tried to keep his steps quiet, but so much weighed on him that he could barely stay upright. He felt himself bearing up under every year of his age, and the heaviness of each failure stored in them. More than ever, he wondered if God would abandon him. Not because of any unrighteousness in the Almighty, but because of Noah's own sins.

He had gone to Ham, just as he felt the Almighty wanted him to. But when he was there, he had still heard nothing—no voice, no sense, no direction. And Ham's arrogance had pulled from him bold claims that only the Almighty could back up.

What if the Almighty didn't appear?

Cold tendrils coiled in the base of Noah's belly as he walked, bent forward, wishing he had a cane to aid him. Elik's hand alighted on his shoulder, and he looked back. The young man's expression showed concern, but also hope for good news.

Noah shook his head. "I can speak no good word," he said.

Elik's eyes dipped, and his hand slid from Noah's shoulder.

"I made a wager I cannot keep, and now I must face Ham at the tower in three days."

In the silence that followed, Noah could practically hear Elik's questions.

"He doesn't know where Japheth is."

"You are certain?"

"No, but what can I do? I'm an old, defenseless fool."

"But you are the prophet of the Almighty! He will protect you."

Noah wished he could believe the young man's words. Wished he could feel confident he hadn't overstepped his authority. But this time was different from when he stood against the God-King before the world was drowned. At that time, he had stood in the confidence of the Voice of the Almighty. Now, he stood only in the confidence of his own voice.

No prophet did that.

He took a deep breath, then nodded. "Let us go back. I must pray."

Elik guided him slowly back to Japheth's home.

...

When they arrived, Gom was standing guard at the entrance. He bowed his head as they neared. "All is well?" Gom said.

"No," Elik said. "But we are alive."

"What happened?" Gom said.

"Are Aran and Zillah awake?" Noah tipped his head around them.

"I showed Zillah to her sleeping quarters," Gom said. "And Aran retreated to his room."

"Then perhaps I will rest as well," Noah said, and he entered the home and ascended the stairs to the male servants' sleeping quarters. He entered the dark room lit only by a shaft of moonlight thrown to the floor through the open window. A chill breeze rustled the bed coverings, and Noah crossed to the window and tried to close the wooden slats before realizing they were broken. He hadn't remembered them being that way.

He turned back and, as his eyes adjusted to the darkness, took stock of the beds.

Every last one was empty.

Strange. Had Aran gone to speak with Zillah? If so, perhaps he should find them first, while the events of the night were fresh in his mind. They would be expecting news and would appreciate knowing that Noah would be staying an additional three days.

He exited the male servant quarters and walked down the hall to the female servant quarters. The wooden planks creaked and bent under his weight and echoed in the silence. As he entered, he tested the beds, for the room was darker with the window slats shut.

As before, they were empty.

"Aran?" he called. "Zillah?"

Silence.

The home was not so large that they would not hear him.

He investigated the rest of the rooms and found them empty, as well. Finally, he returned to the courtyard, where Elik and Gom stood in quiet conversation. They hushed when they saw him.

"Aran and Zillah are gone," Noah said.

Gom's eyes narrowed. "That's impossible."

"I am no liar," Noah said.

Gom clutched his spear in both hands. "Show me."

52

Zillah

As soon as Dedan stepped from the shadows, Zillah knew her relationship with Aran was over.

Because her secrets weren't worth the price of his life. In the end, it was her love for him that had forced her to pierce him.

Still, part of her clung to hope that somehow he would understand. That she could explain why she'd kept her identity secret. That he would be gracious enough to forgive and accept her.

"Zillah," he said, and her entire body shuddered at the tone of his voice. "Who are you?"

She stood, but failed to muster the strength to face him. If he could see her heart at that moment, his soul would surely melt. But he couldn't. And if she tried to explain, he would only see a woman who had been false, who had manipulated and used him, who had kept from him who she was merely to preserve herself.

She closed her eyes and welcomed the burning. "We need to get back to Japheth's," she said. "Before anyone finds us, or Dedan changes his mind."

He stared at her, muscles flexing. "No," he said. "Answer me first."

She turned and faced him, and the sight of him crushed her. She spread her arms. "This is me, just like you wanted to see outside of Erech."

He shook his head. "Who are you, really?"

"Who do you think?" Her voice came out thin and sharp. "The forgotten daughter of the *great lord Nimrod*." She poured all the irony and bitter hatred into her words, letting her fury gnash at her father's name like a lion's fangs against fresh meat.

"I don't understand," he said.

"I knew the moment I heard your mother speak that everything between us was hopeless."

"You kept it from me this entire time." His voice dug into her like a plow into soil.

"What could I have done differently? 'Aran, I'm sorry my father murdered your father.'"

He raised his hand to strike her, but she stood her ground, and he held his fist back. After a deep breath, he closed his eyes and lowered his arm.

"You used me," Aran said.

She pushed away her regret and managed to glare up at him through blurry eyes. "I saved your life. You're welcome."

He stood there, silent. Then, finally, he turned and began to walk away.

What was she going to do? She would die here. She would die in this city alone.

A rush of flames shot down her throat and settled in the base of her belly. "No," she hissed.

Aran turned back and glared at her. "What?"

She willed her expression to chill until none of the rage she felt inside showed. "Dedan said you were spying on him and Seba. What did they say?"

He shook his head and scoffed. "You think I'm going to tell you now after everything?"

He was angry she'd used him. But he didn't realize he could yet use her. And she would gladly offer her life to prove herself true. Even if, in the end, Aran would never forgive her. "Together, we could kill them."

Aran's eyes widened, and he pressed his lips together. "What are you talking about?"

"My parents. Who else?"

"You're mad. You've lost your mind."

"I fled from Babel because my mother tried to sacrifice me to gain a son. She ruined my life, and I've been running from the men she hired to find me ever since."

His eyes widened, and his mouth hung open. He pointed at her. "That's why that man tried to kill us in Erech."

"And that's why I need to finish this. You said they have Japheth. Did they say that?"

He chewed the inside of his cheek and scanned their surroundings. He turned away, and Zillah's stomach dropped.

Was he so foolish? So embittered that he couldn't even see what she was offering him?

If he wouldn't listen, there was nothing she could do.

She could go to Hava alone. She could muster the strength to do what was necessary. She was no coward. She'd ran and hid, until that man found her in Accad and she finally realized that no matter how far she went, she would always be drawn back to the beginning. Over and over again, until everything that had been started was finished.

And I will end it, she thought. *I will end it all.*

She was so deep in her thoughts she didn't realize Aran still stood, hesitating.

Until his voice broke the silence. "Your father has him."

53

Noah

Noah followed Gom through every room in Japheth's home. Elik stayed back to guard the entrance while they searched.

"I told you," Noah said as they began their second round of searching.

"But how could they . . ." Gom scratched the back of his neck as he stood partway up the stairwell to the male servants' sleeping quarters.

Elik called to them from the courtyard, and Gom bounded down the stairs and out the doorway. Noah walked as fast as he could. As he exited, the clouds released their hold on the moon, and its light glowed across a familiar figure striding toward the home.

"Aran?" Noah said. "Where have you—"

Aran held up his hand and said, "I found the truth about who Zillah really is."

"Zillah—what?"

"She's Nimrod's daughter."

Noah's mind spun. He blinked and tipped his head to make certain he'd heard right. "She told you that? Where is she?"

At that moment, he noticed Zillah passing through the gate between Elik and Gom.

"Where have you been?" Noah said. "I thought you had been taken."

Zillah stopped several paces from Aran and Noah. "The city."

"Tell him," Aran said.

Though it could have been the moonlight, Zillah's face looked as white as the wings of a dove. "Aran jumped out the window in the male servant quarters to scout Babel for followers of the Light Bringer."

"What?" Noah said and looked at Aran. "Have you lost your mind?"

"That's not what I meant," Aran said to Zillah.

Zillah raised her brows and said, "You told me to tell him."

Aran said to Noah, "I wasn't going to do nothing while we waited."

"If not for me," Zillah said, "he would have gotten himself killed."

"If not for you, I would have escaped them," Aran said.

"They would have cornered and killed you had I not shown you the way to run. The only reason we were caught was because you took a wrong turn after I *told* you not to."

"Whatever. Even if that were true, we never would have discovered what we did, had I waited around."

"Enough," Noah said. "Aran said your father is Nimrod. Is that true?"

She straightened herself and said, "I told you before that I lived in Babel as a girl."

"And?" Noah said.

"Isn't it evident?"

Noah squeezed his temples. "If it were, I wouldn't need to ask."

Zillah cleared her throat, obviously trying to maintain composure while caught completely off guard—which he knew was the reason she'd attempted to shift blame onto Aran. "I would have told you, but after what happened to Rin . . ."

Noah's heart ached as he realized her periodic sullenness had not been reasonless after all. She had been caught in the middle of an impossible dilemma for days. "I see," he said.

"What happened at Ham's home?" Aran said.

"I asked him where Japheth was, but he said he did not know.

Still, it was no waste of time, for he revealed that in three days they will celebrate the construction of the tower, and representatives from the world will be gathered at the foot of the monument. I will meet him there."

"Why would you risk your life to do that?" Zillah said.

"To meet the end of everything that started me on this journey," Noah said. "Shem is barely maintaining his authority in Erech. Japheth is gone, and my most wayward son has invited me to witness the most significant event in the history of the new world. I don't need you to tell me what is too risky. I will do what I must."

"But that's what I wanted Zillah to tell you," Aran said. "We found out where Japheth is."

Noah's gaze snapped to Aran's. "What? Why didn't you say earlier?" A rush of quicksilver trickled down his veins, making his fingers twitch.

"We didn't know what you'd heard," Aran said.

"Where?" Noah said and grabbed both of their shoulders as hard as his old fingers could. "Where is he?"

"With Nimrod," Aran said.

"Nimrod?" Noah's voice came as soft as a breath. "Nimrod has . . . my son?" He sank to his knees and closed his eyes with outstretched hands in supplication. "Almighty," he said. "Have mercy. Keep Japheth alive."

"We can do more than pray," Zillah said.

Noah opened his eyes. His mouth hung open. He wasn't certain how many more revelations he could endure.

"I can help you rescue him," Zillah said.

Noah ran his tongue over his chapped lips and shook his head. Was this the Almighty subtly speaking to him? "How?"

"It will be much more dangerous than even meeting your son at the tower."

"I am ready to part with my life," Noah said. "I've lived long enough that to risk what little is left on my son is nothing."

Zillah stared at him. "All three of us might die."

"If I don't come," Aran said, "it won't work."

Noah paused, looking between the two. Aran had seemed angry with Zillah when he first explained what he'd found out about her. Now, it seemed that they had already come to some sort of conclusion about this plan to rescue Japheth. "You both are willing to help me?"

"Of course," Aran said. "I have come this far with you."

"And I must settle an old debt," Zillah said.

"But you won't like the plan," Aran said.

Noah groaned and pulled at his beard. "Out with it already! Tell it to me plainly and quickly. I have no time for games."

Zillah nodded. "If you insist it be this way. Then . . . I must bind your wrists and offer you as a sacrifice to my parents."

Noah rubbed his ears to make certain he was hearing correctly. "What?"

"Give me some time," Zillah said, "and I will explain."

Gom stepped near. "Perhaps you should continue inside." And he raised his brow and pointed.

"Yes," Noah said. "Let us go inside."

...

They lit small candles in the female sleeping quarters, for Aran had broken the shutters in the other room, then set the leaning wax towers in the center of the room as they sat cross-legged in a circle.

"To explain what we must do," Zillah said, "I must tell you a bit of history."

Noah picked at the dirt beneath his fingernails and watched the orange glow dance across Zillah's dark forehead and cheeks. "So be it. Only speak quickly."

Zillah licked her chapped lips and began. "I lived with my parents for many years before they turned on me. I was never close with my mother, for she is ruthless and cruel. Even worse than my father, who at times showed me affection."

"Hard to believe, after what I know of him," Noah said.

Zillah stared at him a moment. Noah wondered if he'd offended her. Finally, she said, "Even the worst of men can hold a shard of good in them. But Hava's eyes hold nothing but darkness. From what I've heard, she has been that way since childhood. For me, as a child, she was the incarnation of evil itself."

She cleared her throat and closed her eyes as if trying to conjure distant memories. Aran watched her, silent. Jaw flexed. Scars bending under the weight of his expression.

"After years of trying for children," Zillah said, and nervously glanced for a moment at Aran, "Hava became pregnant with me. A disappointment, for they hoped for a son to carry on their lineage. Still, my father held affection for me, and convinced Hava to keep me. They trained me in their ways and kept me secret from the rest of the city, for they could not admit they'd not had a son. I never saw anyone but those in my parents' inner circle. I was never allowed out. At least one servant watched me at all times except at night, when I was locked in my room."

"You were a prisoner in your own home," Noah said.

"I didn't know any better. I knew only the fear of Hava and, if I disobeyed, Father. Then one day, Father began to avoid me. When I spoke to him, he yelled and struck me. I remember crying in my room, confused and afraid that he would reject me forever. Then Hava entered and began to comfort me. I was frightened, at first, but so distraught that I gave in. She told me not to cry, then took my hand in hers and broke my finger."

Zillah held up her left index finger and showed how it had healed crooked. Noah grimaced, but Aran nodded.

"She wanted to teach me to be calloused, like her. To never cry or embrace weakness. Instead, I wept, and she grew angry with me. But that experience did change me. I began to lay awake at night, pondering the meaning of the quiet words I heard Father and Hava exchange beyond the walls. I couldn't understand what they said, but tried to discern it from the lilt of their voices and the cadence of their speech. I began memorizing the movement patterns of the guards who watched me, and snuck past them through the rest of the house. I listened to my parents' quiet talks and heard plans for their future. I was not surprised to find that most of the ambitions remained Hava's, not Nimrod's. But Father had goals of his own. And I grew to understand those in time, as well."

"Why did he stay with such a woman?" Noah said.

"For a long time, I wondered the same. But the answer lies in their allegiance to the Light Bringer. Long ago, Ham spoke a prophecy. Nimrod and Hava were brother and sister, but the prophecy demanded they marry. It claimed their marriage would be a symbol of the future unification of the world. Once they successfully achieved an integrated world, they would wipe the memory of the Almighty from the earth."

"How?" Noah said.

"How else?" Zillah said. "By slaughtering anyone who followed him."

"Wait, how does that——," Aran began, but Zillah held up her hand.

"Patience. I am going as fast as I can."

Aran let out a grunt and swiped at the wrinkles in his tunic. Noah motioned for her to continue.

"The prophecy claimed that if they separated, the world would never be unified. Nimrod and Hava believed it. But since that day in my room when I wept at my broken finger, Hava has hoped to replace me with a son to inherit the throne. She believes herself barren because of me, for the pregnancy and birth were difficult for her, and she blames me for not being a son. After she realized I would never be like her, she planned to sacrifice me to the Light Bringer to gain a son. To her, human sacrifice is nothing. She believes in dark magic, and that she can manipulate the spirits. But for such a bold request as a son, the sacrifice must be of exceeding value. And so she chose me, not because she finds me valuable, but because I am their only child ——daughter or no."

"Ah," Noah said and felt a ripple of cold shivers darken his thoughts. "I begin to see your intent. You seek to offer me as a sacrifice of exceeding worth, and so win the favor of your parents."

"Yes," Zillah said. "But before they strike, we will have disappeared in the night with Japheth. After all I know of Hava, I think that she will never guess that I would have the boldness to trick her like this. If I guess wrongly, I will be the first to die. Perhaps, if Aran is lucky, he could find a way to escape. But not for long. They believe the tower is the shifting point. The monument that will gather the world and fulfill the prophecy, releasing the followers of the Light Bringer to slaughter a third of the known world."

Noah nodded as he thought of Shem in Erech and the victims of persecution in Accad. Of the suicidal adherent of the Light Bringer who spilled his own blood in Noah's vineyard.

What could ever stop such brutality? Such violent hatred?

He did not know what would become of his promise to Ham, but he needed to attempt to save Japheth. He could not simply stand by as Nimrod and Hava sacrificed Japheth at the tower's coronation.

Would the Almighty bless this endeavor?

He closed his eyes and prayed silently. *Lord, if you wish for me to refrain from this dangerous task, tell me now. Otherwise, I will follow what seems best, lest I forever commit the sin of inaction.*

He waited.

Again, as before, there was nothing.

"How will it work?"

"After I take you there, Aran will take a different route. They will take you to the dungeon, the only place they would feel safe keeping Japheth, and Aran will take the secret entrance I describe to him, and free you both."

"How will you know when we have been set free?"

"I won't," Zillah said. "But I will slip away regardless that night."

"What if you can't?" Noah said. "Or what if Aran fails to free us?"

"Then we will die," Zillah said.

Noah thought this over for several moments. Tumbling the thoughts every which way to see how any of them could mitigate danger. "I will pray tonight and consider all that you've told me. But unless something changes, in the morning you will take me to your father's house and present me as a sacrifice."

He blew out his candle, leaving the others burning, and stood to retire to what had been Japheth's personal sleeping chamber.

54

Aran

Aran stayed with Zillah, staring at the rhythmic dance of the orange tongues of flame atop the candlewicks. Noah's feet made the wood groan as he made his way, until the sound was lost beneath the wind and the ring of Aran's ears.

"Zillah," Aran said. "You lied to Noah. You're not doing this to save Japheth. You're doing it to kill Hava."

For several long moments, neither Aran nor Zillah spoke. Zillah laced her fingers together and breathed soft and slow. Aran frowned and tried not to think of how the candlelight played across the valley of scars on his face.

"How did you get those?" Zillah said.

He traced his index finger across one scar running in line with his cheekbone. "When I was a boy, my father woke me early in the morning. He always drank at night and slept until the sun was high. But that morning, I didn't smell it on his breath. Didn't see it in his eyes. Now that I'm older, I think I know what I saw in his expression. Regret, and the pain of a man who couldn't cope with his own brokenness."

"Aran," Zillah said, and started to reach out to him, but must have thought better of it.

"I thought the beating I received at the market was bad. Then we came home, and he drank himself mad and beat me until everything was gone but my mother's screams. I awoke to her weeping as I lay in a pool of blood." Fresh tears flowed across his scars and dripped to the wood floor beneath the candles. One caught a flame and hissed. "Father thought he'd killed me. So he dragged me into the weeds and told mother where I was." Aran looked up.

"I'm sorry, Aran," Zillah said. Tears pooled in her eyes.

"I loved him," Aran said. "That's why I hated him—because he never loved me back. Not in a way I could take hold of. Do you love your father?"

Zillah's face paled. She swallowed hard and examined her hands. Traced the tip of her index around the outline of each fingernail.

"Can I trust you to give him to me?" Even as he spoke the words, he felt the emotions erupt in his chest like a black abyss. The rabid hatred that had pursued him like a shadow every step he'd taken since leaving the vineyard had only loomed larger as he returned to his home and neared Babel. Now, he wondered if it would swallow his entire world. If he would lose himself to fury and wake only after he'd bathed himself in Nimrod's blood.

It frightened him. The slowly slipping sense of control.

Zillah looked up, and her eyes reflected the candlelight like perfect glass orbs. "So long as you give me Hava."

"I will," Aran said.

"No interfering," she said. "Even if Hava kills me."

He nodded. Then reached out to hold her hand.

She slipped her fingers into his. They were cold and wet. He wondered if his felt the same. They shook hands, but both held on.

"If you are false, I will kill you," Aran said.

The muscles in her neck tensed, and emotion rose in her eyes. Her voice came as a strangled whisper as she pulled her hand away. "You never will forgive me, will you?"

"You expect me to trust so easily?" Aran said. "But I hope you are true."

She stared a moment. "I want both," she said. "To kill Hava and to save Japheth." Then she blew out her candle, leaving only Aran's burning.

He licked his fingers and snuffed the last candle before

standing and walking slowly down the hall to his own room. He needed rest if they were going to succeed in this.

Though he knew as he crept into one of the empty beds that he would never fall asleep. Because the truth was, he could imagine no way that he could both kill Nimrod and save Japheth. In the end, he would have to choose between vengeance and obedience.

Either way, Noah might die. And that brought a pit of despair to Aran's gut. Even if fate smiled on him, and he was given the opportunity to take Nimrod's life . . .

Would the Almighty and his prophet ever forgive him?

55

Noah

Noah laid on Japheth's bed for half the night. Praying silently for wisdom. For insight. Inevitably, as he prayed, his mind drifted to all that had happened. He cycled through the events, the setbacks, the dangers, and found himself time and again returning to the dreams the Almighty had given. He held onto them as his greatest treasure—his only proof that the Almighty hadn't abandoned him.

He felt more certain than ever that Shem's dream pointed to the three of them. Noah, Aran, and Zillah, facing pale light. Could the black holes in their chests be evidence of their broken-ness? Both Aran and Zillah had been abused by shattered families. It made sense, for they had been wounded in similar ways. But what would be the point of including that in the dream?

Did Zillah have another reason to go back to her parents? And what of Aran? His emotions over his father remained tangled. Even as they'd sat in those candlelit sleeping quarters, Noah thought he'd seen a dark hunger in his scarred face. Noah had experienced the darkest side of anger in his younger years and thought he recognized that look as a craving for revenge.

Would Aran and Zillah betray him in this final hour?

He ran his fingers through his beard and wondered if one of the reasons Noah had been pushed on this journey was to support and direct Aran and Zillah down a righteous path.

Had Noah missed another opportunity to speak into their lives tonight?

He sighed, frustrated that he always felt ill equipped as a leader. He wondered if he should speak to Aran before they left in the morning. If he should remind him that violence could never free anyone. That killing would only wound him worse.

He had worried for so long that the Almighty had abandoned him. But in truth, if the Almighty had left him, he'd done so righteously. Noah's only response to that should be repentance.

If Noah were cursed to spend eternity in separation from the Almighty, at least he could die serving the Almighty's ends. Yes, he would spend himself for the glory of the God who had given him life and love and deliverance and joy.

Even if judgment fell about his neck like a millstone.

As he lay there, his eyes slowly closed. The room was so dark that he didn't realize he'd faded until dreams danced on the edge of his awareness.

Then, suddenly, he thought he heard a whisper so close it was as though someone had pressed their lips to his ear. *"Do not fear, I am with you."*

Noah shot up in bed, breaths coming fast and hard, and tossed away the covers. He swung his feet to the floor and stood, lethargic, unsteady. Light peered through the slats over the window. He crossed and opened the shutters to the warm glow of sunrise.

Had he slept through the night?

And what of that voice? *"I am with you,"* it had said.

Or had he dreamed it?

Footsteps sounded and he turned to see Zillah in his doorway.

"It is time," she said.

He nodded. "Just a moment."

He angled past her and made his way to the male servant quarters. Zillah followed and said, "Aran is gone."

But Noah did not listen. The rhythm in his chest sounded in his ears, darkening his sight as he reached the room and found Aran's bed coverings tossed across the floor.

"He left before sunrise with a small bag of money," Zillah said. "He wanted to prepare better."

Noah nodded absently. "Right."

"We should get moving," she said. "If we don't, he might arrive before us and risk disaster. Here, hold your hands behind your back so I might bind you."

Noah did as he was told, wanting to strike himself for failing to speak to Aran before falling asleep.

"Do not fear, I am with you."

Was he really? Or were the words just another extension of his imagination? His hopes and fears manifested in physical sensations by a sleeping mind?

"Do not fear, I am with you."

Zillah coiled a rope around his wrists and cinched it tighter than he thought necessary. Compared to the pain of the rough fibers pinching his skin, the voice now felt distant and false. He peered at her over his shoulder. As much as he knew this wild, haphazard plan their only choice, he questioned the wisdom of putting his life into such a wounded woman's hands.

"I can show no mercy," Zillah said. "Anything less and they will know."

He suppressed a shiver at the cold intensity in her face, which hid a well of dark violence ready to spill over. Now more than ever, he doubted the veracity of the voice.

"I have already spoken to Gom and Elik," she said. "They have left for the outskirts of Babel—for if we fail, their lives will be in danger."

Iron sang as it slid from a sheath, and Noah stiffened as the tip of a knife pricked his lower back. She spoke quietly into his left ear, "Down the stairs."

He began walking, and she held his wrist with her free hand while keeping the weapon pressed to his skin. He resisted the urge to question her. He knew she would need to make certain anyone who saw them exiting Japheth's home would not question her intentions. Because any questions could be fatal for them both, and it was certainly possible that enemies could be watching.

Still, to be rendered helpless in the hands of a woman who

had already proved herself a thief and a liar made the hair rise across his arms.

Nimrod's daughter. Hava's daughter. A dangerous woman.

"Do not fear, I am with you."

Even if it had been no more than imagination, what could he do to change his situation? He had chosen his course, and now must see it through.

So he obeyed every command Zillah gave, until Nimrod's home grew clear in the dust cloud that hung over Babel like a haze.

56

Zillah

As soon as her childhood home came into view, her legs nearly
gave out beneath her, and she pressed the tip of the knife a bit
too deep into Noah's back, drawing a gasp.

She pulled the knife back, but held onto his bound wrists,
nails digging into the rope fibers.

They walked slowly—so slowly—up the rest of the incline,
and at the top of the hill, the gate leading to Nimrod's home
stood closed, made of wide wooden planks studded with bronze
nails. "Open," she said. "I bring tribute for Hava."

For a long moment, they waited. Zillah watched the walls for
any arrows sent flying to slay her. But then the doors opened
slowly, and instead of warriors or servants, Hava walked out to
meet them with a smile on her dark face that sent shivers down
Zillah's body.

She pressed the knife into Noah's back again and yelled,
"Stop, or I'll kill him!"

Noah gasped and said, "Please!"

Hava stopped. Eyes widening, smile faltering only for a
moment. She spread her hands. "Come, now. I know why you
have returned."

"And what do you say?" Zillah said. Despite herself, sweat
beaded across her forehead and slid down her neck. A lock of
hair fell over her eyes, but she blew it away.

"Grudges are for fools. If your gift is true, you bring honor to us both."

"It is true," Zillah said and wondered what Noah thought in that moment. He tipped his head and glanced back, fear written across his face in bold letters.

Yes, she thought. *You should be afraid. Because if you aren't, you're a fool, and we're both dead already, because Hava will notice and perceive everything I plan to do to her.*

"I knew this day would come and even told you that one day you would return," Hava said. "Do you not remember?"

"Indeed, I do."

Hava turned and headed inside, leaving the gate open.

"Go," Zillah whispered. For she knew Hava's twisted mind. She never killed needlessly. Hers was a cold, calculating violence. And right now, unless Zillah was horribly mistaken, Hava had no reason to kill her. The woman didn't fear her. Zillah could hardly imagine anything Hava would fear. Instead, she was driven by cunning, which meant she already had a plan for how she would benefit from Zillah's life, and so Zillah was wary as Noah shuffled forward.

His breaths came shallow and quick, and for the first time, Zillah was struck by how old and frail he really was. His demeanor had always been one of confidence; she never realized how easily she could have overpowered him. It was a strange sensation, to be in complete control of another person's body. She was not accustomed to it, and she wondered if the twinge of pleasure she felt was the same that fueled Hava's lust for control. Zillah grit her teeth and shook her head. Disgusted with herself for even thinking about it.

Only after they entered the gate did Zillah see the servants manning the gate. They did not look her in the eyes, and after Zillah and Noah cleared the entrance, the servants closed the gate behind them.

No turning back now.

57

Aran

Aran stared into the culvert running with defiled water and felt the hard edges of the knife he'd purchased and tied to the inside of his tunic. It was madness to listen to Zillah and enter the shadowed tunnel. He would likely not live out the day. But if he did . . .

If he made it to Nimrod . . .

He unsheathed the dagger and flipped it in his hand. Testing the weight and balance of the blade that reached the length of his forearm. He thrust it forward, into open space, imagining Nimrod's chest the recipient of its tip.

He would kill the man who had destroyed his family and overturned his quiet life. Or die trying.

But no matter what he *wanted* to do, his decision had been made the moment he gave Zillah his assent. He could not abandon Noah, because he was surely being forced into Nimrod's courtyard at this very moment.

Not after all the man had done for him.

But if Noah knew what he would do to Nimrod if given the chance. If he knew the real reason Aran had looked past Zillah's betrayal to do this . . .

Aran was thankful he'd left before sunrise.

"Well," he whispered. "Time to move."

He sunk the knife in its sheath, checked his pocket for the

small, thin nails he'd purchased to adjust locks as Zillah had told him to do, and hoped they were the right size and length to do the job.

Everything depended on those items, and the timing of everyone's movements, though he had no way of keeping track.

He closed his eyes, said a short prayer to the Almighty for guidance, and plunged into the dark.

58

Zillah

Zillah pushed Noah up the stairs through the atrium to the inner garden, which had expanded since she'd seen it last. She glanced at the tasseled grasses and decorative flowers and wondered how so much beauty could exist under the domination of such evil.

But she never let Hava out of sight. After reaching the center of the garden, Hava turned and faced them with that smile fixed like mortar between bricks. A perverse, emotionless expression.

"So," Hava said. "Our wayward daughter has finally returned."

"I've come to pay my debt," Zillah said. But even as the words left her lips, she felt like a fool running into the mouth of a hungry tiger. The way Hava looked at her. The way her teeth glinted in the morning light.

This truly was a desperate, foolhardy attempt.

Still, she was mortally tired, for a lonely life spent fleeing from constant danger was hardly any life at all. If Hava tried to kill her, at least Zillah would die with a knife in her hand.

But Hava would not kill her. Not yet, at least. She would search for a way to twist both Zillah and Noah to her own dark purposes instead.

This time, however, Zillah had a dark purpose of her own.

"You fear me," Hava said.

"I distrust you," Zillah said.

"What do you want, then? You brought Noah. Do you expect to hold him hostage forever?"

Now they came to what Zillah had kept from both Noah and Aran. She kept her gaze on Hava as she said, "I demand to be the one to sacrifice Noah at the tower." She tried to ignore the sudden stiffening in Noah's body.

"Oh?" Hava said and the upward lilt in her voice showed her fascination clear enough. "Why?"

"I have my own requests to make to the Light Bringer. As your daughter, and the only heir to the throne, I deserve to have my request honored." She hoped Noah would forgive her, for there was no other way. She must convince Hava if she hoped to have the chance to both save Japheth and slay Hava.

Hava examined her long. Eyes flittering over her features like a snake's tongue over the air. Finally, she nodded. "Not for long."

Zillah tilted her head. "What?"

"Nimrod has secured for me a more fitting sacrifice than you, so I have no reason to kill you anymore."

"Japheth," Noah whispered.

Zillah jabbed the knife into him hard enough to draw blood.

"What was that?" Hava said.

"You hold no anger toward me?" she said, and prayed her mother hadn't heard Noah.

The subtle smirk on her face spoke otherwise.

Hava examined Noah like a hawk watches a mouse. "Grudges are for fools. Besides, I want you to witness the trans-formation."

"The transformation?"

"After Nimrod spills the blood of Japheth onto my womb, the Light Bringer will give me a son."

Noah jerked in Zillah's hands but managed to keep his expression stoic.

"What do you think of that?" Hava said.

Noah said nothing.

"Answer her," Zillah said.

"The Almighty will judge you," Noah said.

Hava nodded slowly. "And here I thought you'd be more interesting than your son."

Zillah wondered how many would die for Hava's desires. Zillah had spent enough time in the presence of the Light Bringer's inner circle to know that Hava always pushed the darkest agendas. Not publicly. Not in a way that brought attention to her. But trace every initiative back to its source and you would inevitably find her mark.

"Well," Hava said. "My servants will take Noah upstairs while you and I dine. Surely you are hungry?"

"No," Zillah said. Upstairs? Her heart pounded. Why would they take him upstairs? The dungeon was underground, beneath the courtyard.

Four servants arrived, two carrying broadswords.

"Well, you will dine with me anyway. Take the prisoner to my personal bedchamber."

The servants nodded and took Noah from Zillah's possession. Noah looked back at Zillah, and her heart ached at the questions she saw burning in his eyes.

Just trust me. I will come for you.

But she couldn't say that. She couldn't say anything.

Hava motioned her along, and she tried to cleanse herself of remorse and follow, or risk letting everything collapse.

If I fail, Japheth will die. Noah will die. Aran will die. Countless victims gathered across Babel will die, and the legions commanded by the adherents of the Light Bringer will sweep the earth and cleanse the followers of the Old Way with sword and bow.

But I will not fail. I will lie and steal and cheat until I cut off the head of the dragon.

Even if it kills me.

59

Noah

Noah no longer knew what to hope for as the guards led him up the stairs and down a richly hewn marble hall to a solid cedar door locked thrice from the outside.

Zillah had said he would be taken below ground, to a dungeon. Had she been mistaken? Or had she betrayed him as he'd feared?

He closed his eyes and tried to steady his breathing as the guards worked the locks.

Two locks unlatched, but the third was giving them trouble. With closed eyes, Noah's ears clung to the drone of a female voice—low and smooth—exchanging words with Zillah. They were moving laterally beneath him.

"There," one of the guards said, and the third lock fell. The door swung open to a pitch-black cavern, and they shoved him inside.

His arms were still tied behind him, so he stumbled and bashed his knees, falling forward and twisting at the last moment to avoid slamming his nose into the smooth stone floor. The door slammed shut, and the only light came through the crack below the door—not quite wide enough to slip his fingers through.

The locks were returned to their rightful position, and Noah noted how loud they were. In the dead of night, even if the door went unattended, Zillah could never free him without anyone else hearing.

A moan twisted his ear, followed by the subtle hiss of cloth across stone at the far end of the room.

"Who is there?" Noah said.

A man cleared his throat, and Noah could hear a rattle in his chest. Noah's eyes were not yet adjusted to the dark to be able to see the figure.

"Tell me your name," Noah said.

"Japheth," the man said.

That couldn't be. Because the voice sounded as weak as a child's. It had none of Japheth's joyful resonance. Instead, it sounded like a desert wind pushed through brittle branches.

"Son?" Noah said.

There was a pause. Another shift of cloth against stone.

"Is that you?" Noah struggled to his feet and tentatively shuffled his feet forward, so as not to step on him.

Suddenly his toes met a cold puddle, and he gasped and wiped away the wetness on the stone.

"Don't come near," the voice said, and now Noah could hear the distant resemblance to his son. "They harmed me."

Tears came to his eyes. "Son, what did they do to you?"

"Father? Is that really you?"

"Yes," Noah said, and he struggled to push away a wave of sobs that pulled at his chest. "I came for you."

"No," Japheth said. "I am dreaming. My father would not be so foolish as to imprison himself to find me."

Noah twisted and looked back at the door again, thinking of all Zillah had said. She'd sounded so convincing. "Maybe I am foolish. Maybe I am like you and I trust too easily. But we've not reached our end yet."

It seemed Japheth was trying to stand, but he cried out in pain and chains rattled as he fell.

Noah's breath came faster, and he shifted through the puddles and found his son crumpled on the ground. "My hands are tied with rope," Noah said. "You are bound with iron to the wall?"

"Yes," he said.

"How long have you been here?"

"I don't know," Japheth said. "In the endless darkness I lost track."

"I am sorry I came so late."

"Is Shem alive?"

"So far as I know," Noah said. "He was the one who told me you may be in trouble. He's been worried and sent servants to check on you."

"He didn't come to Babel, did he?"

"No. He stayed in Erech to stymie the madness," Noah said.

"Good." Japheth's sigh fell like sand from a cliff. "But why are you here?"

"Hush," Noah said and lowered his voice to a bare whisper. "We are alone?"

"Of course," Japheth whispered.

"Then I will risk telling you. I came to deliver you."

Japheth shifted until he sat upright against the wall. "Every word you speak steals the hope from my veins."

"We have not failed," Noah said. "Not yet, I don't think. I surrendered myself as a sacrifice to find you. But we were supposed to be in the dungeon, not this upper room."

"How confident are you that we will survive this?"

"We will survive if that is what the Almighty wills." A long pause passed between them. Wind beat the home and distant voices droned on beneath them. Noah shifted his shoulder to rest against the wall Japheth leaned on.

"As much as I wish you would not have come . . . ," Japheth said, and he sniffed away tears. Noah shifted closer, and Japheth's head fell on Noah's chest. Noah rested his cheek on top of Japheth's head and remembered holding his son close so many years ago, when he was just a boy.

For the first time since Jade died, Noah felt happy. He felt he belonged. That he was exactly where he was meant to be.

60

Aran

Aran tried not to think about how his feet were splashing through human dung and urine washed down the polished marble slope with buckets of water. Zillah had explained that in the dungeon, they'd built a grate down which they poured human and animal waste. They sometimes stored many beasts for sacrifices and needed a way to easily clean the cells without having to walk the stairs and exit the dungeon every bucketful.

At the end of the tunnel Aran crawled through sat a narrow grate built of brick and mortar. Zillah said the last time she walked the dungeon, much of the mortar had deteriorated from the acidity of what was thrown down it. That was why, besides a knife, Aran had brought a chisel and hammer.

He pulled the tools out as light grew through little slats in a stone wall at the end of the tunnel, barely high enough for him to stand crouched.

Just as he reached the slats, footsteps sounded, and a servant came near with a bucket and slung it through the grate, splattering his legs. Aran pressed himself to the tunnel wall and held his breath.

The man poured a bucket of water to help the sludge move down the chute, and sweat broke from Aran's skin. The smell of fresh refuse threatened to choke a cough from him. He carefully pulled his tunic over his nose and breathed shallow.

Aran listened to his clacking footsteps as the servant ascended the steps and opened the door leading out.

He waited for as long as he dared after the servant left before grabbing hold of the grate and peering to see if he could spot any other guards or servants.

He knew as soon as he broke the grate, he would risk alerting anyone who passed. Zillah said that sometimes servants crossed the dungeon frequently—especially in busy times. And today would certainly be busy.

He had no idea if Zillah and Noah had already made it inside the home. He would need to wait as long as possible before clambering through and trying to free him. But he could hardly hold himself back. Low voices bounced off the walls of the cavern, and he could hear animals bleating as if on the other side of a thick door.

It sounded as though someone were in the sacrificial chamber.

61

Nimrod

Nimrod stood over the star-shaped altar in his underground dungeon and felt the world pulse. The dark desires that had been growing within him since he first encountered the silver boy had reached a shadow pitch. Sweat encased his entire body, and he shook like a crown of leaves in a storm.

"More," he commanded the two servants who were with him. They held back several live goats while three lay dead on the altar already. "It lusts for more," Nimrod said.

He watched as the servants brought the beasts and slayed them on the altar. The swirling red joined the cries of the goats into a river of need that washed his vision and blocked out his hearing.

He was hardly even aware of his body falling forward onto the altar. Neither did he realize that he was drinking the liquid like wine, until the desire waned, and in its wake came a buzzing satisfaction.

His body convulsed on the altar, and the servants looked away, faces flushed, likely terrified that if the goats did not satisfy him, they might be next.

"So thirsty," Nimrod said. "I've been so thirsty. Don't look at me."

What had happened to him? The silver boy had promised to change Hava if he obeyed, but it had changed Nimrod more. He did not like it. He was afraid, for the first time in his life, not of others, but of himself. Of what throbbed inside him.

He feared the cold presence that coiled inside him like a balled-up viper. He felt its desires as his own and knew it was satisfied with his actions. It had woven itself through the very fiber of his being and had become capable of twisting his actions to its own desires.

He wondered if, as Nimrod drank blood, he was actually feeding the silver boy.

Nimrod no longer hungered for food or drink. None brought any satisfaction. Only a cold emptiness. And so he had not eaten in days. Even as he felt his body wasting away.

And so, periodically, he had given in to the disturbing desire to taste blood. Each time, he felt rejuvenated, yet still his muscles withered. Was the satisfaction he felt actually his own? Or merely the silver spirit who now inhabited his body?

He wondered if the silver boy would devour him from the inside out. If he would be destroyed, in the end, not by Hava, but by his own lust for control.

Either way, as he rose from the altar and the servants cleaned the blood from his skin and replaced his tunic with a clean one, he felt a bit of his strength return. The shaking left him, and he walked more freely, as if a weight had been lifted from him.

Satisfied that he had chased away the tide of desire for the time being, he left the temple and walked the long hall of his dungeon. He did not peer into the cells, nor did he look down at the dirty grate at the bottom of the wall. But he said to the servants, "Tomorrow, when we leave for the tower, I want Noah and Japheth to be kept together. And speak nothing of what you saw to Hava. If you do, I will kill you both."

The servants nodded, and he knew they would obey.

62

Aran

Aran nearly collapsed in the tunnel as he heard the voice of what could only be Nimrod—his father's murderer. The man walked with servants flanking either side. Fury throbbed anew like lava through cracks in a volcano, and he had to restrain himself from throwing his knife into the man's chest. If his aim were false, the wound would not be fatal, and Aran would be trapped. He silently cursed himself for not breaking through the grate before.

"Tomorrow, when we leave for the tower, I want Noah and Japheth to be kept together," Nimrod said. "And speak nothing of what you saw to Hava. If you do, I will kill you both."

That could only mean one thing: Zillah had arrived and given Noah as a sacrifice. Nimrod had not mentioned Zillah at all, but that mattered little.

Now was the time to move. But he hadn't seen them bring Noah down. Could it be possible they'd already locked him in the dungeon?

The moment the door shut behind Nimrod and the servants, he put the chisel to the cracked mortar and smashed the end of it with his hammer. The brick gave way and angled hard to the side. A few more whacks and he pulled half the grate away and slipped into the hall.

He tossed the new pair of sandals from Japheth's home back

into the sludge tunnel and cleaned off his feet before walking—to keep from leaving footprints.

He worked quickly and efficiently, peering into each cell and asking the inhabitants their names. There were twelve cells, a freshly bloodied room with a star-shaped altar, and twenty-two men.

None were Japheth.

He looked around and felt panic climb his spine like oil up a wick.

"Please," the voices came. "Help us. Set us free," they said. And the ones who had not been bound clambered at the doors.

Their voices pulled at his heart. But what could he do?

If he attempted to free them, he certainly wouldn't be able to free them all before they were found.

Babel was a massive city, and Nimrod's home lay in the very center of it. If they all fled in different directions, perhaps some of them could survive. But others would certainly die, and Aran would be forced to leave Noah to his death. Along with any chance at killing Nimrod.

He had been so close. He could have reached through the grates and grabbed hold of his tunic as he passed.

He couldn't give up now.

And yet . . .

"Help, my father is here with me, and his leg is broken. They've been torturing us. We don't want to die. Please . . ."

Zillah had been absolutely certain they would be placed in the dungeon. What if—

His breath seized. Could it be possible that Zillah had betrayed them?

His fingers drummed his legs as he worked through the possibilities. None of it made any sense. Now that he was here, even their original plan sounded ludicrous.

Had he let his lust for revenge get the better of him?

He looked again at all the people whose voices and pleading eyes he could not deny. If he'd been fooled, at the very least, he could die doing something useful.

He dug out the little pins he'd brought to pick locks and looked at one of the twelve doors. A single lock separated the two men staring at him from freedom. Two men with lives every bit as valuable and complex as Aran's.

How could he refuse them?

But what if Zillah had remained true yet simply been mistaken about where they would keep Noah and Japheth?

Aran growled and shook his head.

Either way, how could he abandon Noah? He had no idea where Noah was, but he could still try to find him and set him free, couldn't he?

The young man in front of him stared him in the eyes. Brown irises aimed at his scarred face as he rifled through every possible scenario.

He stepped to the door, raised the needle, and let it hover just outside the keyhole.

"Thank you," the man said and tears came to his eyes and wetted his dirty beard overgrown from days spent locked in that underground dungeon.

He pressed the needle into the lock and began fishing for the tumbler as Zillah had taught when suddenly the door at the top of the stairs leading down to the dungeon slammed open.

63

Zillah

Zillah saw her father for a moment before he rushed off again. Only enough time for him to remark that it had "been some time." He looked different somehow. Had the rims of his eyes always had that silver tinge to them?

Hava took her hand and urged her into a dining room where they shared a veritable feast. Zillah made a point to eat only what she saw Hava eating.

"Careful, are we?" Hava said.

"You taught me well," Zillah said.

Hava hadn't asked for her dagger—which disturbed Zillah. It could be that Hava did actually trust her. Or it could be she wanted Zillah to gain a false sense of security.

Either way, they talked little of Noah, or Japheth, or the tower. Bizarrely, Hava chattered about improvements to the home, to the garden, to everything Hava had *never* cared about in her life.

What was she up to?

It made it hard for Zillah to remain conversational.

Because she had more to think about. Like the way the earthenware plate holding a cluster of grapes sat precariously close to the edge of the table. She reached for a pitcher of olive oil and let her arm catch the top of the cluster, sliding it just far enough to the edge that when she retracted her arm, the plate slipped off and broke on the floor.

"Oh!" Zillah said and peered down at the pieces. She huffed and dipped to swipe the pieces away, deftly grabbing a small, rough-edged shard and sliding it between the bottom of her foot and her sandal as she pulled back.

"Don't bother yourself," Hava said. "The servants will get it."

"I don't want to cut my foot on a shard."

"Of course," Hava said, but she watched her closer now.

Zillah went back to picking at the food while Hava droned on. But all she could think of was the feel of that little shard tucked neatly between her foot and sandal.

Her mind alerted her that Hava had stopped talking, and she realized she had lost herself. "Sorry," she said.

"You must be tired," Hava said. "I apologize for exhausting you with all that you've missed since you . . . ran away."

Zillah forced a smile. "It was a long journey back with Noah. Lying doesn't come as easily to me as it does to you. It drains me."

"Pity," Hava said. "It's ever so useful. What about the young man?"

"Who?" Zillah said, and it took her a moment to realize Hava was talking about Aran. "Oh, Noah's servant?"

"You said he stayed in Japheth's home?"

Zillah had never once mentioned Japheth's home. "I'm not sure, though he was there last I saw. It was quite useful that you already had taken Japheth. If not for that, I'm not certain I would have been able to convince Noah to come here."

Hava's smile returned and gained a sly edge. "What did you tell him?"

"That we were going to figure out a way to free Japheth."

It was a bold move, to be so forward about it, but Zillah no longer knew how closely Hava had watched her. And with Noah not in the dungeon, she would need an explanation if Aran were found below. Her attention had indeed shifted to Japheth as the primary sacrifice, and she had ordered her servants to watch every move Zillah made. Hava's knowledge of her presence at Japheth's home was proof enough that Hava could have ordered Gom and Elik murdered, and Zillah taken captive—but hadn't.

"Ah," Hava said and took a bite of boiled root vegetables. "I see."

Why didn't she ask why Noah would agree to be taken hostage? Why didn't she ask any of the obvious questions she should have been asking since the moment Zillah stepped foot on Nimrod and Hava's property?

Because Hava never does anything obvious. Until the moment she put a blade to your throat.

Zillah wondered if this was all just a game to her. Because everything pointed to the fact that Hava could have ordered Zillah crushed days ago. Yet she hadn't.

Could it be that Hava had held back precisely so that Zillah, Noah, and Aran would voluntarily choose to deliver themselves to her? It certainly was the type of idea she would take sick pleasure in.

A servant entered and bowed. "Great mother, we found a fool sneaking around the dungeon with a hammer and chisel, attempting to free the captives."

Zillah was staring at the bread in her hand as she dipped it in olive oil and could almost feel Hava's eyes burn through her face. Had Hava seen the momentary hesitation in her hand holding the bread? She shoved the piece in her mouth and chewed.

"We have bound and placed him in one of the cells. His tools have been destroyed."

"Good," Hava said. "Another sacrifice for tomorrow."

"Indeed," Zillah said and forced another smile. "Tell me, what did he look like? Any identifying features?"

"He had scars across his face. Dark hair and beard."

Zillah slapped the table and forced a laugh. "Mother—please, you must let me do the honor."

"Why would you ever request that?" Hava said, obviously feigning confusion.

"Don't play coy, Mother. You know it's Noah's servant."

Hava smiled, this time with her teeth. "Well of course, my dear." Hava nodded to the servant. "I will grant that—and more."

When the servant did not leave, Hava said, "What else do you need?"

"May I relay one additional detail?"

"Speak," Hava said.

"The cell we put him in had an extra captive in it. Instead of twenty-two captives, there were twenty-three."

Hava stared at the servant for a moment. "Why should I care if there's an additional sacrifice? Begone, before I decide you be added."

The servant bowed low, then rushed away as if Hava's eyes were javelins arcing toward the middle of his back.

64

Aran

Aran's bones ached. He could feel bruises throb across his entire body, for the guards had struck him, but he had been wise enough to resist fighting back. As much as he wanted to defend himself, he knew the only way to free Noah or to get near Nimrod was to let them abuse and imprison him. And he could not risk letting everything fall apart now. Not after they had risked so much. Though now more than ever he doubted Zillah was true. Because both he and Noah were imprisoned, and he could not perceive any way forward.

The cold uneven ground of the prison cell he'd been tossed into dug into his shoulder and hip. Dim light filtered through the small opening in the door, illuminating the tiny space he and the other man occupied. Aran's hands had been tied behind his back with thick rope, and his ankles were tied as well, so that he could not stand or sit without difficulty.

The other man had been bound with iron shackles to the wall. His arms were outstretched at either side, wrists forced within a finger's length of the stone wall. His ankles were bound together and attached to iron shackles where the floor met the wall. In this way, he hung exhausted, knees dropped to one side, body covered in nothing more than a loincloth. His torso bore the stripes from a whipping, and blood had dried to his skin and formed long, fresh scabs.

For hours, they spoke no word to each other. Aran thought only of how to find Nimrod and kill him and Hava—the monsters who had imprisoned and abused so many. He had not come so far to give up so easily. There had to be a way out. A means of escaping. He had gotten himself into this dungeon. He would get himself out. But he dared not give his captors any view of the rage that fueled him, or else they would watch him with increased care.

As it was, they had only bound his hands and ankles with rope, instead of iron, and posted no guard.

He twisted around and began testing the walls for any sharp stones he could dislodge from the earth to cut his bonds. That was when, for the first time, the other prisoner spoke.

"You will find nothing."

Aran kept feeling for stones anyway. He managed to get to his feet and hop to the door. He turned backward to feel the metal bars shot through the small wood opening in the middle of the door—presumably for offering food and water.

Again and again, Aran passed his bound hands over every reachable span of the cell. It would have been easier had his arms not been tied behind his back. But he was careful to be exhaustive in his search. To his dismay, everything he touched was smooth dirt packed hard by the weight of the earth and stone above them.

Finally, exhausted and bruised and bleeding, he sat against a wall and stared at the prisoner in the cell with him.

The man's hair had been cut short, and his beard grew bedraggled. One of his eyelids was swollen shut, making it hard in the dim light for Aran to tell if he were asleep or awake.

Then the prisoner tipped his head toward him.

"You're awake," Aran said.

The prisoner chuckled humorlessly. "I can't sleep."

"How did you get here?"

The man's head swiveled away, up toward the ceiling. He frowned. "I came to see the city and the tower that the children of Noah built."

Aran raised one brow. The children of Noah? A strange term for the citizens of Babel. It made him wonder if the man was a follower of the Old Way. "And this is what you find," Aran said and shook his head.

"I found a people unified against the one true God."

That answered his curiosity easily enough.

"They speak as one," the prisoner continued, "in one language. They work as one, as one people. And if they succeed in this, nothing they propose to do will be impossible for them. They will rule the world. They will stamp out the faithful." A pause. "What happened to you?"

Aran tried to twist the bonds on his wrists, but the fibers rubbed painfully against his skin. "I think I may have been betrayed," Aran said.

"That makes two of us," the man said.

"But I will have my revenge. Even if it kills me."

"Revenge will kill us both. But life is promised to the faithful. Did you know that?"

"So I've been told." He was beginning to regret speaking at all.

The man nodded. "By Noah?"

Aran's eyes widened, and he regarded the prisoner with renewed interest.

The prisoner smiled. "I heard the servants speaking with Nimrod. Not difficult to put together that you came to help him."

After a pause, Aran said, "I see." But now he'd grown uneasy under the man's swollen gaze.

"Do not seek revenge."

He couldn't believe the man's boldness. "I will seek what I will."

"Then you will pay a price too steep for your soul to afford."

Aran continued wrenching at his bonds, but succeeded only in rubbing his skin raw. "You think I should just sit here and give up? Like you?"

"I haven't given up," the man said. "The Lord delivers the faithful. But the vengeful he will destroy."

"Do you not desire justice?"

"I surrender everything to my Lord."

Aran snorted and shook his head. "So did Noah. And now he's going to be marched to his death, same as you and me."

"Everyone dies," the man said. "The question is *how*. I have made my choice. You, however, have not. You think only of killing. But to kill is to become like them. Do you want to be like them? Or would you like to leave the world with your soul unshattered?"

"I would like to leave wielding a weapon toward my enemies."

"Those who live by the sword die by the sword."

"So be it," Aran said. Still, the more the man talked, the more uncomfortable Aran grew. There was something about the prisoner. The way he rested there smiling softly amid horrible discomfort. His wrists bled, raw from hanging in the same position for so long. The muscles and tendons beneath his paper skin were strung taut, likely aching even more than Aran's fresh wounds. And yet . . . he seemed at peace.

He was obviously insane.

But in a bizarre way, Aran wished he were too. Because his chest held only a boiling bitterness. A veritable storm of fury that roiled inside him like an abyss gaping wide, urging every bit of himself to be consumed.

"Who are you?" Aran said.

The prisoner looked up. Shook his head. "I'm just a man."

65

Zillah

The day bled on endlessly as Zillah endured her mother's strange behavior. She took Zillah around every part of their home, showing her additional construction added since she left, as well as the new botanicals in the garden. She commanded servants to clean, or to wash clothing, or to purchase new tapestries to hang in the halls, or to cook food.

Finally, as the sun began to set, Hava took Zillah upstairs.

"I had your old room prepared for you," Hava said. "You will sleep there."

But never once during their day did Zillah hear Hava command the servants to prepare her room. Which could only mean Hava had known she would return.

Slowly, everything was beginning to make sense. Hava had found Japheth and decided to use him as the sacrifice to gain a son. The servants who had followed Zillah all the way from Accad had been commanded to watch her, and to do her no harm.

But what then of the man who had attacked them in the courtyard of Aran's childhood home? Had he not yet received Hava's command to do no harm?

Everything about what had happened made her mind spin. So much so that she nearly didn't realize until too late that they were walking by a room with three locks on it. The room both Noah and Japheth were being held hostage in.

She remembered the shard still lodged between the bottom of her foot and her sandal. Hava was not looking, so she reached down to re-adjust. Then, as they walked past, she angled her foot to the side and kicked soundlessly, sending the shard skidding under the door as soft as the scurry of a cockroach.

If Hava heard, she made no indication.

Three doors down from where Japheth and Noah were being held lay the door to Zillah's old bedroom. Hava opened it and motioned her in with a smile.

Zillah silently prayed that Noah would find the shard and use it tomorrow to free himself.

Still, she had no idea how they would survive this. Aran had been captured. Noah had been taken to the wrong room. And now, Zillah felt caught in Hava's web. She entered her old bedroom, for she could not resist. It felt and looked exactly as it had when she left. The tapestry on the bed, the gold candle-holders burning with fresh candles, the smell of frankincense and cold stone.

"Sleep well, darling," Hava said and closed the door.

A moment later, Zillah heard a second latch sound.

Her heart sank. She crossed to the door and tried it carefully. It refused to move.

66

Noah

The footsteps passed by outside their room at surprisingly consistent intervals. Noah counted time as best he could and realized there must be guards walking a looping pathway continuously, so that the entire house would receive periodic attention without the need for too many personnel.

That was why, as a double set of footsteps shifted by when they shouldn't have, Noah twisted from his position on the floor in the dark to stare at the crack beneath the door.

Shadows flittered past. At the last moment, Noah heard the tiny shift of an item sliding under the door. He waited for several moments, until the footsteps disappeared. He was about to ask Japheth a question when suddenly a female voice said, "Sleep well, darling."

A door shut, and a lock sounded. Footsteps returned and stopped outside Noah and Japheth's door. Noah held his breath as he stared at two black columns blocking the light from entering under the crack—presumably Hava's legs. But she did not touch the locks. Perhaps she didn't have the keys to unlatch them.

Finally, voices called, and the shadow departed.

"Did they pass us food?" Noah said.

"I haven't eaten since arriving," Japheth said.

"Then what did they send under the door?"

"Nothing. Why would they?"

Noah turned and began shifting backward to feel around on the ground with his hands, which were still tied behind him.

"What are you doing?"

"Hush," Noah said. His fingers dipped and ran along the grooves of the stone tile floor as he pushed himself backward. Cold stone, rough edges, smooth surfaces. Nothing loose that skittered as he touched it.

He felt his way to the door, where he almost got his fingers stuck.

"I'm too old for this," he said as he spun around, so that he was facing the door, and pushed away, beginning the process a second time.

"You won't find anything," Japheth said.

But Noah had heard something. Even if it had been a mistake that something had been kicked under the door, perhaps it could be of use. He kept searching.

Three times he checked the entire length of space but found nothing.

Well. Perhaps he *had* imagined the noise.

"I told you," Japheth said. And there was a heaviness in his voice that Noah hadn't heard before. A greater hopelessness than the wounds on his body and the rattle in his chest.

"Did you hear something too?" Noah said.

After a moment, Japheth said, "I'm not certain."

Irritated, Noah shifted his foot to try again, but something sharp punctured his heel. He sucked air through clenched teeth and groaned as he brought his foot back to see what harmed him.

The room was too dark.

"What happened?" Japheth said.

He could feel something—more substantial than a sliver—stuck in his foot. He twisted his leg back hard and rolled his shoulder and wrist until he could just barely reach the shard stuck in his heel. He pinched it between his first and second fingers, then pulled until it slid out. Its length was less than that of his finger, but it was sharp.

"Father?"

"Quiet."

It had a bit of a saw edge, leading to a clean, sharp break. It was earthenware of some kind. He held it in his hands and aimed it down at the rope around his wrist. Using the leverage of his fingers, he tried to saw away at his bindings.

Frays came loose, and Noah felt his pulse pound.

He swallowed and said, "Japheth. Are you certain they are coming for us tomorrow?"

"According to their word."

"Did they mention how they would transport us to the tower?"

"By foot, with guards. It is not far. Don't you remember?"

The tower was so massive that it could be seen everywhere in Babel. It was hard, at times, for Noah to tell how close they were because its magnitude disoriented his sense of perspective. That, and he had been so preoccupied as they journeyed from Japheth's home to Nimrod's that he hadn't thought about it.

If they would be transported by foot with guards watching them, that meant sawing his bindings now would only put them at risk. Noah was too old, and Japheth too battered, for them to attempt to fight for their lives.

What could he do, then?

Almighty, speak. Give me wisdom.

He could hide the shard until later. But where? He wore nothing but a thin tunic. He could not hide the shard in his wrist bindings without risk of them finding it. Especially if they gave them new bindings, as he remembered the slave traders did before the Flood, when evil men chained their captives together in great lines and led them in a procession to be sold like cattle.

Noah's sandals were gone. His hands would be checked. His hair? The shard would certainly fall out. Neither was any man's beard thick enough to conceal it.

He had nothing.

Except for . . .

He dropped the shard on the floor and twisted around until his face was next to it. He bit the shard, careful not to press too hard, then let it fall between the inside of his cheek and his bottom row of teeth.

It just barely fit, the tip of it pressing the inside of his bottom lip.

He hoped no one would notice in the light because it was the only way he could keep the shard on him as they transported to the tower.

"Japheth," he said, voice unclear with the shard in his mouth. Japheth grunted in answer.

"I found something we can use to free ourselves."

"What?"

"Quiet," Noah whispered. "I am storing it in my mouth. It is a shard of something, pottery maybe, with a saw edge. It can cut our bindings. On our way to the tower, I will spit it into your hand. You should be able to cut your bindings with it before passing it back to me, though that may be tricky. Still, it hardly matters whether I'm bound or not. I'll be little help with these rickety old bones."

"But the guards . . ."

"Yes, son, I know. But we must try. I believe God sent this to us. Such events do not happen outside of his sovereign will." He closed his eyes and praised the Almighty. Who could have delivered it but Zillah? It meant she had not given up on him. It meant she was still here, risking her life for his sake.

He had no idea how they would survive. But, for the first time since he left the safety of his home, he felt no fear. In its place came only certainty that this, right here, was the Almighty's will. To be with his son in these final moments, and to continue down this path to the top of the tower.

Lord, I surrender to your will, even if it means I must die. Only protect Aran and Zillah. Keep their hearts from evil. Draw them away from here, and draw them to yourself. Show mercy to this old fool, and don't hold my failures against them. Because I know, now, that if I had been the man you called me to be, they wouldn't be lost in pain and darkness. Free them, Lord.

Free them.

67

Zillah

Zillah crossed to her bed and sat on the edge, feeling like a child in a room too small for her. It was strange to realize she had grown while everything from her memories had remained the same.

She ran her fingers softly over the stitching on the tapestry across her bed. Over the years, she had traced the lines and colors, admiring the beauty of it. Yet its fibers had become entangled with her fears and nightmares. Even now, she felt them sticking through like lances.

She retracted her hand, closed her eyes, and forced herself to lie down, if only to see if it felt the same.

But nothing was the same. Like an umbilical cord at birth, she had severed herself from her old life, and what little warmth left had long since bled away.

She reached up and slid her hand beneath her cushion to support her head, as she'd often done as a child, and felt a cold, hard object.

She rose to a seated position and tossed the cushion away to find a ceremonial dagger.

The blade sat there, gleaming in the dim light, with jewels like eyes at the pommel. A garish, serpentine thing.

A gift from Mother, no doubt. Perhaps an easy way out. A way to take back control of her destiny. Her life.

She wrapped her fingers around it and raised the blade in front of her eyes. How easy it would be to flay her own throat open and end it all. But she wasn't that much a fool. Because more than an opportunity, it was a mocking message.

Look, her mother was saying, *this could free you, but only in pretense. Use it, and you're as much mine as you would have been had you never left.*

Zillah placed it back on the bed, careful to get the angle right so it did not look disturbed. Then she placed the cushion above it and lay her head down, pulling the covers over her shoulders.

The night passed sleepless and cold, like a dead body. For hours, she stared at the angled roof and the wooden poles shot through the stone for support. A slow sickness crept through her belly like so many centipedes as she suffered under the weight of every potential barrier that stood between her and survival.

If she had only kept her tongue behind her teeth, they would easily have lived out the next day. The three of them could have fled into the mountains, crossed the desert, and met the sea. They could have found a new home and survived. Zillah and Aran could have married. They could have built a family, grown into a great people separated from the followers of the Light Bringer. They could have bided their time until strong enough to return. Likely, a hundred years from now they would find half the population culled from war and betrayal.

Because if Zillah knew one thing about the followers of the Light Bringer, it was that they would do anything to get ahead. To gain power. Control. As momentary as it may be.

For to be in control was to be god. And every person who bowed to the Light Bringer tended the desire to usurp him in their hearts.

Still, she had not used her mind. Instead, in the fury and embarrassment of her identity being revealed, she had convinced Aran and Noah to throw their lives away for one foolhardy attempt at revenge.

At least she had sold herself and Aran on the idea of revenge. Noah had been sold on the idea of rescuing his son.

But she had lied to everyone. Even herself.

And now she could do nothing but endure the endless

waiting until the guards came in the morning when she would be forced to the tower to slit Aran's throat and watch Noah and Japheth be murdered. All for the lust her mother held to bear a son.

What a fool.

What a raging fool she was.

But she wouldn't let everything fall apart. Not without a fight.

She reached up and wrapped her fingers around the hilt of the dagger.

68

Aran

After the prisoner refused to share his name, Aran decided to ignore him. He was obviously deluded. Or mad. As if to prove it beyond doubt, in the fourth watch of the night, the prisoner began to sing.

Sing!

And not even any words, but rather garbled gibberish.

"Eli, Eli, lamah azabtani. Rahowq misuati dibre sa agati."

He couldn't deny there was something strangely beautiful about the melody and syllables strung together, but singing at such a ridiculous time made him want to rip the prisoner's beard out. Aran tried to ignore him, but the man kept singing. Outside their door, footsteps and male voices sounded in the stairwell leading into the dungeon. Aran crossed to the prisoner and shoved his shoulder into the man's face, for his hands were still bound.

"Hush, fool. Someone's coming."

Surprisingly, the man responded with calm words. "No need to strike me."

Within a moment, the door opened and guards holding flaming torches entered in leather armor with weapons at their sides and rods in their hands. The guards forced Aran out first and one checked his bindings while two others unlatched the singing lunatic's shackles and bound him with rope.

Other guards led the rest of the prisoners, though one man—
the one Aran had tried to free the previous night—was crying
out in pain, and his son was screaming, "His leg is broken, he
can't walk because you broke his leg days ago!"

Finally, as Aran's co-prisoner hobbled out, one of the guards
motioned him over and said, "You there, carry this man with the
broken leg. Here, we will help him on your back. If you try
anything foolish, we will kill you."

"I won't," he said and looked straight into the guard's eyes
with as much sincerity as an innocent child.

The guard grunted and turned away, scratching the back of
his neck and looking mildly dazed.

Another guard clamped a vise-like hand onto Aran's shoulders and forced him away from the rest. "You will be brought to
the front. Special privileges."

"What?" Aran said.

But the guard smashed his elbow into Aran's temple, bringing
stars to his vision. "Someone put in a special request to kill you
today."

Aran held his tongue—he had no desire to encourage further
beatings. He would need his wits about him if he had any hope
of living through the day.

But who had requested him? Nimrod? Was it possible
Nimrod knew whose son he was?

Perhaps Zillah had told him. Regardless, if he was going to
be brought anywhere near Nimrod, he could not attempt escape
before meeting him in the flesh.

And then there was Noah.

Now more than ever, he considered whether Zillah might
have betrayed them. He just needed one final proof. Because if
Zillah had been sincere, and the plan had gone awry because of
an honest mistake, there was no way she would risk letting Noah
stay in Nimrod and Hava's hands through the night. Noah and
Zillah should be long gone by the time he arrived at the tower.

But if he saw Noah before then . . .

The guard laughed and struck him again, for no reason other
than to indulge in brutality. "You'll be dead soon enough."

69

Noah

Shuffling feet gathered outside their temporary jail cell. One lock fell. Then two. Then three, and the door swung open to a world blindingly bright. For a moment, the guards looked like angels obscured by the Almighty's glory. Then their hands clamped onto Noah's arms and hair, and he was forced back to reality by sharp pain.

They forced him to hop into the hall as the other guards released Japheth from his bindings and brought him gasping into the light. For the first time, Noah was able to see the damage done to his son. Japheth was gaunt. Eyes sunken, rimmed with dark like kohl and olive oil. Bruises mottled his face, neck, arms, and legs, and he was dressed in little more than a tattered undergarment stained with blood from hidden wounds.

Waiting to receive them were a host of guards and a woman who could have been beautiful if not for the way she looked at them like a crow looks at a jewel. "Cut the bindings on his feet," the woman said, and he realized it was the same warm alto he'd heard the night before. Hava, the one who'd stood outside their door. "They won't run."

Noah remained silent, careful to not reveal the shard in his mouth.

The guards cut the bindings at his feet before binding Japheth's hands behind his back.

Hava smiled as she sauntered up to Noah. "Your friend Zillah betrayed you."

Again, Noah said nothing. But he let her know by the look in his eyes how he felt.

She smiled sweetly and leaned closer, her voice a smooth whisper. "I hold your frail little life in my hands." She cupped her hands and smiled as if he lay there. "Do you think I should free you?"

Noah felt fear lace up his spine. He couldn't respond. With her standing so close, she would certainly see that something sat in his mouth.

She grabbed his jaw with frightful intensity, and Noah felt the shard sink into his bottom lip. Her eyes carried none of the intensity he felt in her fingers. She just kept on smiling, voice calm and slow. "We have your servant. The one with the scars who tried to free you from our dungeon last night."

Noah couldn't help it. He struggled against her grip, which only intensified.

"Don't worry. You're both going to end up the same as Japheth before the day ends. Perhaps Zillah too. Speaking of whom." She released Noah and shoved him away. "We must let my daughter know it is time."

Hava walked down the hall a short distance with several guards who unlocked the third door on the right. After a moment, and a few mumbled words from Hava, Zillah shuffled out of the room looking smaller than he remembered. She was wearing the same tunic, rumpled and stained from their journey.

Finally, as one, they descended the stairs and marched through the rest of the home into the outer courtyard, where they found a host of more than twenty captives bound beside half as many guards.

One of the captives, a strong but obviously starved man, held an elderly man on his back, but the strong man's face remained obscured by the shoulder of . . .

Noah's breath nearly stopped when he realized he was seeing Aran, bound by the guards. He wished he could call out to him. But the shard in his mouth held him back.

A guard directed him. "You are to walk at the front."

Noah obeyed and stood behind Hava as a man who he could only guess was Nimrod emerged from the home and joined her. Japheth was arranged behind Noah, but all Noah could think about was how he could ever possibly use the shard in his mouth *now*.

Still, they barely had time to think before they were off, making their way down the hill toward the tower that stood at the bottom of the hill like a naked mountain, unnatural and strange in its perfect symmetry.

He managed one glance behind him and found Aran staring at him, white-faced and wide-eyed.

A massive throng was already milling about the foot of the tower, and some on the steps, just as he had seen in his first dream while still in his vineyard. The hair across his body prickled and straightened. He swung his gaze to the top of the tower and found that today, no blindingly bright star hovered above it.

Instead, there appeared to be a temple.

As they reached the tower and began ascending the stairs, Noah realized what was about to happen to them. They were to be sacrificed at the top of the tower, which was no less than a temple to the Light Bringer himself.

The Almighty's prophet set to be a goat on the enemy's altar.

His throat felt dry, and he thought he would cough and risk losing the shard in his mouth. He tried to clear his throat, but the tickle wouldn't leave. He closed his eyes, which were beginning to water in protest. *Almighty, save me*, he prayed. *Precious Lord, deliver me from this terrifying fate.*

He opened his eyes after nearly stumbling on a step and noticed many who waited on the steps were bound hand and foot, same as him. He let his eyes leave the stairs to run over the crowd and gauge just how many captives were present. If he wasn't mistaken, nearly a third of the crowd would suffer the same fate as him before the moon shone that night.

Noah's foot caught again on the step in front of him and he stumbled and fell, the shard falling from his mouth on the step beside him, bouncing down one, two steps. Panic chilled his chest and the glare of the sun blinded him momentarily. He rolled to his back and winced at the pain while his hands—tied behind his back—searched for the shard, fingernails scraping baked brick. The guards eyed him suspiciously, but he stayed on his back, feigning intense pain while he reached with his hands.

A guard rushed over and lifted him by his armpits just as his fingers clasped the edge of the shard and pulled it into his fist.

The guard pushed him forward and said, "Hurry."

Japheth walked closer, now, body obscuring Noah's hands from view. Noah did his best to make sure none watched, but they were running out of time. He went to work on his bindings, sawing quickly but carefully. The rope was fraying, loosening, until it nearly severed. Noah pressed the frayed edge against his back to obscure it and hid the shard inside his palm. They were nearly at the top, and once they reached the temple, he would need to react quickly.

The stairs ended, and Noah looked back to see the people spread like ants below. Nimrod, Hava, and Zillah broke away from the rest, who seemed unwilling to walk toward the temple.

Hava turned back and raised her hands. All gathered slowly hushed. She held up her hands until the silence of the throng was deafening.

Then she spoke in a clear, strong voice that carried itself on the wind. "Noah, I bid you and your son Japheth to come. For none may enter the temple of the Light Bringer unless bidden. And you." She pointed, and Noah and the rest turned to see Aran standing in the crowd. The others stepped away until Aran could no longer question whether she was speaking of him. "Zillah, my daughter whom for so long denied the Light Bringer, will finally show herself faithful by taking you as her personal sacrifice. Come."

So Noah, Japheth, and Aran joined Nimrod, Hava, and Zillah as they entered the temple atop the tower of Babel, between two guards who stood at the entrance to guard the way.

70

Zillah

As they entered the archways that led into the temple of the Light Bringer, Zillah realized others were gathered by the stone altar. Ham stood at the end, gray beard long, eyes set like hazel gems in his weathered brown skin. Next to him stood Cush, his son, and Zillah's grandfather.

Hava stopped, and Zillah could feel Aran stiffen as she held him back by his bound hands. She resisted the temptation to slip her fingers into his. All she wanted in that moment was to comfort him and to feel his comfort in return. But he probably believed she'd betrayed him after everything that had gone wrong.

If he only knew. What would he do when she finally offered him what he'd been longing for all this time? Would he kill her, as well?

With her free hand, she slowly unsheathed the ceremonial dagger. Aran's eyes shot to the side to see what she was doing. But she paid him no mind, because Ham was raising his hands.

"Today, we consecrate this holy tower to the Light Bringer, the lord of air and earth. Nimrod and Hava will wet the altar with the blood of Japheth. And Zillah, my great- granddaughter, will offer her sacrifice, as well, to finally consummate her entry into the brethren."

Hava and Nimrod pulled Japheth forward and laid him on the altar.

Japheth stared at his brother. Fighting back sobs. "Brother," he whispered. "You have betrayed us all."

Ham just stared at him, face blank, relaxed, almost serene.

Japheth nodded and stared at the ceiling, in the center of which a massive, five-pointed star had been carved. "I shouldn't have believed you. I just wanted to so badly."

Zillah glanced at Noah. What of him? Ham had not mentioned . . .

But then Ham and Cush moved for Noah and led him out of the temple. Of course, they would kill Noah themselves. Nimrod and Hava wanted Japheth for what they believed his lifeblood would offer them—a son. What use did they have for Noah? But Ham had much reason to desire his father's life.

And what a time to take it. To spill Noah's blood on the very steps of the tower, for all to see.

As their shuffling footsteps faded, only Nimrod, Hava, Japheth, Aran, and herself were left in the temple.

Hava laid on her back with her side against the bottom of the altar, pulling her tunic up to reveal her naked belly. A culvert had been carved into the stone altar, presumably to channel the blood directly onto . . . Zillah's eyes widened.

Hava's womb.

Japheth was lying prone on the stone table. He did not shake, and no longer cried. He just laid there, looking fearless as Nimrod took his place at the altar and readied the ceremonial knife.

"In the name of the Light Bringer, I offer this sacrifice!"

Zillah leaned and whispered in Aran's ear, "Remember, Hava is mine."

And then sliced through his bindings.

307

71

Noah

Noah wondered if his heart would break as Ham and Cush led him toward the steps of the tower once more. He knew what Ham was planning. That he had been planning this even when Noah visited him. To baptize the new world in the blood of the father he hated.

Noah knew what he must do, even as he wondered if he would be capable of doing it. Because as he walked, and the city sprawled in front of his eyes and all those countless descendants looked up at him—many waiting to suffer their own humiliating death—he remembered the beginning of it all. When Jade first told him through joy-filled tears that she was pregnant a third time.

They could hardly believe when she had become pregnant with their first after years of barrenness. Then, to have two children and a third on the way, felt like a gift too great to accept.

Noah pondered the intentions of his heart in that moment and felt the growing warmth of shame crawl up his neck. Because he had felt it solely Jade's duty to carry Ham when he was a child. To clean his bottom when he soiled his wrappings. To feed him as he moved from milk to mashed vegetables. To rock him to sleep. To tend him in the night. To do . . .

Everything.

Because in Noah's mind, only he could tend to the new

converts to the Old Way in their small port city at the edge of civilization. Only he could do the work at the dockyard. Only he could design vessels and build them watertight, fit for the work they were commissioned to do—thereby keeping them safe and fed.

How could he possibly be demanded to care for their children?

The rhythmic, tribal chant of the crowd at the foot of the tower brought him back to bitter reality, and he realized that before him was the fruit of his heart. His sin.

For it *had* been sin to abdicate his emotional and physical responsibility of Ham to Jade. And now, the entire world was suffering for it.

It did not matter how such a horror could come about. He could deny it no longer.

He could only accept the fruit of it.

And so, if it were the Almighty's will that he die today, he would not stop it. He would love Ham today, as he had not before, by becoming the martyr his son wanted him to become. By sacrificing his life for his family as the Almighty had asked him to—as he had refused to do. He would not give in to violence as he had as a young boy. It did not matter if Ham's intentions were profane. Noah's intentions were only to obey.

As they stopped atop the staircase, he felt a growing sense of purifying peace. A confidence in the Almighty's word. Because the Almighty had told him, from the beginning, that he was never meant to fight back. His purpose had always been to accompany Aran and Zillah on this perilous, strange journey. To be present.

Because *present* was exactly what he had failed to be for Ham.

Tears fell from his cheeks.

But as one of the guards started to come forward, a captive—the strong looking one who'd carried an injured man—put a hand on the guard's chest and spoke a single Word.

The guard stumbled back as if struck, then opened his mouth and began to spew strange words. He clamped a hand over his mouth as if betrayed by his own tongue.

Ham and Cush turned and examined the prisoner, mouths

and eyes wide. "Where did your bindings go?" Ham said to the prisoner.

Then the guard spoke a second time and, as strange words came out, screamed and tossed his spear before running down the stairs.

Ham continued, "What is—"

But the prisoner who touched the guard turned and raised his hands, and when he opened his mouth, spoke a Word that sounded like a thunderous note of Music.

The thousands gathered at the foot of the tower suddenly roared in response, and then turned toward each other in confusion.

The other guards standing atop the tower tried to speak to one another, but their words came strange as well, and they couldn't understand each other.

The captives saw their opportunity and bolted. The guards dropped their spears in confusion. The crowd stampeded from the tower in panic.

Noah watched, already aware of who the Man—the prisoner —truly was. But not wanting to face him for fear of what he might say. In truth, Noah felt doubly shameful at the sight of him. For the last they had spoken was when the Man washed the world clean in the Flood.

The Man. The Almighty manifested in human form.

Ham and Cush turned toward the Man, who walked slowly toward them. The Man waved Noah forward, and he obeyed.

Ham was staring at the Man, lips quivering.

"You recognize me," the Man said. "From when you stood in the ark, and I commanded the door shut."

"You are . . . ," Ham said.

"Not the Light Bringer," the Man said. "I am God. And I have come to earth to see this little tower the children of man have been building."

Ham was shaking his head, backing away.

"Tell me," the Man said, as Ham looked out and saw his entire empire falling into ruin in the confusion of languages. "Will you return to me, now?"

To see the Man—the Lord of the universe—standing in

nothing but a loincloth, the sinew of his muscles starved from the abuse he voluntarily endured in Nimrod's dungeon, was strange. Noah was struck, in that moment, how embarrassing being human truly is. And yet, the Almighty had chosen to pull on the human form, to show himself present and humble.

"What?" Ham said.

"He has proven himself the victor," Noah said, and tears of thankfulness came to his eyes as he realized why the Man was here in this moment. He faced his son. The son he still loved. "What of your promise to me?"

Ham's face contorted into a grimace. He looked caught between the desire to strike the Man down and fleeing.

The Man frowned, and lifted his palm to Ham's face. "Speak."

Ham tossed the Man's hand away and began screaming what sounded like insults, but as the spittle flew from his lips, he realized the words that came forth were not what he intended.

He shook his head, breath coming in panicked pulses.

Noah held out his hand, fell to his knees, and said through tears, "Please, son, return to us."

But that only terrified and enraged Ham more. He spit on them both and fled down the stairs. Noah fell forward onto his hands, body wracked with grief.

72

Aran

As the bindings fell from Aran's hands, he looked back at Zillah and blinked. "You're not going to. . . ?"

But Zillah was already moving toward Hava, who was standing, pulling her own knife out to meet her with a smile.

"I've been waiting for this moment," Hava said.

Nimrod looked at the bindings fallen from Aran's hands, but before he could attack, what felt like an earthquake shook the temple, and everyone twisted toward the entrance. The guards standing just outside tossed their spears and ran, and they heard the crowd far below roar in panic and confusion.

Nimrod abandoned Japheth on the table and ran out to see what was happening.

73

Zillah

Zillah faced Hava and felt her muscles coil in preparation.

Both held identical daggers. Hava was smiling, but Zillah was not, and she wondered if at any moment the rage knotted like a clot in her chest would collapse on itself, and a hole would erupt, consuming everything.

"Hold it together, dear," Hava said, and though the words she spoke felt new and strange—and from Hava's expression after she spoke, it seemed she thought the same—Zillah found she understood them nonetheless. "I'll kill you quick enough."

Zillah threw herself at the woman she hated too much to call mother. Their blades met and rang as they collided and knocked each other away. Zillah kicked Hava in the thigh with her heel, and Hava grabbed hold of her tunic and pulled hard, yanking her to the side.

She saw Hava's blade flash and lashed out wildly. Zillah's blade caught something hard and fleshy, and her mother screamed. Hava's weapon flew to the side and clanged across the ground. Hava stumbled back, grasping at her arm as Zillah regained her footing.

Blood poured from a stump where Hava's hand used to be. But she did not cry or whimper. Instead, a growl rumbled in her chest as she threw her shoulder into Zillah's abdomen hard enough to send the blade from her hands, as well.

Zillah landed hard on her back, and felt Hava grip her hair in a tight knot and jerk her neck to the side so hard she wondered if it was broken. Blows landed across her abdomen time and again. A bloody elbow landed in Zillah's ribs, and she felt bone crack. Zillah tried to smash her fist into Hava's face, but hit instead with her forearm, which Hava sunk her teeth into.

Zillah screamed again and kicked her mother away, scrambling back toward the dagger on the brick floor. But Hava was relentless, like a rabid animal, and climbed on Zillah's back and smashed her forehead into the stone floor so hard that her eyesight blackened and flashed at once.

The world spun and darkened before she came to in time to see Hava stepping toward one of the blades. As her thoughts cleared, she realized she'd never reach it before Hava. She turned back to find the other dagger she'd dropped.

She found it beside her mother's severed hand and took it up, slick with blood. As she turned, she saw her mother facing her, smiling again.

"I'll finish you this time," Zillah said and shot a hand to her mouth to feel the strange words on her lips. They were not made up of the sounds she remembered, and yet they meant what she intended and flowed out like water.

Something profound had changed since they entered the temple, that much was certain. But she had little time to ponder how, because Hava descended on her like a vulture on a carcass.

74

Noah

As Ham fled down the steps of the tower, Nimrod exited the temple entrance and skidded to a stop, staring out over his city falling to pieces in the confusion wrought by the Man. Aran followed and picked up one of the spears the guards had thrown down.

Noah turned to stop Aran, but the Man held him back with a palm on his chest and said, "Don't worry about him."

And with another Word that sounded like a thousand trees breaking in a tempest, the ground sped away from his feet, until the earth was less than the point of a needle quickly fading in the Light of . . .

The Man next to him, no longer encased in simple flesh, but rather imbued in all the glory and righteousness of the infinite Almighty. When he spoke, his voice thundered. "Do you believe your sin more powerful than me?"

Noah tried to throw himself down, but there was nowhere he could escape the onslaught of those eyes. Instantly, he knew he would be destroyed. He would be crushed by the weight of the Man's glory, that perfect Judge who would decide the fate of the entire universe at the end of Time. Because truthfully, Noah was shot through with sin and had feared his sin too great for the Almighty to mend or forgive.

Then the sound and the fury relented, as if the Man had tossed a veil over himself.

Still, Noah was too ashamed to raise his gaze.

The Man dipped and lifted Noah's chin with the gentleness of a lover. And his voice came in a whisper so tender it felt like a kiss. "Have you so quickly forgotten who I am?"

And Noah remembered how he had stared into the Man's face as the flood waters rose, and the Man had forgiven him for the rage he had failed to let go of in all his years of walking with the Almighty.

Yes, Noah had forgotten the Man's faithfulness, doubted the Man's willingness to love and forgive him, and if not in whole, at least in part, believed the Man abandoned him.

For his own sin, true. But had not the Man promised he would always be with him? That if Noah humbled himself and looked to the Almighty, he would cleanse Noah and restore him?

Had the Man not shown Noah how he listened to every word spoken by human tongues by revealing himself to Noah even when Noah was the Man's enemy? Had the Man not shown him that he knew more of Noah than Noah knew of himself?

Yes, but Noah *had* forgotten.

Who was Noah? A man. A man who failed to be there for his own family.

So how could he question a Man who had never abandoned a single one of his children?

He wanted to throw himself into the Man's embrace. To weep and stay there until the Light burned away every shifting shadow in his heart. Until he could heal in the presence of true perfection and slowly let his soul knit together in the same way the Man was knitted together.

As emotion bubbled over, the Man reached down and took hold of Noah's frayed flesh. Scarred hands against a broken body, tenderly embracing a sin-shattered soul as the Light returned and grew in intensity. Noah tried to open his mouth to speak, but the heat was too great.

Tears glistened in the Man's eyes—too bright to look at without pain. Or was it the Man's pain he was feeling? Yes, he felt in that moment that the veil between flesh and soul was torn away in the Light, which wove their hearts into one like a scarlet thread at the end of a strident needle. The Man knew his pain and cried for it. And Noah felt the Man's pain like a spear thrust through his side, and bitter iron through his hands and ankles, and he wept for the world.

"For you," the Man said. "My pain is for you."

Noah fell forward, into the very source of the Light, hoping it would burn him away and end the suffering, but instead, the pain waned as the last of the dross of him was incinerated and what was left at the center was a little lump of pure gold, molten and rhythmic like a human heart.

"All is not lost," the Man said. "I have not forgotten. I have never forgotten. But you have forgotten."

"I am sorry," Noah tried to say, but he had no mouth left to speak with. He had nothing but that little lump of gold. And the Man cradled the gold in his hands, the yellow liquid falling into the scars in the Man's hands, becoming one with them.

Then the Man spread his arms so the gold-gilded scars reflected the Light in ever-increasing intensity. Like a double-edged sword, those piercing points of Light sliced through Noah's awareness.

Then the Man opened his mouth, but the words that came out were foreign to Noah. Once again, he was afraid. But the Man kept speaking. Voice growing in intensity until each syllable seemed destined to divide the world. Again and again the words changed, but none of the languages came clear to Noah.

Until, at last, the Light rolled away and darkness surrounded him, and he heard the Man speak one final Word, and he was back again, atop the tower of Babel.

75

Nimrod

It was over. Nimrod knew as soon as Noah and that captive disappeared into the air with a glitter of stardust and a crack of thunder that the Light Bringer's plans had been destroyed by Noah's God.

But how could it be? How could everything collapse so quickly, after everything they had built? He had believed the Light Bringer the lord of this world. But now, his servants fled in madness.

"Light Bringer," he said, and his own language came strange to his ears. "Help me."

He felt the pulsing presence of the silver boy uncoil itself inside him like a serpent ready to strike. It slid out of his belly and up his throat until its eyes stared through his eyes, and its mouth spoke through his mouth.

But what erupted was not a string of words, but a guttural scream. Of pain. Of fury. Of murderous hatred as old as the world. It wanted to throw Nimrod's body down the stairs, to break him into pieces.

Nimrod struggled against its desires. Body shifting forward, then back, then to the side, as though he were grappling with an invisible warrior.

He succeeded in thwarting its desire to toss him over the edge, but could not push its presence away. It was rooted too deep. And now he could barely move. He tried to call for Hava to help. For Ham. For anyone. But all that came out was a pathetic squeak, for the silver boy still gripped his voice with an iron fist.

That was when he saw, out of the corner of his eye, the glint of a spear aimed directly at him.

76

Aran

Aran gripped the spear so hard he wondered if the wood might shatter in his fists. He felt the bitterness balled in his chest like an aching pit, as dense as the world yet as empty as the air.

This man, whom he watched shaking at the edge of the staircase on the tower of Babel, was the same who had murdered his father and destroyed his family and oppressed innocent people and planned the genocide of those who followed the Old Way. All Aran had longed for these many days was the opportunity to kill the one responsible for all the pain inside him.

And yet, as he pointed the tip of that deadly weapon at Nimrod and watched the man jerk back and forth as if lost in lunacy, he saw with eyes unclouded by hate that murdering this man would undo none of the pain. If he let his anger pour out and run him through, the emptiness in his chest would only grow.

Still, how could he not kill Nimrod? The man was dangerous. And if Aran let him go, the danger he posed would only grow again elsewhere.

Nimrod's eyes shifted from silver to gray to silver again, and Aran took two steps back, disturbed as a whimpering croak escaped Nimrod's throat.

The look in Nimrod's eyes was one of terror as he looked toward Aran. Not the look of a tyrant, but of a fearful child.

Nimrod managed to raise his hand in invitation. "P-p . . ."

As he got his words out, Aran did not know what they meant. Still, he thought he could understand the look in the man's eyes. It was a look of pleading.

"Help me," he was saying in his own new language.

Then Nimrod pointed to his chest and closed his eyes, as if begging for Aran to run him through.

"Stop it!" Aran said and lifted his spear in preparation.

He wanted to kill Nimrod, but doing so felt obscene as the man's face contorted in madness. Even worse was the possibility that murdering Nimrod could be doing him a service.

Aran lowered his spear. Which was the greater damage? To end the man's life? Or to let him endure the failure of all he had planned? The shame of a life wasted on evil?

Aran remembered Noah's advice to him, then. That to kill would only be to damage his own soul. He felt again the pain and confusion he'd felt after murdering the assassin who had found them in Mother's courtyard. The dark fog of confusion that had settled over his heart after ending the man's life—even though to fail to kill the man would have been to die himself and to let Zillah and his mother die.

Could he willingly submit himself to such darkness and pain once again? And this time without even the reason of base survival to support his decision?

It was the last thing he wanted. Because to murder Nimrod would be self-mutilation, and he hated himself for it. Hated himself for his weakness. For the pity he felt for the writhing man before him.

But even if he tried to claim that letting Nimrod live would allow danger to grow again elsewhere, he knew it would be a lesser danger, for never again would a single man be capable of unifying the world in such a way as he had. Their languages had been confused, and now they didn't understand one another.

The spear rattled as it fell from his hand, then rolled and began to fall down the steps of the tower, clattering and skidding faster as it went.

"Go," Aran said, even as he realized the man could not understand him. So he pointed and said, "Run and suffer the humiliation of this day the rest of your life. Maybe, then, I can find peace." Bitter tears burned his eyes as he watched Nimrod turn and stumble down the steps.

As he watched the opportunity he had lusted after and risked his life for disappear.

77

Zillah

Zillah and Hava ran at each other with suicidal rage. Weapons held high, and then swinging down. Zillah threw herself to the side as she stabbed, and Hava's dagger plunged into the flesh of Zillah's arm as Zillah's blade found Hava's chest and slipped between her ribs.

Hava gasped and coughed, spewing blood into Zillah's face.

Zillah struck again and again as the monster she called Mother fell back and shook with the shock of the wounds. Until Hava stopped moving altogether, and her empty eyes stared at the five-pointed star on the ceiling with motionless intensity.

Zillah hovered over her, shaking with the pain of her wounds. The broken rib. Her bleeding arm. But she felt no satisfaction.

Only an empty, shaking terror.

"This is what you get, Mother!" Zillah screamed. "The wages for your murderous hatred!"

But she was only trying to convince herself that to kill was righteous. Even as her soul screamed that it was anything but. No matter how much Hava deserved it, Zillah had no right to take hold of the retribution her heart had lusted for with the same intensity that Hava lusted for a son.

Emptiness consumed her. She was now completely alone. Abandoned by both father and mother. And she felt that emptiness as if the world had been turned upside down, and she had fallen into the hollow sky.

Who would love her? Now, more than ever before, her mother and father never would.

She realized with a start that she was feeling at last what Aran had felt as he returned to his mother's home and faced the death of his father.

Zillah knelt over her dead mother and for the first time, openly wept. She remembered the boat ride to Babel when Noah had spoken about the Almighty and his forgiveness. That God saw through flesh and bone to the heart inside. And she wept because now she had gone too far. The Almighty would see the hollow clot of darkness she had become and would never forgive her.

She had nothing. No future. No hope.

Only death and emptiness.

Exactly what she had chosen.

78

Noah

Noah blinked and looked for the Man on top of the tower, but saw only Aran standing, staring down the steps. Noah followed the man's gaze and saw Nimrod fleeing as his city broiled in chaos. Some opportunistic men looted and struck people down, though most fled. A few homes had caught fire and raged like torches, their flames licking the air as the roar of the city's strange new languages washed over him like a wave.

Noah looked back at Aran and noticed that the spear he'd taken up was gone. Aran's back was to him, and Noah took the moment to think through everything that had happened.

The Man had confused the world's languages. Ham and Nimrod's kingdom was crumbling. Ham had refused to repent of his idolatry and had spit on him and the Man. Now Nimrod fled, and where was Japheth?

"Aran," Noah said.

Aran turned, eyes shining with such clarity and regal intensity that Noah wondered if he had been appointed the new king of Babel. "I let him go," Aran said. And Noah thanked the Almighty that they could understand one another.

Noah nodded and crossed to Aran. He put a hand on Aran's shoulders and squeezed. "I am proud of you. I know I am not your father but . . ."

Aran threw himself into Noah, clutching him as a boy

clutches his papa. Noah curled his arms around Aran, and the two held each other with all the fury and intensity they felt at a world gone wrong.

Noah knew the difficulty of what Aran had just done. Because he himself had struggled with that very same decision at the end of the old world, before the Flood washed the evil away.

Now, they had endured a second flood of evil. Only this time, the Man had not destroyed the world, for he promised he would not. And the Man was always true to his promises.

For the Man was faithful, even when Noah was not.

Noah released Aran and said. "Japheth, my son."

Aran nodded. "He is still inside. With—" His eyes widened, and they said in unison. "Hava and Zillah!"

79

Japheth

As Hava's daughter wept over her body, Japheth slid from the stone altar and found one of the daggers. Slowly, because his body still ached, he cut his own bindings and stretched his limbs.

The daughter's words came strange to his ears, and he found he could not understand them. Regardless, the girl was growing pale as her arm continued to bleed. Her fingers were laced through her dead mother's hair. It made Japheth's heart ache to see such powerful, mixed emotions.

How cruel that she would be pushed to such a crossroad! How cruel that none had shown her tenderness and compassion. That Hava had used her for such evil.

Japheth crossed to her and laid a hand gently on her back. She did not respond, too lost in shock. He tore a bit of his own tunic and wrapped her wound tight to stem the bleeding.

Then her eyes fluttered closed, and she lay across her dead mother.

Japheth needed to get her out of here. She needed a safe place to rest and recover. Fighting against the pain that threatened to send him to his knees, he picked her up and carried her slowly out. He did not know how far he could carry her, only that he would do what he could.

But even as he made his way toward the door of the temple, Noah and another young man with scars across his face entered.

"She is wounded," Japheth said.

"I will carry her," the man with scars said. And Japheth was relieved to be able to understand his speech.

Japheth handed her over to him, and he carried her all the way down the steps of the tower, into an abandoned home near the foot of the monument, where they rested for the night.

80

Aran

Aran sat beside Zillah's bedside the entire night, waiting for her to wake, for the moment he could talk with her. To apologize for doubting her. And to thank her for what she had risked for them all. But when Zillah awoke, she called out in a strange language, and Aran's heart ached doubly hard.

"Zillah," he said, and she looked at him, confused. "You are safe."

But her expression twisted, and she tried to throw herself out of bed. Her breaths coming in shallow, panicked pulses, hand flying instinctively to her side in pain.

Aran pushed her back and hushed her, though she fought him even harder, and the fear in her eyes felt like a dagger in his abdomen.

So he stopped fighting her and instead slipped his fingers between hers.

She paused, blinking. He took a chance and pressed his lips to hers softly.

He kissed her long and closed his eyes, wrapping his other arm around her neck as she kissed him back.

As he backed away, he said, "Kiss."

She stared at him a moment, face flushed. "K . . . ?"

"K-i-s-s," he said slowly and clearly, and kissed her again.

"K-i . . . k-kiss?" The word came out sounding funny, but it was there.

He nodded. Then raised his hand in front of her face. "Hand."

"H-h . . . han-d?" She shook her head and grimaced. The word was difficult for her to form.

But Aran nodded again. Then pressed her hand to his chest and said. "Love."

She tried for the word but failed.

"I love you," he said, and tears welled in his eyes, and he held her and thanked the Almighty that he had kept them both alive. "I will keep you safe. And I will learn your language and teach you mine."

Noah entered and stood beside them, placing a warm hand on Aran's shoulder. "We will need to move soon. Japheth said the violence has grown greater, but he has found some weapons for us to ward off any attackers as we leave the city."

Zillah watched them, trying desperately to understand, but wincing at the impossibility.

"Where will we go?" Aran said.

"First, we will go back to Erech."

"Do you think my mother . . . ?"

"I believe she is alive. There will likely be unrest there, too, for I believe the confusion of languages reaches to the ends of the earth. But I wonder if Shem has been able to maintain control. He may have become an anchor in the storm. And if that is true, we may find Erech more receptive."

"Japheth agrees?" Aran said.

A nod. "Japheth agrees."

81

Noah

Japheth bandaged up Zillah's arm and helped get a hooded tunic over her in preparation for their journey out of Babel.

"Are you comfortable?" Japheth said, forgetting she couldn't understand him.

Zillah looked at Japheth, eyes searching for a way to understand.

Japheth thought for a moment, then motioned toward his face and smiled, as if to ask her if she was all right.

Her furrowed brow relaxed, and she smiled and nodded. Then she spoke a word in her new language, and Noah guessed that it meant, "Thank you."

"Remember," Japheth said to Noah and Aran. "Keep your hoods low. And do everything in your power to avoid violence."

"No need to tell us that," Noah said, and he looked at Aran.

Aran's mouth flattened. "Indeed."

...

By the time they wove their way through the streets of Babel, many of the citizens had fled. The previous night they'd heard violence spreading again, but after the sun had risen, most had faded into the more distant portions of the city.

Only once before they reached the river did they find another group on the road. It was a family with children. The father was gone, and the mother stood holding a dirty, bruised toddler in her arms, the whites of her eyes gleaming in the shadows of an alley.

Noah stopped and faced her. Held out his hand in gentle invitation. "Beloved," he said. "Can you understand my words?"

The mother stepped back as he spoke and put up a warning hand. She spoke a string of syllables that sounded no more than a baby's gibberish, and Noah felt his shoulders sag. The mother spit in the dirt and turned, pulling her children away in great haste.

Aran, Japheth, and Zillah continued on.

Aran looked back and said, "We need to hurry."

Noah nodded, rubbing his hands together to rid it of the dust that was everywhere in this city. "Of course."

...

When they reached the river, there were no boats. They decided to follow the river's bend toward Erech, where they would need to find some way across.

The journey took them the entire day. As the sun fell, they reached a huddled mass of people who had been waiting for quite some time as boats ferried a few across at a time.

They were obviously from Babel. And some of them still bore red marks across their wrists. The evidence of abuse, and a good sign that they might be followers of the Almighty.

Still, when Noah, Japheth, and Zillah approached the new refugees, only a handful spoke their language, and none spoke Zillah's. After a few moments of trying, Zillah retreated to the outer edge of the gathering, hugged her knees, and cried.

It broke Noah's heart. Looking around, seeing his own progeny incapable of communicating—and it was all his fault. The reason the Almighty had confused the world's languages was because Noah had let his family fall to pieces and chase sordid idolatry. Now these innocent people had been forcibly uprooted from their homes, and many had families to care for. They were terrified and isolated. And Noah could do nothing.

But was that really true? He could not comfort them in that moment, of course, but when the dust of Babel settled, there would be much work to do.

I will do it, he thought. *I will gladly be spent to help rebuild these people's lives. To undo even a portion of the pain that my mistakes have caused.*

...

It was morning before the boat ferried them across. When they landed on the soil of Erech, Japheth wanted to see Shem, but Aran convinced them to first go to Sarah, for he reasoned that Shem would likely be too busy to worry about them.

As they entered the courtyard, Zeck hailed them from the roof. Aran and Noah waved back, and a few moments later Sarah ran out and threw her arms around Aran.

Aran slowly brought up his arms and squeezed his mother back, his eyes closing. They held each other for some time and spoke no words.

Zillah held herself and looked around the courtyard as if one of those evil men would jump out and grab her at any moment. Japheth waited with his hands on his hips. And Zeck watched silently from the rooftop.

"I'm fine," Aran said.

Sarah immediately let go and grabbed his shoulders, examining him hard, face lined with worry. She bit her lower lip and shook her head. Tears grew and fell down her cheeks. She opened her mouth and spoke—but her language, too, was strange.

Aran stepped back, disturbed. "What?" he said, and looked at Noah. "Why her?"

"It struck all of us," Noah said.

"But why does she not speak our language?"

Noah shrugged.

"You're the Almighty's prophet," Aran said, growing more and more upset. "Did he not tell you anything?"

"Nothing that would make sense of this."

Sarah wiped her eyes, closed in, kissed Aran on the cheek, and pointed back toward Erech. "Shem," she said.

"Shem? My son?" Noah said.

Sarah tipped her head in confusion. She spoke again in her own language and acted out placing a circlet on her own head. She puffed out her chest, pointed at herself, and said in a deep voice, "Shem."

"We should go to him?" Japheth said.

Again she was confused. Noah acted out walking, then pointed at the city. "To Shem?"

Sarah nodded and smiled.

"She's saying he's retaken the city," Aran said. "You were right, Japheth."

Japheth reached with his lanky arm and laid his long, dark fingers on Aran's shoulder. "I am sorry, my friend. We will come back again. If Zillah can learn our language, so can your mother."

Aran chewed his cheek and nodded.

They started walking, back into Erech to see Shem.

...

Shem did not hail them at the gate to his home, for he was surrounded by attendants, giving orders, and making important decisions at a rapid pace. As Noah, Japheth, Aran, and Zillah approached, they realized he did not see them, but they heard him speaking in their own language.

"Watch the food stores closely," Shem said. "Ensure that none are broken into. Set a double guard in rotating shifts and strike down any dissidents mentioning the name of the Light Bringer."

"Brother!" Japheth called, and Shem turned and threw up his hands in an uncharacteristic show of emotion. He pushed the servants and attendants aside, pulled up his tunic, and ran to Japheth and Noah, throwing his arms around both.

"I thought you were dead," Shem said.

"You weren't far off," Japheth said. "But we survived, by the mercy of the Almighty."

...

Shem had to return to his work for quite some time. Noah, Japheth, Aran, and Zillah were told to wait inside until Shem was free. They did so and were brought food and wine.

They ate and drank and rested.

In the evening, they sat and ate again with Shem and his wife, Aliska.

After Noah and Japheth told Shem what had happened, the two brothers talked of many administrative details. Toward the end of the night, it became clear Noah, Aran, and Zillah were of no use here.

"Now that I am free," Japheth said, "I will stay here to help you rebuild."

"What of Babel?" Noah said.

"Let it rot," Shem said. "It is a city defiled, cursed from inception."

Japheth nodded and bent forward as if under the weight of his own mistakes. "Yes, now that I see the true aim of those who built the city, I must agree. I scouted Babel and inquired as I could, after everything fell apart. From what I can tell, Ham, Cush, and Nimrod all fled to the north, and a large host of their followers went with them."

"Although some of the followers of the Light Bringer have stayed in Erech and continue to cause trouble. We will deal with them and protect the faithful. We will rebuild Erech and make it into a city to preserve them. That would make Nimrod angry enough—to know the city he previously led is now in league against him." Shem smiled and Aliska agreed.

"I hope he lives to see it," she said.

Shem turned to Noah. "So long as you agree to help us, as well, Father."

Noah nodded. "Of course, my son."

"And to be present, from time to time, to offer counsel and support."

"I will do more than that," Noah said. "I will also support your work with the proceeds from my vineyard. And send the most faithful followers of the Old Way to you, to help you in this."

...

The next day, Noah, Aran, and Zillah bid Shem and Japheth good-bye, and mounted camels—one of them Little Kavel, whom Shem had cared for since—to make their long journey home to the vineyard. But the farther they went from Babel, the more Zillah withdrew, until she wouldn't even abide Aran teaching her new words.

PART III

After The Collapse

291 YEARS AFTER THE WORLDWIDE FLOOD

82

Aran

Aran sat on the waist-high stone wall at the edge of Noah's vine-yard and stared at Zillah, who sat cross-legged in the long grasses in the field, staring at the clouds, lost in memory. The week before, he had finally built up the courage to ask her to marry him, in a desperate attempt to prove his love for her, and to calm her anxious heart.

Footsteps sounded as Noah approached and placed his arm across Aran's shoulders.

"Done working for the day?" Aran said.

Noah nodded. "She hasn't improved?"

Aran shook his head. "I don't understand it. She just can't let it go. I don't know how to help her."

"She only refused to marry you because she believes herself unworthy," Noah said.

Yes. Now, after everything was over, the stains of what had happened still ran too deep. Aran, too, felt the pain of his scars more deeply than before. But he would never let that get in the way of his love for Zillah.

"You told me once that you didn't understand the Old Way," Noah said.

"On the river," Aran said.

"I kept my distance since we returned because I knew you

both needed time. But healing will never be complete until you allow the Almighty to make you whole."

Aran sighed and ran his hands through the tassels of grass leaning against the wall. "How could that even happen?"

"You can't forgive yourself. Can you?"

Aran looked at Noah. "For letting Nimrod go?"

"For killing the man in your mother's courtyard. For hating your father. And every other mistake that mars your past like a reed pen on a clay tablet. Our sins press too deep, Aran. Nothing but the great Potter can make us whole again."

Aran closed his eyes and touched his chest and imagined the clot of darkness removed. That pulsing hole replaced with completeness. Tears came to his eyes. "How?" he whispered.

"Trust the Almighty. Give him your heart. Surrender to his will. Obey his word. Love him more than you hate your father. Choose him over your desire for Zillah. Believe he is greater than your sin. He has chosen you to receive his grace. I am more convinced of this than of anything. Why else would he have given you my language?"

His tears grew, until Zillah's figure blurred and was lost. "And what of Zillah? She still struggles to communicate in our language."

"The Almighty knows to speak in a way we understand. He brought her to you, and to me. Do not doubt his mercy toward those who long for him."

"I do not know his word. I have never heard him speak."

Noah nodded. "I will teach you. I will teach you both. Only surrender. He will see your heart."

Aran slipped from the wall and knelt in the grass. Lifted his hands to the sky. "Almighty," the words caught in his throat, but he forced them out. "Please, heal me. Please . . . heal her."

83

Noah

One week later, Noah decided it was time to bring their first store of wealth—along with a few new servants—to Shem to aid in the rebuilding process. Noah asked if Aran would kindly accompany him, and he had agreed, so long as Zillah would too.

"Let me ask her," Noah said, for he knew that their relationship had grown strained. She had grown to understand enough of the language to communicate simply, though Noah had not made the same strides in her language.

He went and asked her, but she refused.

The morning they were to leave, Noah was readying their camels and a drawn wagon. He was surprised to see Zillah walk out and join them, ready for the journey with a small bag tossed over her shoulder.

She sat next to Aran on the wagon, though she kept to herself and talked little. Still, she stayed near him for the length of the trip, and seemed to draw comfort from his presence.

...

After they arrived in Erech, Aran decided he would stay with Sarah, who also had grown to understand enough of their language, for she had learned how to speak it from Shem's disciples in the Old Way. Zillah was unsure whether to go with him, because she was not family and was not certain she was wanted.

"You are family," Noah whispered to Zillah. "Do not fear. I would have you live in my own home, if you wanted to. I am certain Sarah feels the same."

Zillah just stared at him for several long moments.

"Zillah," Aran called and tried to smile at her. "Would you give me the honor of joining me at my mother's home?"

Zillah turned and seemed to consider it.

Noah put his hand gently on her back and smiled. "Go, precious daughter. Let them love you the way that they long to."

And so she went.

...

They stayed for several weeks in Erech. Then returned home.

On the way back, Noah noticed Zillah resting with her back against Aran's side.

...

Several months later, they made another trek to Shem's city.

Again, as before, Aran and Zillah remained with Sarah, who they said taught them much about the Old Way. Not in word as Noah did, but by the way she lived her life.

A few weeks later, they finally made their way back again.

This time, on the journey home, both Aran and Zillah spent a portion of their time weeping, fingers entwined with each other's.

When Noah asked what they cried for, Zillah said, "We are his, now. For we have seen the goodness of the Almighty."

...

That was how slowly, day by day, Aran and Zillah found healing in community with other lovers of the Almighty. Together, they labored to mend the brokenness of the fall of Babel and formed an enclave for the followers of the Old Way.

Even still, difficulty and strife were common. The confusion of languages strained relationships between cities and violence rose swift like a flashing fire year after year.

Yet nothing could dampen Noah's joy when one month after their second trip to Erech, Aran announced that he and Zillah would be married.

Zillah

On her wedding day, Zillah walked toward Aran with a veil over her face. Their friends were gathered between the rows of grapevines—just how she wanted it—and Noah stood beside Aran, waiting in the shade of a broad tree.

Zillah took her time. She wanted to savor this moment and what it meant for her.

She had first met Aran in Accad and tried to steal from him. Then she had used him as a means of escape. She had lied to him. She had endangered him and Noah. She had come from an evil family and a dark past bathed in wretched idolatry.

And yet these two men had shown her deep, painful love. Noah had become her new father. And Aran had become her best friend.

It had taken her long to accept it. She had so hated herself for how she'd harmed them that their kindness only deepened her pain.

But over time, she realized that the way they loved each other was with the same love they had received from the Almighty, when he forgave them of their darkest evils.

Sarah had been key in the changes in Zillah's heart. For Sarah had spoken to her womanly fears and anxieties like no man ever could. And she had shown Zillah the tenderness and strength of a woman who feared the Almighty.

Even back in Sarah's courtyard, the first time Zillah had met her, Zillah had wanted to be like her. That desire had only grown the more time they spent together.

Zillah stopped a handsbreadth from Aran's chest.

Noah held up his open palms. Aran placed his wrist in Noah's right hand. Zillah placed hers in Noah's left.

Noah crossed their wrists and began to tie them together with a thin vine.

After finishing, Noah pushed Zillah and Aran closer.

Aran looked down at her through her veil with such pride and love that she wondered if her heart would burst. Her face flushed with warmth as she focused on the feel of his chest against hers. The purity of their care for one another had been refined by mutual suffering. And now, for the first time, she felt safe being completely known by another. For the Almighty knew her more deeply than any man ever could—and he loved her.

"What the Almighty joins together, let no man separate," Noah said.

Aran reached up with his free hand, pushed her veil back, and kissed her with the passion of a forest fire that burns and burns and yet does no harm.

And she kissed back.

Epilogue

Aran and Zillah lived in Noah's vineyard for the next thirty years, until the end of Noah's life. After Noah passed, Japheth gained authority over the vineyard, and Aran and Zillah moved to Erech to be closer to Aran's mother, Sarah.

Aran and Zillah had gained much wisdom about the Old Way from Noah and grew to love the Almighty more deeply than many others, for how deeply he'd healed their wounded hearts and filled the aching holes in their hearts with life and joy—and children.

As Aran and Zillah grew older in Erech, they taught many others the Old Way. Aran frequently told stories to the younger children, for children are not afraid of scars like grown men and women are. Aran loved speaking to them. The purity in their hearts, the soft tenderness with which their precious fingers traced the dips and curves of his scars after shyly asking for permission to touch them. It filled his heart with thankfulness and joy.

But then Aran's mother grew sick, and in her old age, Sarah passed away.

Aran had no desire left to stay in Erech, so they traveled south with their family, past the hulking skeleton of Babel to a city named Ur, where they settled for the rest of their days, and Aran continued to teach young children the Old Way.

Though there were many that Aran spent time with, he would remember most a man named Abram, who held a passion for righteousness and a love for the Almighty's word that rivaled that of the man Aran had come to call his surrogate father.

Research Notes on the Story of the Tower of Babel

When did the events at the tower of Babel happen?

Approximately 101 years after the Flood, the Bible claims Peleg was born. Peleg was a descendant of Shem who lived to be 239 years old. The Bible says that in Peleg's lifetime, the earth was divided (Genesis 10:25). We know this does not refer to the Flood or to a split in the continents, because the Flood happened before he was born, and a split in the continents would have caused worldwide flooding all over again—and God promised he'd never again flood the world. The only other significant division we are given in Scripture during this period was the confusion of the world's languages and the dispersal of humanity from the tower of Babel.

There are several conclusions we can arrive at based on this:

1. The confusion of languages at Babel happened when Peleg was born, roughly 101 years after the flood.

2. The confusion of languages happened when Peleg died, 340 years after the Flood.

3. The confusion of languages happened sometime during Peleg's lifetime, between 101 years after the Flood and 340 years after the Flood.

I believe the third option the most likely because the Scriptures say that in Peleg's days (plural) the earth was divided. Of course, that could be too-literal of an approach to interpreting the English translation of the text, and we must keep in mind that the original Hebrew often carries connotations that aren't carried into an essentially literal translation of the text into English.

However, no matter what we conclude, Scripture tells us Noah died 350 years after the Flood (10 years *after* Peleg died). So I believe we can be confident that the events at the tower of Babel happened during Noah's lifetime. This begs the question: Where was Noah when his lineage was rebelling and falling into idolatry?

For the story you just read, I assumed that the bulk of the events happened about 280 years after the flood.

How many people were alive when the events of the tower of Babel happened?

If it is true that the events happened approximately 300 years after the Flood, it is reasonable to assume that Noah's three sons and their families had expanded to a legion of tens of thousands of people spread over many cities. However, because we cannot put a definitive date on the events at the tower, we can never know with certainty how many people were alive.

What do we know about Noah's lineage and what they all looked like?

The genealogical lists in Genesis 10 are focused only on sons, and there is good reason to assume the genealogies are only partial lists important to the ancient peoples Genesis was originally written for. More detailed information was likely passed down either orally or through written documentation, but we no longer have access to these. For example, what of all the "other sons and daughters" of the male descendants listed in Genesis 11? Genesis 11 only goes through one particular line of male descendants, through whom Israel could trace their legacy through Shem to Seth and finally to Adam. What of all the other families of Japheth and Ham? They are hardly listed in any sort of detail. Neither are we told how the sons and daughters of Shem, Japheth, and Ham intermarried. This is because the purpose of Genesis was to trace God's promises through history rather than to give a comprehensive picture of the evolution of human society.

After the dispersal of the peoples from the tower of Babel, ancient documents differ over who went where. Upon deep study, we find that the intermingling of peoples was too complicated and nuanced for us to make clear deductions of what each of the sons of Noah looked like. The only thing we can be reasonably certain of is that likely, all three sons of Noah were dark. Some of Japheth's progeny settled in Africa. Some of them also went east to the Orient, and northwest to Europe. Some of Ham's progeny settled in the far east in China. Some of Ham's progeny also settled in the Middle East and Africa.

Canaan's curse was not that he was black. That is a heresy used by white supremacists to perpetuate racism and human slavery. Some of Canaan's children actually settled in eastern Asia, where many have light skin. Besides, the curse pronounced over Canaan finds its fulfillment in the Israelites conquering the Canaanites centuries after the events of Genesis 9.

How technologically and socially advanced were the people who built the tower of Babel?

We know from earlier in Genesis that people in this time period were building cities and organizing humanity in surprisingly modern ways. For example, even all the way back in Genesis 4, we see city building happening in the first generation. Then, we see the cultivation of livestock (v. 20), the invention and use of stringed and piped instruments (v. 21), and the forging of bronze and *iron* (v. 22). It takes no stretch of the imagination to assume the people who built the tower of Babel were both intelligent and technologically advanced.

Neither is it difficult to assume that the single language they spoke could have been in written form, because without written language, cities are quite difficult to administrate at any sort of scale. If you doubt this is possible, ask yourself which is more difficult: iron forging or written language?

I think the answer is iron forging.

Who was older: Shem or Japheth?

Depending on which English translation you're reading, either Shem or Japheth is listed as being older. But if we look at the genealogies, we see that the timing of Shem's birth, and the timing of the birth of Shem's first son, lock Shem's life in place as firstborn. (Genesis 5:32 and Genesis 11:10)

What does the Bible mean when it says Ham saw his father's nakedness?

We don't know. Some have postulated that Ham castrated his father. Others that he molested his mother. I don't think these interpretations are necessary or even reasonable. It is enough that Ham ridiculed his father's nakedness and drunkenness. I also think it reasonable to assume that Noah became drunk because of the death of his wife, though this is not explicitly stated.

Was the tower of Babel finished when the languages were confused?

According to Genesis 11:5, the Lord came to see the city and tower that the children of man *had built* (past tense). Afterward, he confused their languages, and they left off building the city, but not the tower, which implies that they had already built the tower (Genesis 11:8). City building is perpetual as population grows. Tower building is not. So, it would seem that the tower was finished when the Lord came down and confused the world's languages, though, once again, any definitive answer is difficult to arrive at.

What was the reason for building the tower?

The most obvious purpose we are given is that the tower was supposed to unify the world in rebellion against God's command to spread out and fill the earth. Likely, there was also a purely idolatrous reason for them to build the tower. Many commentators believe that the tower was built to aid in the observation and worship of the celestial bodies (the sun, the stars, etc.). Light-worship is one of the oldest forms of idolatry. And, since Satan is referred to as the "morning star" and the "light bringer," I believe it reasonable to assume that Noah's progeny was engaged in ritualistic worship of the sun, moon, stars, etc.

What we find in a disturbingly large amount of ancient idolatry is that human sacrifice was frequently seen as the ultimate blood sacrifice. The Mayan's, for instance, built massive triadic pyramids likely inspired by the design of the tower of Babel, worshipped the sun, and offered human sacrifices regularly. As did the adherents to Baal and other ancient false gods. Israel even engaged in these evil acts from time to time, sacrificing their own children to false gods.

We view idolatry today as relegated to simpletons bowing to lifeless idols. We forget that the worship of false gods spreads into the worship of actual demonic entities. There are real spiritual effects to this, so I wanted to show the demonic influences over idolatry with Nimrod's possession by the silver spirit, who is the antagonist in all three of the Fall of Man series novels. We pay a price for rebellion, and the reason for the stranglehold idolatry held over early people groups was not that they were simple, but that idolatry holds actual spiritual power.

Did Nimrod build Babel? And can we be certain that he built the tower?

The Bible never says that Nimrod built Babel, or that he built the tower. In fact, it claims that multiple people came together and decided to build the tower in unison (Genesis 11:3–4). I hold the opinion that the tower was likely *not* Nimrod's idea—at least not solely his idea. Originally, Nimrod was a warrior/hunter. Eventually, he held sway over the cities of Babel, Erech, Accad, and Calneh in the land of Shinar (Genesis 10:10). Afterward, he built cities, including the infamous Nineveh, and he seemed to be some sort of leader during the events of the tower of Babel. But we are not told of a definitive timeline, nor are we told whether he built all the cities he held leadership over.

There are insurmountable ambiguities in the text of Genesis, and we must be careful of too literally interpreting the English text, because our English translations do not carry much of the implicit meaning of the original Hebrew, which was orally communicated. For the sake of the story, I chose one particular interpretation. I'm not claiming it's the only one, but it seemed to be plausible based on very careful readings of the actual Biblical text, along with the study of many commentaries and scholarly interpretations.

What was the first language that everyone spoke?

We don't know, and it doesn't matter. If it did, God would have made certain it was written in the book of Genesis. Likely, that language was lost when the Lord confused the world's languages. However, we may be confident it wasn't British English (for those of you who prefer that accent for audiobook readings, hah!).

What's the point of the story of the tower of Babel?

Narrowing it down to just one "message" is foolish. I believe doing so would be a disservice to the Bible. That's why I believed it necessary to write a full novel to explore the themes in it. However, I view the most central themes of the tower of Babel being man's unfaithfulness, God's goodness and gentleness, and the weakness of humanity contrasted with the unlimited power and faithfulness of God. There are additional themes of idolatry, sobriety (literal and figurative sobriety), and the personal responsibility of the father of a family ("Where was Noah during all of this?").

For additional study on the story of the tower of Babel, check out *Tower of Babel* by Bodie Hodge, which is endorsed by Answers in Genesis, and is a careful study on the Scriptures, though I don't agree with every conclusion he draws in the book.

Didn't Noah's Ark land on Mount Ararat?

No. The Bible says that Noah's ark landed on the "mountains" (plural) "of Ararat." Which, in the original Hebrew, is clearly not referring to Mount Ararat in Turkey. Mount Ararat, as we know it today, wasn't named Ararat originally, and first began to be associated with the name in the Bible in the 11th century, when the Armenians began to think of it as the ark's landing place. Obviously, this is long after Genesis was written. In fact, Genesis states explicitly that where the people lived after landing was east of the plain of Shinar. This seems to obviously exclude Mount Ararat in Turkey.

What do you believe about the Bible?

A final note should be made to my belief regarding the authenticity and sufficiency of the Scriptures. The Bible is the only authoritative, infallible word of God, and is sufficient for the revelation of God. I do not believe we need extra-biblical resources, such as the Book of Enoch or the Book of Jasher. Nor do I believe we should consult them as any source of historical or spiritual truth. The church has decried these for many centuries for good reason. Scripture itself warns us of Jewish myths such as these, and I find the recent popularity of these books and the conspiracy theories they've birthed disturbing.

It's perfectly acceptable to apply our imaginations to the Scriptures. But to pass off our imagination as truth is something altogether different from writing fictional stories inspired by biblical stories.

What makes those extra-biblical books different from biblical fiction is that those extra-biblical books *claim to be true*, whereas biblical fiction identifies itself as made-up. This is a critical distinction.

...

Want more? Sign up for my weekly devotional at brennanmcpherson.com and receive a free e-book (Book 1 of the Psalm Series), along with new release alerts when more books are published in this series, and invites to join the launch team and receive new books early.

Acknowledgments

So many people made this book possible. I want to first thank my wife for being so understanding and supportive. She gave me the time I needed to finish this book.

I also want to thank you, dear reader, for continuing to support and encourage me. The only reason I can continue doing this is because you keep buying these books!

My editor, my Master Mind group, my critique group, and all my author friends—your fingerprints are all over this book.

In addition, I want to thank everyone who has contributed to my spiritual growth. I started writing because I wanted to write fantasy books. Falling into biblical fiction was a happy accident driven by the beauty of God's word.

The Bible has drawn me like a magnet, and I am forever thankful to all the people who showed me its beauty, pushed me to engage with it, and helped me live a life changed by it.

Most of all, I'm thankful to Jesus. Words fail to elucidate the outrageous love he's shown me. I pray this book honored him!

Also by McPherson Publishing

Book 4 of the Fall of Man Series is available now!

A coming of age story of biblical proportions...

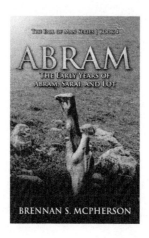

When Abram's brother, Haran, is found dead in their father's field, Sarai, Lot, and Abram's fates become intertwined.

As their family's desires clash, they must discover how to navigate increasingly dangerous circumstances.

From forced marriage, to fleeing the wrath of an angry city-state, and deceiving the pharaoh of Egypt, will they honor the Almighty and find the inheritance God promised? Or will they choose their own path and forge on into ruin?

Find out in this first book on the lives of Abram, Sarai, and Lot, based on Genesis 11:26 – Genesis 13:1.

Go to brennanmcpherson.com to buy your copy today! Or, find it directly on Amazon.

Printed in Great Britain
by Amazon